THE LAZARUS WAR:

LEGION

Jamie Sawyer

www.orbitbooks.net

ORBIT

First published in Great Britain in 2015 by Orbit

1 3 5 7 9 10 8 6 4 2

A CIP catalogue record for this book is available from the British Library.

ISBN 978-0-356-50547-3

Typeset in Stempel Garamond by Palimpsest Book Production Limited,
Falkirk, Stirlingshire
Printed and bound in Great Britain by CPI Group (UK) Ltd,
Croydon CR0 4YY

Papers used by Orbit are from well-managed
forests and other responsible sources.

MIX
Paper from
responsible sources
FSC
www.fsc.org   FSC® C104740

Orbit
An imprint of
Little, Brown Book Group
Carmelite House
50 Victoria Embankment
London EC4Y 0DZ

An Hachette UK Company
www.hachette.co.uk

www.orbitbooks.net

To Louise – because I really couldn't have done it without you

PROLOGUE

"Stop me if you've already heard this one.

"It starts with a legend; with a man they called Lazarus.

"He was Earth-born. American – a Detroit kid through and through. Born with a bullet between his teeth and a pistol in his hand. Pulled up by his bootstraps. Kicked into shape by Life, spat out by Death.

"He was an Alliance Army man but mostly he was Simulant Operations Programme. He craved for the transition; even enjoyed the extraction. He got his callsign – Lazarus – because he always came back for more. Three hundred and something transitions and still going strong.

"Everyone on the *Point* knew the name. But no one knew the man, at least not directly. Always a friend of a friend. If you followed the trail to where the rumour started, you'd find an overheard conversation in a bar – a rumour picked up from a fellow trooper, that sort of thing.

"He went into the Maelstrom, they said. Didn't go alone, either. He took a team of bad-asses with him: a Californian with an attitude, some Venusian Latino, a wiseass Brooklyn kid, and a fresh recruit he was showing the ropes. Chasing down a xeno weapon, or the remains of another alien civilisation: the details seem to change depending on who is telling the tale.

"So, for a long time, he was just a rumour. A legend for rookies and greens to look up to – a figurehead for the Sim Ops Programme.

"Except, you see, he was Lazarus.

"And he came back.

"Riding a Directorate Interceptor, no less. He'd kicked ass and taken names; shown the Asiatic Directorate who was boss. Killed a whole battalion of 'em, as the story goes.

"People started listening. Suddenly the legend wasn't so unlikely, and people started thinking that we could win this war.

"Lazarus came back, man; he came back."

Interview with unknown Alliance trooper, conducted by *The Point Times* reporter, Universal Calendar Date: 21st January 2282

CHAPTER ONE

HARD-DROP

Two years after Helios

I made transition in orbit around Maru Prime; a burning hellhole of a planet somewhere in the Quarantine Zone. Or, at least, what was left of the Zone.

I was inside a Wildcat armoured personnel shuttle. My first act in the new body was to activate the holo-photo inside my helmet: Elena on Azure. The tiny icon was tacked to the bottom right of my face-plate. Reminded of who I was fighting for, I moved on to the mission.

"Squad, sound off!"

Four simulant faces stared back at me through the dark: underlit by green safety bulbs inside tactical helmets.

"Affirmative!" Jenkins bellowed back. Callsign CALIFORNIA; the name stencilled onto the chest-plate of her combat-suit.

"Copy," Kaminski said. Callsign BROOKLYN.

"Confirmed," Martinez said. Callsign CRUSADER. He

clutched a cheap plastic rosary, the beads woven between armoured fingers.

"Affirmative," came the last, and newest, member of the unit: Private Dejah Mason. The name NEW GIRL had been printed onto her chest but she had no other battle honours, rank badges or insignia.

"We have another successful transition, Major," Jenkins said, nodding enthusiastically inside her helmet.

I was still getting used to the new rank and I wasn't entirely comfortable with being addressed as major. I'd been a captain for so long that being called by a different title felt wrong.

"I have eyes on the other squads," Jenkins added. "All five are inbound per mission plan. All on the timeline. Uploaded to your suit."

"Copy that, Sergeant."

Jenkins' grin broadened so that it filled her face. While my new rank felt unnatural, Jenkins had adopted hers without hesitation.

Uplinks from the commanding officers of the other teams scrolled across my HUD: each confirming successful transition, chirping intel on the approach. A full platoon. Each unit was being transported in a Wildcat APS, like us, and was approaching the designated landing zone.

I flexed my arms and legs. Felt the renewed vigour of transition into a simulant body. It was bigger, stronger, just better than my real body. That lay preserved in a simulator-tank, safely ensconced in the operations centre aboard the UAS *Mallard*.

"What's the op?" Kaminski said. He was chewing gum inside his helmet; I wasn't sure how he'd managed to smuggle food into the dormant sim before we'd made transition. I let it slide.

"Didn't you read the briefing?" Mason asked in disbelief. Voice heavily accented with the Martian burr that Standard seemed to have developed on the red world.

"Baby, I never read the briefing."

Kaminski spoke with practised indifference but I knew that it was only skin deep. His vitals danced across my HUD: his autonomics told of a professional. Kaminski worked hard to maintain his false image – ever the wiseass.

Mason hadn't been a soldier for long, let alone a simulant operator, and she didn't know better. Barely twenty, with the body and face of a college cheerleader. Not the sort of trooper Alliance Command used on propaganda recruitment vids: the idea of one of America's finest getting shredded by Krell stinger fire wouldn't sit well with the folks back home. Mason had some big boots to fill and she was already the sixth replacement that I'd taken on – the other five having failed miserably to meet my expectations. I thought, briefly, of Michael Blake – Mason's distant predecessor – but buried the memory as quickly as it surfaced.

"We're approaching Maru Prime," I said, activating a condensed holo-briefing on my wrist-comp.

Maru Prime was an angry red planet composed entirely of molten lava – star-bright, palpably hot, even at this distance. It had no surface, instead being held together by the dynamics of gravitational and tidal forces far too complex for a grunt like me to understand.

A structure came into view in orbit around Maru, gliding above the roiling lava seas.

"This is Far Eye Observatory."

The facility was a painfully delicate lattice-work construction, a collection of bubble-domes, solar vanes and spherical crew modules. A series of huge radar dishes sat on the station's spine: all pointed into deep-space. Many components had taken obvious damage, with large chunks of the rigging punctured and the whole structure leaning at a precarious angle.

"Two days ago," I explained, "Far Eye began to slide from its orbital position."

"It's being sucked off," said Kaminski, sniggering. "Or sucked down, depending on how you see it."

I ignored Kaminski; doing otherwise would only encourage him.

"The station suffered a malfunction in the primary grav-shunt," I said. "As a result, its orbit is in rapid decline. Command wants us to retrieve the personnel. In particular, they want this man."

The image of a thin-faced Sci-Div officer appeared on all five face-plates. Tanned skin; Persian stock. By Earth-standard years he was in his early fifties. He had dark eyes and hair. A beard, rough-grown, peppered grey.

"Our HVT is Professor Ashan Saul."

HVT: high-value target. I'd already researched Saul – who he was, where he had served. It made for interesting reading. Despite his Iranian heritage, his bloodline was long-retired to the Core Worlds. He was a xenolinguist by profession – specialising in the interpretation of alien language. That particular detail had instantly grabbed my attention. There were also huge empty periods in Saul's scientific career: blocks of time when he was inexplicably absent from recorded duty. Nothing stunk of covert ops involvement quite like an unexplained black line through your last posting.

"So they send six Sim Ops teams out into the Quarantine Zone to rescue one man?" Martinez asked. "Seems like over-kill."

"I said we're supposed to bring all personnel back. And it's made more complex by this."

I adjusted the external camera controls, so that a wider graphic of space surrounding Maru Prime became visible. The sector was literally full of activity. Flocks of fighters wove between larger vessels, Alliance ships chasing down Krell bio-fighters.

There were three Alliance warships anchored in high orbit: the *Mallard*, the *Washington's Paragon*, and the *Peace of Seattle*. Assault cruisers with enough onboard firepower to level a small planet. They faced off against six advancing Krell starships of unknown designation, ranging in threat category. The alien vessels were variations on an aquatic theme – black as space, shaped like mutant molluscs.

Both groups were on full offensive: firing torpedoes, railguns, flak cannons. The battlespace within a few thousand klicks was alight with plasma, the immediate and empty explosions of ships dying in vacuum. Tracer fire slid overhead: Alliance tech met with Krell organic equivalents. I picked out the *Mallard* somewhere in the fray – null-shields flaring, laser batteries bristling. Our real bodies, in the *Mallard*'s Simulant Operations Centre, were our vulnerability. One stray missile to the *Mallard*, one missed point-defence reaction, and we'd be open to vacuum.

Our Wildcat was in the thick of the fighting, plummeting to the station below.

"With this much shit going on above our heads," I said, "Command thinks that we will be able to achieve retrieval of Professor Saul without attracting significant enemy attention."

Martinez sucked his teeth. "How long we got?"

I shrugged. "Until Far Eye Station gets eaten by the planet below? Twenty-seven minutes. But we'll be long gone by then. We're going to breach, evac the civvies, then pull out."

"This all sounds a little too easy," Jenkins added. Sarcasm was never her strong point. "What's the complication . . .?"

On cue, something hit the APS.

A warning chimed in my helmet. Direct from the shuttle: CRITICAL DAMAGE DETECTED!

We were hit, hard enough to slam the boat off course.

The APS swung about, throwing me back into my seat. Reflexively, I grabbed the restraints. The shuttle engines started a throaty, unpleasant roaring: the deck underfoot buckling with each new turn.

I checked my heads-up display; the stream of data projected onto the interior of my combat-suit helmet. I was hardwired into my armoured suit – fully powered, sealed, battle-ready – and what data couldn't be relayed onto the HUD was ported directly into my neural-link. *Shit.* Significant structural damage. The main propulsion unit was compromised. I absorbed the information immediately; was already planning how we could stay combat-effective.

"We'll have to do this the hard way. Looks like you get your complication, Jenkins."

"Great."

There wouldn't be time to correct our approach vector. We would miss our landing window. I patched through to Naval command, aboard the UAS *Mallard*.

"Command, this is Lazarus Actual. Do you read me?"

I'd learnt to embrace the callsign; if everyone was going to call me it, then why resist? Since Helios, it was hard to argue with the suggestion that I always came back.

"Copy, Lazarus Actual, but only just," the anonymous voice of Command replied. "Your bird has suffered a hit."

"I know. I guess we just got unlucky."

"There's a first time for everything, Lazarus. It's a glancing bio-plasma impact. You're losing fuel fast. You want to extract?"

"That's a negative. We're going to make a hard-drop to the outpost."

The officer whistled. "Sure you want to risk it?"

"Not like we have a choice."

"That wasn't what I asked. There are five other teams inbound on the same objective."

"So I'm supposed to let some other simulant outfit claim the prize? We're operational and we're proceeding with the mission."

"Your call, Lazarus. Gaia's luck. Be aware that the drop window is closing fast."

"Affirmative."

"You have your orders. Command out."

"Lazarus Actual out."

The cabin lights flickered, signalling radio silence with the *Mallard*. The craft was now descending at entirely the wrong angle; slamming me against the wall of the passenger cabin.

I turned to my squad. "We're hard-dropping to Maru Prime – straight down the pipe."

"You cannot be serious," Kaminski said. When he was anxious, his Brooklyn accent became thick: like he'd just left New York City. Right now, it was the thickest I'd heard it in a long time. "New Girl ain't up to this."

"My name is Mason. And of course I'm up to this. I'm a trained soldier just like the rest of you."

"Whatever, New Girl. Six transitions ain't the same." Kaminski tapped the numeric badge on his shoulder: one hundred and eighteen deaths so far. "Just looking out for you is all. Once you get your Legion badge, then we can talk some more."

"Quit the chatter," Jenkins ordered. "On the major's mark!"

I unstrapped my safety harness, standing as steadily as I could. That was no easy task: the APS was shaking apart now, caught on a drift in the upper atmosphere of Maru. The mags in my boots automatically kicked in: held me to the deck underfoot. I checked everything I needed was strapped down, locked the plasma rifle to my back-plate. Grenades, power cells, sidearm – anything loose was going to be lost in the descent to the station below.

"Suits sealed!" Jenkins yelled. "On the order, people!"

Martinez and Kaminski were up and out of their harnesses, strapping equipment onto their combat-suits.

We were approaching the station fast. The ugly domed structures spun beneath us as the APS tumbled through the sky. The view was heat-blurred and hazy. *It's going to be hot out there. I hope that the combat-suits can take it.* There would be no way that real skins, even in full EVA gear, could operate in those temperatures. My onboard AI informed me that I could withstand six minutes, thirteen seconds before the heat caused catastrophic damage. *That will have to be long enough,* I decided.

"Let's do this."

The rear access hatch of the APS cycled open and I was immediately accosted by a wave of super-heated atmosphere – nearly strong enough to pull me out of the shuttle. I grappled the overhead safety webbing with one hand and fought the urge to cover my face with the other. That was the natural reaction, because Maru Prime's surface was blindingly bright and exuded heat.

"Fall in!"

We assembled at the rear lock of the APS. The craft circled

the base one more time, altitude only a few thousand metres now.

"Don't forget who we are," Jenkins roared over the comm. "Lazarus Legion: prepare for drop."

I took a running jump out of the airlock.

The rest of the squad did the same. Maru Prime had a strong gravitational field – over a gee, according to Science Division's analysis – and I felt it as I launched into the upper atmosphere. The tug of planetary forces was enough to pump the air temporarily from my lungs. My onboard medi-suite issued me with combat-drugs; a mixture of endorphins, analgesics and smart-drugs hit my bloodstream.

My body was like an aerodynamic dart – armoured arms and legs held together to decrease drag. I heard nothing but saw everything. The blinding, furious world beneath me: bubbling, constantly spewing and churning. The prickle of heat on my face, the immediate damp of sweat forming on my brow and my back. The combat-suit attempted to remedy that, atmospheric conditioning working overtime to keep me at optimum combat temperature.

All five of us, in perfect formation, were freefalling to the station below. The actual structure seemed to come up to meet us almost right away, the bare plains of landing bays and storage depots listing precariously.

People, civilians mainly, paid good money for this sort of experience. The serenity of the drop was absolute but it was an acquired taste. One false move, and I'd either be crushed by Maru's gravity, or would fly drastically off course and burn up in the atmosphere.

The trick was riding the momentum of the planet's gravity well *just so*.

"Thrusters!" I yelled.

The Trident Class V was a premium combat-suit, made for battle in space. A full EVA suit but so much more. Of interest to me right now was the onboard manoeuvring system: thrusters incorporated into the backpack unit.

I fired the manoeuvring jets and immediately changed direction. I moved into an upright position, kicked out with both feet and braced to hit the station landing pad. There was a muted hiss as the thrusters fired again, then the wrench of external forces competing with Maru's gravity.

The distance counter inside my helmet began to slow. I held up a hand, watched the armoured glove glow red with heat from the descent. Maru Prime's atmosphere was thin and vapid, so the drop hadn't caused as much frictional heat as it could've done.

"I . . . I'm having some trouble out here!" Mason suddenly broke in over the comm.

Shit. With supreme effort, I twisted my head in her direction. Every muscle in my neck felt locked, every bone fused by the opposing forces pulling at me. Because the Legion had done this so many times before I'd been concentrating on my own drop-technique.

Private Mason had never hard-dropped. She spiralled alongside me, maybe a hundred metres off course. Her thruster pack fired – bright blue against the glaring red of the landscape below – and she spun head over heels.

The combat-suits carried an active camouflage suite, made to mimic the surrounding conditions. Her suit flashed an angry red – mirroring the planet below – then, as her body spun, shifted to copy the black star-field above. The armour eventually gave up completely: the onboard AI must've decided that it was impossible to imitate the constantly shifting environment.

"Told you she wasn't ready," Kaminski tutted.

"You want me to fetch her?" Martinez asked. He panted heavily over the comm; even he was finding this taxing.

"I'm the nearest," I said. This was my problem. "Adopt primary drop formation and secure the LZ."

"Affirmative."

I fired my thruster. My descent was slowing, but I was still moving fast, and that made the lateral shift difficult. I pulled alongside the twisting figure.

Up close, I saw the damage that Mason's uncontrolled descent had caused. Her armour plating was blackened, glowing an incandescent white in places, angry blood-red and orange in others. Inside her helmet, her face was a mask of horror – eyes wide and pallor an absolute white.

"I . . . I can't get . . . angle!" she stammered.

"Breathe deep. Focus."

I issued the orders verbally. In my head, I requested that her suit administer a dose of combat-drugs. Almost immediately, her rhythms flattened. It wouldn't be enough to put her out, or even stop her from panicking, but I hoped that it was enough to keep her alive.

"Help me! Please!"

"Fire the thruster in three short bursts." I was becoming increasingly hot; I realised suddenly how far off course Mason had actually drifted. "Just stay with it."

The thrusters were all thought-activated, and a panicked mind implicitly carried delay. She spiralled again and again, armour glowing hotter with every turn: every exposed angle blistering. Streamers of smoke had started rising from the damaged exterior. Unless I helped her, she was going to roast inside the armour.

"Fire the thruster! Now!"

Mason fired and her descent wobbled.

"Oh shit, oh shit, oh shit . . ." she babbled.

"Keep quiet and keep the comms channel clear. Give me your hand."

Mason reached out to me, her gloved fingers spread. I fired my thruster again, edging nearer to her – I could almost feel the heat coming from her frazzled body, more powerful than that emanating from Maru Prime below.

"I can't reach—"

She wobbled some more, spinning again. An alarm sounded in my helmet: SQUAD MEMBER IN CRITICAL CONDITION. *Thanks, I hadn't noticed.*

I reached for her, the tip of my forefinger brushing her arm.

Distance: two hundred metres.

"Reach again!" I shouted.

Then suddenly Mason was upright, her thruster pack firing pure blue. She ground her teeth. Reached with splayed fingers. I grappled with her hand, locking around her wrist.

Distance: one hundred metres.

"Come on, Private. You can do this!"

She nodded firmly, thruster firing in a steady rhythm.

The distance counter slowed even further and suddenly we were over the LZ. The thruster pack gave one last, monumental fire – allowing me almost to hover above the landing pad. My feet touched down on the deck, absorbed the impact through the rest of my body. I stood for a second, breathing deep, enjoying the fact that I was on solid ground.

"You okay?"

Mason's combat-suit had temporarily locked. She sagged inside the armour, sweated forehead touching her inner faceplate.

"Christo," she whispered. "That was a ride. Thanks."

I didn't answer her, just scanned the landing pad. The rest of my squad watched on with something approaching disbelief. They were assembled outside the station's primary airlock with weapons drawn.

"Maybe Kaminski was right when he said that she wasn't ready," Jenkins said.

"She's alive," I answered, using the restricted channel between Jenkins and me. I didn't want Mason's confidence any more bruised than it already was.

"You really want a ride, maybe I can show you sometime," Kaminski said.

Mason didn't bother with a reply.

"Stow that shit," I ordered, back on the general channel. "Get us inside the station and conduct a sweep."

CHAPTER TWO

TERMINAL DECLINE

The landing pad was on an elevated spar at the periphery of the observatory. It was swathed with hot, ash-ridden winds; and debris from the battle being fought in low orbit had started to rain down, giving the false impression that Maru had a weather system.

"No external security," Jenkins said. "But we've got hostiles inbound."

"I see them."

The sky above was filled with streaking comets – rapidly becoming visible as Krell ships.

"Krell are going to be on-station soon," said Martinez.

The Krell were hot-dropping, just like we had done, to get troops onto Far Eye. Their technology was a fucked-up reflection of ours: their shuttles were living things, whose sole purpose was to deliver as many Krell as possible to their destination.

"'Ski, run a bypass on this door."

"Solid copy."

Kaminski jogged to the airlock, hooking a hacker unit to the door controls.

"Preserve the atmosphere," I said. "We've probably got unarmoured civilians in there."

Kaminski nodded. "Running a hotwire now. It'll take longer than a direct breach, but should keep the civvies happy."

"Update on the rest of the platoon?" I asked of Jenkins.

"Other squads are meeting resistance," she said. "Captain Avis' team has just extracted."

"Avis is an asshole," Martinez said. "Serves him right."

"But more work for us," I said. "Currently twenty-three minutes until the station reaches terminal decline."

"Doors breached!" Kaminski declared.

The airlock outer doors cycled and we moved inside. The inner chamber began to repressurise – jets in the wall hissing as the decontamination procedure commenced, spraying the outside of my suit with a fine white mist. A yellow light flashed overhead, indicating the operation of the cleansing unit.

"Welcome to Far Eye Observatory," started the station's computer system; with a cultured female voice. "Established in 2275, the Observatory is sponsored by the Antares Mining Consortium. Please remain still while the decontamination procedure is completed . . ."

"Cancel that shit, 'Ski."

Kaminski acted immediately, using his wrist-comp and a direct connection to Far Eye's artificial intelligence system. The yellow light stopped flashing and the voice trailed off. The door into the base proper opened to a darkened corridor.

"Double-time it, people. Weapons at the ready."

The squad responded with the clatter of plasma rifles.

We all carried M95 battle-rifles – huge, oversized long-arms only suitable for use by simulant troopers.

"I miss my incinerator," Jenkins absently muttered.

"I don't think that the civvies would appreciate it," I said. I'd ordered rifles only on this operation, to minimise the risk of collateral damage.

"Where is everyone?" Martinez asked.

"Maybe these science pukes knew that the 'Ski was on the force?" Kaminski said.

"Staff were told to gather in the Communications Centre," I said. "Uploading route."

On my HUD, a flashing grid appeared: directing me onwards to Communications. The base was a conglomeration of hab units, laboratories, and observation domes. Living quarters for four times the actual staff numbers but I guess there weren't many applications for postings at the ass-end of the universe. My maps were based on the original configuration of the station, but it had been installed in orbit around Maru Prime several years ago. No telling, in the meantime, quite how much the station had changed.

"Activate drones," I declared.

I carried a full complement of surveillance drones, nested around my life-support pack. About the size of a baseball, the units were equipped with miniature anti-grav generators. The air was filled with an electric whining as the drones came online, swarming around me like flies. Each active drone added to my intelligence network; broadcasting encrypted vid- and audio-feeds, temperature readings, atmospheric fluctuations. The data was streamed direct to my HUD. The flow was temporarily disorienting: the drones were a recent addition to the Sim Ops arsenal and I was still getting used to them.

"Wide dispersal, complete tactical analysis."

The drone army responded immediately, darting off into the shadows. They had a practical range of about a kilometre. That would give us a tactical network sufficient to map and catalogue most of the station, whatever changes had been effected by the staff, faster than even a simulant team.

"Move on to Communications."

With the thump of heavy boots against the metal floor, we moved off.

"Quebec and Falke are out of the game," Jenkins said. "Just made extraction. Contact has also been lost with Captain Yares."

The update flashed across my HUD. Each squad was running autonomously, on the initiative of their respective captain. That was a conscious decision: maintaining regular radio contact might attract Krell attention. They followed comms waves like a shark followed the scent of blood. Supposing that Yares' team was about to make extraction, that left us and one other team. I consulted the mission timeline again: now just over nineteen minutes until terminal decline.

"I'm getting lots of bio-readings," Mason said. She waved at the door ahead. "Concentration of signals in that room, but several more across the station."

That was the problem with the bio-scanner: it couldn't differentiate between Krell and human biological signatures.

Without being asked, Kaminski moved up on the door to the Communications Centre and Martinez fell into a covering crouch.

"It's about to get hot," Jenkins said.

"Fucking A it is," Martinez said. "God bless my hand."

Kaminski slung his M95 rifle over his shoulder, and Martinez nodded to him. He activated the controls and the doors purred open.

"Move on."

Communications was ordinarily occupied by banks of computers and the AI mainframe – most of the running of the station was automated and none of the crew had any dedicated technical expertise. Now, it was crammed with personnel. Clad in EVA suits, ready for immediate evac.

We moved up by the numbers and filtered into the room. I nodded at Jenkins and she dropped back to cover the chamber entrance.

The staff were perched on chairs, huddled in corners, pacing nervously. The group's spokesperson was a pudgy-faced woman, wearing a battered EVA suit, smeared black with burn marks, glass-globe helmet under her arm as though she was ready to make a spacewalk at any moment. Her hair was thinning and receding, an indication that she was used to working in deep-space – experiencing the common side-effect of anti-rad drugs. My HUD aura-tagged the woman as DR JENNIFER ANDERS, STATION SUPERVISOR. Anders pushed her way to the front of the group.

I popped my own helmet, working on the vague assumption that presenting her with a human face – albeit simulated – might allay some of her concerns. It didn't seem to work: there were gasps of amazement around the room as I revealed my simulated features.

"Major Conrad Harris, Alliance Simulant Operations Programme. We're here to effect the evacuation. You are Dr Anders?"

The woman drew back involuntarily. She was tiny, dwarf-like, compared to my physical bulk.

"That's right. We did – have done – as ordered by Command," she muttered, biting the corner of her lip. "They told us that the Krell might be coming here . . . invading . . ."

There was another ripple of gasps through the group, more pale faces glaring up at me and my team.

"They already know," Anders said, nodding towards her staff. She added, haltingly: "But . . . none of us have . . . ever . . . faced the Krell before."

"Let's try to keep it that way," I said, with my best impression of a smile. "Our shuttle was damaged on the way down and I can't guarantee that anyone else is coming. What other transport options do you have on site?"

"We have a shuttle with sufficient capacity for the staff," she said. "It's in the secondary hangar, but it hasn't been used for months."

That could be a problem. I nodded at Kaminski.

"'Ski, get patched in, see if you can remotely activate their shuttle."

"Copy that."

Kaminski went to work again, the civilians parting to allow him access to a terminal.

"Anything else?" I asked.

"There's an evacuation pod, but that only has space for a single passenger."

Her eyes told me that she understood why the Sim Ops team were here: that if only one man could be saved, it would be Professor Saul.

"Show me the locations of both."

Anders called up a schematic on one of the holo-terminals. The shuttle bay was somewhere on the outer rim of the station – beyond a jumbled mass of corridors that didn't appear at all on my official station maps. The evac-pod was, predictably, even further away: on the top of the largest module. That was labelled STAFF LOUNGE. From a technical perspective, to someone who had never actually tried to escape a dying space station, that probably seemed like

F/2382188

a good design choice. But covering either of those distances was going to be a problem: there were now less than eighteen minutes until the station got scuttled.

Rather than demoralise the staff any more, I said: "We'll get you all out of here as quickly as possible. Head count?"

Anders swallowed again. "Twenty-two."

"Professor Saul is missing," Mason said. "All other staff accounted for."

Just then, something creaked ominously in the superstructure of the station. There was a deep, resonant groan: the mournful roll of thunder. The deck listed and my suit activated my mag-locks. Anders grabbed a chair, held herself steady.

"The station's decay is rapidly increasing," she said. "We . . . we've tried to . . . alter our drive pattern, but Maru Prime seems to be—"

"Where is Professor Saul?" I asked, with a little more anger in my voice than I had intended.

Anders set her jaw, face crumpling as though she might cry. "He . . . he's in the primary laboratory. I told him to stay here with the rest of us . . . but he insisted . . ."

"That's all we need: an errant scientist," Martinez said.

"We've been there too many times before," said Kaminski, with a dry chuckle. "Shuttle is active. Engines are online, although I'll need to manually couple the fuel lines."

Dr Anders seemed to wilt beneath my gaze. No point in blaming her, I supposed; it was more important that I actually got these people off the station. I buckled my helmet back into place and activated the intel from the drone network. The drones had invaded every area of the base, throwing our sensor-grid far and wide. No Krell, yet: that meant they were still outside the structure, working their way in. Every room, down to Life Support and Drive Maintenance, had been mapped . . .

Almost every room.

A chamber – one of the larger labs – remained sealed to the drones. A handful of them had gathered outside, and I watched their high-definition vid-feeds. The bio-scanner network, fed with the results of the drone sensor array, pinged a probable result: someone was inside the lab.

"Professor Saul insisted that he continue working until the last moment," Anders said. "I tried to get everyone here, I really did. His work is highly classified, highly specialised. He has a secure entry system in place for his personal lab . . ."

Time was running out fast, but – I reminded myself – we could still complete the mission.

"New orders," I declared to my squad. "I'm going after Saul. Mason, you're with me. Martinez, Jenkins – escort these people to the shuttle. Kaminski, go ahead and make sure that it's ready to leave."

Far Eye Observatory was dying, but not quietly.

Rather than a slow decline into the lava world below, the station was going to have a fast, spectacular death. I knew this, because the ambient temperatures were soaring – the internal atmosphere pressing uncomfortably against the second skin of my combat-suit. *If I'm finding this tough,* I deliberated, *then the civvies must be finding it even harder.* Computer systems, probably adapted for use in the bizarre and threatening environment, were shorting out. Bulkhead hatches flashed hazard warnings. That groaning – the noise that could only be the death knell of the facility itself – had become a constant background accompaniment to my journey.

All of this seismic activity was playing havoc with my sensor-suite. The bio-scanner worked sporadically and communications to the rest of the team were patchy.

I took point and Mason had the rear. Although we were in a state of combat readiness, speed was our priority. We cleared corridor junctions, tore our way through internal doors.

"External surveillance systems are off-line," Mason remarked, as we approached Saul's laboratory.

"Well spotted."

"Conditions outside are getting worse. No way that even shielded tech could survive out there."

I nodded. "Sci-Div probably never thought their facility would get so close to Maru's surface. I'm sure that the Krell will do just fine, though." They always seemed to, no matter what the conditions. "One of nature's bad jokes."

Mason paused, cocked her head. She had a habit of doing that – staring into the middle distance, stopping to inspect her HUD. It was a habit that might cost her a transition in the wrong circumstances. She was so new to all this: using the neural-link data-streams hadn't become second nature yet.

"What's wrong, Private?" I asked, still moving.

"What are the Krell doing here? It's just – well, doesn't this seem all a bit coincidental? I mean, the station is going down – crashing into Maru Prime – and the Krell choose now to invade?"

"Never question the Collective. The Krell can't be predicted. The Quarantine Zone isn't worth shit any more. If Command had listened to me, years back, I'd have told them that it would come to this."

I repressed a memory. *Elena.*

Mason jogged to catch up with me. "In basic training, I read that it costs in excess of a billion Alliance credits to send a simulant team into the Quarantine Zone."

I stopped outside the main lab doors. They were sealed

shut and the corridor outside was now swarming with drones. Whatever was beyond that door was preventing them from mapping the base, and they weren't happy about it.

I turned to Mason. "Command doesn't want the science team. They want Professor Saul. The others are a necessary inconvenience."

"But the briefing from Command referred to retrieval of the entire staff . . ."

"Welcome to your first real lesson, Private. Never believe what Command tells you."

That was something that I had learnt a long time ago.

"Did you read about Saul's background?" I asked. "His expertise?"

Mason nodded. "He's an expert in xenolinguistics."

"Yeah, with a specialism in the Shard."

Mason fell silent. From the expression on her face, she had clearly seen the evidence of the Helios mission: the knowledge that we'd brought back. It was supposed to be classified, but the *Point* was a closed community. Word got around, myth became fact.

"I bet that Command has a plan for Professor Saul," I said.

And if it involved the Shard, then I wanted to know about it – wanted to be part of it.

I popped the laboratory door with a single pulse from my plasma rifle. The metalwork was heavy duty but no match for a phased plasma charge. I created a man-sized hole in the panels, smoking hot at the edges, and prised open the rest.

The drones darted inside and, rifle up, I stalked after them. Mason followed closely behind.

The primary laboratory was jammed with scientific equipment, the likes of which I couldn't identify, and the lights were dimmed. One wall was claimed by ceiling-to-floor reinforced windows, as though this was an observation point. Outside, the rolling red sea of Maru Prime's surface was visible: the view quivering uncertainly as the station shifted on its axis again.

"Professor Saul?" I called into the room.

A tall, lean figure was over one of the workbenches – a man wearing a civilian spacesuit, just like those worn by the rest of the crew. *He's at least got that right,* I thought to myself. He was hurriedly collecting items from around the room: data-clips, slates, disassembled electronic components. An armoured black case sat open on the bench and he was packing the items away.

The drones swooped around the man's head and shoulders. Without any apparent conscious thought, he swiped them away with a gloved hand.

I sighed. *Science types: all the same.*

"Professor Ashan Saul?" I asked. This was nothing more than a nicety, as my suit had already positively identified him from onboard data.

Saul nodded and grumbled something in agreement, continuing to work without looking up. He wore a pair of thick-rimmed spectacles, which at first glance looked painfully archaic. As I got nearer, I saw that these were enhanced vision goggles: recording and playing back data onto the transparent lenses.

"Saul?" I barked, this time turning up my external speaker volume.

Saul jumped and turned to me.

"Yes," he muttered. "Yes, yes. You must be the Simulant Operations team. They said that you were coming."

He eyed me suspiciously; lingering on the Alliance battle-group emblem on my shoulder.

"You are the rescue party, aren't you? Ah, challenge: Chicago."

"Response: claret," I said. I hadn't expected to need to use the safety protocol. "My name is Major Harris. Let's go. There isn't much time—"

"Yes, yes. I understand. The station is capsizing, and the Krell are invading."

His blasé attitude irritated me – such apparent disregard for the efforts it had taken to retrieve him. He waved at the full-length window. The station axis shifted again and now the window showed the airspace above the facility. Krell and Alliance ships continued their assaults.

"I'm almost ready. Shouldn't be much longer."

I inspected Saul. He looked older than he had on his personnel file: beard a little greyer, skin tauter across his cheeks, far more worn out. He had a nasty scar on his left jaw, partially concealed by his beard. His left eye, beyond the coloured projections of the enhanced-vis glasses, was a milky white. His good eye twitched in my direction.

"The station is going down," I said, definitively. "We need to leave."

"Of course, of course," Saul nodded.

A cold feeling gripped me as I looked down at the open case on the workbench. It was filled by printed sheets: starmaps. My vision swam uncomfortably as I took in the tight printed scripture, something so alien that it was impossibly familiar.

Saul moved in front of me, breaking the spell. He grabbed for the case and sealed the outer locks. Attached it to his left wrist with a handcuff.

"It has to be me that carries this. It is my research. Command will want it."

"What is this stuff, Major?" Mason asked, prodding the workbench with the muzzle of her plasma rifle.

I recognised other components, up close. There were scattered hololithic plates pinned to the walls, backlit by light boxes.

Shard scripture.

Saul didn't say anything but he didn't need to. I was looking, I was absolutely sure, at data downloaded from the Key. There were even vid-captures of the Artefact on Helios – grainy, imprecise.

"I thought that this was an observatory?" Mason said.

She was smarter than we'd given her credit for.

Professor Saul nodded absently, almost glumly. "Far Eye Observatory isn't what it seems."

Mason glanced at me. I'd let her fill in the blanks, I decided. Whatever the crew of Far Eye had been working on – it was strictly a black op, established on a station out in the QZ because here it would be safe from prying eyes. It was all about plausible deniability.

Mason looked wounded by the revelation but I'd already decided that Command wanted the recovery of a substantial asset from Maru. Professor Saul, with his experience in such a specialised field, and his research: those were definitely worth risking a five billion-credit simulant team for. It was the sort of conceit I'd not only come to accept, but learnt to expect.

SIXTEEN MINUTES UNTIL TERMINAL DECLINE, my HUD insisted.

"We need to move," I ordered. "Get your shit together, Professor. Stay with us as we move through the station."

"Yes, yes."

I thought-activated the drone swarm: sending them off across the station to monitor our path. At that moment, something deep within the station's structure exploded, giving a reverberant metallic boom.

"And suit up, if you want to breathe."

The professor scrabbled around beneath his workbench, producing a battered plastic safety helmet. He clasped it into place, looking uneasy inside the spacesuit. Then he strapped a solid-shot pistol to his leg.

I linked to Jenkins, moving as I talked.

"What's your status, Jenkins?"

"Clearing the main mess hall now."

The mess hall wasn't far from Communications – the group hadn't made much progress. Damned civvies.

"Not helped by the gravity and atmosphere leakage. Decks three through eleven are venting."

"Just keep moving. You got a bead on Kaminski?"

"His signal is intermittent. I can't get through to him."

"Keep trying."

"My scanner is malfunctioning as well. I can't even pick you up on it."

"Use your good old-fashioned mark one eyeballs."

"Mark twos, actually.

"Stay frosty. Harris out."

"Jenkins out."

We moved through the damaged lab doorway and out into the corridor. The overhead lights gave up – casting an impenetrable gloom over the section. I used my helmet sensor array, a combination of infrared and night-vision, to manoeuvre onwards. I triggered my mag-locks to keep moving. Behind me, I saw that Saul had a similar system incorporated into his suit. He wasn't used to walking with locks though, and stumbled like he was wading through drying concrete. Mason hustled him along, her rifle panning the dark. A shrill keening filled the air.

"That will be the primary drive malfunctioning," Saul proclaimed. "The station was originally tethered into a geosynchronous orbit by the drivers in the lower decks. With those gone, we will reach terminal decline faster than anticipated."

My AI updated almost immediately: TWELVE MINUTES UNTIL TERMINAL DECLINE.

"Damn. We're losing time."

I was using the updated intel from the Communications Centre. The path to the shuttle bay was now mapped by my HUD and the continuous visuals from the drone swarm. Roughly half of those had now gone off-line; either no longer broadcasting, or perhaps destroyed by the chaos erupting across the facility.

"What would cause such an occurrence?" Mason said, still moving on. "Didn't your station AI predict that you had several minutes before safety parameters were breached?"

Saul gave a soft shrug. Through the plasglass helmet, his thin face was sweating profusely. A disabling layer of condensation had formed on the interior of his face-plate.

"Maybe the AI got it wrong. I've never really trusted her. Nothing that intelligent should be fully trusted. Or maybe some external force—"

Before he could finish the sentence, the bio-scanner illuminated with a wave of soft targets – potential organic life-forms in our vicinity.

There was no time to shout a warning.

In front of me, a six-inch-thick metal bulkhead suddenly exploded. Debris showered us – boomer-fire pouring through the destroyed door. Bright as plasma, just as deadly: multi-coloured laser lances, scorching the floor and ceiling.

"Brace!" I ordered, rolling aside as Krell flooded the corridor. "Shields up."

Another piece of new kit: the personal null-shield generator – one of Research & Development's more useful innovations. I locked my left arm in front of my face, plasma rifle aimed with my right, and watched as the generator activated. The actual tech was encased somewhere in my backpack, powered by the same generator as my life-support package. An oily shimmer appeared in front of me. As it went up, the shield began to hum angrily – made my skull bones vibrate.

"Get behind me, Professor," I ordered.

Three targets presented. Krell gun-grafts – technical designation "secondary-forms". They were slower than the primary-form warrior caste but armed with larger and longer-ranged weapons. The nearest drone caught a decent image of the lead Krell: armed with a grafted bio-cannon – a boomer – complete with an ammunition sac that trailed between its stomach and gun-arms.

The Krell group moved as a single entity. They poured through the door and fired. They looked vaguely confused – if they were capable of experiencing such an emotion – as their shots hit my null-shield.

Upgrades, fucker! It felt good to get one up on them for a change, although I knew that it wouldn't last. The null-shield generator was new tech – once the Krell had faced the gear a few times, they would devise a counter-measure. Individually, the Krell had limited tactical awareness, but the Collective was the best battlefield database in the universe.

Incandescent pulses fired on both sides. The Krell advanced regardless. The lead xeno caught a round to the chest – leaking blood and ichor across the floor – and began to close the distance between us.

Mason primed a grenade, scattered it towards the Krell.

It breached her shield temporarily, bounced off the wall as the station axis shifted again. The secondary-forms had no mag-locks and grappled with whatever terrain features they could to stay fixed to the deck. The lucky distraction was enough to throw them off balance: the grenade exploded amid the trio of aliens. Suddenly body parts and gore covered the corridor. Two of the aliens went down, although the third was rallying for a further attack.

This was a kill or be killed situation; no cover, nowhere to run. There was little point in stealth, little purpose in trying to effect a retreat. I rose up, cycled three micro-grenades into the underslung launcher of my plasma rifle. New tech is good, but sometimes the old ways are best: I launched the incendiary grenades at the Krell attackers.

"Down!" I yelled to Saul, grinding my teeth in expectation.

The professor rolled sideways, the deck listing beneath him like that of a ship at sea, and the incendiaries went off.

The remaining secondary-form exploded. It fired its boomer as it went but every shot went wide.

"More incoming," Mason said.

This time a primary-form darted through the smoke. It moved with an alien grace: a bio-form obviously adapted for life in or near water, a theory supplemented by the xeno's sharkish features. The xeno didn't pause and I caught its movements only in freeze frame. Despite their physical bulk, the primary-forms were seriously fast.

Mason slammed the xeno aside with a volley of shots from her plasma rifle.

The primary kept coming, tumbling to within a metre of our position – holes smoking in its chest and head. The body eventually collapsed.

"Just follow me and stay safe," I ordered, and was already up and moving.

CHAPTER THREE

I ALWAYS COME BACK

A swarm of hostile signals – blazing hot on my HUD – followed us through the skewed corridors. Elsewhere, pestering my hindbrain like a hot needle, the drone army sent regular alerts: going off-line faster than I could follow, broadcasting a stream of unpalatable images.

Far Eye Observatory was now filled with invaders. The whole pantheon of Krell xeno-forms was present: from primary-forms, through to secondary-forms, even a handful of the dedicated leader-forms.

It was a pleasant surprise when friendlies appeared on my scanner – identifiable by their IFF beacons – and even more of a turn when I realised that the survivors weren't Lazarus Legion.

"Hold your fire," I barked at Mason, waving a hand behind me towards Saul.

Three troopers made their way through the smoke and dust. My suit flagged them as the team under Captain Baker, and as they approached I saw that he was still in command.

"Moving on objective, sir!" Baker rumbled. He saluted me.

I sighed, shook my head. "Ah, the fabulous Baker Boys. Is this all that's left of your outfit?"

All three survivors were battered, covered in xeno gore and severely rattled. Behind his face-plate, Baker looked much like he did in real life: middle-aged, grizzled, a veteran soldier a little past his prime. He pulled back his thin lips and flashed a toothy grin.

"Yes, sir," Baker said. He shook his head. "Fish heads got us on the way down. Lost two skins before we could get on-station."

"Doesn't look like the other teams even touched down, so you have that honour at least."

Baker indicated towards Saul. "But it's the Legion that claims the HVT."

"Only the best need apply."

He eyed Mason, saw her blank combat-suit. "So New Girl isn't official yet?"

"Well, if she fucks up she can always apply to join your outfit."

I clocked the two behind Baker, both in unmarked suits.

Baker flared his nostrils and sighed. "I'd have her any day of the week, but that's another story. Ready to assist on the bounce when you are, sir."

"That's appreciated. We're moving on the shuttle bay." I uploaded my tactical plan to Baker's suit. "Less than three hundred metres."

"Solid copy." He turned to the two fresh-faced simulants behind him. "You heard the man – move out!"

Visibility had improved, but only slightly. There were flashing blood-red emergency lamps in the walls and ceilings, but black smoke pumped from the air-recyclers.

"This station is experiencing a critical emergency," the mainframe AI repeated, over the PA. "All hands evacuate."

"Where's your sergeant, Laz?" Baker asked me, as we picked our way through the corridor. "Has she gone and left—"

Before he could complete the sentence, another primary-form sprang up ahead. The Krell slammed into Baker, knocking him sideways. One of his squad opened fire but in the tight confines of the corridor lost his nerve. The Krell slashed its enormous bladed forelimbs through Baker's body, ripping open his combat-suit. The station atmosphere had not yet fully drained, but was seriously depleted: Baker started gasping for air, clawing at his face-plate.

"Oh fuck!" one of the fresh-faces shouted.

The Krell whipped its head around, double-jointed jaw opening to expose row on row of shark teeth. I fired, sending bright lances across the corridor, but the xeno was too fast. It cleared the dead captain's body, vaulted right into one of the privates. In less than a second, all of Baker's squad had been reduced to bloody ribbons.

I put three more shots into the xeno's armoured body. Carnage complete, the alien was dead.

I caught the panicked look in Saul's eyes; the look that asked, "Am I actually going to make it out of this alive?" But he didn't voice the question and I had no time to baby him.

I activated my comm. "Jenkins! You read me?"

The comm-link hissed: "Affirmative. Moving through Filtration."

"Casualties?"

"Negative, but it's been damned close."

"We're coming up on your six."

"I read you on the scanner."

Mason, Saul and I jogged into what was once a filtration plant. A tangled network of pipework sat under a heavy plasglass dome. I guessed that water on Maru Prime was a serious commodity, perhaps more so than it was elsewhere in space. This was a recycling centre that had now fallen into disrepair. Liquid gold, lost to the war, pumped from exposed plumbing. Between the sagging remains of two protective plastic tents, the survivors crouched. Jenkins half-stood on our arrival.

"You took your time, Major," she said with a dark grin.

"Multiple kills en route."

"Some men will use anything for an excuse."

"We met Baker, too."

"How is the old bastard?"

"Dead. Bought it with two rookies."

"Figures."

The staff huddled between Jenkins and Martinez. Professor Saul went to join them, patting Anders on the back and muttering something over the private comm. Anders had been crying; her face was streaked red.

"What's the plan?" Jenkins asked.

"Clearest route to the shuttle bay is through the maintenance deck. You got ears on Kaminski?"

Jenkins shook her head. "Negative."

Looking back at the terrified civvies, and at the flashing warning on my HUD – SEVEN MINUTES UNTIL TERMINAL DECLINE – made me decide to break protocol.

I switched comm channels. My combat-suit was a command model; I could order a protocol override to boost my signal.

"Kaminski, you still alive?"

"Affirmative, Major, but only just. Hangar is seeing some action, but I'm lying low."

Jenkins shook her head, laughed to herself. "That'll be the day."

"You're hiding?"

"Affirmative. That's one way of putting it."

"Is the shuttle prepped?"

"Primed and ready for evac."

"Then stay alive, whatever way you can. We're less than a minute from your position."

"Solid copy. Kaminski out."

The staff began shouting and hollering.

"Stay calm, people!" Martinez insisted. "God will protect you. You're all going to be all right—"

I wasn't sure that the Almighty was listening. Martinez meant well, but his words were no counter for what the group had witnessed.

The ceiling of the filtration plant was domed – made of reinforced plastic-glass, gridded with metal supports. It presented a good vantage point to observe the developing space battle in low orbit. Some of the survivors had been watching the sky – the multi-coloured explosions, the bright streams of flak, the plasma pulses – but suddenly all faces, in unison, were turned to the spectacle above.

Something enormous exploded.

A brilliant, eye-scorching light filled the blackness. It sent numerous miniature sub-detonations through space. The dying vessel couldn't have been far from our location, because very rapidly we were being showered with burning debris. Chunks of starship slammed into the plastic dome, assaulted the rest of the station.

"*Gracia de Dios . . .*" Martinez whispered.

The pattern of the explosion could only mean that it was an Alliance vessel. Not a fighter: had to be one of the assault cruisers. I took some minor reassurance from the fact that it wasn't the *Mallard*, or we'd all be dead right now. But it did mean that the war in heaven wasn't going as well as planned and that we had even less time to make the retrieval.

"Everyone up!" I declared, shouting over my loudspeaker and indicating with my hands. "Mag-locks on! Follow us. Squad, combat formation—"

The dome above began to crack. Very noisily, very dramatically. Escaping atmosphere began to hiss, then shriek.

"Mason, you take the rear!" Jenkins ordered, locking her boots and helping some of the civvies up. "Martinez, you take left flank. We've got to get these people out of here now! Go, go, go!"

The dome suddenly exploded outwards. Glass, metal and frozen liquid were sucked out. I braced, grabbed Saul. His civilian-issue mag-locks were torn off the deck and he flapped around like a child's doll. Anders sailed past me. Mason reached out a hand to catch her. Too late: the female doctor's arms windmilled as she flew by. Mason fumbled with her rifle, maybe thought about discarding it to go after Anders, but I warned her against it.

"Don't, Mason. She's already gone."

The hurricane of escaping atmosphere cost us most of the survivors – bodies spinning out, catching on the remains of the dome, slamming into assorted debris raining from the sky above. I barely gave them a thought. Saul was all that mattered.

I might be expendable, but right now I had to survive. If I died, then Saul had no chance of survival. Certain tactical and operational considerations become far more relevant once a human, non-expendable asset is present in the theatre of war.

I have to get Saul out, I repeated. The safest way to do that was to ensure that I remained viable for as long as possible. With the station collapsing around me, that was becoming an increasingly difficult objective to achieve.

I thought of all this as I cajoled the remaining survivors through the ruined facility.

FOUR MINUTES UNTIL TERMINAL DECLINE.

The station's AI gave up with the warning – probably shut off, maybe diverting what little power remained to the essentials of trying to keep Far Eye Observatory upright. If that was the plan, it wasn't working.

As we scrambled towards the shuttle, two more Krell appeared ahead – this time, firing stinger-spines. Poisoned flechette rounds, propelled by organic rail shooters. About as powerful as an Alliance-issue armour-piercing round.

"Repressing fire. Move on the shuttle bay – next junction. We don't have time to get into a firefight."

"Affirmative," Jenkins said.

The volley of fire hit our activated null-shields. We fired back with plasma rifles, from the hip, always advancing. One of the secondaries went down. Despite being riddled with plasma wounds the remaining xeno was still combat-effective.

"More hostiles incoming!" Jenkins roared.

More primary-forms swarmed us from the same direction. Two big bastards slipped through the shimmering protective shields without pause – made for firearms and energy weapons only, these did nothing to stop them. I dropped one of the two with a volley from my rifle but the other descended on the group.

"By Gaia!" Saul shouted. He fired his pistol into the approaching alien.

Great: an Earth worshipper. That's all I need.

Whatever ammo he was packing, the rounds bounced off the armoured head of the nearest Krell. The xeno turned in his direction, mouth split with rage—

"I've got this one," Martinez said.

He grabbed at the target, jamming his rifle into the creature's underside. The xeno moved faster than him, bladed forelimbs punching right through his torso. He managed a yelp in surprise – it's always surprising when they get you – and was lifted straight off the ground.

Martinez's biometrics leapt into overdrive. Even if he didn't know it yet, he was already dead.

"Good journey," I whispered.

I used the momentary pause in the assault to fire through Martinez's body: a full auto stream of plasma pulses. His armoured suit ran like water, super-heated by the impacts, and he stopped trembling. The Krell on the other side of his body exploded.

"Martinez is out," I said, to anyone who cared.

The shuttle-bay doors were ahead. I dispensed another xeno with a quick blast from my M95, waved on Jenkins with the remaining civvies. Saul was among them.

I caught a glimpse of the interior of the shuttle bay. It was a large, mainly empty hangar. The blast-shutters were ahead, promising escape from the dying station – embossed with hazard warnings, suggestions not to open without prior approval. The shuttle sat on the apron. It was a basic runabout – probably the oldest piece of technology on the station. Snub-nosed and worn-out, the name MARY-SUE was stamped on the hull. The model was a not-too-distant relative of our own Wildcat APS, but a strictly civilian version. Although a quad of thruster engines sat at the rear, the shuttle had no quantum-drive capability at all – it wouldn't be capable of fleeing into Q-space. I just hoped it would be enough to get us off the station.

Kaminski had set up shop at the aft access ramp. His rifle was up in a braced crouch.

"Keep moving, people!" he shouted. "Not much further—!"

The shuttle creaked with the see-sawing motion of the rest of the station. It was moored into place by fuel feedlines. One of those burst under the renewed motion, spilling pressurised fluid across the hangar bay floor. The fuel was highly flammable, meant to be handled under restricted circumstances.

A pool had already formed on the deck.

I froze, detected that something bad – very bad – was about to happen.

The base tilted further on its axis. It had done that already – had been doing that for several minutes – but this was more extreme.

This time, the tilt didn't correct.

A metal cargo crate slid past me, moving fast enough to send a trail of orange sparks as it went. The crate smashed into the shuttle, another feedline disconnecting.

The fuel ignited.

Violet flame licked the air. In low atmosphere, fire was usually a limited concern; but the shuttle fuel was super-combustible. Fire poured over the deck almost immediately.

Then everything that wasn't bolted down began to slide towards the exterior bay doors. Those were still sealed shut – would require something big and heavy to cause significant damage.

Oh fuck. The shuttle.

Seemingly in slow motion, it slid towards the bay doors. The noise was deafening: that nerve-jangling shriek of metal grinding against metal. I watched as it capsized.

"Get anchored – now!" I ordered.

The station continued that interminable tilting, almost vertical now.

The shuttle hit the bay doors with an enormous boom.

It settled there for a long second, collected with other detritus from the bay.

"I think the doors might hold—" Kaminski started.

He never got to finish the sentence.

The blast doors creaked, then spectacularly failed. The shuttle fell right through them as they gave way in the centre.

Kaminski scrambled to get free of the shuttle but it all happened too quickly.

Shuttle, Kaminski, any hope of evacuation from Maru Prime: all tumbled through the destroyed doors.

The ship fell side-on, nose down. Kaminski spiralled out of the hatch – waving his hands frantically, his plasma rifle falling with him – to the awaiting lava flows below. There was no way that the shuttle could be preserved, nothing that could be done.

The wave of heat from the open doors hit me like a fist. My mag-locks held me upright, on a wall that had seconds ago been a floor. Debris fell all around me, through the open hangar doors. Krell bodies, station staff – all and sundry were being sucked out.

I lost sight of his falling body and Kaminski's vitals flat-lined. I scanned the area, desperately making an assessment of what damage we had suffered, who was left.

Two staff members remained: one aura-tagged as PROFESSOR SAUL – PRIMARY ASSET. He was locked to the deck, near the entrance door. The other – a middle-aged man – staggered about on his mag-locks. He clutched towards Jenkins, reaching out desperately, arching his back.

"Please!" he screamed. "Don't let me die!"

Jenkins was attached to a cargo anchor point on the floor. One hand wrapped around the pin, she went to grab for him with the other.

"Jesus," she moaned, "why is nothing ever easy?"

The man managed to grasp her forearm, just as his mag-locks gave way. Jenkins lost her balance momentarily, but managed to stay attached to the anchor.

Mason was upright, locks holding, terrified behind her face-plate. She was still squeezing off pulses from her M95 into the mass of following Krell.

The fish heads had fared well in the confusion. Some clung to the ceilings, others leapt between sparse cover on the walls. Gun-grafts assembled in the distance – clambering into the station through the destroyed blast doors. Krell fire began to cover the area – stingers, boomers, shriekers. I returned fire with my rifle – sending a volley of explosive grenades across the hangar-bay doors. Xeno bodies dropped from the station in hordes but there were always more.

"Mason!" I ordered. "Cover Saul – get him back towards the entrance door."

My comm crackled to life: "Lazarus Actual, do you read?"

"This is Actual," I said,. "I read, but I'm busy right now."

"Command reads your position. Team appears compromised."

"Negative. Hostiles present. Shuttle has been lost."

"We saw that. Suggest that you make extraction. Call it a day, Lazarus. It's over."

"Fuck that."

I thought-commanded the station map onto my HUD, still firing away at the encroaching Krell. It wasn't over; it couldn't be. Saul was alive. There was still a chance that the mission could be redeemed. *The evac-pod.* A route to the pod lit on my map: back through the main corridor, through the living quarters.

"I can make it to the evac-pod. I can do this."

"The station is crawling with hostiles, Lazarus."

"Then why are we wasting time talking? I have a job to do."

"The extraction is hot. More Krell are inbound. We're bugging out in two minutes, tops."

"Fuck you. Lazarus Actual out."

Jenkins grunted beside me. She was still holding the unknown scientist, one hand locked around the man's wrist, the other grappling with the anchor point. The civvie bashed against the deck—

Jenkins slipped again, and then she was gone.

No more ceremony than that: even in a sim, she couldn't hold the man's weight any longer. She spun along the deck – out of the shuttle doors, the blue-suited civvie beside her, and into the inferno below.

Mason had Saul. He was still teetering on his mag-locks, that ridiculous armoured case swinging back and forth.

A Krell stinger-spine clipped me. The round lodged in my shoulder and the impact threw me backwards. It carried a poison load – enough to kill Saul, enough to seriously injure me. My locks gave out, and I started to slide the way that Jenkins had just gone.

"Not me, you bastards!" I shouted.

I immediately let go of my rifle. Irrelevant now; staying alive was far more important. In exactly the same way as Jenkins, Martinez, everyone else I'd lost on this damned mission, I started to claw at the sky – desperate for something to grab on to.

Sim Ops taught me how to die but Special Forces taught me how to survive. I learnt my craft as a soldier during covert ops; using my environment and adapting to it. You don't forget those skills.

I connected with the deck and grabbed at the space between floor tiles. One hand caught – by the tips of my fingers. Then the other hand caught as well. I roared with the exertion – all of my armoured weight held on my finger-tips – but held tight.

"Glove mag-locks!" I roared.

The magnetic strips in my gloves were weak, not intended for use in these circumstances, but they would have to do. Anything to help me stay put.

Above me, Mason and Saul were still on their feet. Mason was shooting at the Krell – now below me.

"Not today . . ." I whispered to myself.

Out of the corner of my eye, the semi-translucent picture of Elena was still on my HUD.

She's why I have to do this. She is why I can't give up.

One hand over the other, I began to climb towards Mason and Saul. Behind them, the bay entrance door was still open – and that was a route back into the station, to the evac-pod. My gloves were fully powered and I began to dig my finger-tips into the metal flooring. I made finger holds of the gaps between every tile. As I prised each one up, I moved on to the next handhold. Meanwhile Krell fire rained all around me and my bio-scanner went berserk with incoming hostiles.

"Fall back towards the door," I ordered.

"Affirmative," Mason said.

Her null-shield lit with sidearms fire. It was only a few steps to the bulkhead but in these conditions it seemed impossible. Mason was now bleeding, I realised, from several stinger impacts.

STATION IN TERMINAL DECLINE, my AI declared.

SHUT UP, I commed back.

As I got nearer, I heard that Saul was praying. He wept in great, chortling waves; a man afraid that he was about to meet his maker. His exact words were unclear but he sounded resigned to his fate.

Another Krell weapon hit me, dragging me back to precision of thought. My medi-suite complained that safe drug administration levels had been exceeded. I overrode those warnings, fed more endorphin and adrenaline into my system. I was going to shut down soon – crash and burn. The world had started to take on a dreamlike quality: edges blurred, everything moving in slow motion around me.

Mason lurched over Saul, protecting him from more bio-weapons fire. Her shield suddenly gave out and she disappeared under a wave of flechettes. A secondary-form, attached to the ceiling – now parallel to my position – streamed a shrieker down on her. Even in the low atmosphere, through my helmet, I could hear the weapon's distinctive sonics: a pitched scream. A jet of super-heated flame scoured over Mason and coated her armour. The flechettes opened her up, the flame cooked her: the perfect combination of weapons.

Mason's vitals flatlined on my HUD – no doubt, she was dead. Even so, she stood upright in her baking suit for a second or two. Her face boiled through the melted plate of her helmet; skin and bone and plastic. I was quite sure that it was a death that she would remember and the image of her standing there was something I would struggle to forget as well.

This isn't a dream, I contemplated. *It's a nightmare.*

Mason's body had acted as a shield for Saul. I finally reached him and grabbed him by the arm. I hauled him alongside me. Through the door, back the way we had come.

It was dark inside the station and even emergency power had failed. My suit-lamps flickered on, threw out bright pools of light. I vaguely registered that I wasn't carrying an active weapon, and unholstered my PPG-13 plasma pistol.

Keep going. Keep going. Command sent you here for a reason. You saw Shard material in that room! Saul might be a step nearer . . .

Krell were dropping into my path, through the murk and debris. I slaughtered them all: my plasma pistol laying down a precise curtain of death.

At the end of the main lounge, the objective loomed. There was writing on the wall but it was at the wrong angle. In my impaired condition, it took me a second to recognise the words.

EMERGENCY EVACUATION POD.

"Holy Gaia," Saul cried, "please protect us through the cold voyage to the stars—"

"Shut up!" I slurred. "I'm all that's left."

Another round impacted my shoulder. Stingers pitted the wall around the evac-pod entrance and ricocheted around the chamber.

I reached for the pod activation controls. Bashed again and again on the door stud. The machine wasn't made for careful or considered operation, didn't require much to operate. With painful slowness, the doors began to open.

My lamps lit the inside of the pod and I conducted a cursory examination. It was a one-man unit with a tightly padded interior. Not exactly luxurious: no navigational controls, the aim was to evacuate the passenger from a station emergency, and to keep him or her alive long enough for a rescue party to pick them up.

"Get inside," I said.

Saul scrambled up the deck, tossing his spent pistol into the pod. The gun hadn't done him any good anyway. Angrily, I grabbed him by the legs and pushed him in. The case was still attached to his arm. He turned back to look at me; through his scratched and battered helmet. The comm-line had been cut between us, maybe at that moment or maybe somewhere else along the way. His mouth moved silently – forming words that looked like "thank you".

I slammed the ACTIVATE POD control. The doors rapidly sealed.

TERMINAL DECLINE, my AI repeated.

"The station or me?" I laughed.

A stinger caught me in the leg, knocking me over a dead Krell. My lamps flashed over more bodies in the dark. There was another primary-form beside me and a gun-graft was poised on the ceiling.

From my prone position, I grinned up at them.

"Filthy xenos!" I shouted.

The primary moved off towards me. I emptied the pistol power cell – hoping to achieve nothing more than pointless butchery. The primary-form disintegrated under the hail of plasma.

The lounge had no view-ports and I couldn't see outside. My suit was trashed – all systems failing, my entire sensor-suite off-line. There was no way for me to know whether Saul had made it off the doomed station.

I was tired. The bio-toxins were rampant throughout my system. There was nothing else to be done. The secondary-form overhead sneered at me, aiming the grafted boomer in my direction. There was a sea of Krell forming in the room now, watching.

"I'm Lazarus," I shouted. "I always come back."

The secondary-form opened fire.

They say that a man's life flashes through his mind's eye as he dies. That you consider all of your regrets, all of your mistakes. People important to you, frozen moments in time, those events that make a man who he is.

The moment of extraction – although it is not a moment at all, but rather an infinitesimal segment of time – is an interesting one. No scientist can really explain what happens to the human mind, as it extracts from a simulant body: it has to be experienced to be truly understood.

It's like dying, because you do see those important milestones – those iconic occurrences that have shaped you – but there is also that niggling suggestion that you will have the chance to change all of this. A second shot: that things can be undone.

I only saw one face as I made extraction. Snapshots of Elena – as she'd been on Azure, before she left for the Maelstrom. It was a chance to savour those memories that I tried to keep sealed away. I had too many regrets, had made too many mistakes. They would weigh me down, hold me in the dead simulant body, if I allowed myself to dwell on them.

"I'm sorry, Elena," I whispered through lips that didn't even exist any more.

Then I heard it: the sound. That signal, so fragile that when I concentrated on it the sound evaporated.

The Artefact.

It was all over in a picosecond, less than that even, and my consciousness retreated across space into the waiting ship.

I woke up in the simulator-tank, aboard the *Mallard*.

My hands clawed at my shoulder – where that last secondary-form had fired a boomer into me – but it was an automatic reaction. *There's nothing there,* I told myself. *It's done.* I steadied myself against the plastic canopy of the tank.

There were faces out there, watching from the relative safety of the medical bay, but for a long while no one seemed to do anything. They just looked on; slack, emotionless faces.

No, not emotionless: just uncomprehending.

I blinked the wash out of my eyes, let the tank purge. With trembling fingers I plucked at the cables from each of my data-ports. The transparent tank door opened and I staggered out.

"What the fuck's wrong with you people?" I rumbled.

My arms, legs, voice – none of it seemed willing to bend to my commands. I glared at the nearest medtech, who jumped and passed me an aluminium blanket – shot me up with a hypodermic of post-extraction recovery drugs. But then she retreated again, and stood in the same stunned silence as the rest of the room.

The Lazarus Legion were present, as well as Avis and Baker, and their respective teams. All just looking at me.

"That was . . ." Martinez broke the silence, shaking his head, "fucking unbelievable . . ."

"What are you doing standing around?" I said, uncomfortable with the attention. "There's a war going on."

A communicator blared in the background, broadcasting clipped Naval squawk: *". . . that's a confirm on pick-up for the evac-pod . . ."*

"Solid copy. Primary asset is in the hold."

"Issuing retreat order, moving off at sub-light speed."

"Copy that. Breaking orbit now."

"Great work, Lazarus," Baker added. "We were watching the whole thing, through your suit-feeds. Never seen anything like it."

"We'll have you people back on the *Point* within the next

day or so," the communicator bleated again, this time directed to the medical bay. "Good job."

I just stood, trembling, shaking.

"I need a damned drink."

CHAPTER FOUR

PSYCH

We pulled out of Maru Prime. Two Alliance ships – the *Mallard* and the *Peace of Seattle* – made good the escape and left the Krell to it. The Alliance had given as good as they got, and left behind the carcasses of several Krell starships. Whatever their reason for the abrupt and brutal incursion into the QZ, the Krell didn't pursue. Maybe they were licking their wounds, maybe biding their time; but several hours into the retreat Naval control confirmed that the Krell had bugged out of Maru Prime as well.

Astronomically speaking, Maru wasn't far from the Alliance border with the Quarantine Zone. The journey back took less than a day, cruising at FTL speed. I was glad that we could avoid the hypersleep capsules for such a short trip.

It had been a successful operation. Saul had been picked up almost as soon as his evac-pod had been fired out of Far Eye Observatory. He'd survived the ordeal without life-threatening injury, although I had no doubt the experience would be life-changing. He'd been witness to things few Sci-Div staff had the misfortune of seeing; brushed death so closely that the bony fingers had left their mark deep on his psyche.

I considered searching him out – asking him about the subject of his research, why Far Eye had been chosen as the location of a black ops project – but dismissed the idea. I had a feeling that our allocation to the retrieval operation hadn't been a coincidence.

Of course, not everything had gone to plan. There had been losses.

There are always losses in war, the Directorate AI tacticians would no doubt say. Victory is all that matters.

I didn't doubt that but recognising what we'd lost was what made us human. It separated us from the Krell. The mission had cost us an Alliance warship. Likely several hundred personnel onboard; gone to the cold void. Two of the simulant teams under my command had been located on the *Washington's Paragon* when it went down. I was sure that their families would receive comfortable compensation packages and "Dear John" letters from the Department of Off-World Affairs.

The *Mallard* had taken fire during the battle over Maru Prime, and made dry dock on arrival at FOB *Liberty Point*. My squad gathered in the umbilical tube between the *Mallard* and the *Point*'s dock.

The Far Eye operation had taken less than a week of objective time, but coming back to the *Point* always reminded me how long I'd been away on Helios. So much had changed in that time, and it wasn't the place that I remembered. There was extensive construction work now: scaffold, welding teams, Army engineering units. The *Point* had grown to be the biggest station not only on the Quarantine Zone but in all of Alliance space. It was suspected to be the largest in all of human space, although the Directorate weren't exactly willing to confirm that.

Soldiers and crewmen were dutifully lined up for clearance. The Sim Ops teams were dressed in Army khakis, Sci-Div in white smocks, maintenance techs in orange overalls, Navy in formal blues: all neatly separated by rank and role. Everyone had the tired air of having worked hard for a short period, and now riding the downer at the other end of a sudden adrenaline spike.

My squad had the same vacant, slightly misplaced expressions on their faces. It was a gaze that simulant operators developed over time, an implacable wrongness that a man should never feel when he is piloting the body he's born in.

Kaminski jostled with Martinez next to me, agitated to get on base.

"Another successful operation," Martinez said. "Another victory for the Lazarus Legion."

"Does Mason get her badge yet?" Jenkins asked, in a disinterested sort of way.

The squad, save for Mason, had fabric badges stitched to the shoulders of their uniforms. The badges were an old Army tradition – awarded for achievements as simple as basic combat training, or more complex accomplishments like capsule-dropping or courage under fire. My original team members had a large variety of awards – topped by the Lazarus Legion badge, giving our official Alliance Army designation.

"Absolutely not," Kaminski said. "No fucking way. She's only got seven transitions under her belt."

A holo-patch on the chest indicated the number of transitions each of us had made. Whilst the Alliance Army had medals and honours and everything in between, the patch was the closest thing that Sim Ops Programme had to a dedicated decoration. It was the only statistic that mattered between operators.

"So? She did good."

"The regs are quite clear," Kaminski continued, "and she has to prove that she's Legion material before she gets the badge."

"Fuck off, Kaminski," Mason said.

She cocked her head in his direction. She was a good deal smaller than the rest of the group, and stood rubbing her elbows, arms crossed over her chest. Her platinum-blonde hair was tied up behind her head, making her neck look painfully slender.

"She knows how to handle you already, 'Ski," I said. "And I thought I was Lazarus? Why are you the one making up all the rules?"

"Look, we can't have every wet-behind-the-ears, greener-than-puke, freshest recruit, claiming that they're Lazarus Legion. Take the guy before her – what was his name?"

"Omar," Jenkins said. "He was nice."

"Yeah, well nice doesn't cut it with the Legion. How long'd he last?"

"He managed two ops," Mason said. "I read all about him. He dropped out."

"Couldn't keep up with the A-game," Kaminski said. "So you have to prove you're good enough."

I said nothing. It was just a bit of fun; something to keep Kaminski engaged between operations. Although she'd done a good job on Maru Prime, in truth I wasn't sure whether Mason was Legion material either. She had the makings of a decent trooper but I'd been there. I wanted to make sure she was stable enough to stay on the team before I made her permanent.

"We did show them our A-game, *mano*," Martinez said, shaking his head. "But I got questions."

"Such as?" I asked. Although I was tired, the circumstances of the last mission didn't sit easy with me.

"Like why do the Krell keep coming into the QZ?" Martinez said. "Since we got back from Helios, we've been there too often. The QZ isn't exactly quarantined any more."

"I'm quite sure that Command know exactly what they're doing," Jenkins said, adopting her most cynical tone of voice. "And that grunts like us shouldn't ask questions."

"Well, it's good to be back," Kaminski said to the group at large. "Nothing like recycled air and bad beer."

The docking doors chimed and the tube opened to *Liberty Point*. I gathered up my duty gear in a canvas bag and stalked down the ramp. The air felt and tasted familiar, more metallic than that on the *Mallard*. There was a slight gravitational shift as well: just enough to let me know that I'd stepped between artificial gravity wells.

"Do you ever hear from Tyler?" Jenkins said.

Jenna Tyler was the sole civilian survivor from Helios. She'd been gone for months; back Corewards after our debrief, to be settled somewhere nice and quiet, with a decent severance package, where neither the media nor the Directorate could get to her.

"She went to Alpha Centauri, I think," Kaminski said. "For a civvie, she was okay."

I fell in step beside Martinez, cricked my neck painfully. I didn't yet feel completely at ease in my own skin. Each breath was alien, each heartbeat foreign. I knew that it would get better with time, but the acclimatisation back into my real body was unpleasant.

"You okay there, *jefe*?" Martinez asked, under his breath. The rest of the team were moving off ahead of us; maybe Martinez was trying to talk to me without them overhearing.

"As I ever am," I said, quietly.

Martinez gave a gentle nod. "Maybe that extraction, you know, jarred you or something?"

"Maybe."

Martinez didn't quite have it right, I decided. It wasn't the extractions that were getting worse; it was the transition into my real body. The sense of not belonging in my own skin was increasing.

"It's been getting worse since Helios. What about you?"

"Helios changed everything," Martinez said, pulling a concerned face but at the same time trying to keep our conversation private among a sea of people. "No shame in admitting that. You still having the dreams?"

I sighed. "Sometimes."

"Go see the medtechs. They might be able to give you something."

"Think I'll do that."

We were greeted by a fleet of security drones, and the conversation was over. These were bigger than the combat models we had used back on Maru Prime – tasked with checking biometrics and immigration status.

"Please remain still while your Alliance citizenship is confirmed," bleated the nearest drone. "Please remain still while . . ."

The human flood mostly ignored them and we were no different. They did their best, weaving between bodies and lighting up exposed skin with data-sensors, but it was a losing war. I caught sight of a couple of familiar faces in the crowd. I'd been seeing them a lot, recently. Before I could make any enquiry, the faces were gone: swept along with the tide.

On aching legs I stumbled back to my quarters.

After my promotion to major, I'd been assigned a new cabin. That sounded grander than it really was: my original quarters had been reassigned while I was on Helios. Someone in Logistics had decided that I was probably KIA, that Command would shortly reach the same conclusion, and that my old quarters should be reallocated. It wasn't a big deal – I hadn't been particularly attached to the room – but it was another change, another indication that while I had remained the same the rest of the universe had moved on.

I swiped my palm on the entry scanner and the AI chirped: "Welcome home, Major Harris."

The lights inside the suite were dimmed, and that subtle smell of sweat and used clothing crept into the back of my throat. Told me that there was someone else in my quarters. I dropped my bag to the floor, walked straight through to the tiny washroom. The harsh electric lighting flickered on, tracking my movements. I had three interconnecting rooms, and from the main bedroom there came the crackle of a tri-D viewer: the jangle of a commercial news-feed.

"Today marks the sixteenth day of hostilities on the Rim – and the possible reignition of armed conflict between Alliance and Directorate forces . . ."

"Harris?" a female voice called, from the room.

I watched my own ageing reflection in the mirror over the sink. The damned mirror that I'd told her to get rid of—

". . . President Francis, speaking from Olympus City, Mars . . ."

"That you?"

I closed my eyes. For just a moment, I could imagine that it was her: that the speaker was Elena. It was a sublime self-delusion.

Maybe that's the lie that I'm trying to live?

". . . *We will not be cowed. I am in direct communication with Director-General Zhang, and I will not allow the compromising of Alliance interests . . .*"

"It's me," I eventually answered.

A shadow padded up behind me, the gentle slap of bare feet on the tiled flooring.

"*Is he the man for the job? It's an interesting question. Some commentators have suggested that Francis is too old, been in-seat for too long. His empty threats have been ignored before, after all . . .*"

The news-feed snapped off in the background.

When I turned around, there was no one there at all.

Just a figment of my imagination.

I activated the tap. Splashed cold water over my face, allowed it to drip onto my uniform.

"I can tell you the story again, if you'd like," Dr Viscarri said, shaking his head. "I was the first man to examine you when you got back from that damned mission . . . I'll dine out on that story for years."

I was in the *Point* medical bay; a special wing dedicated to monitoring and certifying Simulant Operations crews. Such a familiar setting: the beige walls, tired metal bunks, exhausted medical teams. Viscarri sat on a stool opposite me, completing the assessment. Most tests were done rcmotely via the subdermal chip in my neck but some assessments like blood-work were still conducted manually. Viscarri had done most of those. His diagnostic kit was on a table between us.

"I couldn't believe it was really you," he said. "We all thought that the mission had gone wrong, that you'd been killed in the Maelstrom . . ."

"It was supposed to be classified."

"You think 'classified' means anything to an old man like me? I have my methods, Harris."

Viscarri chuckled to himself. The doctor was a senior medico, white coat straining against a frame grown flabby over the years. He shook his head a lot, which made his sagging neck shake. Viscarri was the lead medical examiner for the Sim Ops Programme. Something of a *Point* fixture, he'd held the job for as many years as I could remember. That said, he was genuine enough: knew a lot about me, had been my assessor before and after the Helios mission.

"My blood all good?" I asked, eager to get this over and done with.

Viscarri was more interested in retelling the story of my return – as some *Point* commentators had termed it, my "resurrection".

"When I first examined you," he said, reading now from a data-slate he had perched on his knees, "you had a recently healed injury to your right thigh – possible deep tissue infection, although an inexpert attempt to remove that seemed to have been made. You had multiple rib fractures to the right of your cage. You'd a gunshot injury to the right shoulder, causing damage to your collarbone." He paused, sighed. "The things you soldiers do to yourselves. Let's not even get started on your face: the broken bones and nose."

"I didn't do anything to myself. I had some help."

"Of course you did," he said, shaking his head again. He sipped from a cup of cold coffee. "Whatever happened out there, you were damned lucky to be alive. You escaped the

Asiatic Directorate. Few Alliance troopers can say that. The last prisoner of war who was returned to the *Point* by the Directorate came back in bags."

"A body bag?"

"No. Grip seal bags."

"What a way to die . . ."

Viscarri sighed. "Oh no, he wasn't dead. It's a new Directorate interrogation method. Keeping the body costs storage space; the mind can be probed without the rest. Try explaining that to the family, eh?"

I shivered. Wasn't sure what to say to that.

"I'm an old man," Viscarri said. "Too damned old. I go back to the Core, next rotation."

I stood up from the bunk and rolled my sleeve into place. I'd miss Viscarri; he always did his duty with good humour. Many physicians might've taken a dimmer view of my health; certified me as unfit long ago. At least Dr Viscarri had kept me working and for that I was grateful.

"Going anywhere nice?" I asked.

"I have a retirement plot on Alpha Centauri. It'll see me out until Gaia takes me back."

"Who'll bust my chops when you're gone?"

"A new doctor. Young, blonde."

"Then I should like her."

Viscarri rumbled a laugh. "You won't like *him*. Now, listen: you often skip these tests. Why did you really come down here today? Surely can't have been to see an old man off on his lonely retirement . . ."

How best to phrase it? I'm experiencing hallucinations of the woman I love – a woman that I lost to the Maelstrom – and I never feel at ease in the body I was born in.

"Nothing," I said, lying easily. "I just wanted to be sure that I'm in good health is all."

"You're getting older, Harris." He flipped through his data-slate again. "Forty-two objective years. Given that you've spent so long in hypersleep, your subjective age is a matter for debate. What's this really about? Are you expecting another mission?"

"Always."

"Is what happened on Helios still getting to you?" Viscarri asked. "I could—"

"No need. I'm fine."

"There's nothing physically wrong with you, Harris. Just look after yourself."

The psychiatric evaluation chambers were uniformly small, no bigger than a Detroit Metro cube. An estate agent would probably call them "personal" or "intimate".

What went on in them was often intimate.

I sat across from the psych. There was a metal table between us, surface covered with childish graffiti.

FUCK A FISH HEAD.

MAKE WAR, NOT LOVE.

IF I FUCK THIS LIFE UP, CAN I HAVE ANOTHER?

A picture of a pyramid – wavy lines emanating from an open eye at the tip—

"What is troubling you?" the psych asked me.

There was a slight lilt to her voice, not quite placeable. *Russian? French?*

I always found these sessions awkward. I didn't know where to start. If it wasn't for my urgent need to get the

62

episode off my chest – out of my head – I'd have terminated the session right there and then.

The woman waited for my response. She was stock-still, except for her eyes. Those gently darted between me and the data-pad in front of her. Such pretty eyes.

"Would you rather that we spoke another time?" she asked.

She was unobtrusively attractive, with a full face and a lightly brazened complexion. Early thirties, probably, although her age was hard to place. She tapped the pen from her slate on the table: a nervous tell. She always did that.

Tap, tap, tap.

The ticking of a clock. A reminder that time was finite, that I had to make the most of it.

"We can talk about anything you like. I'm here to help you."

I let out a long sigh and leant back in the chair. It creaked under my weight. I slightly over-adjusted, because I was used to living in a body much larger than the one I currently inhabited.

"It's complicated."

"Go on."

"I'm having dreams."

"Of a sexual nature?"

I snorted. "No. More like nightmares."

"Of a sexual nature?"

"I said no!"

The psychiatrist nodded sagely, wasn't disturbed by my tone. "These sessions are confidential. We can talk about your work if you like. Where did your last mission take place?"

"It wasn't the last mission."

"But I take it that your concerns are work related?"

"It happened on Helios III. In the Maelstrom."

"I understand," the psych said, although she really didn't. No one did.

I told her everything, everything that I could remember. When I'd first started having these sessions again, it had been a painful experience. Reliving those memories: dwelling on the discovery of the Shard wreck out in the desert, on the death of Michael Blake. Then the revelation that Dr Kellerman was a Directorate agent, and retelling the battle at the foot of the Artefact itself. By the tenth session, the memories had dulled in their intensity. I only really remembered the detail in dream and nightmare – bad enough, but not the same as a conscious retelling.

"What did you learn from the mission?" the psych asked me. She shifted her body under the table. I imagined that I could feel the tip of her shoe brush my trouser leg.

"That I should never trust Command. When I got back, I was interrogated for months. They wanted me to revisit every aspect of the Helios mission, of Operation Keystone. They picked apart my responses."

I'd answered all of their questions as best I could, but it had been wearing.

The woman looked down at her slate again. "What did you bring back with you?"

"The Key. That's the only physical evidence of the Shard – all that's left."

"When was this?"

"Over eighteen months ago. Objectively, it happened two years ago."

The realisation disgusted me: that I'd been back from Helios for eighteen months. When we'd been retrieved by a salvage team, after the trip from Helios back to Alliance space, I'd handed the Key over to Science Division. I hadn't seen it since then. Sci-Div had been ecstatic with the find; promised that it would bring a new era of understanding to the Alliance. Months on, there hadn't been any progress at all.

Except for, just maybe, Professor Saul.

Between missions I spent hours pacing my quarters – hoping, expecting, needing some discovery to be made about the Key's astrocartography. As the days became weeks, weeks became months: nothing. The discovery had been taken from me, coveted by Sci-Div.

"How did it make you feel to have your version of events questioned by Command?"

I grunted a laugh. "I've told you this a hundred times. I had no other choice: we were stranded on Helios, and the only way to escape was to use the Directorate Interceptor. The Artefact's signal was interfering with the starship's navigation systems, and so we destroyed the Artefact with the onboard plasma warheads."

The psych paused for a moment. Then looked up at me, over the rim of her glasses. That look: so familiar. "Are you perhaps being paranoid?"

I leant across the table. I could smell her scent: sweet and intoxicating. It made something in my groin stir. "If I'm being paranoid, tell me why I'm being followed? Surveillance drones down in the dry dock. Everywhere I go, they're watching me."

"Is it possible that you have some form of transient brain damage?"

"Believe what you want. You've seen my brain pattern scans and I've been certified for active duty for several months."

"What do you want to do about all of this?"

"I want to follow Elena. Kellerman told me that there were other Shard sites. There might be other Artefacts out there. I want to go back into the Maelstrom."

"Do you really think that is possible?"

"Maybe. If Command authorises another strike team."

The psych nodded solemnly. "Is there anything else that you wish to discuss?"

"I'm still hearing things."

"Auditory hallucinations?"

"At night, since I came back from Helios." I shook my head, struggling to order this. "I'm remembering things. Memories I thought that I'd long-forgotten. Painful things." I sighed. "Sometimes I think I can see and hear Elena. Other times I can hear the signal. I think that I'm going mad. I destroyed it. But what happened there – I still carry it."

"Would you prefer to forget the encounter? I can refer you to a psychosurgeon for a consultation at a low, low price—"

"I don't want to forget! I want to understand."

"What about friends, family? Perhaps visit a sibling. Have you considered some shore-leave?"

This was a topic that the psych returned to every session: a persistent suggestion. I always dismissed it.

"I'm not talking to you about my family," I said. "I'm not here to discuss what happened to them."

"Very well. My working diagnosis is post-traumatic stress disorder. Regular exercise and a course of barbiturates will improve your mental state. Based on your alcohol consumption, you might be a functional alco—"

The woman froze. Stylus poised over pad, chest slightly pushed out, lips parted ready to speak.

"*Thank you for using Weller Enterprises psychiatric*

services. Bringing better mental health to Liberty Point, *in association with the Alliance military."*

The voice was male and very annoying: piped into the room from speakers somewhere in the ceiling.

"You can continue this session with the psychiatrist for a low, low price of only fifty Alliance credits: good for another ten minutes. To choose this option, please say 'yes' now."

"Fuck you," I said, leaning over the table and swiping a hand at the psych.

My hand passed harmlessly through the holo: a perfect reproduction of a real woman, probably downloaded and decoded from somewhere Coreside. I doubted that the real model had ever been a psychiatrist. Her reactions and responses were controlled by the chamber's medical AI.

"Thank you for your business," the room said. *"Based on the subject matter of today's session, can I suggest that you consider using the Weller Enterprises sexual experiences programme? Available at a low, low price; just select option three from the touchscreen menu, or say 'sex' now . . ."*

I got up to leave the room, but as I did the psychiatrist came to life again. Just a recording now, she wasn't responding to anything that I had done or said: gyrating in front of the metal table, grinding her hips back and forth, tearing at her blouse to reveal her breasts—

I left the chamber, the door shutting behind me.

As a simulant operator I was entitled to free and proper psychiatric intervention – indeed, the psych-evals were supposed to be obligatory. But I'd rather pay for private medical care, because I didn't want to tell the medtechs about what had happened since Helios. The consequences of that might be revocation of my active duty certification.

No. That would never do. I had to be ready for Elena, ready for Command when they sent for me: when they gave me the all-clear that I could follow her. That I could use the Key.

The boulevard outside was choked with soldiers and sailors. Overhead, a surveillance drone watched me go.

CHAPTER FIVE

ANY VODKA

I might have been on active duty but until I had a new mission my time was my own.

Seeking the familiar, I wandered down to the District.

But even that had changed.

Enormous view-screens were mounted in the ceiling, far above: set to show news-feeds. Concerned news reporters, ticker-tape headlines shuttling along the bottom of each screen. Lots of the news was months old, sent on the civilian feeds. We were so far from the Core, even a decent FTL broadcast took that long to reach the *Point*. The military had their tightbeam transmitters – their instant comms – but the civilian networks were still catching up. It was the same old news.

A colony-shuttle collision with Ganymede Docks.

Escalating political tensions between the Alliance and the Directorate.

Chino and American talking heads, promoting pro- or anti-war sentiments.

A new viral outbreak on Ventris II.

Carrie had been on Ventris II. *Turn away. Don't think about her any more.* My only sister. The damned psych had stirred something up – reminded me of a memory long forgotten. Reminded me that I was supposed to care about things outside of the spinning top that was *Liberty Point*.

"Unless we stand united, the Krell Collective will consume us all!" a voice rasped across the crowd.

A clutch of religios on the corner of Main and Ninth Intersection. Proper old-school priests; unkempt, with dirty beards, eyes like sapphire.

"This universe is ours to inherit, but we will only get one chance!" the lead prophet shouted. "Great Gaia has ordained our supremacy! As her children, we have a duty to wipe the xenos from existence!"

I paused for a moment, looked at the bedraggled figure. God only knew how he had got onto the *Point*; it was supposed to be reserved for military personnel and civilian support staff. But more and more of these sorts seemed to be seeping through the cracks. The appearance of the religios was one of the more unusual developments that had occurred on the *Point*. A wide range of new sects had sprung up: Krell worshippers, Gaia Cults, post-humanists. I didn't understand any of them. This wasn't religion as I knew it, nor as Martinez knew it. These people harboured a fervent, dangerous passion: born of the desperate will to carve a bloody empire into the stars. It had spread out from Old Earth, from the Core Worlds, and was enveloping the rest of us like a tsunami – like one of the Directorate's lab-borne viral attacks.

The preacher stared down at me, from atop a makeshift pulpit of cargo crates, and there was something almost knowing in his eyes.

"There will be no resurrection," he said, his voice lowering in pitch. "Those that have already been taken are lost to time . . ."

I walked on. The sector was swarming with off-duty military personnel; full of light and sound.

I used a comms-booth to put in a call to Kaminski, to see if he wanted to join me, but he didn't answer. The same went for Jenkins and Martinez. They had other lives, I guessed, that didn't involve fixation on the next resurrection. Maybe Martinez was more than a little fixated with that but not in the same way as I was. Although I thought about calling Mason, the idea of drinking alone with the young trooper didn't appeal.

So I pushed my way through the crowd, past the street hawkers and local marketeers. The throng parted easily: I'm a decent six foot even skinless, and although I'm past my physical prime I'm no slouch.

But the reaction wasn't about that, and I full well knew it.

"Uh, sir," someone said, pausing in front of me.

A young-faced trooper saluted. He wore Sim Ops Programme fatigues; likely one of the newer recruits. He stood with three other troopers, all almost identical. Collectively, they looked a little shell-shocked by the District experience. One of the troopers pushed the leader in my direction, encouraging him, and he awkwardly took a step towards me.

"Can I just say," he started, "what a damned inspiration you are to us all, sir?"

"Yeah, sure."

He saluted as well. "I mean, two hundred and twenty-three transitions? Man, you are one mean bastard. We all heard about what you did on Helios – with the Krell, and the Directorate and all. Jesus Christo, that was some serious shit."

It was actually two hundred and twenty-four, including today, but I chose not to correct him.

"As you were, troopers," I said, trying to brush the group off.

"Our outfit is new," the kid called to me as I went. "Indigo Squad. Just got our approval from Command. We're going to be just like you, sir."

I glanced back at him once, at the four identical faces. They were all younger than Blake when he had died; probably barely had a hundred transitions between them. They'd never be selected for an operation in the Maelstrom, probably hadn't been soldiers before induction into the Programme.

"Nice to meet you, sir," the trooper said.

I was already moving off into the crowds and the noise swallowed anything else that he had to say.

I found myself in front of a wall-sized view-screen, showing President Francis' disembodied head. Some things hadn't changed at all. I sniggered to myself. President Francis was still in power; still head of the Alliance and all things good. It seemed that he was a constant, the rock around which the river flowed.

"What's the saying?" I asked the president as he griped about the free market conditions on the Core Worlds. "The best medication is self-medication?"

Francis didn't answer me. He just kept talking: that perfectly quaffed black hair, that award-winning smile—

I was being watched.

I clocked them before they saw me. From across the sea of faces, two familiar pairs of eyes peered back at me. I'd seen the guys before – down at the dry docks. They were good tails but not good enough.

Before I could get a proper look they were gone again.

* * *

I found a bar and went inside. My regular haunt had closed during my time on Helios, to be replaced by a fast-food joint with a fake attitude. So instead I just found somewhere that sold alcohol and would tolerate a tired old veteran.

"Good evening, sir," the robotic bartender said. It was just a mech-job; all gleaming steel and plastic, a vid-monitor for a face.

"Vodka," I said. "I need vodka."

"We've got a good range of vodka-based spirits. Just had some decent-quality Tau Ceti import delivered. Or, if you'd prefer something a little fruitier, we have several flavoured vodkas—"

"Any vodka, neat."

"You want a double?" he asked, rubbing a dishcloth over a glass: some bizarre programming affectation. "I can wire your unicard."

"Give me the bottle," I answered, slumping over the bar. The money didn't matter: I'd accrued a decent credit balance while I'd been in the freezer.

"You sure?"

"Just the one for starters."

"You want to talk about it?"

"I'm done talking to robots."

The plain glass bottle and clean shot glass sat in front of me. I poured myself a drink and downed it.

"This is the first drink I've had since I died."

An electronic face formed on the vid-monitor and the robot gave me a sad, almost disapproving look.

"I get it: Sim Ops?"

I nodded, and downed another shot.

* * *

"You know the worst part?" I asked, slurring my words.

"Yes," the robot said. "I'm pretty sure that you've told me this already."

"The worst part," I continued, regardless of the response, "is that there's not a damned thing I can do about it. Command has the Key. They call the shots."

"I'll bet," the robot said. Just one of the programmed responses I'd heard a hundred times already, but was too drunk to recognise.

It must've been early morning, although I'd lost track of time. The bar was almost empty: just me and a couple of shadowy stragglers over a corner table. A tired-looking hooker – naked, blonde, and equipped with the most perfect rack I'd ever seen: nipples flashing with psychedelic patterns – cruised past. The robot gave her a vague nod; face shifting into a reproachful frown that told the girl she was best off giving me a wide berth.

I slammed my shot glass down on the bar, maybe a little harder than I had intended. Looked to the vodka bottle: empty.

"Give me another bottle."

"Don't you have a girl to go home to?"

"Haven't you been listening to me?"

The robot paused, gave me another of those sympathetic looks. "You could be President Francis himself, and I wouldn't be able to serve you. Sorry, chump, but you've had enough."

I exhaled and glared at the machine.

"I said: get me another bottle of vodka. I fought the Directorate on Helios. I killed an enemy agent. I brought back evidence of another alien species. And I want another drink!"

The robot gesticulated with its metal shoulders. "I can't serve you. Go home. It'll be kicking out time soon, anyway."

Anger spiked in my blood. I reared up from the stool, brushed aside the vodka bottle and glass. Both slid off the bar top. Smashed noisily on the floor somewhere.

"This place never closes!"

"We do for you, pal."

"I'm not your pal. I'm a goddamned major in the Alliance Army!"

The room spun a little. I was more drunk than I'd realised. No matter: I still wasn't drunk enough—

"We'll take it from here."

I whipped about, fists up.

The stragglers from the corner table stood beside me. Up close, in a moment of drunken clarity, I recognised them. The tails from the dry dock, from outside. I immediately flagged them as military, but an entirely different breed to me. Dressed in pristine khaki uniforms, officer caps held tightly under their arms. Holstered pistols that looked like crude children's toys next to the hardware we'd been throwing around back at Maru Prime.

"Having a good night, Major?" the lead asked. "I'm Captain Ostrow. This is Lieutenant Pieter."

"You're MI?" I asked.

They had to be Military Intelligence. Spooks: the age-old interior intelligence service. Neither even tried to deny it. I'd been expecting this, but that didn't mean I wanted to go through it. Or go through it again.

"Let me guess?" I roared. "You want to ask me some questions?"

The captain shook his head. "Not any more. But just for your information, Operation Keystone – the Helios mission – remains classified. I could arrest you for discussing it in public."

He shot a glance over at the bartender. The bot was intently looking down at the floor; probably hoping to avoid a RAM-wipe.

"That why you want to see me?" I drawled.

"We can only erase the local psychiatric services so many times before someone will get wise to what you're discussing, but not today. We have papers to serve on you, sir."

Pieter slid a sealed envelope across the bar.

Sweet Jesus. It's finally happening.

I felt suddenly and very firmly awake and sober.

"We'll escort the major back to his quarters," the captain said, nodding to the bartender.

"I didn't hear a thing," the robot said.

"Good."

Mili-Intel were notoriously bad company and the other soldiers were silent all the way back to my quarters. Although it only took a few minutes, Ostrow and Pieter made sure that it was as uncomfortable as possible. They accompanied me to the door – probably under orders to make sure I didn't do anything harmful to the new mission. Maybe they'd read my personnel records, or perhaps my reputation preceded me. Either way, they were wise to make sure I got home in one piece.

I scanned my palm against the controls. The two men watched from the end of the corridor; the shadowy captain nodding to me.

"We'll be in touch," he said. Added: "Sir."

Nothing and no one touched the MI; not even Lazarus. I gave him the finger and lurched into my quarters.

I could barely wait to pull the orders envelope from my pocket. The auto-lighting activated and I read from the single sheet of plastic.

```
*** EYES ONLY ***
TO: MAJOR CONRAD HARRIS (SERIAL CODE
   93778)
FROM: ALLIANCE MILITARY COMMAND (ARMY)
SUBJECT: GENERAL COLE INBOUND
   (HARDCOPY) - NEW MISSION ORDERS
"OPERATION PORTENT"
ORDERED TO ATTEND BRIEFING SESSION AT
   0800 (OH-EIGHT-HUNDRED) HOURS
RESTRICTED INTELLIGENCE: NOT FOR
   DISTRIBUTION
ADDRESSED PERSONNEL ONLY
```

"Fuck. It's for real. It's happening."

I slid down against the inside of the door, head in my hands. Sat there, listening to the wheeze and hiss of the air-conditioner.

For the first time in a long while, I slept without hearing the signal, without hearing her voice.

But I remembered something else almost as painful.

CHAPTER SIX

CARRIE

Thirty-four years ago

"Psst!" came the voice. "You want to see something cool?"

I was in my bed.

The apartment had three rooms: the bedroom that my mother and father had shared, in the little time they lived together as a couple; the combination kitchen-diner-lounge; the room that I shared with my sister. The whole tenement had that same smell – not specific, just the scent of decades-old decay – and our apartment was no different. The smell of too many animals living together, huddling in too close a space.

Except that these animals were human.

We were lucky, my mother used to say. There were plenty out there with even less.

It had been a few months since she'd died.

Carrie leant over me, on the edge of my bed. Her scraggly blonde hair escaped all over the place: big and unkempt. She never bothered to wash it.

She was – what? – maybe eleven.

Which made me eight, Earth-standard. Terms like subjective and objective ageing meant nothing to me, because I'd never left Earth. So, eight years was eight years – but at that age, nearly nine was better. Which made Carrie my older sister.

I bolted up in bed. The window was open, broken shutters allowing in the milky early-morning light. I was dressed in last night's clothes – my school jumpsuit, though I hadn't actually attended the local education centre in over a month. *There's nothing they can teach me there that I don't already know,* a voice – the voice of my eight-year-old psyche – told me.

"What's up with you, Con?" Carrie asked. "You been at the meth again? Jonathan will have you if he finds it."

Jonathan Harris. My father. Carrie always called him by his first name, mostly because it irritated him. The more he complained about it, the more she did it.

I shook myself awake. "All good. And you know I don't do that shit."

"Hmm. You look kind of sick?" Carrie said, tilting her head. She had the annoying habit of raising her voice at the end of a statement, so that everything she said sounded like a question.

"I'm good. Honest."

"Don't worry; Jonathan's been drinking again." She slung a thumb towards the broken door to our bedroom. "He's in the lounge."

I nodded. I'd seen that too many times before to bother going to investigate.

Carrie zipped up her jumpsuit. The same deep blue as mine, except that the edu-centre badge had been torn off the sleeve. Whether she'd done it herself, or one of the other children on the block was responsible, I couldn't remember. She had become an easy target for bullies.

"What the fuck is up with you, Conrad?" Carrie asked again, pushing her face right into mine. "You want to see something cool, or not?"

"Okay. I want to see something cool."

Our apartment was on the twenty-eighth floor, overlooking the mass conurbation that had become known as Detroit Metropolis. When I'd bothered attending school, I'd learnt that in earlier times this whole region had been known by a different name – that the Metro had once been regarded as an affluent area of Detroit and Michigan. Right now, that seemed hard to believe. We darted through the tenement communal hall, past the jeering street prostitutes and drug-pushers. Even though we were kids, they'd harass anyone: easier to keep your head down and get past them. Carrie led the way. Out into the bombed-out main plaza, the communal area between three apartment blocks.

It wasn't long past nine in the morning but it was hot. The air carried the promise of another muggy July day. The sun was still a brittle haze in the sky, burning off low cloud cover. Where the clouds were thinnest, where the sky was a dirty blue colour, it was just possible to make out a fine black matrix. I put my hand to my forehead, squinted to make out the detail.

The Skyshield.

An orbital defence network – the answer to the Asiatic Directorate hostilities. The metal framework was in reality a collection of satellites gliding overhead in loose formation, in low orbit.

"Hey, Con!" someone shouted from across the plaza.

A man shuffled through the crumbling remains of a

dried-up water fountain, a communal feature that the municipal authorities had long since turned off. His age was indeterminate, to me at least, but he was indisputably ancient: bony shoulders poking against a worn green T-shirt, skin like torched parchment. He pushed a shopping cart filled to the brim with papers and magazines, old bottles and rags, that produced an uncomfortably loud scraping noise as it moved.

"Hey, Con!" Joel called again, with a genuine smile. "It's gonna be a hot one. A real Detroit summer."

That had become a joke among the city folk: a Detroit summer. Carrie waited at the edge of the plaza, looking back – encouraging me to hurry up.

"When is it not a Detroit summer?" I asked. That was the punchline, apparently: I'd heard the joke, didn't really understand the meaning.

"We get promised a nuclear winter," Joel went on, waving his hands at the sky, "but that doesn't seem to have cooled things off much."

I was only eight. I didn't recognise that sort of terminology. But I understood well enough the pictures on the newscasts and vid-feeds: the graphic images of New York under fire. The buildings, the emergency vehicles, the politicians and scientists demanding retribution.

"Let's hope that this fucking Skyshield keeps us safe," Joel added.

Of course, I knew that it hadn't worked; had only made the whole ugly war go underground. All it did was force both sides to change their tactics. Instead of dropping bombs from the sky, they'd turned to dirty bombs, sleeper agents, attacks on civilians.

"Come on!" Carrie shouted. "Leave Joel to it."

I waved Joel off and followed Carrie down to the highway.

* * *

We took a shortcut through an abandoned factory. The name MACMILLAN-FORDSWELL MANUFACTURING was printed in fading letters on a signpost out front. Story went it used to produce ground cars but I hadn't seen many of those without armoured plating in recent history, and the factory didn't look capable of making the sort of vehicles I saw on the streets. The windows had been stolen and there were holes in the walls. None of the factories here were operational any more: anything of value was produced off-world – Mars, Alpha Centauri, Epsilon Eridani – or on the orbital nano-factories.

"You're slow as fuck today," Carrie said.

"Leave it."

She led us down to the riverside. That was what the local children called it: the riverside. It was really a storm drain. Now parched dry, it gave easy access to the sewer system.

That was where Carrie was headed. She picked her way down the bank of the storm drain, clutching the dry concrete side with dirty fingers. I followed her – smaller, more nimble. We reached the basin at the same time.

"Too slow!" I gabbled at her.

Carrie tutted. "Not like you know where we're going, anyway?"

"Show me then."

She pointed at one of the run-off drains set into the side of the basin: a big black rectangle. A little taller than me, probably protected by a door or gate that had been torn off at some point. A corrugated rusty tin roof – a makeshift porch – sat crooked over the entrance.

Carrie stooped to get into the drain. Her uncontrolled hair clipped the frame as she went.

"Come on."

I stopped at the entrance. I could smell the scent of real,

present rot: that malodorous spoor. Clinging to the back of my throat. I knew that whatever had died in that storm drain was bigger than a rat or a wild cat – was big enough to give off a pungent wave of decay. Even old Joel's smell was a preferable alternative.

On automatic, I followed Carrie into the dark.

There was a body inside.

The drain entrance led to a tiny chamber, not much bigger than the body itself, lined with further drains. A filthy fabric shoulder bag lay in one corner, the remains of a small fire in another. The place likely smelled bad at the best of times but the odour of death was undeniably coming from the corpse.

The body was on its front, face concealed, and dressed in a black costume. Good-quality boots, I noticed. The flesh beneath strained at the outfit; had bloated through exposure to the elements. I could see one bare hand poking from the sleeve of a black fatigue cuff.

I'd never seen a dead body before. There was some significance that this man wasn't coming back and it was paralysing; more impactive than the smell and the press of the sewer walls.

Carrie knelt down beside the body. She didn't seem frightened by him – by it. She grinned up at me.

"You'll like this."

She attempted to shift the body, with obvious difficulty. When she couldn't do it on the second try, she scowled at me.

"Come on, Connie. Get the other shoulder. We have to turn him over."

I didn't want to. I shook my head, mute.

"He's like Jonathan," Carrie said. "A soldier."

On automatic again: frightened at eight years old that she would tell someone else about my fear of the corpse. So I went to the other shoulder, careful not to brush my jumpsuit against the mouldering walls, and in unison we turned the body over. In life the man might've been small and compact but in death he had become heavy and swollen.

Carrie was right: he had been a soldier. He wore fatigues, of a type even I recognised. Directorate People's Army. A winged emblem had been sown onto the lapel of his blouse. Carrie reached for that, tugging at it.

"Might be worth something," she said.

When it wouldn't come free, she moved on to rifling through his pockets. He was carrying a unicard and a couple of scrunched-up twenty-dollar notes. Some more money that we didn't recognise.

"Don't," I said. My voice faltered. "You'll get into trouble. We . . . we should tell someone about this."

"Why?"

"It's serious."

Carrie rubbed the notes between her fingers, like she was testing whether they were real.

"Won't get us a fucking packet of smokes, let alone a ticket out of this joint," she said, shaking her head. Again, adult language that she didn't understand how to use: parroting back what she'd heard older children saying.

"Maybe soldiers don't earn much," I whispered. Stayed a respectful distance from the body, eager not to disturb it any more than we already had. "Dad doesn't earn much."

"Jonathan is an asshole," Carrie said. "That's why he doesn't earn much."

The soldier's face was big and white. He'd been dead for a while. Days out in the storm drain. I couldn't see how he'd died. Maybe flu or something viral. Maybe a shot from some backstreet pusher. The eyes were wide open, lids peeled back: so dry that they hurt to look at. The expression was sad and lonely.

"He's a damned bad guy all right," Carrie said, hands on hips. "We should burn him."

"How do you know that he's bad?"

"Look at his uniform! They all wear them. Black uniform, bad guy. They killed Mom."

"You – you don't know that," I said. The futility of my argument was obvious: the Directorate had killed my mother. But I couldn't muster much animosity towards this pathetic thing in the drain. "Doesn't mean that *he* did it. He might've been different."

"They killed her," Carrie repeated. "The Chino. This one is probably a deserter."

"Maybe he didn't want to go to war."

"That makes him even worse." Carrie kicked the corpse. "Fucking coward. Won't fight. My old man has to go to war, and you get to stay in this drain?"

"Don't do that, Carrie," I said. Then reiterated, impotently: "We should tell somebody."

"This one is a scumbag. Probably wants independence for Mars and all that shit. Help me drag him out of here. We should definitely burn him."

"Please don't."

"You've got to toughen up, Con. This sucker would kill you in a heartbeat."

"He's dead."

Carrie shook her head in disgust. "He killed Mom, and you don't even have the guts to burn him."

Outside, it had started to rain. The droplets made a distinctive sound as they hit the tin porch roof: pitter patter, pitter patter.

CHAPTER SEVEN

OPERATION PORTENT

With the dream about Carrie so fresh that I could almost smell the storm drain, I woke early the next morning. Much earlier than I needed to. I'd only had a couple of hours' sleep but that didn't matter. I languished in the shower unit. The hot water was refreshing; one of the few luxuries that I missed while I was in the field. As a major, I got subsidised water and heat rates: I made the most of both.

I felt the scars on my torso; those reminders left from my time on Helios. The skin was still puckered and white in places – keloid scars, tissue grown proud – although the pain had faded. I only really felt that in my leg, and only if I thought about it.

With a careful precision that belayed my fraught nerves, I arranged my smart-suit uniform and got dressed.

By the time I'd finished with my preparations, I looked halfway respectable: a reasonable facsimile of a military officer.

The chamber AI chimed just before oh-seven-forty-five. Captain Ostrow waited outside, Lieutenant Pieter just behind him. Both wore dark glasses but otherwise appeared unchanged.

"Good morning, sir," Ostrow said, saluting briskly.

"I hope so."

"If you'd like to come with us, we have a mule waiting."

Pieter drove and Ostrow sat in the back with me. The mule was a basic anti-grav buggy, used to ferry material and personnel around the *Point* when the public transport system wasn't appropriate. Lieutenant Pieter regularly sounded the electric horn to scatter soldiers and sailors out of our path. I tried to ignore the flight of sky-drones that followed us across the station. *It's in your head,* I insisted. Whatever the truth was, the drones peeled off shortly after we left the officers' quarters.

"Where are we headed?" I asked.

"The general hasn't declared his attendance on-station," Ostrow said. "He wants to meet in a neutral environment."

"Which is where?"

"Tactical Command Centre."

"So he thinks we're enemies?"

"Right now, everyone is an enemy."

The mule pulled into the Command deck and Pieter leant back in his seat. "You've been away from the *Point* for a while, haven't you?"

"You've read my file."

Pieter smiled. The expression was painfully practised. "I don't mean to pry. I just wanted to offer some advice."

"Go on," I said, curious.

"General Cole is different now," the officer said. "Since the accident."

"I heard," I said. It was public knowledge.

Security troops approached the mule, before we had a chance to finish the conversation.

"You go straight through, sir," the captain said to me. "When you're done, we'll be waiting here."

The elevator doors slid open and I walked out into the Tactical Command Centre. I was anxious, and fought to control my heart rate.

Two voices vied for dominance.

Don't overthink this: it's probably nothing.

No, this has to be something.

The Command deck was located on the outermost ring of the *Point*. Maybe that was deliberate: beyond the observation windows, the Maelstrom glittered garishly – a sparkling reminder that the Krell were still out there, across the gulf of space. Inside, the deck was filled with holo-displays and working command consoles. Officers of every stripe crammed the space. The business of coordinating the Alliance Army, Navy and Aerospace Force elements was not an easy one: requiring the presence of almost every nationality united under the Alliance banner.

A young male officer peeled off from the mass of personnel and saluted me.

"This way, Major. General Cole is waiting for you."

We walked a metal gantry, over the heads of the staff below, and into a discrete sub-chamber.

"A spy booth," I said. "Very clichéd."

The military aide said nothing but as we went inside the noise levels immediately dropped. There was a pitched hum and a box on the wall above the door flashed with green lights. The ultrasonic vibe in the air denoted that the anti-surveillance field was in effect. The aide retreated, the door sliding shut behind him, and two Military Police privates took up position beyond the transparent door.

General Mohammed Cole stood in the middle of the

room; one hand resting on the corner of a hololithic display table, the other propped on a walking stick. As I entered, his face seemed to brighten a little, and he shuffled to greet me. He was dressed in a blue and gold-rimmed, near ceremonial, officer's uniform. It hung off his frame. I tried not to make it obvious that I was surprised by his presentation. I hadn't seen him since he'd briefed me on Helios, but time hadn't been kind to Cole. His dark hair had almost fully greyed – it off-set peculiarly against his coffee skin – and he'd lost a lot of weight. *He's finally earned his moniker "Old Man Cole"*, I thought. There was more to his ageing than natural atrophy: even the dynamics of time-dilation couldn't explain his appearance.

"Sir," I said, abruptly saluting.

"Morning, Major Harris. As you were."

A survcillance drone hovered at Cole's shoulder; kept a respectful distance.

"Permission to speak freely."

"Always."

"I'd like to relay my condolences for what happened."

Cole gave a tight-lipped nod. I certainly didn't begrudge him his aged appearance: he'd survived an assassination attempt on Epsilon Ventris II. *People die on Ventris II,* I thought. *Even those that don't deserve it.* The Directorate had claimed responsibility for the incident – an orbital launch on an Alliance military station – that had cost five hundred lives.

Cole had survived.

His wife and children hadn't been so lucky.

"Fucking Directorate," Cole muttered. "Happened while you were away. We're going to shift some personnel in that direction, make sure that the Directorate knows that Ventris II is Alliance true and through."

"Yes, sir."

"Can't go anywhere without these damned things now," Cole said, waving his stick at the drone. "I'm a class-one political target, apparently. I'm not quite sure what a drone would do if I was attacked, except record my death for posterity."

I nodded. This explained Cole's secretive arrival on the *Point*; his decision to take an unscheduled shuttle, to keep this *sub rosa*.

There were two other personnel in the chamber. Cole pointed them out in turn.

"This is Admiral Joseph Loeb, of the Alliance Navy."

I took the man in for a moment. Older; mid-sixties Earth-standard. Dressed in immaculate Navy blues, he was freakishly thin but barrel-chested, as through his proportions had grown all wrong. I'd seen the body-type before. It was caused by long periods in micro-G, back before they'd made the gravity generators so reliable. The exposure to reduced grav caused variation to the skeletal and muscular structure – made the human body all screwed up. It immediately marked Loeb as one of the old guard; as a long-term sailor.

"Major," he grunted.

"You already know Professor Saul."

Saul gave a tight smile. He was dressed in civilian clothes: grey slacks and a crumpled shirt. His glasses rainbowed with colour, that one white eye staring blankly at the info-feed. A heavy gold pendant hung around his neck.

"Earth's praises be upon you, Major Harris," he said. "I wanted to see you as soon as I felt well enough. My thanks to you for your efforts back at Maru Prime."

Cole rapped his walking stick on the metal-plated floor, giving Saul a sharp look. "Let's get down to business."

All parties were gathered around the tactical display. It

showed a variety of different images and read-outs. Cole manipulated the controls and an image of familiar space spread out to fill the table.

"You probably recognise this as the QZ," he said, waving at the hologram. Several markers appeared on the graphic; all clearly inside the Zone. "These are the locations of recent Krell–Alliance engagements."

Statistics on each engagement floated alongside the markers and I recognised a few of the names. Most recently there was Maru Prime, but there were other sites of interest as well. Naval engagements, the occupation of certain star systems. The QZ didn't look good.

"Have the Krell reneged on the Treaty?" I asked.

"Not formally," Saul said, "but then again they've never formally recognised it either."

"Then why the change in behaviour?"

"It's impossible to quantify the reasons for these inter-actions," he said. "Some of my associates feel that Helios is the primary aggravating feature, but I'm not so sure."

The display shifted again, showing a much wider tranche of space: the QZ, the border with Alliance territory, the Maelstrom.

"This is only a projection, and considering the erratic move-ments that we have witnessed so far, it is difficult to place much weight on the prediction," Cole said, "but we anticipate that within the next two objective years, the QZ will collapse."

That prediction hung in the air for a moment. The display animated, showing movement of large Krell Collectives through the Zone, directly butting up against *Liberty Point*. The other associated, more minor, FOBs – "forward oper-ating bases" – faced a similar fate. War-fleets spilled into human space, both Alliance and Directorate.

"With all due respect, sir," I started, "what do you expect

me to do about this? I went into the Maelstrom as ordered. I've sat through numerous military psych-evals, and I've given you all the detail that I can—"

"This isn't a blame game, Harris," Cole said gruffly. "I want to show you what's at stake here. I'm losing men out there – real and simulated. We're adopting a change in policy. The discovery of the Key – your discovery – has changed our approach."

He manipulated the controls again and the star-map was replaced with a graphic of wider space. *The Key's star-data.* The graphic displayed a broad overview of the Maelstrom, of Krell Space. There were hundreds, if not thousands, of star systems within that glittering eye. Just as many black holes, pulsars and quasars: a churning mass of live space. I noticed that Admiral Loeb – who had so far been still throughout the briefing – visibly flinched at the image. Navigation through the shifting time-space of the Maelstrom was every captain's worst nightmare.

But this image was different. An overlay appeared; a spider web of calm white light superimposed over the Maelstrom. Like a net, taming the ferocious beast.

"This is the result of our research into the Key," Saul said. "We've discovered, and safely tested, a number of Q-jump points throughout the Maelstrom."

This had been Dr Kellerman's dream. A network of operational Q-jumps, taking human ships into the Maelstrom and beyond.

"It's time that you had some answers," Cole said. "I certified your most recent mission into the Quarantine Zone because we couldn't afford to lose Professor Saul. He is a significant asset, and he has primary experience of several Shard sites. Far Eye was a deep listening post. We were tracking another potential objective."

"Another Artefact?" I asked.

"Yes," Saul said. "I'm almost certain that I've found another Shard Artefact."

"We're calling this Operation Portent," Cole said. "And I want you to have full disclosure. You'll know everything that we know."

"Far Eye wasn't an observatory in the traditional sense," Saul continued. "For the last three months, we have been searching for something inside the Maelstrom. Using the star-data, downloaded from the Key."

Saul pointed to a holographic representation of stamps. The astrocartography I'd seen him with back on Far Eye. Those maps had been so important to him that he'd risked his life to retrieve them from the lab. Holos of the Key flitted over the display: scrawled with imagery – somehow both crude and highly advanced. Ancient circuit-prints, finely detailed.

"The data from the Key suggests the presence of another device," Saul said, leaning into the display. "Another Artefact."

"And that was what you were listening for?" I said.

"Exactly," Saul said. "But this Artefact isn't transmitting."

Thirteen indicators showed the locations of Shard sites. The most familiar to me was Helios III, caught in the orbit of Helios Primary and Secondary. The other locations were spread far and wide across the QZ and to the best of my knowledge I hadn't been to any of them.

"Where is the new Artefact?" I asked.

The tactical display shifted again. A close-scan area of space that I didn't recognise at all. I got the impression that this was an area that I didn't want to recognise. The reaction was immediate and overwhelming.

"Welcome to the Damascus Rift," Saul said.

A collection of blue stars – ancient and cold – circled the phenomena. They threw dying light across a series of sterile grey planets, trapped in a death-dance with the Rift. Moon-sized pieces of debris tumbled through the schematic.

Then there was the Rift itself.

A fissure in time-space; one of so many stellar phenomena found in the Maelstrom that human science was unable to classify properly, let alone understand. It shimmered with balefire, brighter than the stars that circled it. The debris in near-space gave the impression that it was being gently pulled into the Rift, and, on a glacial scale, that was exactly what was happening. Those stars, those worlds and moon-fields: over the millennia all would be claimed by the Rift's insatiable hunger.

Space is collapsing in on itself.

Cole went on: "Professor Saul thinks that he has a basic understanding of the linguistics used by the Shard. He can translate, broadly speaking."

"The Key suggests that another Shard Artefact is located within this sector," Saul explained. "It's largely wilderness space, unexplored to any degree. The logistics of moving a fleet into such a perilous area would ordinarily be insurmountable, but the Key changed all of that."

"We can use the star-data to reach the Rift," Cole concluded. "But there is more."

Cole and Saul exchanged knowing glances.

My mouth suddenly felt dry, palms sweating. My data-ports positively burnt: so eager for activation.

"What do you know?" I queried.

Cole swallowed. "A tachyon trail has been identified around Proxima Altaris V. It leads to Damascus Space, and was left by an Alliance ship."

"The *Endeavour*?" I asked. "Elena's ship?"

Cole nodded. "We have quantum-space jump data. This route was taken by Dr Elena Marceau's expedition, during the founding of the Treaty."

Tachyon spills were left behind when human ships entered and left quantum-space. It was a virtual trail of breadcrumbs, an indicator that a ship had made a Q-jump somewhere nearby. Other than recognising that they existed, I didn't know the science behind the tach trails. Even so, my mind raced with the disclosure. Krell ships used Q-space in just the same way as human vessels, but their technology was different and they didn't leave behind a tach trail. I consulted the tactical display again, noted the location of Damascus Space. It was well within the Maelstrom, certainly further than I had ever gone before.

I breathed out slowly. This was it. At last: some solid evidence of where Elena had gone.

"When the UAS *Endeavour* left for the Maelstrom," Cole said, "their rendezvous point was suggested by senior members of the Krell Collective." He pointed to a location on the edge of the Maelstrom. "But we know that they left these coordinates shortly after making contact. It appears that they jumped to Altaris V, then from there likely to Damascus."

"Why did Elena go into Damascus Space?"

"We aren't sure," Cole said.

"Although we have yet to find proof of life," Saul picked up, "we know enough about the Shard to consider the species a continuing threat to Alliance security. It's possible that the Krell have the same perception. I'm reasonably certain that the Damascus Artefact is a transport hub of some sort. As you Americans would say, a Grand Central Station."

The graphic spun, showed routes across the region of space.

"In theory, if activated – if harnessed – it could be used as a Q-space jump point for Alliance ships, right into the heart of the Maelstrom. That might explain why the *Endeavour* took the journey."

"Our goals are, for once, your goals," Cole said. "We want to secure the second Artefact, and then to use the Q-jump point to access the inner Maelstrom. You want to follow Dr Marceau – the *Endeavour*.

"And we won't be doing things by halves this time. You will be mission commander, but you'll have the full might of the Navy behind you. A big team; a fleet. I've assigned a proper warship to the operation; the UAS *Colossus*, under Admiral Loeb. He's assembled a fleet with sixteen other ships."

Holos of the seventeen warships appeared on the display, spinning and scrolling with data-reads. The *Colossus* was a ship to be reckoned with and the assignment of the ship to Operation Portent demonstrated Cole's commitment to the project. The other sixteen ships – cruisers, corvettes, a couple of battleships – were formidable too. Their names floated across the holo, but I didn't have time to take in all of the details.

Loeb had said hardly anything throughout the briefing but he let out a pained sigh. "It's a nine-month journey time between the *Point* and Damascus Space, give or take. All those resources tied up in one project."

Cole ignored the veiled criticism – I strongly detected that Loeb disagreed with Operation Portent – but built on the comment.

"This Artefact might be our last chance to turn the tide of the war," Cole said. "You'll be able to pick your simulant team. Whatever personnel you want. Maybe a new candidate for the girl's post – Mason, is it? Or a replacement for that unruly trooper."

"Kaminski," I said. "His name is Kaminski."

"As you wish. Your second in command will be Captain Lance Williams; an experienced Sim Ops man. I selected him myself. He's not unlike you, I suppose: he'll break the rules if it gets results. He has already been assigned to the *Colossus*, with a four-man team. They call themselves the Warfighters – while they're no Lazarus Legion, the extra personnel should assist in meeting your mission objectives."

"What are my objectives?" I asked.

"I want the old Lazarus magic. Secure the Artefact, then support the science team in studying it. We want to know how this thing works; what makes it tick. Once you're in-country, we want results as soon as possible. Take too long, and there might not be anything to come home to."

Saul gave a nod of his head, a mild smile. "I will also be accompanying the expedition."

Things didn't go so well for the last Sci-Div officer that followed me out to the Maelstrom, I considered, but said nothing.

"I believe that this Artefact may also interact with the Key," Saul said, adjusting his glasses. "And as such, I'm procuring it. I'm particularly interested in the activation process." There was a flash of excitement behind his one good eye. "The side-effects of a dormant transmitter were extensively catalogued by Dr Kellerman, but his mental state towards the end of his, ah, tenure make his data unreliable."

I'll have to watch him, I thought. *Could he be another Kellerman in the making?*

"This device is not transmitting at all; the reasons for that are unclear at present," Saul continued. "These are all aspects which require further analysis."

"I'll need some time," I said. "Before we leave the *Point*."

That was a lie: it wasn't me who needed time at all. I was

ready and willing, would've suited up immediately. I wanted to speak with my squad, to ensure that they knew what they were signing up for. They might need the time, if they were coming with me – this was, after all, a volunteer-only op.

"We can't give you much," Cole said. "As Admiral Loeb says, huge resources have been sunk into Operation Portent. We haven't been back to Helios. The Directorate might have access to whatever was left there. We aren't the only ones listening and watching. Will forty-eight hours be enough to get your team together?"

"That'll be fine, sir."

Back into the madness.

I couldn't wait.

CHAPTER EIGHT

SHE'S HIDING SOMETHING

I left the briefing room and found the Mili-Intel team waiting for me outside. Both soldiers lounged over the mule.

"All done, sir?" Ostrow asked.

"Nearly. I need to take the mule."

Pieter shrugged. "You want a lift somewhere, sir?"

Afraid to let me off the leash?

"No. I need to do this alone."

Pieter paused. Looked to Ostrow.

The captain tossed me the activation card. "Try not to crash it."

"Don't bother following me," I said.

I went to see Sergeant Keira Jenkins first. She was my second in command and it only seemed proper that I explain the mission to her before the others.

Jenkins had a cube in the NCO barracks; somewhere near the station hub, where there was only artificial light. The overhead strips intermittently flickered and the deck had the slightly sickly smell of recent sterilisation. It was a warren of corridors and anonymous troopers' quarters. I passed a grumbling utility robot, tasked with clearing up the remains of some trooper's stomach from a particularly raucous night out. This area of the *Point* reminded me of where I'd grown up; of the crumbling apartment blocks of Detroit Metro, of the decaying inner city.

I found Jenkins' cube and rang her buzzer. The room had an outer display unit, originally equipped with a surveillance eye so that the occupant could see who was calling. That had been smashed and blinked at me ineffectually.

After a long delay, I heard someone moving around behind the thin plastic door. Jenkins appeared through a crack between the door panel and jam.

"Major?" she asked. She ran a hand through her dishevelled dark hair, and still had last night's make-up around her eyes.

"Catch you at a bad time, Jenkins?"

"No," she said, shaking her head. She didn't sound very convincing. "Not at all. It's just . . . I . . ." She paused, rubbing her eyes. "It's early, is all."

"This can't wait. I need to speak with you."

"Sure. Come in."

She opened the door a little more, and I saw that Jenkins was dressed in an oversized San-Angeles speedball shirt. She wore it well; draping off her trim figure, falling to her thighs. Barefoot, she had obviously just woken up.

"Present from my folks back home," she said, with an awkward smile to the shirt. "Fuckers can send parcels, fuckers can't visit."

Jenkins' cube was in stark contradiction to her military state of mind. It was small but unkempt: clothing strewn across the floor, mingled with food wrappers and alcohol bottles. The door opened straight into the living quarters and a bunk filled the space – heaped with bedsheets and more clothes. An open-plan kitchenette adjoined the room.

A wall-screen dominated the panel behind the bunk: showing the sunrise over some Californian beach. How the West Coast used to look, how a great-grandparent would describe it; not the fallout-ridden seaboard my generation knew.

I wandered into the room, failing to hide my disbelief at the disarray. Jenkins slid the door shut behind me. Nudged a tequila bottle out of the way with her foot.

"Sorry about the mess. I'm still settling in to the new quarters."

I raised an eyebrow. "We've been back on operational duty for eighteen months, Jenkins."

"I've just been . . . you know . . . busy."

"Was it a good night?"

"Something like that," she said, voice cracking. Last night hadn't claimed its dues just yet: she continued kneading her scalp.

"Anything to drink round here, Sergeant?"

"Yeah, sure. There's water in the kitchen. I've paid up the sub."

I laughed. "I was thinking of something a little stronger."

"Whatever you can find then."

I plucked the half-full bottle of Martian tequila from the floor, tilted it to check that the contents were as labelled, and searched the tiny kitchen worktop for a clean glass. An opened packet of stimulant tabs – ALLIANCE APPROVED, GUARANTEED NON-ADDICTIVE FORMULA: TROOPER'S FRIENDS – sat beside the piled-high sink, and I flipped a couple out of the wrappers.

"Maybe these will clear your head," I said, passing them to Jenkins.

"I think I should definitely give alcohol a miss today," she muttered. She dry swallowed the medication.

"We'll see how long that lasts."

I swigged at the tequila. It tasted hot in my mouth, burnt on the way down. Martian spirits are uniformly rough but they get the job done – a lot like the Martian people.

"You in a rush today, Jenkins?" I asked.

She reached back a little in the bed, over the heaped covers. There was something awkward in her presentation and it wasn't just the hangover. I'd seen Jenkins with enough of those, and in any event with smart-meds and stims she'd be on her feet within the hour. This was something else, something different.

She's hiding something.

Jenkins reached back again, feet dangling over the edge of the bed: back arched. "No rush. Just tired."

"I don't believe you. Have you got someone under there?"

Her face immediately turned scarlet. Simultaneously, something moved under the pile of bedsheets. *Someone* coughed.

"Just – a – friend," Jenkins stammered, cheeks burning an even brighter shade, still trying vainly to hide whoever was in the bed with her.

"Kaminski?" I asked.

Jenkins was still for a long beat, then let out a sigh.

The bedcovers peeled back and Private Vincent Kaminski appeared from beneath them: bare-chested and grinning inanely, no hint of embarrassment on his face.

"Hey there, sir."

"Morning, trooper."

"Only just," he said, nodding at his wrist-comp.

Oh-nine-hundred-thirty hours.

I laughed out loud, slinging back the rest of the tequila.

* * *

This was unbelievable, but now – seeing Kaminski and Jenkins sitting in the bed together – it also seemed strangely inevitable. Troopers worked hard and played hard.

"How long has this been going on for?" I asked. I was enjoying the mortified look on Jenkins' face, which contrasted so comically with Kaminski's unabashed grin.

"Not long," Jenkins managed.

"On Helios? Before then?"

"After then," Jenkins said. She shot Kaminski a look and he nodded in agreement. "Are you angry?"

"It's a disciplinary offence. You're lucky I don't report you."

"Are you going to?" said Jenkins.

"You know that I won't. You're the best damned troopers I've ever had, along with Martinez."

"And Blake," Jenkins added. "Don't forget Blake."

"How could I forget him? What you two do in your downtime is for you. Off ops, spend your time with whoever you like. As long as it doesn't interfere with work, then it's all good with me."

Jenkins gave a relieved smile, and some pressure even seemed to escape from Kaminski's vacant face.

"I might question your choice in men though, Jenkins. Maybe I'll suggest you get an additional psych-eval. Any woman who chooses to go with 'Ski must need some work."

The atmosphere in the cube suddenly relaxed and all three of us were at ease. I'd never actually seen my crew like this before, in all the years we'd served together.

"Now," Jenkins said, back to her usual self again, "it's always nice to see my CO – on or off duty – but care to tell us why you're here?"

I sat on the end of the bunk and looked at them earnestly.

"I need to speak to you, to both of you. Command wants us to go back into the Maelstrom."

I explained everything that I knew. Told them what had happened at the briefing, of the second Artefact and the Damascus Rift. They listened intently, rarely interrupting my account.

Of course I was willing to risk my life, do whatever it took to follow Elena, but it wasn't just my life on the line out there. My squad deserved not just more intel before making an informed choice: they deserved complete disclosure.

But when is a military op ever that easy? a voice in my head persisted.

Kaminski and Jenkins sat up in bed now, close together.

"So that's everything I know," I said. "Command wants to send us back into the Maelstrom, to secure the Artefact. I'm going, with or without a team, but Cole has promised I can have whoever I want. If I'm going back into the hot zone, then I want you two with me."

I left out Cole's snide remark about Kaminski. He might well be a bad comedian but he was a good trooper. Whatever had gone down in debrief, Cole could never know what my squad had collectively faced on Helios.

"If you want some more time to think about it, then I can ask for longer."

"I've got your back," Jenkins said, without hesitation.

She offered her fist to Kaminski. His face broke into another grin and he gently tapped knuckles with Jenkins.

"*We've* got your back. No way I'd let you go out there without us."

"This is your choice, troopers. I won't think any worse of you if you decide to stay here. After Helios, I can probably swing you a rear echelon post somewhere – not necessarily outside of Sim Ops—"

"No choice to be made," Jenkins said. "Look: we all suffered on Helios. We all brought something back with us. And left something behind."

Kaminski and Jenkins had pained expressions. I realised then that I'd been selfish, that for a long time I'd been wrapped up in my own memories of the Artefact. But my team had been there too. Neither of them would say it, but I immediately knew that they had the nightmares as well – that they remembered all too well.

"This will be a chance for closure," Jenkins said. "A chance to put some things right."

Although I could barely admit it to myself, I'd been dreading asking my crew to go back into the Maelstrom. More than anything, I'd secretly feared that they might say no: might decide that after what had happened on Helios, enough was enough. And who could blame them for that decision?

"I'm going to ask Martinez as well. You think he'll agree to go?"

"No question," Kaminski said. "He'll take any opportunity to bring his righteous fury down on the infidels." Kaminski crossed himself. "God's way and all that. What about the fifth member of the squad?"

I rubbed my jaw. That wasn't an easy question to answer. Private Dejah Mason was young and inexperienced. Should I take Cole up on his offer of some old blood in the post? There would be very little time to train with another soldier, even if we remained on the *Point* and opted for a virtual-reality simulation. But I saw something in her, something that I didn't want to lose. She reminded me of Blake.

"I'm going to ask Mason," I said, definitively.

"Is that a good idea? She's still green, sir. Seven transitions, including the last one. And that hard-drop from the Wildcat nearly messed our shit up."

"She'll polish fine. I'm going to ask her. Maybe you'll get your wish; she might say no."

"No to a posting with Lazarus?" Kaminski said. "Not likely. The average sim operator would kill for a posting to the Legion."

I nodded: didn't need Kaminski to tell me that this was on my head.

"When do we leave?" Jenkins asked.

"You've got forty-eight hours to complete any formalities." *Write a will, send a letter home.* "Cole has a starship assigned. Some real hot shit, apparently."

I moved for the door and stepped over piled clothes. "Maybe you can use the time before we disembark to clear up this mess. And since you two are so close now, maybe Kaminski can help out. That's an order."

I left them to it.

Next was PFC Elliot Martinez.

There were areas of the *Point* where not even I felt safe. It had always been that way, in reality, but my time away had cemented the belief. It was a growing, ever-evolving outpost, with its own ecosystem and populace. Communities rose and fell within the wider structure, little empires and kingdoms splintering under the general Alliance military umbrella.

On larger outposts, it wasn't unknown for whole sectors to fall through the cracks. The District was an example of that: originally a civilian recreation zone, designated for the use of contractors and visitors, it had evolved over time into an open-all-hours drinking spot. Sometimes, areas of a station were abandoned and took on a purpose that the original builders hadn't intended. Real estate in space is precious.

The Ghetto was such a sector, and I knew that was where I would find Martinez.

I took the requisitioned Army mule down through the habitation decks. Large signs insisted CARRY YOUR BREATHER AT ALL TIMES! RISK OF ASPHYXIATION! Gradually, the character of the station changed. The stark military corridors became dirtier, some sectors even graffiti-covered. Old propaganda holo-posters jumped to life as my transport glided past: calling out to me to stay behind. The very few view-ports located in the walls were plastered over with maintenance signs or sealed with breaching foam. Much of the works had been started but left unfinished; funded by corporates that had long gone out of business, for military projects that were terminated before they had even started. Just one of the many peculiarities of time-dilation.

I approached a couple of troopers in old and worn-out Army fatigues, sitting around a burning oil can. They carried shock-rifles and one of them slowly flagged me down. I pulled my mule up to the checkpoint.

"Sir," the trooper said. "You got business in this sector?"

"I have."

"Such as?" the other asked.

"Here to see a friend."

The rifles were worn on the hip, safeties off: charge level set to DEBILITATION. One chewed a toothpick, rolling it around his mouth as he looked over my vehicle.

"Can't take a mule down there, sir. It's a restricted area."

"Then I'll walk. I'm here to see Private Martinez. Either of you know him?"

The lead trooper gave a lazy smile. "Why didn't you just say? Scares a trooper out of his mind, seeing a Sim Ops major turn up on a mule at this hour of the morning." The soldier turned to his colleague. "Take the major through."

The sections beyond the checkpoint were mostly lit by portable units. General power had been cut off to this area of the *Point*; officially, it didn't exist. Didn't mean that the place wasn't busy though: a multitude of troopers and service personnel milled about down here. The occupants of the sector were made up of a mixture of military agencies. Neither rank nor organisation seemed to matter. Only kudos, reputation, face.

The two troopers showed me through to a storage room, partitioned into several smaller chambers by cargo crates. Some of those were opened: stacked up with older-model plasma rifles, power cells, Sci-Div flak-vests. Destined for onward distribution via strictly unofficial channels. I turned a blind eye to all of it; Logistics could do their own dirty work and it was nothing to do with me. The place smelled dank, caused by a flood from the central water recycling plant a few years back.

I found Elliot Martinez playing a card game with others around a table. It was real old school, proper antique-level shit: plastic cards were positioned in front of each player, with a pool of crumpled American bank notes in the centre.

All of the group were tanned, with dark eyes and hair. They were Venusians; immigrants from the Cloud Cities – the ugly orbital habs that so many poverty-stricken had been attracted to in the early days of the Second Space Race. There had been a time when those had probably sounded exciting, romantic even. Generations on, the reality was anything but: cramped, dirty, the occupants trapped in the cycle of destitution by the corporates and governments that owned not just their homes, but indirectly them. Cloud Shanties,

Martinez had once called them. Even so, the Venusian people had a strong identity: behind Martinez, a split Venusian–American flag had been pinned – loud and proud.

A young Hispanic woman was draped over his shoulder, her Naval uniform open to expose her cleavage. She passed him a drink, held out a cigar for him. He set his jaw, nodded. Threw some cards into the pool. Barked something in Spanish, speaking too fast for me to follow.

"Martinez," said one of the troopers who had showed me in. "Got company for you."

The other players turned as one. Looked up at me as though I were a Krell primary-form, invading the *Point*. All of them had gang tattoos. The Naval officer tending to Martinez had a Widow identifier on her cheekbone; three small spiders dripping from her eye like tears. The Black Widow gang were relatively innocuous – had helped clear up Venus during the initial colonisation, even been made semi-official as a law-enforcement agency.

"It's okay," Martinez quickly said. "He's okay."

"Lazarus?" the man opposite Martinez said. He had an Odeo's Crew marker on the nape of his neck – a large star drawn around the primary data-port. He was Sim Ops as well, I realised. "Come to the Ghetto to rough it for a while?"

The trooper's allegiance to the Odeo Crew could get him a life term back on Venus but out here regulations were a little more lax.

"Just leave us to it, troopers," I said.

No one moved though. Not until Martinez gave a nod. I was a stranger here: I didn't feel like a major, but Martinez was a king. Seems I wasn't the only one whose reputation had been enhanced by what had happened on Helios. The gamblers filed out past me. The woman reluctantly disengaged herself from Martinez and followed them.

Martinez looked like he'd been awake all night. He pushed a hand through his sweated hair, reshaped his black goatee.

"Good to see you, *jefe*."

I sat down in one of the ancient metal chairs. It was warm to the touch and creaked precariously under my weight.

"Come to join my church?" he asked. "Maybe St Maria can persuade you to attend one of our meetings."

I laughed, although Martinez didn't. "No, it isn't that. I need to run something past you."

"Go on."

"Let me make it clear that this is not an order. You have a choice."

"I'm still listening, *cuate*."

I explained everything.

"Kaminski and Jenkins are in, but don't let that influence your decision."

"Do I get danger pay?"

"Of course."

"It's not just about the money, but I got mouths to feed back on the City."

"I didn't know that you had children."

"I'd never get a licence, but that wouldn't stop me," Martinez said, smirking. He was referring to a child licence, to allow a legally registered birth. The authorities on Venus were probably the strictest in Alliance space. There were as many unregistered births as there were registered, though, and I doubted that the lack of a government licence would impede a man with Martinez's initiative. "I mean my family. Things on Venus are bad, Major. Real bad." He threw both hands up. "I do what I can to help."

"Well, you in?"

"I'll go with you."

"You sure?"

"We're Lazarus Legion. We stick together."

"I'm going to ask Mason as well. Kaminski has doubts, thinks that she won't be able to handle it, but she deserves a chance."

Martinez nodded. "Girl is okay by me."

"Good. You've got forty-eight hours to put your affairs in order." I stood to leave and eyed the weapons crates. "Any of this stuff stolen?"

"Better not to ask," he said. "If you don't know, you can't tell."

I was escorted out of the Ghetto by two Latino troopers, and I took the mule right over to the training sector.

I found Dejah Mason in one of the simulator ranges.

There were whole banks of virtual-reality machines down there, specifically for troopers running training programmes. A soldier could jack-in via a machine and access a range of drills. Of course, the training was fully VR – because of their enormous credit value, no actual simulants were involved. But the theory went that if you could shoot well enough in a fully immersive VR environment, then you could shoot in a real simulant. They were both simulations, after all.

I stress theory, because the reality wasn't anything so simple. The neural-link between simulant and operator rendered everything actual and so far as I was concerned the only experience worth a damn was to do this for real.

I checked in with the systems technician overseeing the training and he directed me to the relevant tank.

Mason was just finishing up and towelling herself dry from the simulator amniotic fluid. Other troopers were noisily chest-bumping around me – the atmosphere was something like a high school locker room after a speedball match – but Mason looked a species apart. The sys-tech must've commed her to tell her I was inbound, because she didn't look surprised to see me.

"Morning, sir," she said, going to salute.

"Cut that shit out."

Mason was a new breed of soldier. Someone who had never been to war in her own skin, whose only experience of the Krell was through her simulant. The rest of my team all had real military history – had been soldiers of differing stripes, before induction into the Sim Ops Programme. Kaminski and I had even served as Alliance Special Forces together.

Mason slipped into a black bodysuit and swept her blonde hair back from her face. Despite the defiant pout on her lips, she still looked like a kid playing soldiers: the sort of fair-weather trooper that'd be paralysed with fear by the Krell if skinless.

"Walk with me," I ordered.

We fell in step and walked around the simulator chamber. The place was noisy; both the mechanical and electrical hum of so many tanks working at once, and the whooping and hollering of troopers coming and going. Occasional glances in my direction informed me that everyone down here fully knew who I was.

"What training programme were you running?" I asked as we walked.

"I was doing a hard-drop. Sixteen simulations. All successful landings. I've worked really hard on this, and I can guarantee that the incident on Maru Prime won't happen again."

"Incident is a very neutral word to describe it, Mason."

"I know that it was serious."

"You did good. Don't worry about it." To be fair to

Mason, Kaminski had warned me against making her go through with it. "Hard-dropping from high altitude isn't easy. Especially under fire."

Mason nodded. "And there was a lot of enemy fire."

"Affirmative. We can agree on that."

"Then you're not here to take me off the squad?"

I laughed. "No. It's more complicated than that."

She looked both deflated and relieved, her small shoulders sagging. "Go on, sir."

"I've been made an offer, by Command," I said. Wasn't quite sure how to put it; I wanted to give her full disclosure, but didn't want to scare her off the mission, if she really wanted to go. "The opportunity to go back into the Maelstrom."

To follow Elena.

"You want me to come?" she asked, her voice rising sharply. "If you'll have me, then I'll willingly go."

"I can give you the details, such that I know. But make no mistake; this won't be a cakewalk. They've found another Artefact, and if Helios is anything to go by – it'll be hell."

"The others have told me what happened out there," Mason said.

"It's probably worse than you've heard. No point in dressing this up. Out there, in the Maelstrom, there won't be any room for mistakes."

"I want to be Lazarus Legion. I won't let you down."

"See that you don't."

Mason nodded. I really hoped that she appreciated what she had just signed up to.

At least, if it all goes wrong, I thought to myself, *you can rest assured that you gave them the choice. That they decided to follow you.*

But that wasn't much assurance at all.

CHAPTER NINE

I DON'T WANT TO DREAM

I woke up in the brig.

"How the fuck did this happen?" Kaminski asked me.

I couldn't answer the question because I had very little memory of the previous few hours. The only real evidence of our last night on the *Point* was my pounding, aching head.

"Just get some sleep, *mano*," Martinez muttered.

We were all in the same holding cell. Two drop-down bunks were attached to the walls; I occupied one, Kaminski the other. Martinez had taken up a position in the corner of the cell, lying flat on his back, hands clasped behind his head. Eyes tightly shut, he had removed his fatigue shirt and rolled it up to use as a pillow.

"Hey Martinez?" Kaminski said "This must be just like old times for you."

I cracked an eye open and looked down at Martinez. His chest was marked with scars, from real military service, but there were tattoos there as well. An old analogue watch-face without hands; a Black Widow spider on his shoulder; an

Alliance Marine Corps bar-tag. All memoirs of his past life, scrubbed away on joining Sim Ops.

"Fuck you, 'Ski. I left all that behind in the Cities."

"Sure you did. Like you can ever really leave that behind. What'd you do again? Didn't you get a stretch for driving an air-car through a pressurised dome?"

"Like I said, I left that behind. Did my dues same as everybody else."

"Yeah, whatever."

"You're one to talk, 'Ski," Martinez said. "Didn't you do time for hacking that bank in Queens? Those in glass domes shouldn't throw stones."

"Or air-cars," Kaminski said. He laughed at his own joke.

"Can it, 'Ski," I said. "We've all done things that we regret. But my head hurts too much to listen to your bullshit."

"Who says I regret anything?" Martinez asked.

Just then, there was a rattle at the cell door. The wicket opened. The facility was sturdy and used such old-fashioned tech. A face appeared through the grate-covered window. A stern-looking female MP – the ever-present *Point* Military Police – peered into the cell. She nosed us for a second, like she was checking that the three of us were still in there.

"I got good and bad news for you," she said.

"We'll take the good first," I said.

"Seems it's your lucky day, boys. The Navy ensigns you trounced last night don't want to press charges."

"That's good," Kaminski said, "even if I can't remember doing anything wrong."

"They didn't want to press charges against the so-called Legion," the MP went on. There was more noise as she manually unlocked the cell door. "If it was me, can't say I'd feel the same way."

Kaminski was already up, bouncing towards the door. Martinez and I were less enthusiastic; as I stood, another wave of nausea caught me.

"Whoa, whoa," the MP said. "That was the good news."

"The bad?" I managed.

I noticed that there was a whole squad of Military Police outside the cell, all wearing full body-armour and bulky helmets: carbines slung. *So they're not taking any chances,* I thought with a smile.

"Your transport off-base leaves in less than an hour. I got a direct order from Command. Do you know how often a dumb-shit MP stationed on the *Point* gets a directive like this from Command?"

Kaminski shrugged and grinned. "Most weeks?"

The MP gave him a cold stare. "Never is how often. I'm ordered to get your sorry asses direct to a waiting transport shuttle."

That had to be something. We weren't going to miss the flight.

We were hustled down to the dis-bark deck by the MP squad, led by the female sergeant. I guessed that I – or maybe we – had been watched by Mili-Intel, because our luggage was already packed and palleted for onward transport. The deck was busy again, filled with bustling personnel being ferried to and from other awaiting ships.

Jenkins and Mason stood with a couple of MPs. Jenkins waved through the crowd.

"So it wasn't just us that ran into trouble?" I asked.

"No," Jenkins said, shaking her head. "This was a Legion affair."

"Even New Girl?" Kaminski asked.

"Even New Girl," Jenkins said.

"I tried to break it up," Mason said, "and got involved by accident."

"Girl's got balls," Martinez said.

"Whatever, assholes," the female MP said. "I would've hoped that a major would know better." She looked me up and down; I hoped that I didn't look as exhausted and hungover as I felt. "Or maybe not."

A Naval ensign approached, holding a data-slate. Looked flustered and embarrassed as she scanned each of our barcode tattoos – I bared my wrist. She smiled nervously at the MPs.

"These are your priority passengers," the MP said. "Can I leave them in your care?"

"Sure thing."

The MP eyed us one last time. "Guess you'll be off the grid for a few months. Can only hope that it'll quieten things down around here. Now get the fuck off my station."

"Yes, ma'am," Kaminski said, saluting. "Thanks so much for the bed and breakfast."

My squad sniggered and the MPs disappeared into the crowd.

Around us, the crew was being herded onto an umbilicus, boarding a transport ship moored somewhere in the *Point*'s near-space. A series of pallets passed by. Those were loaded with plasglass capsules: a hundred perfect and naked simulants. Improved versions of the Lazarus Legion.

"If you'd care to come this way," the ensign said, "we'll get you aboard the shuttle."

"My head hurts," Kaminski interjected.

"Whatever, 'Ski," Jenkins said. "At least we know it can't be brain ache."

I noticed that Kaminski and Jenkins kept a professional distance from each other when the rest of the squad was around. In some ways, I felt I'd rather not know about their dalliance: that I was complicit in the deceit of the rest of the team.

A squad of Alliance Marines in full battledress – helmets, goggles, the full deal – trooped by. The unit was in formation around a sealed metal crate, transported on an anti-grav sled. Although I couldn't see inside the crate, I immediately knew what it contained. *The Key.*

It wasn't just me who could detect it, because Kaminski piped up: "Just think what the Directorate would do to get hold of that thing . . ."

"Way to go to give Martinez nightmares," Jenkins muttered.

"Nothing's going to give me nightmares," said Martinez, with an almost accepting stare. "I'll sleep like a baby. The Chino want to come kill me in my sleep? Then I'll go happy. God'll be my witness."

I didn't know whether that was meant as a joke, but no one laughed.

Professor Saul broke into an awkward run behind the Key's entourage, and when he saw us he waved and dashed in our direction.

"I was conducting some last-minute diagnostics on the monitoring equipment," he said, catching his breath. "The Key is endlessly fascinating . . ."

The ensign shook her head in dismay. "You're all running very late. The *Colossus* is almost fully loaded. I need to get you boarded as quickly as possible."

She pushed aside other queued personnel and led us down the docking tube into a waiting shuttle.

Together with a handful of last-minute Navy stragglers, we were ferried over to the UAS *Colossus* in a Wildcat APS. Near-space around the *Point* was full of commercial and military starships, a disparate variety of names and nationalities. Even though not all of these ships were for Operation Portent, I took the opportunity to soak in the detail of the Naval fleet. Mostly United American but there were also a couple of European and Antarctic Republic vessels.

But as we got nearer to the *Colossus*, it became increasingly difficult to focus on anything but the warship herself. The ship had the identifier UNITED AMERICAS STARSHIP *COLOSSUS* – ALPHA CENTAURI BATTLE-GROUP, 3rd NAVAL SUPPORT ELEMENT printed on her armoured hull. American and Centauri flags sat beneath the ID tags.

Her name was appropriate: she was a titanic vessel. Numerous hangar bays lined her flanks, tiny shuttles and fighters coming and going – moving between the other fleet elements. Town-sized railguns sat atop the exterior landing stations. Deployed missile silos stood ready to fire. Communications, radar dishes and antennae sprinkled the outer hull. Even from this distance, it was plain that the vessel had a standing crew of several thousand personnel. The *Colossus* looked less like a starship, more like a living city. Not a city, I corrected, as we moved nearer: a fortress. She was indomitable – a true feat of Alliance engineering. She stirred a false sense of hope, of security, in me.

"You ever seen a ship so big?" Mason asked.

"Only in my pants," Kaminski replied.

"Fuck you, 'Ski," Jenkins said.

"Hey Major," Kaminski said. He waved at the starship's pocked hull. "Check out those drop-troop bays. Brings back memories, huh?"

"And not good ones," I said.

The *Colossus*' belly was pitted with tiny launch bays. Not much bigger than a man, each individual tube was capable of firing a drop-capsule: an old military tactic that had long fallen into disuse. The deck looked capable of firing a hundred drop-capsules at once. When the *Colossus* had been built, her makers had obviously bought into the old drop-troop tactical doctrine. Kaminski and I, during our time in Spec Forces, had used the drop-capsules. Looking at the empty black holes in the underside of the warship conjured the smell, the sense of confinement and the anxiety.

Just then, a squadron of Hornet space fighters flew past. The MSK-60 Hornets were long, sleek attack ships, made for ship-to-ship combat. The flight circled ahead of us, performing sudden but intricate manoeuvres.

Saul jumped as the Hornets passed us. Looked away from the view-screen.

"Don't worry, *padre*," Martinez said. "Those ones are on our side."

"Still, that's a hella lot of firepower," Jenkins said.

"Made to breach starship armour," Mason murmured, almost to herself. "Even military-class plating."

"Will you check out New Girl?" Kaminski said. "She's a regular bookworm. You Martians have always been proud of your navy."

"Damn straight," Mason said. "Best in the Alliance."

Some of the ships performed a swift ballet, while two hovered near enough to our location that they could put us down if necessary.

"They're just showing off," I said.

The fighters adopted a fixed formation and approached the *Colossus*.

My team, together with the other passengers, marched out of the Wildcat's aft ramp. The *Colossus*' hangar bay was awash with deckhands and maintenance crew, feverishly working to prepare for launch. Utility robots began to decant rows of cargo crates from the Wildcat's belly, carefully lining them up for onward processing.

A group of soldiers immediately approached us on our arrival.

"Attention on deck!"

The speaker was an officer, dressed in the shipboard uniform of the Alliance Army. Captain's rank insignia on his shoulder patch, Sim Ops Programme badge on his lapel.

"Captain Lance Williams," the officer said, eyes forward and salute held, in a motion that seemed entirely unnatural to him. "Commanding officer of Williams' Warfighters. Reporting for duty, sir."

"At ease," I said.

Williams looked relieved to drop out of the salute and grinned boyishly. He was tall and lanky, with ruffled sandy hair, like he would be more at home on a surfboard than a starship. When he spoke, it was with a familiar Californian twang, the same dialect of Standard as Jenkins. Whereas she was a disciplined and motivated trooper, Williams looked anything but.

"Welcome aboard the *Colossus*," Williams said. "I wanted to ensure your successful docking before I ordered the Warfighters into the sleepers."

"This your team?" I asked.

Williams nodded. "Yeah, sir. These are the Warfighters."

I heard Kaminski cluck his tongue from somewhere behind me.

Williams' Warfighters were a ragtag bunch – young and bullish. The first was of proper Martian heritage; a big bastard, both tall and wide. He had a beard and a mohawk of hair that reached down to the nape of his neck. One side of his face was covered in Martian Clan tattoos – from before the Unification. He was trying too hard, I decided. The other two were young women, almost identical: slim but muscled, with shaven heads and blunt features.

Williams' team was line infantry and the troopers were in their real, hardcopy bodies. *Cole wasn't wrong when he said that the Warfighters were no Lazarus Legion,* I thought to myself. I hoped that they'd look a little more organised in their simulants, because right now they didn't exactly fill me with confidence.

"Captain Williams," I said, "meet the Legion, and our adviser on this mission."

I commenced a round of introductions with my squad and Saul. When I got to Jenkins, she slightly faltered. Williams' face illuminated.

"Keira Jenkins?" he asked. "That really you?"

"Yes, Lance," she said, begrudgingly; a lukewarm and very unconvincing smile on her face. "Nice to see you."

"Same here," Williams said. "It's been such a long time."

"It has," Jenkins said. "Years, in fact."

"Too long! We should catch up, Sergeant, if your CO will allow it. Chew the fat and all that."

Jenkins gave a curt nod. There was something of substance to their connection; I parked that knowledge and reminded myself to find out about their history later. Right now, on the cargo deck, Jenkins shot me a frosty glare that clearly told me *don't ask*.

Before I could say anything more, a small woman in an oversized Sci-Div smock made herself known.

"Welcome aboard the ship," she said. "I'm Dr Marie West, lead researcher assigned to the *Colossus* and aide to Admiral Loeb."

Late fifties, West had pale skin, brilliant blue eyes and wispy grey hair.

"Will I have the opportunity to see Admiral Loeb before we set off?" I asked.

"Unfortunately not," Dr West said. "You are running rather late. Our launch window is less than an hour away."

Maybe last night hadn't been such a good idea. I'd missed out on preliminary briefings with Admiral Loeb and Captain Williams. I guessed they would have to wait until we reached Damascus Space.

"Is the relic present?" Dr West said.

"It's called the Key," Saul replied. "It should be on our Wildcat. Please ensure that it is properly secured in the main laboratory."

"Certainly," Dr West said.

From nowhere, a dog started to bark: loud enough that it could be heard over the industrial din of the cargo deck. A black and brown animal pushed between the crowded personnel, slid across the polished metal tiles.

"Here boy!" Mason said, brushing past me to see the dog.

He was big, and I immediately recognised him as a genetic crossbreed – German shepherd and husky maybe. He barked some more, almost exclusively in the direction of Professor Saul, who positioned himself behind me, grimacing at the animal. The dog seemed to settle a little as Mason ruffled the fur behind his ears.

"This is Lincoln," Williams said. "Admiral Loeb's dog, retired from the combat division. Dumb mutt."

None of the *Colossus'* crew paid any attention to the dog.

"Last call for sleepers!" an officer yelled across the deck.

The *Colossus* had numerous hypersleep suites – each a vault big enough to house hundreds of sleepers – and we were led into one of them. Multiple rows of freezer units lined the bay: sometimes piled atop one another to make use of every possible space. Robot lifters were already stacking filled freezers; the canopies frosting, vacant human faces peering out. The hiss and churn of mechanical movers filled my ears; the crisp, cold smell of active cryogenics units filled my nose.

As I lay in my hypersleep capsule, hooked up to the device by intravenous drip and my data-ports, it occurred to me that I hadn't actually been into the sleep since Helios. We'd been on other operations since our return but none of those had required a long journey time. Expectant anxiety crept into my bones; the idea that anything could happen once I'd fallen asleep.

You might never wake up.

Or you might wake up in ten years.

Maybe the war will be over.

Fat fucking chance.

The Legion lay in their own capsules, dressed in medical gowns and attached to machines. Martinez had already fallen asleep, whereas Mason was nervously fidgeting.

"First cold sleep for you, Mason?" I asked.

"Second," she said. "I was frozen between Mars and the *Point*. How many times for you?"

"Too many, but you never get used to it."

Mason fell silent. A pretty blonde medtech approached my capsule, with a placatory smile.

"Major Conrad Harris?" she asked. "You'll be going into the sleep in a few minutes. Are there any travel requests?"

"Such as?"

She tapped the capsule lid with a fingernail. "These are new hypersleep capsules. They can assess brainwaves, encourage REM-sleep. It's all very advanced. I can create an artificially induced dream for you."

And you don't need to know how it works, the smile on her face explained. *Lousy grunts.*

"I can download a dream-sequence, if you'd like. It's non-intrusive; the system engages with your data-port—"

"I'll have the Fortuna deluxe package," Kaminski said. "And you can join me if you like. Something wet and wild."

Jenkins scowled at him.

"I'm afraid that's not possible," the medtech said, continuing that painted smile. "But you'd be surprised how many passengers make the same request."

"Jog on, girl," Jenkins ordered. "We'll all take the same – a beach holiday, something simple."

"Nothing for me," I said. *I don't want to dream.*

The medtech busied herself about the procedure.

Whatever she did was happening in the dormant psyche – on a level not consciously appreciable, at least until we were under. But I could feel the cryogen being pumped into me; the gentle throb of the fluids entering through the IV.

"See you in nine months," Jenkins said.

"Sooner," Kaminski replied, "if something goes wrong."

"Fuck you, 'Ski. Fuck you."

CHAPTER TEN

BADDEST GANG

Thirty-four years ago

"What was I supposed to do?" I asked.

"What were *we* supposed to do, don't you mean?" Carrie replied.

She was pissed with me.

Pissed big time.

It had stopped raining a couple of hours ago. The sidewalks were still glazed with a layer of moisture, not yet cooked off by the cloud-wrapped sun, but the cloying warmth that had come to define the Metro had returned.

Carrie paced the storm drain. She shook her head. Crossed her arms over her chest, rubbed her elbows. Such adult affectations. She looked a lot like my mother. Hard to believe that she was not yet twelve.

I sat on the bank of the storm drain, watching the circus develop around us. It was interesting – made a change from the usual daily tedium, if nothing else.

"I can't believe that you called them," she said again.

"It's fucking embarrassing, Connie. Embarrassing, you know?"

I sighed. "I . . . I don't get what the problem is."

"You called them, Con. That makes us rats."

The nearest spinner sat further up the storm drain. The vehicle was a deep blue with white panelling; the words DETROIT POLICE printed in bold lettering on the flank. The motto AUTOMOTIVE CAPITAL OF THE WORLD: MAKING DETROIT A SAFER PLACE TO LIVE, WORK AND VISIT had been painted over, but scratches to the bodywork allowed the forgotten lettering to show through. When it had landed, the cops aboard had used the siren. Now the roof-mounted cherry light flashed soundlessly. It was hypnotising; and for a kid like me it was exciting. They had even brought along a robot. Clad in the same blue-and-white livery as the spinner, it was much bigger than a man and stood stock-still, watching the proceedings with electronic eyes.

"I remembered the number," I said, "and I phoned them. They can deal with him." I swallowed. "With it."

"That was our thing," Carrie scolded. "Don't we deal with our own shit round here? We should've told Adelia. She always says: anything goes wrong, come tell me. I'll get it sorted. This is something going wrong, isn't it?"

I played with a piece of grass I'd torn up from the drain floor.

"Adelia isn't cops," I said. "Adelia is a hooker."

"Yeah, but she knows people. Knows the people who run this sector. Who do you think the cops are, Con? Another damned gang. Just a bigger gang than the rest, is all."

"I wanted to tell Dad – but, you know . . ."

"Fat lot of good Jonathan would do," Carrie replied. "Worse than the fucking cops."

"This needed biggers. This needed cops. The baddest gang."

"Baddest is right," Carrie said.

It was a pretty big deal. For starters, it was the first dead body I had ever seen in person. The neutrality – the loss of any emotional response – to seeing the dead would come later.

"I've seen them on the viewer," I said. "On the tri-D."

"Who hasn't? They're everywhere, except the Metro."

"So what was it doing in the drain?"

Carrie frowned at me angrily. She had probably been talking about police, I realised; whereas I'd been talking about the dead soldier. At the time, there was no reason I could imagine why a uniformed Directorate soldier would possibly be in a Detroit storm drain.

"Maybe they're invading," I suggested.

"Shut up, Con. Just shut up."

It wasn't as though there were ranks of enemy soldiers in the downtown. They had never landed in New York, Washington, San-Angeles: only dropped their terrible bombs.

"That's why I called them," I offered. "Because I can't figure it out."

"And they're going to?"

There were lots of cop and other cars I didn't recognise. At least six spinners – air-cars, designed for low-altitude flight. A couple of ambulances as well – throwing their own flashing lights over the walls of the storm drain. In the distance, beyond the multi-coloured light arcs, street people had gathered. They peered on with undisguised curiosity.

I was just as intrigued. I watched as the men and women milled around the sub-drain, flitting in and out of the tiny chamber in which we'd found the Directorate soldier. Some were in padded white forensic suits: faces covered with masks and goggles. Others were in blue flak-vests, POLICE printed over the chests. One wore a long brown trench coat, pulled up around his dusky unshaven chin. He was pointing things out to people, nodding a lot; telling them what to do. I decided that he was probably the boss.

"You ever see a cop this close up before?" I asked as I looked on. "They never come this far into the Metro."

"No, and I damned well never want to," she said.

"That robot is kind of cool."

"It's stupid."

The cop-leader looked down at a data-pad, then up at us. Carrie shirked back – withering under the gaze of the law man. The cop only smiled at us: a tired but pleasant expression.

"Don't go anywhere, kids," he called. "I'll have some questions for you later. Be with you as soon as I can, all right?"

"Now you've fucking done it . . ." Carrie muttered under her breath, quiet enough so that only I could hear it.

The cop went back to that dark rectangle of the drain entrance and we waited on the verge until he was ready to see us.

That turned out to be a lot longer than we'd expected.

Several hours passed. No one spoke to us.

Day turned into night.

The skyline became a dirty orange blaze, the sun setting uncomfortably on another day. Seemed to do nothing for the heat but a breeze began to filter down the exposed drain – sending off a fine skeet of grit. Overhead, warning beacons on the Skyshield occasionally flickered: a reminder of the UA government's unwavering vigilance. That hadn't seemed to deter the little man in the storm drain, whoever he was.

The flashers kept flashing: reds and blues, more imposing by night.

Carrie had given up complaining about my decision to call in the cops. Instead she was just hungry and tired, and had decided to focus on that. I tended to agree with her on both counts.

The cop in the trench coat eventually separated from the rest. Putting on his best and brightest 'I'm a cop, but I'm okay' smile, he approached us.

Carrie sat beside me, hands clutched in front of her knees, feet together. She looked a lot younger, all of a sudden.

"I'm Detective Romero," the man said. "Pleased to meet you both."

He held out his hand and I gingerly shook it. I'd seen adults doing that so it seemed the proper response. He did the same to Carrie but she edged backwards without explanation.

"You kids did the right thing calling us," Romero said, nodding along with his own spiel. It was obviously working for him, even if Carrie didn't buy it. "What you found is very interesting and important."

He twitched his nose, rubbed it. Like all of the other cops, the boss wore a full filter: plugs jammed into both nostrils, a white-fabric face mask dangling loose around his neck. His voice sounded a little muffled behind the gear.

"Don't you kids got filters?" he asked. "You should be wearing them outside. Whole lot of fallout in this sector, especially at night."

We both shook our heads, mutely. I vaguely understood that fallout was bad and should be avoided, but not much more than that.

"Well, let's see if we got some in the car. I'm sure that we do. Come with me and we'll have a chat."

Detective Romero was a slight Latino man; maybe once handsome, but face now lined heavily from too much hard work and exposure to the Detroit elements. Not as old as my father, not a young man either – Romero was clearly a seasoned officer. His clothes looked like him: weather-beaten, downtrodden. His black-leather boots were badly scuffed, and his trench coat was battered and lacerated.

One of the harness-bulls – that was what my father always called the beat-cops: in their heavy armour jackets, with their mirrored protective glasses – stood over by the lead air-car. As Romero approached, he nodded, and the uniformed cop opened the car. The gullwing door cracked with a creak of the hinges.

"You ever been inside a cop car before?" Romero asked me.

"No," I said.

"Then this'll be something new."

He ushered me into the passenger side. Carrie scrambled into the car behind me; the front seat was easily wide enough to accommodate both of us. Romero went around the other side of the vehicle, opened his own door and slipped into the driver seat. With both doors closed, it felt like we were in a protective cocoon: warm, safe from the outside world.

This must be how cops feel, I thought.

"Guess this must be kind of nerve-wracking for you?" Romero asked. "Finding that body and all."

"I don't know what that means," I said. "But it wasn't very nice."

Romero laughed: a not-unpleasant sound, but not convincing either.

"You kids see the robot?" Romero said, pointing out past the windshield at the metal support bot. "He's always a hit with the kids."

"Yes," I said. Copying my sister, I added: "It looks kind of stupid."

Romero laughed. "Well, you know, he is a little stupid. That's the thing about robots; they don't think like people do. You tell Big Ron – our police bot – to do something, he'll do it for ever. He'll do it until his batteries run out."

"I guess," I said.

"You're not much older than my nephew," Romero said.

The car dashboard was an enticing combination of flashing diodes, tri-D projections, and exotic controls. Taped above the main police scanner was a creased and stained photograph: Romero and several young children. The picture looked old. He held two fingers together; kissed the tips, then touched the picture. I noticed that his hands were worn and tired. A sector tattoo – some police unit badge – coiled around his wrist.

"That's him," he said, referring to the photograph. "His name's Diego. Gone off-world now, to the Cloud Cities. They say it's real nice up there."

Romero fished in the pocket of his coat. Pulled out a chocolate bar, broke it in half. He passed the first chunk to me then leant over me to give Carrie the second. We both took it and started eating immediately. Even at eight years old, I knew a bribe when I saw one – but I was so hungry that I didn't care.

"You kids ever think about going into space?"

Carrie and I both shook our heads.

"That's a shame. I'm sure that you'd both like it. They say that Mars is lovely right now. Been terraformed and all."

"Okay," I said, finishing the chocolate.

"Now, let's talk about what happened," Romero started. "First, you don't got to worry: you're not in any trouble."

"I told you, Carrie," I whispered.

She nudged me in the ribs. "Shut up, Connie."

"That your name – Connie?"

"Conrad. And she's Carrie."

"That so?"

"Yeah. I'm Conrad Harris. She's my sister."

"That's nice. Having a sister or a brother is nice. Family is important. How was the sweet?"

"Good," I said.

"Glad to hear it. Like I was saying, you don't got to think you're in any trouble. You did the right thing calling us. You kids probably know that we don't got to answer call-outs from the Metro any more."

I nodded. I didn't really understand why that was but the change had happened some months ago. The cops just stopped coming out this way; stopped answering calls for help. The politicos talked about better resource management, about "handing the streets back to the people", but mostly it just meant that the police had given up on the Metro.

"I made an exception, because you two sounded like good kids," Romero continued. He was staring out of the wind-screen, looking at the cordon now formed around the drain door. "It's important that you understand what you saw down there. That you realise what it actually was."

I nodded. Swallowed down the last of the chocolate. It left a greasy aftertaste in my mouth. The man's voice had changed: developed a harder edge. I'd heard that change in an adult's voice before, and I didn't like it one bit. It was the voice that my father used when he was angry. It was the voice that he used when he spoke to my mother, before she had died, when I heard them talking through the bedroom wall.

Romero fidgeted in the driver seat. His trench coat bulged

at the chest – obviously fitted with flak armour plates but also something else. He pulled a pistol from a concealed holster. Slammed it onto the dashboard.

"You kids know what this is?" he asked. He removed his hand from the weapon and let us get a good long look.

"Yeah," Carrie whispered.

"Our daddy – dad – has one," I said. "He's in the Army."

The gun was big and silver. Multi-barrelled. Shiny like it had been looked after, polished. I'd seen more than enough guns for my age. But while I'd seen them around, I didn't know what it really was: other than dangerous and threatening.

Which was, I guess, exactly what Romero intended it to be.

Carrie's body had gone rigid beside me. She was never good at hiding things. Her fear was like the worst contagion and I felt my heart rate quickening too. We were in a closed space, trapped in the car.

Is he really going to shoot us . . .?

"Like I say, you need to understand what you saw down there. It wasn't what you think, for starters."

"What did we see?" Carrie asked.

Just as I'd been hypnotised by the flashing lights outside, now she was hypnotised by the silver gun. Her eyes were pinned to it as she spoke. She was asking a smart question, I figured, because it told us exactly what we were supposed to think.

Romero laughed. "Nothing, really. Some kook in a soldier's costume. A prank in bad taste, is all. What would the Directorate be doing in the downtown? Doesn't make sense, does it? Important thing is: what you saw wasn't real. What you saw wasn't a proper Directorate soldier."

We sat in the cop car for a while.

All I could hear was Romero's heavy breathing.

"Now, some of my colleagues down there suggested that I might need to take you to an all-night surgeon. A proper head-man, get you wiped. I told them you weren't like that. I told them you were good kids."

"We are," Carrie said.

She sniffed loudly. I couldn't bring myself to look round at her, because I suspected that she was crying. Not my Carrie; crying in a cop car.

"So there's no need to take you to see the psychosurgeon, get a mind-wipe. All right? We got an understanding?"

"Yeah," Carrie answered for both of us. "We understand."

"That's a deal then, and we don't go back on deals. Did either of you take anything from the drain?"

"No," Carrie said. "Nothing."

I didn't disagree with her.

"Good. Make sure this stays between yous two. Don't tell anyone else, all right?"

"Yeah," Carrie repeated.

"That's real important – the most important thing of all. No talking about it." He tapped the gun, sitting just above that creased photo of his family. "You seem like good kids. I'm sure that you won't talk. But if you do, I'll know it. I got people on the streets, even if I don't answer call-outs. I hear any chatter, I'll know it was yous that talked. I got your names now; I know you."

Down in the storm drain, two of the forensics officers were carrying something bulky between them. It was a black body bag, I realised. They quickly moved between the drain and a waiting ambulance, doors shut immediately. Had to be the soldier. Gone in seconds. The robot was up and walking now, with big imprecise strides: eyes panning the storm drain. The thing looked frighteningly unpredictable.

"Cease and desist," it blurted in an electronic voice, loud enough that we could hear inside the cop car. "Disperse immediately."

Other officers were already clearing away the yellow crime tape, erasing any physical evidence that they had been here at all. The street people responded to the threatening cant of the metal man, and they had evaporated just as quickly. They wouldn't talk, for just the same reasons as us: because they were scared.

The radio crackled, and Carrie and I jumped.

Romero laughed again. "So glad that we got that all cleared up. You kids want a lift back home? It's getting late. On a warm night like this, street dogs'll be out."

"No," I said. "We'll walk."

Carrie and I attempted to walk from the drain quickly and naturally, in a wasted attempt to maintain our dignity. I'm sure that it was pretty obvious we were shit-scared. As soon as the reflections of the flashing lights were no longer visible on the sidewalk, we broke into a frantic run. Took whatever back-routes we could to make ourselves invisible although no one gave chase. The cop's message had been received loud and clear.

"I told you it was a bad idea," Carrie hissed at me, as we slowed down – a block or so away from home. "You going to listen to me next time?"

"I might. But no one will know that we called the cops. They didn't want us to tell anyone, so they won't tell anyone."

"People will know. We stink of cop."

"No one will know. The stink will wear off."

"You even ate cop food."

I laughed. "So did you. And you were crying in that car."

Carrie rubbed at her eyes. Both were red-rimmed. "I had something in my eye, shithead."

"We didn't get the nose-filters."

"Fuck nose-filters. Only pussies use filters. Fucking cop pussies."

Carrie shook her head and tutted.

I stopped, watched her walking ahead of me.

"What?"

"Nothing. You just remind me of Mom sometimes."

Carrie bit her lip, sighed. "That's not a good thing. Mom was a stupid dipshit who got herself killed by the Directorate."

"Don't talk about her like that."

"Jonathan is no better."

"You still think about her?"

"All the time," she said. "I wish I could forget. Sometimes remembering is more painful."

She put a thin arm around my shoulder, hugged me tight. She smelled of sweat and fear but the human contact felt good. That was what I missed most about my mother, I decided.

We walked on through the plaza.

"Did you believe that cop?" she asked me. "About the soldier, I mean?"

"I don't know."

Carrie fumbled in her pocket and produced something. She pressed it into my hand.

"That look like something a kook would carry around?" she said.

I stared down at the scrunched-up and clammy banknote for a long time. I didn't recognise the writing, nor the etched and ignoble face that was printed on it, though I'd come to do so one day. Eventually, I'd know both the image and the text very well. The UA had mostly filtered banknotes

137

out of circulation – the unicard was the only official currency. Even so, I knew that this was something else completely.

A Chino banknote.

In the distance, the street dogs howled and howled: hungry and angry and left behind. Old Joel trilled a song in the shadow of the tenement. By now he was too drunk to bother with us.

Carrie ran ahead of me, feet pitter-pattering on the steps of the stairwell as she went.

"You're too slow, Con!" she shouted, and I raced to catch up with her.

CHAPTER ELEVEN

THE DIRECTORATE

Pitter patter, pitter patter.

Rain on a tin roof.

A child's feet on stairs.

No. Something else.

I awoke with a start.

Cold.

Dark.

The capsule had drained of cryogenic liquid, but only recently: I could still smell the cloying odour and feel the frost on my skin. It limed the glass canopy just inches from my face. Such that I could see, the world beyond was still dark.

Has the ship woken up? Why am I awake?

Thawing liquid dripped in heavy rivulets down the canopy interior. I shivered. I was naked. Still wired to the capsule I'd called home for months – or was that years? Time had passed, but how long was conjecture. A feeder tube – responsible for pumping my stomach with nutrients during the long night – rattled against the side of the capsule. I wanted to call out: to attract some attention, get help, an explanation. But an animal instinct instructed me to stay quiet. That sixth sense that you can't justify following; that you can never adequately describe. The same sense that you learn to trust when you're under fire.

Except that I wasn't under fire.

I was in a hypersleep capsule—

There was a light above me. A brief stab of illumination. I reacted by closing my eyes.

Instinct, that wily old beast, told me to *stay the fuck alert*.

Voices outside. Harsh, disciplined.

Speaking a language that I didn't understand.

My skin began to prickle.

More lights. I recognised rifle-lamps.

That meant soldiers, aboard the ship.

Then more noise. Boots on deck plating.

So multiple soldiers.

Oh shit.

A figure stood above my capsule. Through the layer of frost and excess cryogen, it was nothing more than an outline. The lamp beam stopped moving, focused on my capsule now.

A black-gloved hand reached for the canopy. Wiped at the frost, cleared the layer of condensation left by an age in the sleep.

I could see out.

He could see in.

Horrifying clarity hit me.

A soldier, wearing full vacuum gear: a helmet with attached combat goggles. Those two bug-eyes stared back at me. Red light played across the inside of those lenses – relaying data to the wearer.

For a long second, the soldier and I just looked at each other. That gear? It wasn't Alliance issue.

I knew those eyes.

Directorate.

An alarm sounded.

It took me a few seconds to register the noise – to appreciate that it was real, not a waking dream or nightmare. *An alarm is a bad noise*, my subconscious insisted. *If you want to live, you've got to wake up.* Even in my drug-addled state, that made sense. Hands balled into fists, I started to slam against the inside of the canopy. Again and again. So hard that my arms ached.

Got to get out of here! Got to get—

Nearby, someone was shouting. It sounded like the noise was coming through water: distant, fuzzy. I couldn't make out the words, but didn't stop to try. Getting out of the capsule had become my priority. While I struggled to understand what was being said, I could easily understand the tone: desperate, panicked.

Inside my hypersleep capsule, I was still attached to the unit by a plethora of cables and pipes, plugged in at the base of the spine. My vision was blurred; eyes aching from the abrupt awakening. Everything was so white. The strip lights above were too bright for me to handle. I pounded both fists against the plastic canopy again. It was frozen cold, heavily frosted so that the outside world was just a haze.

"Open up!" I shouted.

With a mechanical whine, the canopy began to rise.

There was no soldier above me and there never had been.

I was surrounded by capsules. Some of those were opening now as well; the sleepers rising from their temporary caskets. Pale from the long sleep, all exchanging confused glances. Some of those turned to angry scowls now, responding to the alarm. The ship's crew, I realised, were waking as well. That was something else to add to the list of things wrong with this picture: the Navy crew were almost uniformly awoken before ground troops.

Holy shit. Something is very wrong here.

A message was being repeated over and over, broadcast through the ship's public address system. It took me a few tries to follow what was being said – to understand the message.

"This is not a drill. Emergency awakening in progress. All hands report to the bridge."

I forced myself awake, shook out the freezer chills. I pulled out the attachments to my arms and legs – broke the connection to the hypersleep machinery. Climbed out of the capsule.

Martinez appeared over me. Clutched my shoulders.

"You okay, Major?"

"Yeah. I'm awake."

Checking that the old man hasn't died in his sleep?

Unplugged, I felt reality suddenly take on a new dimension: the absence of the hypersleep preservative had an immediate effect. This wasn't the way things were supposed to be done – waking from the cold sleep was supposed to be a long and gradual process. A sudden awakening carried with it risks, carried with it the possibility of serious side-effects or even death. I swivelled my legs and slammed my feet down on the metal plate flooring.

Kaminski, Jenkins and Mason were doing the same.

"What the fuck's going on?" Kaminski shouted above the alarm.

The ship's PA shifted loop.

"There is a hull breach in Sector Three."

I frowned. Stared up at the wall.

Words were printed there.
SECTOR 3: HYPERSLEEP CHAMBER.

The bay wasn't filled to capacity but there were sixty or so sleepers. Just as many personnel were still in the freezers, either fighting to wake up or still in hibernation. The AI was attempting to awaken us all and through some quirk of programming this was being done in reverse: ground troops first, then medical staff, finally Naval crew.

Not everyone woke up. Perhaps that was a small blessing. Better, I told myself, that they passed sleeping than face what was about to happen. But I knew that this wasn't how I'd want to go. Asleep in a capsule, somewhere in the Maelstrom, without a fighting chance. Snuffed out, just like that: regardless of what you've done with your life, who you are or were.

I probably had that programming fault – the error that had caused the ground troops to awaken first – to thank for my life.

The floor beneath me began to rumble gently. Heavy rain on a tin roof: pitter patter, pitter patter. I recognised the sound too well.

"Jenkins!" I yelled. "Door – now!"

Jenkins was nearest to the main bulkhead, thirty metres from our position. She stumbled towards it.

There were two red emergency boxes located on the far wall. Those were sprinkled throughout the ship, labelled BREAK IN CASE OF EMERGENCY! Crammed with the sort of safety gear I'd normally ignore but which had suddenly become incredibly relevant. Martinez dashed for the nearest box. I went for the other, willing my legs to move-move-move.

The floor continued to vibrate.

"Everyone – get out!" I shouted.

Confused faces stared back at me. Like geriatric patients, dressed in identical white robes: pale as ghosts.

A whistling sound filled the chamber. Despite my order, most of the inhabitants stopped to listen. Stupid fucks, one and all. Small black dots appeared on the ground. A man next to me – rank and role unascertainable in the gown – leant over one of the dots, inspecting it. He looked down, then looked up at the ceiling.

"Sweet Jesus . . ." he groaned.

Some of the hypersleep capsules wouldn't be opening at all. Those canopies were peppered with the same shotgun pellet pattern – flecked about with brilliant red blood.

"We're going to lose atmosphere in here very soon!" I shouted.

"Move people!" Mason yelled. "Get to the other side of that bulkhead!"

The hypersleep suite was about to become depressurised; provided that the corridor outside hadn't been hit as well, we could use the bulkhead to seal off the area.

I smashed a hand into the emergency supply box, yanking out a vacuum-packed emergency environment suit. It was a brilliant yellow, condensed down to a package the size of my hand. I hit the USE button and the suit began to pop up.

Not a moment too soon. More peppershot hit the deck. Harder now: holes the size of my thumb appeared in the floor, reciprocal damage to the ceiling.

Meteor shower.

The Maelstrom was replete with meteor and asteroid bands – constantly shifting due to the gravimetric storms and stellar winds. They came in all shapes and sizes, capable of causing minor damage to a ship or completely hulling it. There was no telling how severe this storm was until we'd weathered it and from inside the hypersleep vault there was little to nothing that I could do to evaluate the threat.

"We're being hit in every direction!" Martinez yelled. He was half-dressed in his own suit.

I caught sight of Kaminski and Jenkins hustling sleepers towards the door. A man exploded in a bright red haze, punched through by a piece of debris no bigger than my little finger. People were screaming now.

The vac-suit was ready for use and I stuffed a leg inside. I clipped the hood into place, sealing myself in. It had a face-shield that inflated immediately, but also fogged with each breath. This wasn't how I was used to operating: the tech wasn't battle hardened. I was a blunt instrument and I needed my tools to withstand proper punishment. Inside the vac-suit, I was also out of communication with the rest of my team.

Jenkins reached the exit to the chamber. She looked increasingly pale, had started to tremble.

I knew that we had to get out of the chamber and we had to do it now.

Martinez nodded at me, starting off towards the bulkhead door as well.

Jenkins slammed her hand onto the control.

Nothing.

Another handful of scattershot hit the ship.

Fuck.

She hit the control again.

Nothing.

The door sat resolutely shut, an emergency lamp overhead flashing red. From my position it looked like her face was covered in blood – like she was weeping from the eyes.

Maybe she is, I thought.

I reached the door, bounding along on the spongy soles of the built-in vac-suit boots.

"Won't open," Jenkins gasped.

"Try it again!" I shouted, exaggerating the formation of my words: hopeful that Jenkins would see what I was saying even if she couldn't hear.

The control console flashed with a red light.

LOCKED.

Kaminski, Jenkins and Mason stood at the door, all dressed in those ridiculous medical gowns.

"Nice knowing you!" Kaminski mouthed.

The nearest sleeper to me had started to asphyxiate. Atmosphere was almost gone from the room.

I pushed past the group, slammed my hand onto the control panel again and again.

LOCKED.

LOCKED.

LOCKED.

"Martinez! Get a tool from the emergency box! Anything!"

Martinez frowned at me and I motioned to him with my hands – pointed at the control panel. Maybe we could overload the unit, force the door open. If Kaminski was in a suit, he might be able to hack the box: fool the AI into opening the lock.

But he wasn't. I was, and my team was about to die in that chamber unless I could get them out.

Around me, sleepers were wailing, bashing fists against the door. It would do them no good: probably use up what little reserve of stamina they had left.

Martinez bounced to the door, holding a powered wrench. He tossed another to me and I caught it. Activated the tool with a stud on the shaft and began working on the box.

"Please hurry!" someone shouted.

The whistling from the punctured hull had become a wailing now. The room lights were flashing erratically.

Something had gone so very, very wrong.

I hit the box, watched it spark momentarily. In the depleted atmosphere any ignition from the device was passing.

Why haven't the null-shields protected us?

I hit the box again.

Martinez was doing the same; faster and faster. Rage built up behind his face-plate, spittle flecking the inside—

Both controls shorted.

The lights overhead flashed off.

Everyone seemed to pause for a moment.

Then the door gave an enormous rumble and started to lift into the ceiling.

The human wave poured through into the corridor beyond.

There were four Alliance Marines outside the room, in full vac-proofed battledress. Not sims: hardcopy soldiers. They hurried all of the survivors out of the chamber. When no one else came out, they sealed the doors shut.

At least they're Alliance, I thought, remembering my dream of the Directorate invasion.

The sleepers variously fell against the corridor walls, passed out on the floor, or fell to their knees. There were gasped prayers and thanks to a variety of deities; even some puking.

I tore off the vac-hood. Underneath, I was pouring with sweat. My hands were shaking; not from the effects of oxygen-deprivation but with plain anger.

"Clear," the lead Marine said. He spoke into a communicator, one hand to his ear. "All survivors are out the chamber."

"What the fuck just happened?" I yelled, my voice ringing in my ears and down the corridor.

"Hold on a second, sir," the Marine said. He nodded. "Fine. Purge the chamber."

"There could still be survivors in there," I shouted.

"Hold on, sir!" the Marine yelled back at me. "We're dealing with an emergency right now."

Jenkins sat at my feet, wiping blood from her nose.

"You okay, Jenkins?"

"I feel like shit."

"Better than being dead, I guess."

"It's a close run thing right now."

I took in my squad. All four were alive, but a sudden panic gripped me.

"Saul! Where's Saul?"

The Marine sergeant cocked his head, gave me a disapproving look.

"He's on the bridge. Admiral Loeb wants to see you when you're feeling up to it."

I grabbed an oxygen bottle from one of the soldiers and clipped it to the harness of my vac-suit. The whole ship seemed to be awakening: lights and recycling units whirring to life, not just in the hypersleep chamber but the adjoining rooms. The alarm continued; unexplained and intrusive.

"Stay here," I ordered. "Jenkins, you're in charge."

"Affirmative," Jenkins said, still sitting on the floor, back rigid against the wall. "For all the good it'll do."

Still wearing the ridiculous vac-suit, I stormed onto the bridge.

On a smaller Naval starship, the command centre and bridge were often combined. The *Colossus* was so big that division was not only possible but necessary. There were dozens of stations but most stood empty, with only a handful of crew working. Those crewmen looked as though they were not long out of the freezers.

I found Loeb at the helm. Dressed in simple shipboard uniform, he was yelling orders at the crew. But there was a calm coldness in his voice, and something in his eyes that I hadn't noticed during the briefing back at *Liberty Point*.

"Bring us point-five port side!"

"Aye, aye!"

The ship's view-screens were dominated with the same image: a field of bright white lines, sparks thrown across near-space. A billion rock particles struck the null-shield, aerating the energy field. We were still travelling at an insane, Einstein-denying speed: the minuscule rocks were punching against the ship's armour, acting as kinetic rounds. It was inevitable that some of the debris would get through, even if the null-shield was at maximum polarity.

Saul sat beside Loeb, in the same attire I'd seen him wearing back on the *Point*. He was strapped into a station and gripped the armrests with enough force that his tanned knuckles had gone an unhealthy white.

"*Point*-defence lasers firing, sir!" another officer called to Loeb.

"Shields holding, XO?"

"Affirmative, sir."

"Are we clearing the field?"

I watched the view-screens for activity and breathed a sigh of relief. The storm was slowly subsiding; impacts becoming less regular, particulate striking the null-shield and not the ship herself.

"All clear," an officer declared.

Loeb held his rigid position for a moment, eyes fixed on space outside. Then, slowly, he grasped at the data-cables jacked to each of his forearms, yanked them free and tossed them aside.

"Sweet Mother Earth," Saul groaned. "That was too close."

"We're through," Loeb said. "The course correction will take us well out of the field."

"What just happened?" I asked. "The hypersleep suite is a damned mess – you have multiple casualties."

Loeb sneered at me from the command console. "We hit a meteor field. One of the many – and unavoidable – hazards of this fool's errand." He jabbed at a terminal in front of him and the alarm abruptly ceased. "For your information, only two of the hypersleep bays were hit. We managed to make an evasive manoeuvre, which saved a number of other decks from serious harm."

"It appears that the navigational AI developed a fault," Saul said. "We were thrown off course by a storm in Ypress Sector. I've tried to repatch the ship's AI. Yes, yes – not my specialty, but I've done what I can."

"That easy, huh?" I quivered with anger. "Tell that to the dead."

Loeb ignored my protestations. "Some of the cargo holds weren't included in the course profile. Cargo holds six and nine are carrying a full load of military equipment. The course projections allowed for empty modules."

Such a simple error, such enormous ramifications. Making Q-jump – technically translating from Q-space into real-space – required a precise calculation of weight and mass. The specifics were arcane, usually computed by highly advanced AIs. A minor error was enough to send a ship off course. In well-plotted Alliance space, that was bad enough: you could end up translating into a moon or find that the screwed-up dynamics of Q-space cost you a decade of real-time. Stories about these errors were commonly traded among Alliance space forces – usually anecdotally. In the Maelstrom, as with everything, the consequences could be so much worse. We'd made translation off course and the result had been we'd strayed into a meteor storm. Looking down at a holo-map of the surrounding sector, there was at least one black hole and the remnant of solar storm within a parsec of our position.

"This is the first time that the *Colossus* has suffered such a fault," Loeb said. He nodded at a nearby officer. "XO, I need an immediate assessment of the damage. It looks like we've maintained structural integrity, but I want a sitrep on the rest of the Operation Portent fleet."

"Aye, sir."

"Better yet, get me visuals," Loeb corrected.

"I can do that, sir."

The holo filled with ten or so glowing icons: the *Northern Pledge*, the *San-Ang's Finest*, and the *Midwest*, among others. I recognised those names as American ships, from the briefing back on the *Point*. There were other multi-nationals among the flotilla, and I noted that the Antarctic Republic and the Pan-African Union vessels had made it through as well.

"No damage reported, sir," an officer responded. "Looks like it was only us that got hit. We're still waiting for three further ships to make translation from Q-space."

"When are we expecting complete battlegroup conversion?" Loeb asked.

The same officer paused, reading from his terminal screen. "Within the next hour."

"Good. Maintain course vector to the rendezvous point."

"Aye, sir," the XO replied.

"Is the battlegroup still mission able?" I asked.

"Preliminary indications are positive," Loeb said. He sounded almost dismissive of my question.

"Another of the perils of the Maelstrom . . ." Saul added. "Praise the Divine Earth Mother that we got away so lightly."

"What about our sims and tanks?" I asked.

I recalled what had happened on Helios: losing my sims, the damage to the tanks, going into battle in my own skin. I dreaded that happening again.

"Only the hypersleep suite has been hit," Loeb growled. "Your equipment was stowed in cargo bay fifteen – it's fine."

I nodded, tried to hide my relief. Despite Loeb's reassurance, I knew that I'd take the first opportunity to check on the gear myself – to see the simulants with my own eyes.

Loeb shook his head. "Get a clean-up crew down to the damaged bays. I want confirmation that those hull breaches are sealed within the next fifteen minutes."

"I'll make it so, sir," another junior officer said, scuttling off the bridge.

Loeb turned to me. "I want to see you in my chambers before we reach Damascus Space. You should probably have breakfast, see the medtechs. I'll let you know when I'm available."

"Whenever you're ready," I said.

I can't wait, I thought, and stalked out of the chamber.

CHAPTER TWELVE

IN ENEMY TERRITORY

Despite Dr West's objections, I skipped the medical evaluation. Instead, I hit the showers and got dressed. By now the whole ship was awake: corridors flooded with crewmen, the ship's systems running as though the incident in the hypersleep suite had never happened.

The first meal after a long sleep is important. Hypersleep messes with the body's natural rhythm: although you're pumped with sufficient nutrients to keep you alive, long-term the experience is debilitating. The side-effect was the gnawing in my gut that reminded me I hadn't eaten for nine months. It inevitably took its toll, to the extent that Loeb's directive to go and eat was actually welcome.

After getting lost twice, I found the mess hall on one of the lower crew decks. It was a large and busy room; lined with metal tables and chairs, enough for maybe a couple of hundred personnel to be fed at the same time. The place had a relaxed ambience, with a clutch of big green trees occupying one corner. Full-scale observation windows claimed a wall, gave a decent view of near-space. The stars looked alien to me, and they were: we had passed over into the Maelstrom now. Space was full of colours, full of disarmingly beautiful spirals and multi-hued stars.

A constant reminder that we are in enemy territory.

Sailors and support staff were catching meals; the ship had a real servery dispensing proper cooked food from a kitchen at the end of the hall. The smell was welcome – I wasn't used to real food aboard a ship. Mostly MREs and vac-packs were the order of the day. I picked up some kind of geno-modified fried meat and a pureed potato paste. I decided to skip the Centaurian insect-bites, grabbed a nutrient shake. Wasn't any breakfast that I'd ever heard of but I needed carbs and sugar badly.

The Legion sat around a table, all drawn and tired – hunched over trays of steaming food. Saul sat with them, working on a data-slate, but he wasn't eating.

"All in order, Major?" Jenkins said.

I grimaced. "As well as it's going to be. We're out of any immediate danger."

"Immediate?" Jenkins said. "That sounds real encouraging."

"We're in the Maelstrom," Kaminski said. "Being out of immediate danger is the best that any of us could ask for."

He'd probably meant it as a joke, but for once Kaminski was actually talking sense.

"Scuttlebutt is that we got hit by a meteor shower," Jenkins said. "Care to confirm, Major?"

"Yes," I said. I chewed on the steak. It was a vat-grown clone source, and the texture felt wrong. The techs never seemed to get the little details right. "Your intel is accurate."

"How bad is it?" Jenkins asked.

"From what I could see, just the hypersleep suite," I said. "A couple of bays. Ours happened to be one of them."

Jenkins whistled. "We really do get all the luck."

"Loeb is putting it down to a cargo load error," I said. "That sent us off course, apparently. We wandered into the storm."

"How's that possible?" Mason said. "The cargo mass is calculated by the ship's AI. There's virtually no room for error."

I sighed. "You want to go and argue with the admiral, be my guest. Loeb is a piece of work."

"We heard that his nickname is the Buzzard," Kaminski said, swallowing down a mouthful of hot food. "And that he doesn't like Sim Ops."

"Well he certainly doesn't like me."

"We thought maybe he'd invite you for breakfast in the officers' mess . . ." Jenkins said.

"That isn't going to happen anytime soon. How are the quarters?"

"Clean, small, quiet," Martinez said. "Good."

"How far are we from Damascus Space?" Jenkins asked.

"A few days. I didn't get the chance to ask properly."

"It's that bad, huh?" Jenkins said.

"Pretty much," I answered. "We'll need to get to work soon. This new guy – Williams – what's he like? Sounded like you knew him."

I smiled at her, teasing the point.

"I know – or knew – him," Jenkins said. She stared down at the potato-substitute on her plate. "Sort of."

"You didn't mention it," Kaminski added, otherwise oblivious to the significance of the comment.

I recalled Jenkins' reaction to Williams when we'd boarded the *Colossus*, and I suspected that there was something more to Jenkins' comment. Williams and the Warfighters ate breakfast a few tables away. His team was younger, probably fitter than mine. They were boisterous and seemed to have thrown off the thawing already. I noticed that Williams was regularly looking over in our direction: trying to make eye contact with Jenkins.

"'Ski," Jenkins said, her voice dropping to that authoritative tone that made her such a good NCO, "I want you to escort Professor Saul to the cargo bay. Do an inventory check on the Sci-Div crates."

"Sure thing," Kaminski said. "Just as soon as I finish this."

"*Now*," Jenkins said. "It's a priority; Admiral Loeb will want to check on any damage. Martinez, you go with him."

Kaminski looked nonplussed. Martinez didn't argue and stood without argument. He hauled a very confused-looking Saul to his feet.

"Come on, Professor," he said. "Sergeant has a good point."

The three quickly disappeared out of the mess.

Once she was sure they'd gone, Jenkins looked over my shoulder, at the Warfighters. Sipping a fruit juice from a foil pouch, she began to talk again.

"This Captain Williams: we were in Basic together."

"And?" I asked. "So what?"

Basic training was the standard infantry course that all Alliance Army went through – that had been so for as long as the Army had existed. There had to be more to this than just two soldiers training together.

"We had a thing."

"Right . . ." I said, waiting for more.

"Nothing serious. It only lasted a few weeks."

Mason broke a smile. "Is that all? Basic is a different world. It must've been years ago. Captain Williams probably won't even remember you."

Jenkins looked offended. "Thanks, Mason. And there was me thinking that we had a sisterhood thing going on here."

"I didn't mean it like that—"

Jenkins cut her off. "He obviously remembers, but I haven't seen him in a very long time."

"Nothing sinister in that," I said. "The *Point*'s a big place."

"Yeah, maybe." She looked at me awkwardly. "I'm pretty sure that someone will be pissed to hear an old boyfriend is on the scene."

"Kaminski?" I asked. "He's a big boy now, and he'll just have to deal with it. But if you were in Basic together, Williams made captain fast."

"I know. It surprised me too. He has a background in technical training."

"Now he's on a crucial operation into another Artefact," I said. "Cole spoke highly of him."

"Well, he must be doing something right. Maybe he's changed." Jenkins slurped down the remainder of her juice. "Just thought that you should know."

Loeb called an orientation session shortly after breakfast. It was an expected inconvenience and most personnel were required to attend. Navy officers briefed us on safety measures aboard the ship, on emergency exits, on the flight decks. The blurb was standard: evacuation pods are clearly signposted; do not collect your belongings in the case of an emergency; please try not to activate the airlocks without permission. It all washed over me pretty easily and I was sure that my team ignored most of it too.

"Communications between the fleet are restricted," droned a junior officer with a penchant for his own voice. "And comms back home are completely prohibited. Such broadcasts could attract the attentions of the Krell, and we want to avoid that if at all possible."

"What if they find us first?" Kaminski called.

"Shut up, 'Ski," Jenkins hissed. "Let him talk and let's get this over with."

"We have a procedure called the 'dark protocol'," the officer continued. "In the event that a significant Krell war-fleet is discovered near our location – a Krell Collective with a threat-range the Damascus battlegroup is unable to deal with – then we simply go dark."

"We hide?" Kaminski said. "All this firepower, and that's what we do? Just hide?"

"Exactly. We hide and wait for the threat to pass."

Just as boredom was starting to set in, and the crowd was beginning to turn against the Navy officers, Admiral Loeb took the podium. He scanned the room, jaw set. He was, in many ways, the very epitome of an old-school Navy officer. The room fell into a nervous hush.

"I know that everyone has heard about this morning's fiasco," he started. "Sixteen personnel were killed in Sector Three."

He let the words breathe, kept those eyes pinned on the crowd. Although it could've been paranoia, it felt like a good deal of his animosity was directed at me.

"We flew into a previously uncharted meteor storm. Unfortunately, that's the reality of travel in the Maelstrom. Before the rumour mill gets out of control, allow me to spell it out: we are still mission capable and we are pressing on to the objective. Professor Saul assures me that we are approaching the designated coordinates in Damascus Space."

Saul sat a row away from the Legion. Some faces turned to look in his direction. Uncomfortable with the sudden attention, he quickly nodded in an attempt to diffuse it.

"As we move closer to the Rift," Loeb said, "cosmic radiation counts will increase. Dr West will be arranging anti-radiation drugs and appropriate smart-meds. I want complete compliance with the medical team.

"There will be a remembrance service for the dead – for today's casualties – at seventeen hundred hours tomorrow evening." Loeb lingered on the words "today's casualties" as though he suspected that there would be many more before this fool's errand was done: again, the barb of his criticism was directed towards me. "My office is distributing the list of names. All are welcome to attend.

"That'll be all."

The Legion filed out of the auditorium, appropriately admonished by the admiral. The corridor was jammed with personnel; several looking at the list of deceased crew displayed on a terminal screen outside.

"Major Harris?" someone called.

I stopped and turned, took in the man following me. He was an aerospace pilot, and a real flyboy at that; dressed in a bronze-metallic flight-suit, mirrored helm under his arm. Tall, handsome and the better side of thirty standard. He threw me a crisp salute and smiled broadly.

"Lieutenant Andre James, Alliance Aerospace Force," he said. "I wanted to introduce myself and my team. I'm commander of the aerospace group."

A badge on his shoulder marked him as the "CAG": this man was in charge of the *Colossus*' space force element, the fighter ships that we would rely on in the event of enemy action. His flight-suit was covered in varied and colourful insignia. The largest was a comic depiction of a rad-scorpion, tail arching to stab at a star.

I nodded down his salute. "At ease."

"It's an honour to meet the commanding officer of the Lazarus Legion," James said.

"Ah shucks," Jenkins said. "We've got a fan."

"Scorpio Squadron – my boys – are the best." James tapped the scorpion insignia; obviously his squadron badge. "We've got a whole wing of fighters aboard the *Colossus*: we fly Hornets, Dragonflies, Wildcats. Whatever your team needs by way of space support, we're at your disposal."

At least this reception is better than that I got from Loeb, I thought. His presentation was a good deal better than I'd seen of Williams' Warfighters as well. If nothing else, at least James was enthusiastic and seemed behind the operation.

"Glad to hear it," I said. "Was that you outside on the approach back at *Liberty Point*?"

"Damn straight. Sorry about the acrobatics. Something for the ladies." He gave a surreptitious glance in the direction of Jenkins and Mason. James had a precise and sinewy physique, like most flyboys that I'd known; I'd heard that it came from a lifetime of space runs at high-G. "The squadron likes to stretch its wings every now and again."

"Don't we all."

"Admiral Loeb thinks that we're unlikely to see any proper action during this operation, but I'm not so sure—"

Lincoln bounded into the corridor. The old dog was barking and growling; had worked himself into a real rage. I realised that his vitriol was directed specifically at James. The pilot shooed the dog away with his booted foot, growled back at him.

"He doesn't like you much," I said.

"It's not personal," James said, "he just doesn't like simulants."

I paused; felt the rest of my squad doing the same behind me.

"Simulant?" Jenkins asked. "But you're not in a sim . . ."

James gave her a perplexed stare. "Did the hypersleep scramble your head or something?"

He pointed to an emblem on his shoulder: SIMULANT OPERATIONS – AEROSPACE FORCE DIVISION.

I'd heard of testing – expanding the Programme beyond front-line troops – but nothing more than that. *Liberty Point* exclusively ran simulant combat operations; I'd never heard of simulant space pilots before.

"I'm on the Programme," he said. "I thought that you knew."

"How could we?" I asked. "You look – well – like a flyboy."

"I'm just the same in my own skin," he said. Gave a brief look down at Mason: on automatic, her cheeks flushed red. "Except, some say, a bit better looking."

Dr West appeared beside James and patted him on the arm like he was a piece of meat. Which he was, in a sense.

"Lieutenant James is operating a next-generation simulant. I expect, Major Harris, that you and your team are conversant with the combat-simulants. The next-gens are the newest models. The project has been in development for several years, and we're finally seeing the results. The next-gens are being used for various alternative military roles, other than direct combat."

"I'd call flying a Hornet direct combat," James muttered. "You try getting one of those things to do as it's told." He laughed; typical flyboy humour. "My whole flight wing is skinned up. There are thirty-two of us. We have our own dedicated Sim Ops bay. I'll show you around some time, if it interests."

"That's some impressive shit," Jenkins said, moving in closer to James. "You look completely real."

On looking at him up close, I felt a strange chill. Not because he looked unreal, but because he looked *too real*. Down to the pores in his face, the speckling of stubble on his chin: a perfect replica of a flyboy. The combat-grade sims were based on the operator's genetic footprint, but they were obviously upgraded: homo sapiens mark two. James' body appeared to be indistinguishable – any upgrades that Sci-Div had worked into him were well hidden. *But it's more than just that,* I considered. I was discomfited by the fact that Sim Ops was moving on. I knew – or at least thought I knew – everything about Sim Ops, and yet here was a specialist division about which I'd only heard rumours.

Dr West took over. "We've achieved a number of deviations from the standard combat-simulant model. It would be possible to create an almost precise copy of your actual body, Sergeant." This was obviously her specialism; the discussion illuminated her aged face. "The technology exists and it could be done, but I'm not sure why you'd want to do so. The advantages of using a simulant would largely be lost. For instance, muscle-mass requires a larger frame – a body at your size would have only a nominal muscular increase."

"The next-gen models have other advantages though," James went on. "I can withstand increased G-force and I have improved eyesight. I can fly further and faster than I can in my own skin. Like your combat-sims, but in a more refined package. Can't have the Army stealing all the best inventions."

"And you're disposable . . ." Kaminski said.

"Not if he can help it," Dr West said. "The next-gen sims are as expensive to clone as your combat models."

"How long can you stay in that sim for?" Jenkins asked, intrigued.

"As long as I want," James said.

"The next-gen models allow for an almost indefinite operating period," Dr West said. "Provided that the operator is kept in biomass; and obviously the simulant requires feeding and watering, as any other biological vessel."

"Not standard food, of course, but we have specialised nutrients."

"Can you drink alcohol in that skin?" Kaminski asked.

"I could, but it wouldn't have much effect," James said. "The liver is improved, works double-time. I'd filter out the good stuff before it had a chance to act."

"As you can imagine," Dr West said, "we're very excited about the potential of these advances on the standard simulant model."

"Can you make me one?" Kaminski asked. "I'd quite like a copy of myself."

"We don't want to know what you'd do with it," Martinez said, with a chuckle.

Dr West missed the joke completely and shook her head with a matronly smile. "Sadly no, Private. The technology to replicate bodies isn't available aboard the *Colossus*. We have to rely on simulants being imported from *Liberty Point*."

"What about making him a James copy?" Jenkins asked. "I'm sure that'd be easier on the eye."

Dr West shook her head again. "The genotype must match, just like your combat-sims. This is another area that we are seeking to research, but at present only the real Lieutenant James can operate a simulated copy of himself."

The dog barked at James again, and Dr West gave a high-pitched whistle.

"Lincoln!" she called.

Lincoln reluctantly went to the aide's side, but kept eyes on James.

"Loeb spoils that dog," said James, "and he has the run

of the place. I'd suggest that you keep away from him when you're skinned up. It's something about the pheromones simulants produce that drives him crazy."

"We haven't quite cracked that one," Dr West said, with an apologetic smile. She turned to me. "Major, the admiral would like to see you in his chambers."

I followed Dr West through the *Colossus'* corridors.

The ship was immaculately presented; floors a polished sheen, bulkheads oiled to perfection. The same could be said of the ship's crew. Officers and enlisted men passed by, nodding and saluting as appropriate. Loeb's dog padded on beside us, occasionally pausing to sniff the air.

"Despite the size of this ship, I find myself wearing two hats," Dr West said. "I'm acting as aide to the admiral, and he wants to see you before you settle in."

"Good."

Dr West's pace slowed, and she half-turned to me.

"A word of advice, Major," she said. Her voice was hushed, almost conspiratorial.

"I'm listening," I said, not quite sure where this was going.

Dr West smiled. "No one wants to stay here longer than absolutely necessary. No matter what General Cole has told you: the admiral is keen that you conclude your mission here as quickly as possible."

"I understand."

"That might explain the admiral's current disposition. You'll probably find that he can be, well, difficult."

"I've seen that already, and I'm used to difficult."

"He can be *very* difficult. He's rather set in his ways, and I don't think he values this posting."

We passed into another corridor and the character of the ship changed sharply from austere and military to almost homely. The floor was carpeted. There were three chairs in a line against the wall – real wood, probably imported from the Core Worlds.

Dr West noticed me looking at the decor and gave me a slight smile. "Just like I said, set in his ways."

The door to the admiral's quarters slid open. Loeb appeared there.

"Come," he ordered.

West watched me and Lincoln go inside.

Loeb's room was modern and spartan. He strode across it and positioned himself behind a large glass desk. One of the self-cleaning types, not gaudy or cheap. A selection of data-slates, transparent films and other stationery lay across the surface; Loeb leant in and touched one item, moved another. Lincoln followed after Loeb, then settled down beside him.

Loeb nodded at one of the chairs in front of his desk. "Sit."

I took a chair.

"Coffee," Loeb ordered, waving a hand at a junior orderly waiting nearby.

"None for me," I said.

Loeb stared at me with small, very dark eyes. His nose was hooked, beaklike. He did, I decided, look very much like a buzzard: his nickname was more than appropriate. His features were aged, his greyed hair shorn very close; a shipboard Navy cap positioned precisely atop his head.

"This ship has history," Loeb said. "Some of her elements are over a hundred years old."

"Is that so?" I said, although the tone of my voice made plain the comment was not made out of curiosity.

"It is so," Loeb replied. "And it's an old Naval tradition that when a ship dies, the parts of her that can be saved are recycled. She's born again, you see: whether by reuse of a data-coil or an engine component – her spirit lives on. She's resurrected. Reborn."

"I've never heard of that before."

"Well, you wouldn't have, because you aren't Navy," Loeb said. He had a habit of retaining eye contact; like he was staring me down. "The *Colossus*, or parts of her, have fought in many of the Alliance's defining military engagements. She was at Titan when the Directorate were defeated. She was on Mars during the Rebellion."

The orderly delivered Loeb's coffee, then retreated in silence. Loeb smelled the drink for a long moment before continuing.

"The *Colossus* was once a drop-troop transport for the Alliance Army. She carried real, living human troopers: to whom life and death had a meaning."

"Why exactly are you telling me this?" I asked.

"Because I can remember when war was real. When we didn't run around chasing alien Artefacts, wearing skins that we weren't born in."

"Those days were a long time ago."

I tried to weigh Loeb up, to get the measure of him. He wore a short-sleeved deck-issue Navy uniform, probably far less ostentatious than many senior officers would favour. Beneath the sleeve of his right arm I caught an ancient ink tattoo: a trident symbol, surrounded by stars. *An old Navy SEAL, perhaps?* The formation was now long gone, but the traditions lived on. *Is he a relic?* I asked myself. *Does he think that this war can be won with boots on the ground rather than bodies in simulators?* Lots of the older military organisations had been disbanded as a result of the success of the Sim Ops Programme. Many did not go quietly.

"My point, Major," Loeb continued, "is that the Navy,

and the *Colossus*, has history. Things work because of it. People do what they've done for generations and they do it better as a result. The Simulant Operations Programme, on the other hand, doesn't. Maybe things work all right when the right man is in charge, maybe things fall apart when the wrong man is behind the controls."

He sipped at his coffee, eyes closed as he savoured the taste.

I scanned the photos behind his desk. Most were famous framed holographics – Mustafa Islam, the first man on Mars; the atmosphere-processing grid on Alpha Centauri; a hard-copy of the Alliance Constitution – but something niggled. Last in the row was a graduation shot. A dozen or so young Naval officers, dressed in formal blues: smiling for a photographer. A familiar face, much younger than when I had known him, stared back at mc.

Captain James Atkins.

GRADUATION CLASS OF 2261: GANYMEDE NAVAL OFFICER SCHOOL.

Former captain of the UAS *Oregon*.

It was like seeing a ghost: a reminder of how Helios had gone wrong. In the forefront of the picture, a rakishly thin man stood with his service cap in his hands. A much younger Admiral Loeb, I realised.

When I looked back to Loeb, he was staring at me again.

So that's what this is all about.

"I know that a lot of people think you're some kind of hero," Loeb said. "But there's a fine line between heroics and negligence. I haven't yet decided on which side you fall. I've read the Helios debriefing. I know what happened to James Atkins. He was a damned good man, and he died – along with his ship – because people took risks. I won't let that happen to my fleet, to my ship, to my crew."

"Captain Atkins was a great man . . ." I said, my voice trailing off.

Let Loeb believe whatever he wants. I couldn't defend my actions because to do so would be an attack on Atkins; would undermine Atkins' valour. Loeb hadn't been on Helios and no matter what he'd read about it, he could never know what had really gone down. Captain Atkins had made a brave sacrifice – the ultimate sacrifice – and it was one that I would never forget.

"Listen, Lazarus or whatever it is you call yourself. I run a tight ship out here. We're in enemy territory. I won't be taking any risks. I don't want any drama."

I breathed out slowly. "I have a mission, and I'm going to complete it to the best of my ability."

Loeb waved at a view-port set into the wall, at space beyond. "Then I'll make this clear. Our – my – commitment to Damascus Space is a waste of resources. There are seventeen battle-ready warships in this fleet, and those ships would be better deployed on real operations. Those seventeen ships are my responsibility, and they are my resources. I want to be killing Krell, Major Harris. First chance I get: I'm off this operation."

"Understood."

"To ease your transition – forgive the word – into ship-board life, Captain Williams will acquaint you with the facilities aboard the *Colossus*. I'm sure that Lazarus, and his Legion, will want to utilise everything at their disposal."

Loeb poured scorn into the words, emphasising *Lazarus* with contempt.

I stood from the desk. Loeb remained seated, watching me from under the brim of his cap.

"I'll be seeing you, Admiral," I said.

"I'm sure," Loeb replied, as I left his quarters.

CHAPTER THIRTEEN

THIS IS THE UAS *ENDEAVOUR*

Williams was waiting for me outside the admiral's room, lounging in one of the wooden seats. When he heard the door open, he jumped up and tried to salute.

"Don't bother with any of that shit around me," I said. "I'm not that kind of major."

"So I hear," Williams said. He smiled sheepishly. "Did the admiral chew you up?"

"Something like that. He doesn't seem very sold on the idea of Sim Ops."

"The Warfighters got the same reception when we first arrived, but I think that I've won him around."

"How did you do that?"

"Loeb is just real angry, man." He motioned with his hands – the whole of him seemed to be in movement – and tapped the side of his skull with his index finger. "Doesn't like it out here. The best way to handle him is to keep your head down."

We passed through a junction and made our way to an elevator shaft. Two Marines in combat gear sat at the end of the corridor. Both had shock-rifles slung over their chests.

"When the Buzzard is around, you've got to look like you're doing something," Williams said. "He likes busy people, see."

"I see," I said. I really didn't. "So you're afraid of hard work then, Captain?"

Williams shook his head. "It isn't like that, man. It's just that you need to know when to work." It was almost as though Williams had forgotten that I was his CO. He rapidly tried to explain himself. "Don't get me wrong. I'm Sim Ops, through and through, but I've never been a foot soldier, and never wanted to be one. I'm only interested in the glory work."

"I'll remember that."

I'd have to watch Williams. He struck me as a liability and I wasn't quite sure why a trooper like him would be assigned to such an important operation. I stayed quiet, allowed Williams to activate the elevator controls – selecting a destination in the upper decks of the *Colossus*.

"This is a restricted area," the ship's AI warned. "Security clearance red required for access."

Williams tutted, swiped his thumb over a combination DNA and fingerprint scanner set into the elevator wall.

"User not recognised."

He cursed, swiped again. There was a brief pause, then a light on the panel illuminated green.

"User recognised: Captain Lance Williams. Destination accepted. Note that your presence in this location will be logged."

"Yeah, man. Just get us up there."

Over the course of a couple of hours, Williams showed me around the ship. We toured the command intelligence centre – the CIC – and the bridge, which I'd already seen. I saw the navigation arrays, and the analytical engines – machines tuned to monitor the arcane energies of the Damascus Rift. He showed me the armoury, the barracks and the flight decks. I got an idea of the firepower that the *Colossus* could wield, if she was given a free rein. She was constructed over maybe thirty or forty decks, although many decks were dedicated to engineering, maintenance and other closed functions. Despite that, the ship was easily the largest upon which I'd travelled.

"How long have you been assigned to the *Colossus*?" I asked.

Williams sighed thoughtfully. "Six months? Well, fifteen with the time-dilation. We were in the Eskari Sector. Fighting's pretty hot down there."

"That so?" I questioned. I hadn't heard of any activity in that sector of the QZ, but the Zone was big enough that combat action often got missed. That, and time-dilation, made casual observation of the war a difficult task. "Guess that kept Loeb happy."

"But I miss home pretty bad. I'm Earth-born too; Californian. There are so few of us left these days. Don't know if Jenkins told you, but we knew each other."

"She didn't mention," I lied.

"Really? We had this thing together in Basic. She was sweet on me, man. Had it real bad. I had to let her down gently."

"I'm sure."

"These things – relationships – just don't last when you're both on long-term deployment. But Jenkins is a nice chick. It's good to see her again."

"Right," I said. I was indifferent to what Williams had to say: I already felt like I knew more than enough about

Jenkins' past life. "What physical facilities does the *Colossus* have?"

"You mean like a gymnasium or something?"

"Anywhere I can work out."

"Sure, man. We got everything here. You like to run?"

"Most days if I can."

"Then you'll like the Buzzard's Run."

That piqued my interest. "Show me."

Our destination was the very upper deck of the ship.

". . . Lots of personnel use this as a run," Williams said. I'd tuned him out: he talked a lot. "We got anti-gravity exercise devices, a whole gym dedicated to muscle-mass and tone. You'll find the Warfighters down there often, but sometimes the old ways are the best." He turned to me, pointedly said: "You strike me as a man who appreciates the old ways, Harris."

The elevator doors opened to a long, straight corridor. But this corridor was different: the walls and ceiling were composed entirely of glass, ribbed by metal supports. Beyond the glass, there was nothing but space. I swallowed, felt an intense wave of agoraphobia. The place was so utterly open. It gave the impression that I was walking through space.

A shadow fell across the deck for a moment and I turned to see a Hornet space fighter coming in to land. The corridor was on the very spine of the *Colossus*, and below us there was a vacuum-landing strip on either side. I watched as the fighter slowed down, caught by the gravity-runs of the strip. It eventually disappeared into the awaiting hangar.

"If you want to get a good view of the fighters coming in to land," Williams babbled, "then take Vulture's Row."

He pointed out the tower almost directly above us. The Row was a regular feature on most space fighter carriers; a popular location for visitors and off-duty Marines to witness the spatial acrobatics of show-off jockeys.

"I'll pass," I said. I'd seen it all before.

Williams nodded. "This is what I wanted to show you. It's a challenge, see? This end of the Run has a full decompression survival kit – first aid, an emergency respirator, the works."

Williams jogged ahead of me. He pointed out a red box beside the elevator door, then the other end of the run. There was an empty space beside the corresponding elevator door, where the first had a supply box.

"That end has nothing. Aerospace crew removed it, to make the Run more of a risk. That's where you start the Run."

I'd seen similar games on other ships. If, unlikely though it was, you got caught mid-run, you'd have to finish the course in a decompressing environment. There would be no purpose in turning back, because the way you'd come from would have nothing to help your survival.

"Has the corridor actually ever decompressed before?" I asked.

Williams sniggered. "Not so far as I know, but there's a first time for everything."

"And I guess it's called Buzzard's Run because the admiral uses it?"

"You're smarter than you look," Williams chided. "Yeah, the old man uses it every day – oh-six-hundred sharp. Try not to be here when he is."

"Doesn't strike me as much of a runner. I reckon that I could take him."

"You're joking, right? He does good for a man of his age. The Run is exactly two hundred metres. He can clear it in twenty-five seconds."

I raised an eyebrow. "Really?"

"Really. He's a machine, is old Loeb."

"And what's your best time, Williams?"

"Twenty-two." He eyed me cautiously. "I've got the record. Some of the flyboys have set up a score table: you can patch in with your wrist-comp."

"Maybe I'll do that."

The day's tasks dealt with, I wandered through the maze of corridors to my assigned stateroom. The deck felt as cold and lonely as that of the Buzzard's Run.

My away-bag had been unceremoniously dumped on the single bunk. A pile of smart-meds sat on the small terminal in the corner, printed plastic instructions sheets indicating appropriate use.

My body was exhausted but I didn't feel like sleeping. I'd been under for nine months. Mentally, I felt as though I'd slept for long enough. So I took to the decks. I found the anti-grav gymnasium occupied by the Warfighters – the big Martian lifting weights – and decided that I'd give that a miss. I tried the Buzzard's Run. Thought about inviting Martinez – he often ran with me, between ops – but decided to try it on my own first. Predictably, my time was atrocious. My wrist-comp put me on the leaderboard somewhere in the middle; well behind the entire Warfighter squad.

I considered that I might need something more cerebral to put me under. So I found a disused communications pod at the aft of the *Colossus* and claimed that as my own. The walls were soon plastered with mission papers and I hooked my slate up to the ship's terminals. Started running analyses of our approach, checking near-space for any more surprises.

The comms-pod was meant to be manned by two staff. Crammed full of electronics gear – mainly passive listening and scanning devices – the place was comfortably tight with a single occupant. A tiny view-port sat in front of me: a slice of outer space moving by at sub-light speed.

I'm preparing for the mission, I told myself. *Doing what any good commanding officer would do. That's why I'm here.*

"You're becoming a good liar," I whispered in the dark. "Even to yourself . . ."

I knew that mission prep wasn't the real reason for my withdrawal from shipboard life.

I spent the hours tuning and retuning the comms receiver. Fragments of long-lost communications swept over me. Some in hot, fractious static. Others crystal-clear, as honest as the day that they were sent. The transmissions rarely had visual elements – but the audio was enough. Impossible to date, but likely sent at the end of the First Krell War.

It was like stepping back in time.

"I shouldn't even be sending this," came a disembodied voice – female, faltering. "But I wanted my children to hear me speak one last time. I want you all to know that I love you, that I'm sorry that I left . . ."

"This is the UAS *Atreides*." A strong male voice: the voice of a Naval officer. "We have fallen back to the Rift. The Krell continue to give chase. Our Q-drive is damaged . . ."

". . . Help us all! God help us all!"

The messages were retained by Damascus Space: by the triangulation of space debris, so many moons and planets, and the presence of the Rift itself. They would bounce around for ever, trapped in the void.

I discarded all of those messages. I knew exactly what I was listening for, even if I didn't really want to admit it.

This was where Elena disappeared.

I was searching for Elena. For her ship, for some scrap of who she used to be. I needed to know what had become of her.

I cycled through the tuning bands, searching every possible frequency, to no avail. Eventually, my body won the war against my mind. I drifted into a fitful and shallow sleep.

And just then, I heard a voice.

"*. . . This is the UAS* Endeavour. *We've found it. The results of our examination have proved inconclusive . . .*"

The speaker was a reedy male voice; pitched, frightened. It wasn't Elena, but just the mention of her ship – the *Endeavour* – was enough. Although I tried to wake up, my limbs were solid, as inert as a disused simulant's. I didn't know whether the voice was real, or a fabrication of my imagination. I wanted to investigate, to find the provenance of the transmission. But more than anything I wanted to believe that Elena was still out there.

In the twilight between wake and sleep, the voices kept coming from the squawk box, and all I could do was listen.

"*I am sending messages home, to our loved ones. These people deserve a proper funeral. We have their bodies in the freezers. If we ever make it back, they can be honoured. Christo protect us all . . .*"

CHAPTER FOURTEEN

FUNERAL

Thirty years ago

A few years after we found the soldier in the storm drain, my father died.

Killed himself.

Committed suicide.

Dress it up however you like. Only in retrospect could I recognise that finding his body had been one of the most difficult things in my young life. He'd been on Mars for a long time, only back home a week.

What with my mother gone as well, it was rough on Carrie and me. At the time, being so young, the experience was difficult to process properly. Because it had hurt so much, I made sure not to let anyone else know. Carrie and I became insular; became guardians of each other's pain. Outwardly, I was a street tough just like the youngers around me. Just another face on the street with too much time on my hands and a hungry stomach. Carrie was going down an even darker path. She hadn't long turned fifteen when it happened. I was an adult eleven.

There was no money for a proper ceremony, so one of my father's old squad mates arranged it. He was an ex-Army vet, settled somewhere out in the Michigan state, who called himself Nelson. He booked the local church – the old religious centre on the corner of Baker and Eighth – and although it was only a few minutes' walk from our apartment, Aunt Beth insisted that she couldn't attend.

"Not right, what he did," she would regularly say, shaking her old head. "Leaving you two behind to fend for yourselves. Not right."

Although she mostly kept her beliefs to herself, Beth was a devout Latter Day Catholic. The topic of my father was one of the few on which she would express very strong views.

"Suicide is wrong, all wrong. Not God's way. He wouldn't be pleased. It'd be wrong if I attended the ceremony. Make me a proper hypocrite. You wouldn't want to make me into one of those, would you?"

"No, Aunt Beth," Carrie muttered. "Of course not."

I didn't understand what hypocrite meant, and I doubted that Carrie did either. We were still only children.

The signpost outside the church declared that the place was THE HOUSE OF THE BELOVED BRETHREN. It felt like an impression of a church – nothing particularly denominational about the place, nothing particularly spiritual. Didn't make me feel beloved or like brethren. Just a building dressed up as a church. Lifeless and drab; it would've disappointed Martinez. The LED board outside – dripping with half-thawed snow – showed a list of funerals being conducted that day. The name JONATHAN HARRIS (UA CITIZEN) was at the top.

"No one ever called him Jonathan," I whispered. "Except for you."

"That was his name," Carrie bit back.

Inside, the centre was all white-washed walls now filled with cracks and plastic graffiti-scrawled pews. It smelled vaguely of urine.

Nelson and another man attended.

"Be brave, kids," Nelson said, nudging me on the shoulder.

Nelson wore a khaki Army uniform with frayed fabric medals on the lapels. The outfit looked older than him, but had matured a deal more graciously. He clutched his service cap to his chest; as though it was a shield against the rest of the world. I vaguely recalled meeting him a few times before. He'd been drinking in our apartment.

The other man was also an Army veteran – about the same age, equally used up. He milled around nervously in the background.

"Thanks for coming," I said to Nelson. It sounded like the right thing to say.

"Wouldn't have had it any other way."

Something had changed about Nelson, since the last time I'd seen him. From the cuff of his left shirt sleeve poked a prosthetic hand. Not a good prosthetic, either – not an organic graft, rather a metal and plastic hybrid. An ugly claw-hand: functional, made for anything but looks. Nelson's silent colleague had the same affliction, except it was his right hand that had been replaced. When he noticed me looking, Nelson covered it with his good hand – smile becoming fixed, embarrassed. I smiled back; didn't want to press him for an explanation.

"Sit down," Carrie said to me, tugging on my arm. "Let's get this over with."

*   *   *

It wasn't a long service. My family weren't religious sorts in life and in death they were no better. The priest gave a brief eulogy about grief and loss, trying his best to avoid talking about God. Thin, haggard and tired: he wasn't much of a public speaker.

The attendees for the next funeral were waiting in the foyer. That sounded to be a bigger and bolder affair; with much wailing and gnashing of teeth. I kept looking to the back of the room, glaring at the big woman who was crying uncontrollably.

Carrie just sat, eyes forward, emotionless.

"We commit this body to flame, in accordance with Michigan state law, and we remember the deceased for the man that he was . . ." the priest finished. He looked down at the terminal set into his pulpit. "Jonathan Harris. May his memory be everlasting."

Then the casket disappeared into the furnace and Jon Harris was gone.

We slowly filtered out of the centre – not through any sign of respect, but because the Spanish family were so tightly crammed into the entrance hall.

It was February and had been snowing. Just as the Detroit summer could be hot, the winter could be damned hard. Dirty white drizzle coated the buildings; had turned to a yellow frost in places. It looked like ash – grey powdered fallout, the remains of the New York bomb. *Maybe that's what it really is,* I thought. The second bomb had only fallen a few months ago: a Christmas present from the Directorate that the people of NYC had never asked for, and certainly never wanted.

The four of us – Carrie, me, and the two Army vets – stood in a huddle, shivering in the cold. Nelson and his colleague looked particularly affected by the weather. They didn't even have winter coats.

"He was a good man," Nelson said. Nodded back into the church. "Shame he felt that he had to do that. He'll be missed."

"Sure," Carrie said, with feigned indifference. She was getting so good at that. "We know."

"Take these," Nelson said. "You two look like you need them more than me. Least that I can do."

He produced two yellowed ration vouchers from his jacket pocket, thrust them into my hand. I knew that Beth would be grateful for the slips and so I took them without comment.

"Sometimes," Nelson said, shifting from foot to foot to ward off the cold, "life just happens like that. Your pa was on Mars with me. He saw things; real bad things."

I found my sightline drifting unconsciously down to Nelson's metal hand. He did nothing to hide it this time. I noticed, with mild repulsion, that the claw was polished and clean: like some perverse badge of honour, the marker of some great sacrifice to the Alliance and the military.

"We were the lucky ones," he said. "The Directorate are unkind. They know the right buttons to push."

"And I think that they will keep pushing them," Nelson's quiet colleague added. "They'll be damned angry over what happened on Mars."

Even at eleven, I knew about the Martian War. The Rebellion, I'd heard it called. It had been quelled the month after the NYC bombing.

"The Directorate sure do have their ways," Nelson said. For a moment, I didn't know whether he was referring to the Rebellion, or to the metal hand.

The Alliance and the Directorate had fought long and

hard over that turf, both sides eager to prove that they could hold the objective. If you ignored Earth, Mars had been the last shared Alliance–Directorate holding. In a sense, it was the final possible bridge between the two super-pacts: the last demonstration that the power blocs could work together.

I already knew that my father had been there. Before my mother had died, late at night, I'd heard the word shouted through the tenement walls. Usually happened when they were arguing – when the shouting was at its worst.

"We don't agree with the war," Carrie said, definitively. "We're pacifists."

"That ain't no way to be," Nelson said. His voice sounded sad and his face contorted into a confused scowl. "Your father wouldn't want to hear you talking like that."

"He's dead," Carrie said. "He can't do anything about it."

Nelson looked on with that same expression, but said, "You two need anything, just let me know. I don't live far out-state. Got a decent place in the hills. I'd be glad to help. There's a veterans' association. They might be able to get you two somewhere to stay."

"We'll be fine," I said. "We already have somewhere."

"Come on, Con," Carrie said. "We have places to be."

She turned to leave. I immediately followed.

The two old men walked off down the road, taking it slow and easy through the ice.

Icicles had formed on the roof of the religious centre. Some of those had started to thaw: drip-drip-dripping onto the ground below. The liquid looked like falling tears.

That reminded me that I had forgotten to cry at the ceremony.

* * *

We didn't go straight home – or at least, we didn't go straight back to Aunt Beth's. That didn't feel like home: nowhere did any more.

Instead, and without explanation, Carrie guided us to a street diner. She picked a table by the window and settled down. The close press of so many patrons made the diner warm inside.

The waitress eyed us cautiously but Carrie made clear that we had a means of payment.

"Let's put those ration vouchers to good use," she said, loud enough so that the old woman could hear.

The waitress gave a blunt nod.

Carrie ordered us two cups of black filter coffee and a minute later we both sat huddled over the potent sludge. I breathed in the fumes. The stuff smelled overpowering.

"What are we going to do?" I asked.

"Keep going. Stick together. Do what we always do."

"Without Dad?"

"What difference will that make?" she said. Strands of steam played around her face, made her cheeks flush. She sighed, sipping at the scratched plastic cup. "Jonathan was out of your life more often than he was in it."

She was right, of course, but that didn't mean that I wanted to hear her say it. My father had been taking more and more distant tours of duty. I'd barely recognised the man who came home to Detroit on the last occasion. Not just emotionally, but physically.

"That's what time-dilation does to a man," Carrie added. "Someone has to pay the debt."

I'd heard it called that before. "The debt": that ever-increasing gap between objective and subjective time. That distance that serving soldiers put between themselves and their families. My father hadn't aged right: had fallen out of kilter with those around him. Those were the combined and very real effects of relativity, of the Q-space drive and of protracted periods in hypersleep. I involuntarily shivered, despite the collective warmth of the diner.

"It was his choice," Carrie went on. "He decided to live his life that way."

"So you have all the answers now?"

Carrie smiled. "Just some."

"I don't want to end up like that."

"Like Jonathan?"

"Like those old men. The vets."

The vision of the two old soldiers with their crippled hands had struck an unpleasant chord. Maybe affected me more than the funeral itself.

"Probably in our genes," Carrie muttered, sipping at the coffee again. "Maybe war is a Harris family tradition."

"Then I'll break the tradition."

"Yeah, just like Granddad? That didn't end so well for him."

My grandfather had been a veteran as well, had served in Cambodia and on Charon. He'd mustered out of the Army but civilian life hadn't suited him. Last we'd heard, he'd been sectioned in a medical centre somewhere upstate. My father had forbidden any discussion about his condition and I suspected that there was more to his sudden incarceration than I knew.

"We'll be okay," Carrie said. She waved over the waitress, who begrudgingly refilled her cup. "Whatever happens, we have each other. Like I said, we'll stick together. Just like before."

"There has to be a way to change all of this," I said, not really listening to her any more. "I don't want to end up like them."

Carrie nodded. "Me neither, little brother. Me neither."

CHAPTER FIFTEEN

EQUIPPED FOR WAR

Two days after the meteor strike, the fleet assembled in Damascus Space.

Admiral Loeb summoned all command crew to the CIC. The Legion, the Warfighters and most of the Sci-Div staff attended.

I watched as the *Colossus* moved on the Rift. It was, I supposed, a significant achievement. Save for those poor souls who had fled here during the First Krell War, very few expeditions had made it this far. That it was now possible was the Key's legacy; the result of the Helios operation. But more than that: I was retracing Elena's journey – a route that her ship had taken years ago.

"Battlegroup adopting approach formation," a lieutenant declared. "We have open comms throughout the fleet."

"Good," Loeb said, still ensconced in his command throne. "Keep it that way. Maintain battle readiness."

"Aye, sir. Shields at maximum polarity."

The fleet comprised starships of varying designation but all made the approach at the same ponderous speed. The battlegroup adopted a pattern – a perversion of the fighter squadron aero-acrobatics, played out in slow motion. Every vessel was running null-shields and the oily shimmer of their protective barriers was just visible against the blackness of space. The shields overlapped in places, creating a nigh-impenetrable wall for any spaceborne attacker to overcome. Hornets and Dragonflies swarmed between the bigger starships.

One of the Dragonflies broke formation, conducted a brief series of zero-G manoeuvres.

"That'd be Lieutenant James, I guess," I said. "He's probably out there leading the charge . . ."

"Deploy buoys," Loeb ordered.

"Aye, sir."

Vacuum buoys floated in a wide cordon around the fleet, flashing amber warning lights.

Saul sat beside me. His anxiety prickled about him like an aura; more than once Loeb had told him to sit still and be quiet.

I felt the same nervous energy. Was Saul's intel correct? All of this might be a terrible waste of time – something for Loeb to use against Sim Ops when he took his complaints back to Command.

"Any returns on the scanners yet?" Loeb asked.

"Just one, sir. A weak energy signal."

Saul almost leapt from his seat.

"Easy, Professor," Martinez said.

"Take us in," Loeb said. "Nice and slow."

Beyond the assembled flotilla, I could make out withered blue stars. They cast a muted, dying light over the ship hulls. Several planetoids hung in surrounding space. All of them looked dead: populated by swirls of grey desert and empty lunar plains. Those worlds seemed closer than they really were, but near-space was a tumble of rocks, shattered moonlets and jagged-edge asteroids. Beyond, dwarfing all, was the green glow of the Damascus Rift.

"I want eyes on that signature," Loeb rumbled.

And suddenly, he had them.

The Artefact drifted almost serenely among the flotsam and jetsam.

I had expected it to look like the Artefact on Helios. Vast, angular; upturned like a knife to the sky. This was nothing like that, nothing at all. Although it had been hewn from the same material, the shape was all wrong. Broadly spherical, the outside was irregularly studded. At this range I couldn't tell what those features were. It was bigger than any Alliance starship and cast from blackest obsidian – from something blacker than space itself. As it moved, the starlight flickered over cuneiform patterns all over the structure.

All gathered personnel fell silent for a long moment. *Shard machines tend to have that effect on people,* I thought. The Artefact emanated a sense of age; so strong that it was almost overpowering, the aeons pressing down on me and my tiny heritage as a member of the human race.

Finally, Loeb spoke up. "Looks as though you have your wish, Major."

I nodded. "Let's get this thing secure."

Over the next few hours, Loeb painstakingly deployed his fleet in a wide net around the Artefact.

Several warships were tasked with the unglamorous job of detonating rogue asteroids, to ensure that the immediate vicinity was safe for the fleet. Meanwhile, Saul and Dr West conducted scans on near-space and the Artefact itself. As far as they could ascertain, Damascus Space was deserted:

no Krell presence, no other immediate hazards. *Being this close to the Rift is bad enough,* I reminded myself.

"This is where our work starts," I declared to the Legion and the Warfighters. "Assemble for briefing in one hour."

The *Colossus* was well equipped for war. Not just a small directed expedition like this, but proper old-fashioned and man-heavy military operations. The briefing room was huge; an amphitheatre with four hundred or so seats arranged in a horseshoe formation and a full audio-visual set-up in the well of the chamber.

My team arrived on time and shortly thereafter Loeb filed in: damned dog sniffing and mewling as he tagged at Loeb's heels. A small cadre of *Colossus* officers had also been summoned and they arrived together with the Sci-Div contingent. The flyboys, led by James, assembled at the back of the room. Back from their recent foray off-ship, the jockeys were exuberant but disciplined. They had obviously enjoyed the opportunity to do a recon run.

Williams and his team were late. They noisily burst into the chamber, laughing and joking, barely reacting to the glares of disapproval from the Naval staff.

As mission commander, I started the briefing.

"Simmer down, people," I said, and the chamber fell quiet. "Welcome to Operation Portent."

I ran through General Cole's mission objectives: that the expedition was to explore the Artefact, find out how it activated, without doing so until it was deemed safe.

I turned to Saul. "What does Sci-Div know so far?"

"It isn't transmitting," Saul said. "At this range, we're detecting an energy signature but not much else. I'm not sure whether it's operational. We'll need to board it to make any real progress."

"Which is where we come in," Kaminski said. "As always."

"Given the likely age of the structure," Saul said, "the fact that it is still operating at all is miraculous."

"How old exactly is this thing?" Mason asked. She was the only member of my team taking notes, with a data-slate on her lap.

"Carbon-dating from the material found on Helios suggests thousands of years. We are working on the assumption that the Damascus Artefact is of a similar age."

"But we don't actually know?" Mason followed up.

"As Major Harris says, the overall objective is to insert a science team. Once we have people aboard the structure, I'll be able to provide a more accurate picture. The area needs to be secured first."

"Do we know what the structure looks like inside?" I asked.

Saul manipulated the tri-D. Now it showed the honey-combed interior of the Artefact.

"These maps were produced by long-distance scans on our approach. They might, or might not, be reliable. I'm especially eager that we investigate these locations." Saul tapped a number of sites; left flags on the display. "They represent possible energy signatures. The Artefact is probably in a dormant mode; sleeping perhaps. These sites are possible activators – that would be consistent with research on the Helios Artefact." He marked the very centre of the Artefact – through a labyrinth of twisted corridors and apparently empty chambers. "This is our final objective: likely to be a control chamber of some sort. The Hub, perhaps."

"All this is fascinating," Williams suddenly chirped up, "but what is this thing? I've read the debrief from Helios. This," he waved a hand at the display, "doesn't look anything like what the Legionnaires found."

Dr West gave another of her trademark apologetic smiles. "We're dealing with the unknown, Captain. It is undeniably of the same construction, of the same material, as the Helios Artefact. But the nature and purpose is different."

Saul slid his glasses along the bridge of his nose. "My best guess is that this is a space station, or an outpost of some sort."

"So we might find survivors?" Williams said. "We might find some Shard?"

"Do we get to kill them?" the big Martian roared. He thumped a hand on the table in front of him. The Warfighters dissolved into whistling catcalls.

"The Warfighters will abide by first contact protocols," I said, cutting through the noise. "As will the Legionnaires." Back to the science team: "Do we anticipate that there will be anything alive in there?"

"That's unclear," Saul said. "Biological scans have returned indeterminate results, but life can take many forms."

"Care to explain that?" I asked.

Saul gave an uncomfortable half-smile. That simple gesture informed me that he knew more about the Shard than he was willing to let on: that even though Command expected us to carry out this mission, to die in the process, they were still unwilling to show their hand of cards.

"Yes, yes," he said. "But it is complicated. The Shard sites suggest that they might have been mechanical – inorganic – in composition. Where machine ends and life begins is not always clear."

"Do we have any idea what the Shard looked – or look – like?" Mason probed. "Even a hypothetical would be useful."

"Yeah, because then I know what I'm supposed to kill," Williams yelled.

"Quiet," I shouted back. "Don't take this lightly, people. If the Shard are aboard the Artefact, they might not appreciate us making contact."

No one answered back this time.

"To answer your question, Private," Saul said, "we have no idea what the Shard look like. We've never found any viable remains."

Saul let the line hang and the debate was over. I pressed on with the briefing.

"This is our approach plan." I called up some tactical overlays and flight plans. "It's simple: we drop down to the Artefact in Wildcat shuttles. The Wildcats will be automated; we won't be using flight crew. But Lieutenant James' fighter squadron will escort us."

James nodded. "With two Wildcats, six fighters should be sufficient. We'll keep the rest in reserve, as a contingency. Fire support will be available if you need it."

"We land here and here," I said, pointing to locations on the hull of the Artefact. "Overlapping arcs of fire, in case we meet hostiles."

"How are we going to get inside?" Jenkins asked. There was a flash of interest behind her eyes. "Demolitions?"

I smiled. "You get to do your thing, Jenkins."

"The structure on Helios responded to plasma warheads," Saul added. "A well-placed nuclear charge should be sufficient to breach the outer hull."

"Once inside, the two teams establish a beachhead in these chambers," I said, pointing to two larger caverns inside the Artefact. "Williams' Warfighters takes this location; the Lazarus Legion takes the other. Environmental pressurisation will be a priority. We can deploy drones to map out the structure. After the threat level has been assessed, and if necessary contained, we can consider moving hardcopy personnel aboard. Until then the combat-suits will be broad-casting video-, audio- and scanner-feeds directly back to the *Colossus*. I want eyes everywhere: anything of interest, record it with your suit."

"Are we confident that we can broadcast out?" Martinez asked. "On Helios, that didn't work so well . . ."

"The Helios Artefact was transmitting," Saul replied. "Its signal blocked local comms traffic. Until this Artefact becomes active, I am hopeful that we can remain in contact."

"Hopeful?" Jenkins said.

Saul shrugged. "It's an unknown."

"And that about sums it up," I said. "Any more questions?"

"Not until we get out there," Kaminski replied.

"All right. Are equipment and weapon checks complete?"

"Affirmative," Jenkins said. "Simulants are loaded into the Wildcats, ready for deployment. The Legion will go down in the first, Warfighters in the second."

Loeb suddenly stood from his seat, turning to face the gathered personnel.

"Be advised that you are all here at my leisure," the Buzzard said. "And that I have ultimate sanction on this operation. If anything you do presents a risk to this fleet, I will take immediate action. In particular, do not even attempt to activate that Artefact." He jabbed a finger at the screen behind him. "Based on Major Harris' previous experience, I have strong reason to believe that operational Shard machines pose a threat to the security of this battle-group." He scanned the faces of every man and woman in the room, drilling home his message. "That Artefact is alien technology. If it starts to broadcast, it'll call every Krell ship within light-years to our position. I can't allow that. The *Colossus*' weapons officers have a standing order to open fire in the event that the Artefact becomes operational."

Saul stood again. "Dr Kellerman's findings on Helios indicate a potential—"

Just then, Lincoln scrambled down from the upper auditorium, snarling at Saul. Teeth bared, eyes wide, the old dog looked quite ferocious. Before Saul could retreat, the dog bowled into him. Two massive paws landed on his shoulders, and the dog's head reared back to bite the professor.

I went to assist, but Loeb made a high-pitched whistle. Lincoln retreated from Saul. The scientist was left on his back, dishevelled, glasses skewed, but otherwise uninjured.

"You okay, Professor?" I asked.

"Yes, yes. I – I'm not good with animals."

I helped him to his feet.

"I would have thought that you had an affinity for all Earth's creatures," Martinez said. He had a self-satisfied look on his face. "Gaia and all that shit."

"Maybe just not a dog man," James said. "But hey, it's nice for us to have a break from the damned thing. Now he has a new best friend."

The flyboys laughed among themselves.

Loeb grabbed the dog's collar and the moment passed. Lincoln went back into the upper auditorium.

"Let's wrap this up," I ordered, bringing the meeting back on point. "Sim operators to the SOC."

The Simulant Operations Centre was the largest that I had ever seen on a starship, all clinical bleached walls and glowing holo-consoles. Most of the SOC was taken up by the simulator-tanks – twenty of those in all, although only nine had been activated. Each tank had been designated for a particular trooper; recently shipped in and sparkling under the bright med-bay lights. The bay was just for the combat-sim operations: the flyboys had their own facility somewhere else in Medical, running their own gear.

I ached to get back into the tanks.

A handful of medical staff milled between the simulators, jotting readings on data-slates.

"We need data-readings, proper prep, for the transition," Dr West said, meekly.

"Death has to be properly logged and monitored," Kaminski joked.

Let's get on with it.

I proceeded to strip off, while West oversaw the connection to the simulator-tanks. Cables were jacked to my dataports. My simulator powered up. I fixed the respirator over my mouth, attached the ear-bead communicator. Once all of that was done, I slid into my tank. The amniotic fluid inside had grown pleasantly warm. Just the scent of the stuff triggered potent chemical reactions in my brain – it was impossible to divorce the smell from the promise of making transition.

The rest of my team did the same. I noticed Williams eying Jenkins as she undressed: a little too interested.

Dr West checked each tank in turn, confirming with each of us that we were good to go. Jenkins, Kaminski, Martinez and Mason were all jacked in and ready.

"Do you read me, Major Harris?" she asked, tapping on the transparent canopy of my tank.

"I copy," I said. Her voice was clear through my ear-bead.

"All vitals are good," another tech remarked. "Establishing link to CIC."

"This is Admiral Loeb," the CIC declared. "We have a solid line."

Locked inside my simulator, I realised that there was a bank of controls inside the tank. While some of the controls were familiar – EMERGENCY EVACUATION, REQUEST ASSISTANCE and so on – I saw that others were not. In particular, there was an easily accessible activator near my right hand, labelled COMMENCE TRANSITION.

"What's with the new controls?" I asked. I'd seen virtually every type of simulator-tank, all kinds of modifications, but I'd never seen controls like this inside a tank.

"These are custom tanks," Williams answered. "Real new shit. You can initiate your own transition."

"No impediment to launch," another voice confirmed.

"Establishing remote link with simulants. Link is good."

"Commence uplink when you are ready."

"We are good to go. Commencing uplink in T minus ten seconds . . ."

Do it! Do it now!

I couldn't wait any longer and slammed the COMMENCE TRANSITION button with the palm of my hand before the countdown had even finished.

I could tell that I was going to like these new tanks.

CHAPTER SIXTEEN

WALK IN THE FUCKING PARK

There was a sudden jolt through my nervous system.

One mind, two bodies.

The brilliant clinical light of the med-bay.

The dimmed interior of the Wildcat.

The transition was almost instant.

A battery of senses awakened within me. My perceptions improved beyond the ken of a human body. Touch, smell, sight, hearing: all were super-alert. The texture of the insides of each combat-suit gauntlet. The smell of the brand-new tactical-helmet. Then the flood of fresh data, pouring into my mind as though it were an extra sense – unreadable in a human body, an additional faculty in my simulant body. A sense that I hadn't been born with, but that I was by now so deeply acquainted with that it felt unnatural to be without it.

I growled – a deep, throaty animal expression – eager to try out this new body. I flexed my arms and legs.

"Transition confirmed. Sound off!"

My team were inside the Wildcat cabin and all confirmed successful transition.

"Williams, you copy?" I asked.

"Affirmative, sir," Williams said. "All reads are nominal."

Something about his tone made him sound more like a soldier; as though the transition had brought something alive in him as well. A simulant body does that to a man. I couldn't see him or his team but knew that they were mounted in the second Wildcat, ready to launch alongside us.

"Lieutenant James, do you read?" I said, switching channels to the fighter squadron.

"This is Scorpio One," James replied, "and I read loud and clear. Scorpio Squadron has green lights across the board."

"Lazarus Actual," a more distant voice chimed in on the communicator-network, "this is *Colossus* CIC. We have a confirm on your departure. Launching in five . . ."

The countdown ticked down rapidly.

Then I felt the Wildcat moving; the tug of G-force as the shuttle began to leave the mothership's launching bay. I was pinned into my seat. Somewhere beside me, Kaminski crooned a line from a song that I didn't recognise.

AUTO-PILOT ENGAGED, my suit declared.

The Wildcat hurtled out of the belly of the *Colossus*, streaking across Damascus Space. In zero-G now, I stayed buckled in. I followed our progress on the exterior cams, patched direct to my HUD. Our shuttle took point with the Warfighters following a safe distance behind.

"Clearing *Colossus* null-shield," James said. "Adopting escort formation."

There was no sensation to indicate that we were moving beyond the perimeter of the protective sphere, but I felt the psychological burden. The Wildcat was a transport shuttle and had no shield of its own.

Scorpio Squadron – six Hornet space fighters – fell into a tight pattern around the two shuttles. The Hornets were short-winged and delicate; carrying a single pilot, encased within a mirrored canopy. A GE-908 Starcannon – a heavy-duty laser – sat at the nose of each vessel. Beneath the wings, they carried a restricted load of plasma warheads.

"Walk in the fucking park . . ." a voice whispered over the comm. It sounded like someone from Williams' team.

"Keep the line clear, people," I ordered.

"You heard the man," Williams said. "Radio silence."

As we moved into our designated approach path, I saw our target. This was why we were here: what we were going to crack. *The Artefact.* I manipulated the camera controls, magnifying the image. The picture was patchy, fuzzed with lines of interference, but I could make out the basics. The outside was rough-hewn and sand-blasted. As we moved closer, on inspection the entire hull was etched with scripture. The markings flickered erratically. That might've just been a trick of the light caused by the Damascus Rift; but the effect was strangely disconcerting, like the structure was alive—

WARNING, my suit insisted.

A marker flashed on my HUD. I frowned, examined the feed. We were still on target, moving on the Artefact at a good pace. The problem was with the fighters.

"One of the Hornets has fallen out of formation," Jenkins said.

I patched into James' frequency. "Scorpio One? What's happening to your people?"

Another marker flashed on my HUD. Another ship was off course now.

"Lazarus Actual," James said. His voice was unclear, whining with static. "We are experiencing some technical difficulties with Scorpio Four and Five."

My skin prickled. The noise behind that interference: I recognised it. It was a ghostly whisper of the Artefact's signal. I swallowed hard, fought back the urge to call this whole damned thing off.

Two of the fighters were dangerously off course. Their running lights flashed intermittently. *They're losing power,* I concluded. Our attack party suddenly seemed painfully vulnerable and underarmed; insects to the enormous Shard device.

"Oh shit . . ." someone whispered.

Scorpio Four dropped into an uncontrolled spin, end over end towards the Artefact . . .

My cams were still magnified. I saw something that no one else had noticed.

The Artefact was changing.

Structures rose from the hull.

"Anyone else seeing this?" one of the fighters queried. "Looks like some kind of—"

Weapon mounts suddenly studded the Artefact. Concealed turrets peppered the hull. As we drew nearer – into the kill zone – the weapons sprang to life, tracking incoming signals. The cannons weren't any weapon that I could identify but the muzzle calibre was big enough to throw out a decent energy output.

Which is exactly what they did.

"Oh, fuck!" said the same voice. "We're taking fire out here!"

"Hostile is active. Repeat: hostile is active—"

"Evasive manoeuvre! Hot fire on your six."

A brilliant beam whip-cracked across my vision; gone before I even recognised what it was. The beam licked Scorpio Four. Punched straight through the armoured undercarriage.

"James!" I said. "Evade!"

"We're experiencing systems failure," James said. "Not sure what—"

That meant no null-shields, no electronic countermeasures. No defences at all. No nothing.

Another flash of light: Scorpio Five was suddenly in two pieces. The pilot babbled like crazy over the comms, managing to loose a missile. The plasma warhead corkscrewed in the direction of the *Colossus*.

"Danger close!" Jenkins screamed. "Danger close!"

A tiny, short-lived explosion marked the death of Scorpio Five. Debris rained across the dark hull of the Artefact, more turrets tracking the larger remnants. Where the ship hit the structure, fire poured over it.

"It's awake," Martinez declared. "I'm getting readings . . ."

An energy beam scythed into the hull of our APS.

Cut through the triple-plated ablative armour.

Went right through Martinez's combat-suit and torso.

Left a hole in him as big as my head: immediately cauterised. The beam proceeded through the cabin roof.

"Shit!" Jenkins yelled. "Martinez is out and we're open."

Warning alarms began to sound in my head. The shuttle lurched into a spin.

"Seal suits!" I ordered.

The exterior cams were fried but they suddenly weren't necessary. Through the gaping puncture in the hull, I saw the scene develop with my own eyes. The turrets poured beams into the approaching Alliance expedition. The fighter squadron was in total disarray. There was debris everywhere, fighters spinning out of control. None of them had managed any meaningful return fire.

I mag-locked my boots, held myself at the edge of the hull breach. It was a long way down; a vertiginous drop.

Anti-sickness drugs flooded my system and kept me from throwing up inside my suit.

The sensation passed but suddenly the opposite became a reality: the Artefact spiralled beneath me, coming up far too fast. A crash-landing on the hull would be fatal.

"We're taking heavy fire out here!" Williams reported.

"What exactly are we supposed to do about it?" Kaminski said.

To shut up and die.

The second Wildcat was lit up by a beam. It hit the engine. The fuel reserve must've been breached because the entire shuttle exploded.

My HUD flashed with confirmations that the Warfighters had made extraction.

Then Scorpio Squadron were all gone.

We were all that was left.

Our shuttle banked again – the AI making an irrelevant and futile attempt to avoid enemy fire. We were thrown towards the cabin ceiling. I slammed into a support strut, felt intense pain blossom in my back. *Broken spine?* It was agonising.

"Prepare for emergency landing!" I managed.

Another turn; another blistering impact against the cabin wall. Mason's suit was breached and she clutched at a rent in her stomach.

I was almost glad when an energy beam caught our flank.

Moving at speed, firing thrusters and jinking, the superstructure fractured. There was a brief wave of heat over my combat-suit – I saw components exploding as the innards of the shuttle broke apart. Something heavy slammed into my chest. I grappled for purchase, tried to stay standing, but my mag-locks failed.

Mason was screaming, then she abruptly went silent.

Jenkins was still shouting orders. It was all pointless. I wasn't even sure when Kaminski had bought it.

My body was flung clear of the wreckage, towards the Artefact. This could only go one way. I picked out flashes of light as the Artefact's defences fired: again and again.

Either because I wasn't a threat, or because I was a spent force, the Shard weapons completely ignored me.

The hull came up fast to meet me—

I was back in my simulator, screaming so loud that my vocal chords burnt.

Above me, floating on a viewer-screen, scrolled text:

```
WILLIAMS' WARFIGHTERS
CAPTAIN LANCE WILLIAMS: DECEASED . . .
CORPORAL DIEMTZ OSAKA: DECEASED . . .
PRIVATE ALICIA MALIKA: DECEASED . . .
PRIVATE REBECCA SPITARI: DECEASED . . .

LAZARUS LEGION
PFC ELLIOT MARTINEZ: DECEASED . . .
PFC HAYDON MASON: DECEASED . . .
PFC VINCENT KAMINSKI (ELECTRONICS
   TECH, FIRST GRADE): DECEASED . . .
SERGEANT KEIRA JENKINS (EXPLOSIVES
   TECH, FIRST GRADE): DECEASED . . .
MAJOR CONRAD HARRIS: DECEASED . . .

ALL OPERATORS EXTRACTED . . .
MISSION TIME: 73 SECONDS . . .
```

All dead. All gone.
The tank canopy popped open.

A team of medtechs reached over, wrapping an aluminium blanket around me, whispering soothing words. I shoved them away, collapsed out of the tank. My vision was spinning and I clung to consciousness: if I passed out I didn't think that I would come back.

Williams stood beside me, out of his tank and holding a blanket around his naked body. He grimaced – his face full of red lacerations, the reminders of how his simulant had just died.

Debrief was short and to the point.

No one knew what had happened. Saul had detected some internal energy signatures but couldn't tell us anything else.

"No shit," Williams said. "Those were some big ass lasers, Professor."

It was hard to disagree with him on that.

The atmosphere aboard the *Colossus* felt subdued. News of the disaster spread through the ship like wildfire – with the rumour that the Shard were maybe not as dead as we'd expected. Not even the *Colossus*, with all her massed firepower, could stand up to such an enemy. The Hornet space fighters, absent from the hangar bay, were evidence of that.

Everyone avoided the mess hall that night. Warfighters, Legion, even Scorpio Squadron.

I wanted to check on the Legion but they had gone to ground. It wasn't an official visit, so I didn't bother comming them. I just took for granted that they were all wrapped up in their own private hells: reliving the sudden and brutal dispatch we'd just experienced.

Almost as an afterthought, I went up to the Vulture's Row. The Row was a tower-block construction, and by elevator it took almost a minute to reach the top. The deck itself was empty, save for a lone figure standing at the end of the observatory.

Mason started as I approached, wiped her face.

"Good evening, sir," she said.

"Is it?"

"Well, the view is okay." She leant against the safety rail. "I've never been on a ship like this before."

"The others will think that you're a tourist, if they catch you up here."

"Maybe I am. I like watching the fighter-ships taking off, coming in to land. Scorpio Squadron has been running security patrols."

It was so easy to forget that not everyone was like me. Not everyone had seen this all before; not everyone was so tired, jaded and bitter. Maybe it was even a little refreshing to meet a trooper who was still impressed by such simple things.

"There will be a good deal fewer of those ships," I said, "given what happened today. The simulants – next-gen or otherwise – are expendable. The ships are not."

Mason laughed. "Did today go as you expected?"

The Artefact lingered at the corner of my eye. I didn't want to look out at it, didn't want to face it tonight.

"Of course it didn't. I think that you can guess that."

I'd expected it to be easy. I'd expected this Artefact to be just like the one that I had known on Helios. But this Artefact was different.

Unconsciously Mason rubbed her stomach with the palm of her hand. I had no doubt that the pressure still dwelt there – the pain that had killed her just hours ago.

I found myself choking at the memory – because that was all it was – and struggling for breath.

"Is it always like this?" she asked.

"Not always," I said. "Sometimes it's worse."

CHAPTER SEVENTEEN

STEEL COFFINS

I called a general assembly early the next morning.

"Let's work on what we know," Saul said, pacing the CIC.

The Warfighters and Legionnaires sat around the enormous tactical holo-display. Loeb, Dr West and James were in attendance as well. The Artefact's response to our first approach had seriously altered the game.

Saul lapped the display, one hand poised beneath his bearded chin, the other used to punctuate every point he made.

"The Artefact has a defensive mechanism of some sort. Likely an automatic response."

For likely, I heard possibly.

"Have you seen technology like this on any of the other Shard sites?" I asked.

"No, no. None of the other sites have yielded working xeno-tech."

James tapped the display controls, rewound the feed. Each Hornet in his squadron had been recording and broadcasting as they went down. In tri-D, we watched the fighters being torn apart by the Artefact's defences. Brilliant beams criss-crossed the sky, leaving destruction in their wake. James winced as the last of the fighters went down. He and his team had made immediate extraction. They were now back in new bodies; I hadn't seen them in their real skins yet. His new skin was indistinguishable from the last.

"Probably some form of laser weapon," he concluded. "Maybe plasma."

James looked somewhat crestfallen by the turn of events. I got the distinct feeling that Scorpio Squadron hadn't suffered a defeat like this before.

"Doesn't much matter what it is," I said. "We know that it kills us."

James nodded. "Not only that. Immediately before we got hit, the Hornets suffered general systems failure. It wasn't targeted; we were all hit."

"That suggests a 'dead zone' around the Artefact," Saul said, "which is consistent with existing research on Shard tech. Perhaps Shard tech is capable of producing an anti-electronic field."

I watched the last few seconds of our demise. Scorpio Squadron now gone, the feed jumped to footage from the Wildcats. They had barely lasted longer than the Hornets.

"They took out everything," Williams said, shaking his head.

"Not quite . . ." I said.

The last few seconds of the feed played. Burning wreckage showered the Artefact's hull. The Artefact used more energy beams to break up the larger elements, until there was nothing left at all.

Not quite nothing.

I watched as my simulant sailed out of the Wildcat. I

could still feel the muscle-memory reaction. Flash, flash. The remains of the Wildcat were annihilated. The feed jumped to my combat-suit – a jittery, poor-quality stream that I knew would imminently terminate. Another simulant – maybe Mason or Jenkins – flew past me, also thrown clear of the APS.

"There . . ." I said.

My body fell to the Artefact.

There was no response from the cannons.

I froze the display. An operating Shard turret sat within metres of where my body had fallen, but it did nothing. The video abruptly terminated in a wave of static as I smashed into the Artefact.

"It reacted to the incoming ships. But it didn't react to me, or the other falling simulants."

"So, what are you suggesting?" Williams asked. "We're a long way from the Artefact, man. How the hell are we going to get down there? Jump?"

His team laughed, but nervously.

An idea had begun to form.

"The *Colossus* was a drop-troop ship, wasn't it?" I said. "Admiral Loeb: does the *Colossus* still have drop-troop launch tubes?"

Although I'd seen the tubes when we'd first boarded the *Colossus*, I didn't know whether the starship still had the necessary internal loading mechanisms.

Loeb frowned at me, as though the question was some insult to him personally. "Command doesn't consider drop-troop assaults a good use of resources any more. We haven't used the launch tubes in years. When the Simulant Operations Programme gained favour, Command more or less abandoned the drop-troop initiative."

"But do the tubes work?"

"All of the original features of my ship are still functional."

"What are you thinking?" Jenkins asked, a half-smile on her lips.

Kaminski leant over the table, grinning as well. "The Torus Seigel manoeuvre?"

"The very same," I said.

Exactly an hour after the briefing, I clambered back into my tank and jacked myself in. Around me, through the watery prism of the tank, I saw the Legionnaires and the Warfighters jacking in as well.

"Are all simulant operators ready for transition?" Dr West called.

"Of course we're ready," I said, and activated the internal tank controls.

Back in the early days of the Alliance space forces, the drop-troop delivery method was considered the pinnacle of shock tactics. The Alliance had used the strategy on Epsilon Ultris, on Barnard's Star, even during the Martian Rebellion. Tacticians had long regarded the orbital delivery of a large-scale infantry force to be an admirable but impossible goal.

The development of dependable anti-grav technology changed all of that. Imagine it: a thousand Alliance troops raining down from the sky, landing in precise formation and taking the fight to the Directorate's front door. The mothership, the drop-troop base, remains in high orbit – lending fire support to the ground pounders. No need for costly dropship insertions any more.

That was the theory, at least.

Now the reality. The trooper is loaded into a drop-capsule: an armoured shell, not much bigger than the soldier encased inside. Wholly dependent on Naval intel to make sure he is fired at the right moment, to make sure he lands on target. The period between launch and landing in enemy territory? It lasts seconds but I can tell you, it's hell. Anything could go wrong: your capsule might not fire, you might get hit on the way down, or you could land off-target. Coming out of the capsule, you're likely to be under heavy enemy fire. You better hope that the Navy boys – safe in their warship, just visible on the horizon – have tracked you on the way down as well. You can just as easily end up being hit by friendly fire.

As I lay inside the capsule, I silently considered all of this. The capsule was Iron-Horse pattern, manufactured by some long-defunct Earth corporation – through some twist of coincidence, the same type that I had used on my last hardcopy mission. Torus Seigel had been a hellish drop-troop operation, a true meat grinder for the Alliance Army and, in particular, Special Forces. It had been a planet of strategic value to both the Krell and the Alliance, into which each species had poured millions of lives to achieve a bloody stalemate. The memories came flooding back. I remembered being trapped inside one of the flying caskets as it launched over Seigel. I hadn't thought about that op in an age, but now I could recall every detail of the mission . . .

I snapped back to reality. I was in utter blackness, body held rigid by webbing across my arms, legs and torso. That was for my own safety. A crippling sense of anxiety overcame me, made me want to thrash out – to break the webbing, to be free from the drop-capsule.

Relax. You've done this a hundred times before. You know the drill.

And I did know the drill, too well. The only difference was that this time I was simulated.

At just that moment, my tactical-helmet came online. The

HUD illuminated. Glowing graphics confirmed what I couldn't physically see: successful transition for the rest of the operators.

"Sound off!"

There came a barrage of "affirmatives" from the rest of my team, as well as Williams' Warfighters.

"Countdown initiated," Dr West confirmed.

Nine steel coffins, in a tight grid formation. Several other dud capsules were being launched as well, filling out our numbers: extras in case the Artefact took offensive action.

"Stay together and stay cool," I ordered.

My heart beat fractionally faster, containing an impossible fear that a simulant body could never know.

Five . . .

Four . . .

Three . . .

Two . . .

One . . .

"Yee haw!" someone shouted over the communicator, generating enough feedback that my ears ached.

Feet first, I was launched from the *Colossus*.

No sound, no visuals.

It made the hard-drop to Maru Prime feel like child's play. The sudden rush of the launch, pushing down on every organ and bone of my body. Such that I felt it would squash me flat, for just a second, then—

Nothing.

My HUD indicated that I'd broken free of the *Colossus'* gravity well. The other troopers were in staggered formation, some launching with me, others pausing for a second or so. The theory went that this would maximise the chances of a successful drop. But staggered launches meant nothing to an enemy with no tactical awareness, and where the

Shard were concerned I was minded to abandon all tactical assumptions.

The outer shell started to slew away; metal plating flaking from the exterior. The safety webbing began to relax.

CLEARANCE ACHIEVED, my HUD stated. PREPARE FOR LANDING.

As fast as that: probably a few seconds of freefall.

I braced for the Artefact's attack, but realised that we'd made it past the perimeter at which the Artefact had commenced the assault the previous expedition.

Now I had work to do. In a controlled planetary drop, the outer capsule protects you from damage caused by atmospheric re-entry. That can be lethal, even to a simulant. But when the drop is being conducted in a vacuum, when there is no atmosphere, it serves a different purpose. The capsule can withstand small-arms fire, can block your IR signature.

I was a few hundred metres from the Artefact.

INITIATING DESCENT PROCEDURE, my HUD stated.

Although the Artefact had no significant gravitational pull of its own, the *Colossus* had fired me at speed. The momentum generated by the launch meant that I'd have to slow my descent if I was going to actually land on the structure, as opposed to being splattered across it. I fired a burst from my thruster unit, mounted on my back. Twisted in zero-G and began to decelerate.

"Mason, you clear?" I asked. I remembered too well what had happened back at Maru Prime.

She breathed hard but answered: "Affirmative, Major. I'm in formation."

Practice makes perfect, I thought.

"Kaminski, Jenkins, Martinez?"

"All in formation," Jenkins answered. "Coming up on the Artefact now."

My backpack thruster activated again and I landed gently on the hull. My mag-locks kicked in: anchoring me to the metallic plating underfoot. In zero-G, I barely felt a thing.

Still, I wasn't taking any chances.

"Weapons free," I said.

We were all carrying the same standard-issue plasma rifles. I fluidly unlocked my M95. The battle-rifle camera system activated but there were no targets to be identified.

"Sweet Christo!" Kaminski chuckled. "That was something."

We had landed in a dispersed formation, within a square kilometre of each other. My HUD illuminated with the locations of the rest of my team.

"This is Captain Williams, sounding off. We're all down safely."

I tuned my communicator to the *Colossus*.

"This is Lazarus Actual, do you read?"

"We copy," Saul replied. "Fascinating, fascinating."

"We're down. Do you have audio and video?"

"Patchy, but the feeds are holding."

That would have to be good enough. "Keep comms contact to a minimum," I directed. "If there are Krell in there, I don't want them homing in on us."

"Understood."

"Moving to breach point. Lazarus out."

"*Colossus* out."

I moved along the hull, towards the rest of my squad.

"Check those cannons," Jenkins ordered.

Although I was cautious, the Shard weapons sat inert.

"Just keep a safe distance from them," I said.

Nothing about this structure felt predictable.

Williams' Warfighters fell into position alongside my team. This was the first time that I'd seen them skinned up. Their camo-fields were deactivated and I took in the personal modifications that each of them had made to their gear. They had their own squad badge: a surfboard, riding a blue wave. Maybe some reference to California.

The suggested breach location was flagged on my map. Both squads slowly converged on it. Dr West and Saul had selected a circular structure of unknown design, simply because the scanner returns had suggested that this was a weaker point in the hull.

"Permission to deploy demolitions," Jenkins asked.

She was especially loaded up and must've been crammed into her drop-capsule. Two large demo-charges were strapped to her back, together with a heavy breaching tool and other explosives kit. Saul could give his best guess, but since no one had been aboard the Artefact yet, we didn't know what tech would be necessary to breach it.

"Set a charge," I nodded. "Warfighters, fall into covering position."

Just as we didn't know how easy it would be to breach the Artefact, we didn't know what would be waiting for us inside.

"Warfighters!" Williams barked. "Form up! On the man's mark!"

Kaminski was crouched beside me, panning a bio-scanner unit over the hull, searching for signals.

"Any movement inside?" I asked him.

"Hull's too thick to penetrate with handheld kit," he said. "But I'll keep trying."

Jenkins moved towards the circular structure set into the hull. The diameter was twice, three times my size: obviously made for something far larger than a simulant. There were no obvious controls or other mechanisms.

"I'll blow the central seam," she explained. "That should weaken the panel—"

"Hold position!" Kaminski suddenly said.

Jenkins paused over her demo pack.

I stepped back, battle-rifle up and ready to fire. Only now could I see what it really was: a portal. An enormous airlock, with panels made from overlapping metal leaves, as black as the rest of the structure. Those had been contracted tight, sealing the entrance. Along with the rest of the Artefact, it was difficult to scan – had probably been hidden from the *Colossus'* sensor-suite. Up close, the purpose was obvious. The portal began to open. Each individual metal panel rotated, relaxing: retreating into the hull.

Eight heavy plasma rifles aimed into the darkness inside. Ready for what might be about to come out.

"How did it do that?" Williams whispered. His breathing was restrained. "Why did it do that?"

"Maybe it wants us to go inside," Martinez said.

There was another sub-chamber, much bigger than a man: leading to a further ominous doorway. A fine mist of ice crystals floated into space, the remains of whatever atmosphere had been captured inside the chamber. I crouched at the lip of the portal and activated my rifle-lamp. Bright light flashed over the inside of the Artefact, probing the abandoned room.

"Looks empty," I said. "And it has a gravity field."

My body was being gently tugged into the Artefact; if I allowed myself to lean too far forward, I knew that I would be pulled inside. Williams knelt beside me. It was like we were both at the edge of a yawning black pit, a glimpse into the abyss. *Thousands of years, and this old crate is still working.* I briefly wondered whether anything that the human race had built or created would last so long. The gun turrets were one thing – possibly explainable as an automatic defence response. But a functioning airlock was something completely different.

"Maybe it isn't as dead as Saul thinks," Martinez offered.

"Still no bio-scanner returns," Kaminski said. "And I'm getting a decent field inside the structure now."

The darkness called out to me. A single toneless whistle sounded over my comm-link. My HUD fuzzed for a second; systems jumbling.

"Anyone else hear that?" I asked.

"Hear what?" Kaminski said.

That was answer enough. "Nothing. Just interference."

And it's only going to get worse . . .

"I should take point," Williams said, readying himself to move inside. He turned to my helmet-mounted camera – pulled his best video-face: "This is a big step for the human race, contact with another alien species—"

I put a hand to his chest, to hold him back. "No. I want to be first in."

I stepped over the boundary into the Artefact.

I'm finally here. I'm back again.

Felt the gut punch of a gravity shift. Down and up became confused. My brain tried to interpret otolith signals and I was temporarily paralysed with nausea. The sensation passed rapidly: before I could really appreciate it, my medi-suite had already administered the necessary drug combination. Down really was down, and my mag-locks automatically deactivated.

Behind me was an infinite star-field – the Alliance fleet just visible – and ahead of me was the interior of the Shard Artefact. I suddenly felt a very long way from the rest of the human race, let alone the Alliance.

"Watch the shift," I warned the others. "Gravity approaching full-G in here."

The sub-chamber was abandoned and crystallised dust lined the walls and floor. *Could this have been Elena's route?* I asked myself. I searched for footprints – for some indication that someone had come before us – but there was nothing. The place was pristine in its desertion.

The others filed into the corridor beyond the portal, through the sub-chamber. I kept my eyes ahead: only saw the movements of the rest of my squad on my HUD scanner as blips.

"All troopers in formation," Jenkins confirmed.

"I'm inside, but I'm not believing it," Kaminski said. "Why'd it let us in?"

"Fuck knows. But this is definitely an airlock. Which suggests that – at some point – whoever built this structure needed an atmosphere."

"But there are no controls . . ." Williams said. "Maybe the whole place is automated."

As if in response to his comment, the airlock door slid shut behind us. With the access door shut, it was pitch-black inside. Not just dark: nothingness black. My tactical-helmet shifted into night-vision mode: drawing the corridor in filtered greens and greys.

There was movement up ahead.

Both squads were combat-ready, weapons trained in that direction.

The inner lock door slid open. I couldn't hear it, through my closed tactical-helmet, but I could imagine the groan of the ancient mechanism – the *schtick!* as the panels retreated into the walls.

"Move up. By the numbers."

Both squads darted through the inner door. The lock led

into a tunnel – wide, ovoid. The walls and floors were lined with more cuneiform, just like the outer hull. The inside of the structure looked a lot like the tunnels under the desert on Helios, and I struggled to deal with those memories. My heartbeat increased; that sudden emotional response that not even a simulant could protect me from. My suit AI instantly noticed the shift in my presentation.

"You okay, sir?" Mason asked.

She must've seen my biorhythms too. It took a second for some corrective chemical concoction to hit my bloodstream, administered by my onboard medi-suite.

"I'm fine," I said.

Martinez was tapping his wrist-comp, taking readings from his external suit sensors. "This place has atmospherics."

Kaminski verified his findings. "Jesus. Crusader's right. Decent oxygenation, low nitrogen levels."

"Everyone stay buttoned up until I say otherwise. Move on to objectives."

But Kaminski and Martinez were right. There had to be some sort of concealed life-support system in place, but I couldn't see any evidence of it. However the atmosphere was being maintained, it was optimal, approaching Earth-standard.

"How'd it know what we breathe, man?" Williams asked.

There was no answer to that. There was no way that the Artefact could know. The structure itself offered no answer: the interior was horrendously quiet.

I separated from the group, moved up on the next junction. Tapped the suit-camera mounted on the side of my helmet: broadcasting in real-time back to the *Colossus*. I knew that the Sci-Div complement would be eager to see what was happening.

"This is Lazarus Actual. Are you reading me, Saul?"

"Loud and clear," Saul replied. "I'm getting everything. Can you pan around left and take in that wall?"

I did as he asked. My camera recorded whatever I was seeing. Although the cuneiform all looked the same to me, I hoped that Saul could understand some of it.

"That good enough?"

"Yes, yes. The vid-feeds are being analysed by the xeno-linguistics AIs. Can you commence mapping of that corridor section?"

"Fine. Lazarus out."

I broke the connection.

"Deploying drones," I said. "All troopers copy."

My combat-suit carried a full complement of surveillance drones, and on my mark they deployed around me. The swarm scattered immediately. The others did the same; soon the area was flooded with electronic eyes.

"Execute mission plan. Legion move on the primary objective, Warfighters take the secondary objective."

"That's an affirmative," Williams said, and moved off with his squad.

Our designated coordinates were a few hundred metres inside the Artefact.

"Drones report no biological or mechanical activity," I recorded. "Anyone else getting any readings?"

"Nothing here," Mason said.

"Same here," Jenkins said.

"Same," Martinez reported.

"Nothing," Kaminski said. "But this place is heavily shielded. I'd like to know what the hull's made of. There's hardly any background radiation."

That was surprising enough: we were so close to the Rift,

the place should've be bathed in cosmic rays. Outside, my suit had detected a significant rem reading.

"Moving into surrounding corridors," Jenkins said. "Provide covering fire to the major, people."

Williams and his Warfighters were behind us now.

A soft chime sounded in my head.

MICRO CHANGE IN AIR DENSITY, my HUD warned.

What the fuck is that supposed to mean?

"Combat formation!" Williams roared over the comm.

The urgency in his voice, that edge that couldn't be faked, made me drop to one knee. I scanned the corridor.

"Speak to me, Williams!"

He was only a couple of corridors away, almost on the Warfighters' objective. The glowing blips representing his squad abruptly fell into a tight perimeter at a junction, trying to cover every opening.

"Williams, fall back down the main corridor," I ordered. "You've got too many approaches to cover there—"

"Drones are down!" Martinez called.

One by one, each of my drones went off-line. In the course of maybe three seconds, their feeds were terminated. *That's impossible!* I argued. They had been spread across the structure, several hundred metres apart. But it was much worse than that. My drones weren't the only units affected. *All* of the drones were gone. The implications were clear: there was something else inside the Artefact with us. Hostiles fast enough to take out the drones before they could even be registered.

Even so, save for picking up the rest of my team, my bio-scanner was completely dead .

The enemy doesn't show up on scans.

"Watch those corners!" Williams called. "Executing your order. Tight formation, people . . ."

The Legion did the same. Formed a defensive perimeter, back to back, covering the wide corridor. It was dark, the walls pressing in on us—

"One of Williams' team is down," Kaminski said.

There was a nervous, pregnant pause as the others consulted their suit systems.

"Jesus, he's just gone!" said Mason. "My diagnostics report that his signal has vanished."

"What's happening, Williams?"

This is fucking stupid, I insisted to myself. *There's nothing in here*—

"Do we fall back to the exit?" Mason asked.

"That's a negative," I whispered. "Null-shields up. There's nowhere to run."

There really wasn't. If we did fall back, would the Artefact let us retreat? I didn't think so. We were trapped.

Martinez tore a flare from his combat-suit, and lit it. The area was dowsed in angry light – jittery spider-web shadows thrown over the walls. The others copied him: soon the corridor was full of unpleasant, blood-red luminescence. Our null-shields were visible as overlapping red spheres.

The floor was softly vibrating, filtering through the soles of my combat-suit. A humming began to fill the air, barely perceivable, but quickly building. It felt – impossibly – like the structure was breathing.

"Welcome to the war!" Williams declared, his voice now crackling with static. "Incoming!"

Then the communication network descended into screaming, and the calm was well and truly broken.

* * *

There was weapons fire – lots of weapons fire.

The sound of heavy plasma weapons discharging bounced off the walls. The structure acted as an amplifier, creating nightmarish echoes. Something began to shriek in the distance: something not Krell, not human. It tore into my subconscious, was almost disabling.

The Shard are still here.

"What's happening in there?" Saul insisted. "We're getting some massive energy readings."

"Get off the line, *Colossus*!" I roared. I didn't have time to deal with technical queries. "Now!"

Another of Williams' team died. No explanation. The corresponding blip disappeared from my tactical display.

"Trooper down!" someone shouted over the comm.

Impossible to tell who it was.

Then Williams' whole team was gone.

Just gone: extracted. Their respective life-signs vanished from my scanner.

They will be coming for us next . . .

I panned my rifle over the walls, the floor.

"I see it!" Martinez yelled. "It's above us!"

He fired into the ceiling, into shadow.

Whatever it was, the thing was only a metre or so away from me. But even with the multi-vision cameras in my tactical-helmet, even with the targeting-AI of my battle-rifle, it was still too fast for me to capture.

"They're all around us!" Mason managed. "I can't get a fix—!"

Then the thing was suddenly inside Mason's null-shield. It lifted her body with ease. She struggled, her armoured limbs thrashing.

"Stay still!" I ordered.

I brought my rifle up, trying to get a clean shot at the

blur of motion that had her. But before I could fire, before Mason could get free, she was slammed against the wall. Again and again, so fast that she had almost become invisible. Her neck, chest and arms snapped. The force was sickening – enough to rupture her suit and pulverise the body inside.

Jenkins put two shots into Mason; either accidentally or as some small act of mercy. Didn't much matter, because we were all about to die in the tunnel. Of that I was certain.

It tossed Mason aside. Her body landed with arms and legs at the wrong angle, combat-suit crushed beyond recognition. I'd never seen armour suffer that much damage.

By the time I managed to loose a shot, the shadow had already moved on. My pulses scorched the walls and ceiling.

"I have it—!" Jenkins said.

Then Jenkins was off her feet as well.

Kaminski twisted about, and perfectly illuminated her with his suit-lamps.

Jenkins brought her rifle up to fire at something that was breaking from the dark. And for just a split second, I saw what was hunting us through the Artefact's dead tunnels.

A sculpture of living metal.

A thing of black chrome.

A shadow within a shadow, glistening like oil.

Whatever it was, it grabbed Jenkins.

For a moment, the construct was rippling, amorphous dark. Then, without warning, it became precise – so fucking defined – and punched a limb right through Jenkins' shoulder. Her armour did nothing to protect her: the shadow sliced into it with ease.

"No!" Kaminski roared.

Jenkins' face exploded as the construct put a tendril through her helmet. The face-plate shattered noisily and bloodily.

Kaminski and I fell back, desperately trying to get a bead on the thing. It never seemed to stay still.

In a perverted lover's embrace, Jenkins' arms and legs shook in the ecstasy of death. She was wrapped in viscous strands: ensnared by a poisoned web of mercury. The dark spewed ten twisting pseudopods, needle-tipped limbs.

"Fuck you!" Kaminski shouted.

He opened up with his rifle. Plasma pulses impacted the dark all around. He was firing without discipline, driven by pure rage. The living metal pitted and twisted as each shot hit home; but reformed just as quickly.

"Get back," I said.

It didn't have the effect that Kaminski wanted. As the volley hit, Jenkins' body twitched. Probably born of the wish to end her simulated suffering, her finger pressed on the trigger of her rifle. Uncontrolled plasma rifle-fire poured over the area – washed over Kaminski. He was hit, reeling backwards. I only just managed to dive out of Jenkins' fire arc, and predicted what would happen next.

Kaminski's grenade harness went up almost immediately. He was loaded with explosives – carrying more than regulation would allow – and his whole body went off. His torso vanished beneath the first explosion and the second set off the power cell in his own plasma rifle.

By the time that the third went off, there was nothing really left.

Martinez was showered with frag from Kaminski's dead body, and stumbled back the way we had come. He laid down a sloppy shower of plasma with his rifle to cover his retreat.

"*Gracia de Dios!*" he shouted.

The Shard-thing finally dropped Jenkins.

It speared Martinez with a hundred sharp appendages. It

was everywhere in the corridor, flowing from the cuneiform: a thing of absolute nightmare. Martinez's body slumped to the floor, oozing simulated blood and loose organs.

I was in here alone with the thing.

The Shard reared over me.

"Come get me, asshole!" I yelled.

I began to fire. I knew that it would do no good; that my weapons were useless.

In a flurry of motion – movements so fast that I could barely track them – it was done.

CHAPTER EIGHTEEN

THE GRIM REAPER

No one took the extraction well.

That included me: for hours afterwards, my body ached – echoes of the ghost injuries I'd suffered aboard the Artefact.

I called a debrief in the SOC and everyone except Loeb attended. Following today's disaster, I imagined that he was counting the hours until he could justify pulling the plug on the whole op.

Dr West and Saul sat at the back of the centre, already working on the data we'd collected from the operation. Vid-feeds showed the final moments of our demise, broadcast direct from the Artefact. The tri-Ds looked like postmortem photos; remains decanted from a Midwest serial killer's hideaway. Busted and punctured combat-suits, blood everywhere, severed limbs.

"It was so damned fast," Williams said. "I've never seen anything like it."

His squad rumbled agreement. For the most part, the Warfighters had become withdrawn and sanguine. *Strange*, I thought, *how a taste of death could have such a calming effect.*

"Your people never had a rough extraction before, Captain?" Kaminski asked of Williams, with a put-on sneer.

"We've made plenty of extractions," Williams said. "Two hundred and nineteen is my magic number – two-twenty after today." He patted the big Martian on the shoulder. "The big man has a couple hundred under his belt, and the girls are nearly there as well."

"But nothing like this . . ." one of them whispered.

The images of the Shard – whatever it was – were always out of focus, usually blurred. The thing was a moving shadow; definitely not Krell. It seemed to pour from the ceiling and fluidly move towards the camera.

"So that's what the Shard look like . . ." Kaminski said. "A real nice species. Makes me almost wish that we could have the Krell back."

"Was that one of the Shard?" Mason asked.

"There are many possibilities . . ." Saul said.

"Then explain," I said. I was fed up with Sci-Div games.

Saul chewed the inside of his mouth. "Perhaps it is another defensive response; an advanced electronic sentry. Maybe some form of nanotechnology? That might explain the ability to reform and absorb energy discharge."

"It enjoyed the slaughter," Martinez said, shaking his head. He looked over at Kaminski, still shirtless. There was a grinning skull tattooed on his chest, sightless eyes peering out at each of us. Martinez nodded at 'Ski. "That thing was the Grim Reaper."

"Whatever it was, it attacked in sequence," Saul offered. "Suggesting that the Reaper, as Private Martinez calls it, is a single entity."

"How do you know that?" I said.

"I've analysed the vid-feeds and the suit data captures.

The Artefact's structure interferes with comms, but I'm certain that there was only a single specimen."

He indicated the computer monitors. A timeline, stitched together from each of our vid-feeds, showed the rapid demise of all nine simulants. Although the thing moved at lightning speed – with barely milliseconds between some kills – there appeared to be a single Reaper.

"Why'd the Reaper let us in," Kaminski said, "only to kill us?"

"Perhaps it is a foreign-body reaction," Dr West suggested. "Falling into a programmed sequence, then reacting to your presence once it realises that you are intruders."

"An allergic reaction," Williams muttered. "Like a living machine."

"A machine that has been alive – functional – for thousands of years," I said. "It knew those tunnels well."

I pointed to a cut-away map of the Artefact, on one of the viewer-screens. There were probably hundreds – if not thousands – of kilometres of chambers and tunnels. If we were going to meet the same reception every time we entered the Artefact, the idea of mapping the place was beyond daunting. There, in the very centre of the map, was the Hub: the control chamber.

"If Saul is right, and we're dealing with a machine," I reasoned, "then what about an electromagnetic pulse?"

Saul paused. "An EMP? I don't know. The Reaper might be shielded. Given the abilities that the specimen has demonstrated so far, even if the grenades are effective, I doubt that they will do much more than temporarily disable it."

"Got to be worth a shot," I said. "Do we have any EMP grenades aboard?"

"The *Colossus* armoury has most things," Jenkins said.

"Those grenades have a very small blast radius," Mason muttered. Her gaze was fixed on her own death-scene. "We're going to have to get personal with that thing if we want to have an effect."

"If that's what it takes . . ." Kaminski replied.

I turned to Saul. "What about the combat-suits? Are they shielded?"

I didn't much like the idea of being trapped inside a non-effective combat-suit, aboard the Artefact.

"The armour is EMP-proofed," he said. "Although the grenades will probably disturb your transmission capability."

"Good enough," I said. I nodded at Jenkins. "Distribute the EMP grenades among the simulants."

"Affirmative," Jenkins said, her back arching now, the embers of her dedication stirring. "Sounds like a plan."

"Get some rest, people. We'll try again tomorrow."

Later that night, I went to the comms-pod again.

I found the same pod as I'd used before, but it irked me to find that my mission papers had been removed. *Must've been cleaned by one of the maintenance crews*, I decided. I tried a search of the comms bands – tried to find any evidence of the *Endeavour*'s ghost transmission – but it yielded no results. Indeed, there were no transmissions at all. Every frequency was full of squalling, bubbling static: not so much as a human voice among the madness. *Maybe I imagined them*, I considered. *Wouldn't be the first time.*

Angry with myself, I decided to take a different tack. I would speak to Saul. He was the key to real progress. I hadn't been entirely convinced by Saul's responses today. It still felt as though he was holding back, like he knew more about the thing aboard the Artefact than he was willing to let on. *Watch him*, a voice suggested to me. *He could be*

228

trouble. I tried to dismiss the whispers, but it wasn't that easy. I was tired and frustrated with the progress we'd made so far: finding a human face to blame was an appealing prospect. We had weapons, we had armour, we had technology. I could handle the pain, the dying: it was the unknown that I couldn't deal with.

So I took an elevator down to the laboratories. The lab complex adjoined the SOC and it was as well equipped as the rest of the starship. This late into the night-cycle, the deck lights were dimmed – mostly lit by view-screens and monitors, machines set to run tests while the Sci-Div staff got some shut-eye. There were metal gantries and catwalks above me, criss-crossing the larger chamber, and a nest of sub-labs fed off the main facility. *Place'd be a nightmare to assault or defend*, I thought to myself.

In the centre of the room, concealed behind multiple layers of reinforced plasglass, was the Shard Key.

I felt a surge of adrenaline in my system, caused by my proximity to the device. I hadn't seen it, in person, since Helios. *Christo, it's just as I remember it*. A dark-metallic dagger blade, engraved with Shard glyphs. Occasionally, those illuminated – a miniature spark of lightning reaching out against the glass wall. Suspended inside the prison, it gently twisted as if caught by an unseen stellar wind.

Saul wandered about the lab. Although he lacked the vac-suit I'd first seen him in, his presentation immediately reminded me of our meeting on Maru Prime. He was buried in a data-slate, mumbling to himself, the light of a data-read reflecting off his glasses.

"Good evening, Professor."

Saul nodded, but kept reading for a moment, walked right past me.

"Professor?"

"Hmmm?" he started. Then he looked up, jumped. "Yes, yes, Major."

"You're working late."

"Aren't we all?" He smiled; a toothy, forced reaction that was vaguely unsettling. "So much to do. So much to learn."

"Find anything useful in the data-reads from today?"

"It's all useful, Major. Every little bit."

I paced the Key's glass prison. A quad of sentry guns were mounted overhead. The high-calibre plasma weapons were augmented by a bio-sensor and motion-tracking AI. The guns twitched, following every motion below. The Key was the last remaining evidence of Helios, of an operational Artefact – a device of untold value to the Alliance. Security here was even tighter than in the rest of the ship.

Saul activated something on a nearby terminal. An image of the Damascus Artefact, gliding through space, filled one of the wall-screens. The image was jittery, frequently dipping out of focus. But I could see flashes of red light on the outer hull: could make out squadrons of drones drifting over the structure, investigating the hull.

"What are the drones doing?" I asked.

"Those?" he said. "Just intelligence-gathering drones. I ordered their deployment after your mission. Didn't think to bother you. We have several thousand of them, working on the cuneiform patterns. Provided they remain on the hull, the Artefact appears to ignore them. Whatever the Shard were, this appears to be their method of communication: they recorded everything." He sighed. "I'm sure that we will eventually understand it all, but it will take time. This lab has some of the most advanced AI systems poring over the texts day and night.

"I'm very interested in the markings on the outside of the structure. Before Dr Kellerman . . ." – he paused, as

though carefully considering his next choice of word –
". . . uh, passed, he provided Sci-Div with images from the
Helios site. I have access to the sum total of Command's
knowledge. The language repository is proving very helpful
in understanding this Artefact."

"Then what is this place? This thing?"

"Probably a very large machine, a computer made to link
with other nodes in the network. A long time ago, Damascus
was a busy star system: several planets, each of those with
several moons. This might've been a major Shard holding."

"Any idea what they were? After today, anything might
help."

Saul paused, rubbed his chin. "I've told you everything
that I know: they were machines, and they hated the Krell."

"Is that supposed to be enough?"

"It makes them a potential ally."

"Not from where my people were standing."

"I'm sure that the Reaper's reaction can be explained."

Saul placed his data-slate on a nearby terminal, tilted his
head as he looked at me. "Is there anything else I can help
you with, Major?" he asked. "I have so much to get on
with."

"I wanted to ask you about the *Endeavour*'s tachyon
trail. Have you found anything new?"

Saul nodded. "I expected you to ask that, sooner or later."

He punched some keys on a keyboard. A golden dust
trail appeared on the view-screen; alongside the Artefact. I
watched on, felt my heart begin to race – begin to beat
again. That feeling, that Elena was tantalisingly close, almost
overwhelmed me. *Stay with it*, I told myself.

"This was the *Endeavour*'s trail. I can be sure of that.
But it seems to have just disappeared."

"How is that possible?" I asked. I was desperate for more

information. "Surely a starship of that size couldn't just disappear from time-space."

"It was here, now it is not," Saul said, shrugging. "It's unlikely that the *Endeavour* was destroyed."

That possibility had barely occurred to me, but I discarded it immediately. I'd done my research on the *Endeavour*, and she had been a city-sized starship: had she been involved in a fight, she would've caused a debris field the size of the United Americas. There would be plenty of evidence of that. Her battlegroup had also included numerous warships for protection – a fleet much larger than the Damascus operation.

"What about if she jumped to Q-space from here?" I offered.

"There isn't any evidence of that. I'd expect to see a further tach trail if the ship used her Q-drive."

"Then what happened?"

"It is one of the many mysteries of the Maelstrom, Major. Maybe it is linked to the Artefact's purpose. Until we can understand that, it's impossible to track where the ship went."

I sighed. I knew all of this already, had expected the same answers.

"Rest assured, I would be most interested in understanding why the *Endeavour* was here," Saul said, staring at the view-screen: light flashing over the insides of his enhanced-vis glasses. "And I'd like to know where she has gone."

"You and me both," I said.

I needed a clear head, so I took the Run again. This time, Martinez insisted on coming with me. I found him waiting for me beneath the shadow of the Vulture's Row.

"Nice view, *jefe*."

"Guess so."

I pointed to the other end of the corridor. It looked a distance away; the elevator door impossibly small. The red emergency supply box winked a warning light.

"You heard about this place?" I asked.

Martinez nodded, limbering up. "Some of the space jocks told me about it."

"Then you know about the challenge?"

"*Si*. I reckon I can beat the Old Buzzard's record." Martinez pulled a face and lifted his shoulders. "He's fast, but I'm faster."

"Just try to keep up with me."

We sat at the end of the Run; drenched in sweat and panting for breath. The physical exertion was punishing, but it felt good: that lactic burn in my arms and legs, the thundering of my heart. I slid back against the cold floor, put my hands behind my head.

Martinez gave a deep laugh. "What did I tell you?" he said.

"It was closer than you think."

"Check your wrist-comp. It wasn't that close at all."

He had beaten me by several seconds, pulled away into the lead somewhere along the mid-point of the Run.

I'm getting old and out of shape.

My wrist-comp flashed with run completion times. Williams still sat at the top of the leaderboard, swiftly followed by some of the space jockeys. There was the Buzzard: well up the leaderboard, run-time several seconds ahead of mine.

"That's a fucking joke," Martinez said. "The jockeys are using sims. I could do this run in half the time if I was skinned."

"I reckon I could get used to that," I said. "Being skinned up twenty-four hours a day."

Martinez considered the idea. "I'm not sure. It might be too much."

"You'd be okay; you can sleep in them."

We stood together, walked to the nearest elevator. Another of the ubiquitous DNA and fingerprint scanners sat beside the door. I thumbed the well-worn panel and activated the elevator call.

The machine chirped an error. "User not recognised. Please retry."

"Let me try," Martinez said, and swiped the panel.

"User recognised: PFC Elliot Martinez."

The elevator door slid open.

"Fuck you, too," Martinez said, as we entered the waiting elevator. "You want to try again tomorrow?"

"Sure," I absently answered.

CHAPTER NINETEEN

COMPROMISED

The following morning, the Warfighters and the Legion gathered in the SOC. I outlined my new plan.

"We'll split up and go in alone," I said. "If Professor Saul is right – and there is only a single Reaper – then we'll stretch this bastard thin."

"So it has to move around the structure . . ." Jenkins said. She was getting it, saw where this was going. "More targets means longer inside the Artefact?"

"Exactly," I said.

I turned my back on the operators, activated one of the view-screens. The by-now familiar schematics of the Artefact appeared, indicating thirty or forty structures randomly spaced across the alien hull. They were the same formation as the portal we'd used the previous day: it was a reasonable assumption that each represented an airlock of the same design.

"We're going to approach the Artefact separately. Based on yesterday's experience, the airlocks will likely respond in the same way." Glowing markers indicated the landing sites for each sim. "We go into the structure alone, carrying EMPs. When the Reaper hits, each of us holds it off for as long as possible."

"So we're buying time, then?" Williams asked. "With our lives?"

"Isn't that what we always do?" Kaminski offered.

More simulants were loaded into the drop-capsules and we were in turn installed into our simulator-tanks.

"Are all operators ready for connection?" Dr West asked.

"All operators are engaged," reported a technician.

"Establishing remote link with simulants."

"Link is good."

"Commence uplink when ready."

"We are good to go. Commencing uplink in T-minus ten seconds . . ."

"See you on the other side," Jenkins said.

That flash as I made transition: between bodies.

Then the sudden plunging sensation as the drop-capsule fired from the belly of the *Colossus*.

This time, my HUD showed a different drop-pattern. I made the same approach as I had on previous drops, but the other capsules diverted on alternative routes. I plotted the dispersal on my HUD, traced the nine capsules as they each made the approach.

"Lazarus Actual, transition confirmed. Making descent."

The Legionnaires all called in as expected. Mason's voice shook as she reported. Could be that was just the vibration of her capsule, causing vocal distortion; more likely it was fear. We were each going to be aboard the Artefact alone in the dark. Even I felt trepidation at that. Something like anxiety swept through my simulant body. Skinning up usually deprived me of such base reactions – it had been a long time since I'd felt that sort of emotion inside a sim. Yesterday's experience with the Reaper had changed that.

"Warfighters confirmed," Williams said. "On target."

My capsule shed the outer layers and I made the LZ. In a replay of yesterday's landing, I anchored myself to the Artefact's hull and approached the airlock. On my own now, the sense of desolation was almost overwhelming. I focused on the small manual tasks – broke the approach down action by action.

The airlock opened in front of me. I wondered whether the structure would respond differently this time – whether the Artefact might deny us entry. But as I fired my thruster pack, and crossed over, the airlock hummed to life. The outer door contracted to allow entry.

"Is everyone getting the same response?" I asked over the comms.

"That's an affirmative," Jenkins said.

"Then double-time it to interior coordinates," I ordered, "and stay in touch. Ready on the EMPs. On first appearance, I want complete coverage."

"Copy that. You heard the man."

Glowing blips appeared on my scanner, each representing a different bio-sign. All troopers had successfully crossed over.

My objective was the same as the previous day – a chamber a few hundred metres inside the Artefact.

I stalked down the corridor. The Reaper could be anywhere. There were so many shadows for it to move through. I pulled long-burning flares from my webbing. Activated, I dropped them to the ground. On a logical level, I knew that it was wasted effort – that, inside my sim, I was truly expendable – but I was motivated by some primal need to know my way back, to have an escape route.

I held the EMP grenade in my left hand, my rifle in my right. My thumb covered the grenade firing stud and I felt an unconscious twitch; an urge to use the device.

"What's the tac sit, people?" I asked over the general comm band. I desperately wanted – needed – to hear the chatter of friendlies.

"Nothing from me," Kaminski said. "But I'm ready for it. I owe this motherfucker one . . ."

Watching Jenkins being ripped apart by a shadow had affected him, even if the death was only simulated. Couldn't blame him: I could still remember the look on her face as the machine-thing had taken her.

"Drones away."

My drone flight disappeared ahead. Sonar pinged chambers beyond my location. The interior was a jumble of ovoid corridors and caverns.

"I'm seeing machines," Mason reported. "But everything is real old."

The nature of the corridors was changing. Here and there, ancient machines grew out of the walls. My suit-lamps flashed over the decrepit interior – searching for some clue that the facility was occupied. But the devices were covered in an eternity of dust, unlit—

There was a whisper from somewhere ahead.

I paused, rifle up.

Nothing. Turned up the gain on my pick-ups.

A child's voice.

"Anyone there?" I asked, using my suit-speakers.

Something answered me from the darkness: a young girl's whispering.

I grabbed another flare, tossed it down the corridor. It

scattered metres away. Sent fizzing shadows across the walls and floor.

The corridor was still empty.

Get a grip, man. There's nothing there.

"I know what I heard . . ." I said to myself.

My helmet chimed.

One of Williams' team had extracted. There were seven blips on my scanner, instead of eight.

No gunfire, no chance to fight back.

Just gone.

"I've got a man down," Williams said. "Be on alert."

My drones dropped off-line in sequence. I flashed through their feeds on my HUD – eager to see the last frame before each was terminated – but there was no explanation.

Just like yesterday.

"Stay frosty, people . . ."

Ahead of me, the route became dark: the length of this section of tunnel unclear. Although I couldn't see them, my suit sensors picked up shafts above me reaching deep into the structure. It would be impossible to cover every entrance. So many damned places to hide—

Then the girl's voice came again. This time, I was sure that I'd heard it—

The communicator devolved into a babble of shouts and death-cries.

"Hold your positions!" Williams ordered. "All of you! I said hold positions—!"

Oh shit.

Two more Warfighters vanished from my HUD. Williams lasted a second longer, then he too flashed out of existence.

My team were faring only slightly better. Mason was moving. Her suit status indicated that she'd managed to get off a couple of the EMP grenades. Probable locations of the Reaper appeared as glowing red markers.

Then Mason's vitals flatlined.

The Reaper was moving again, now towards—

Jenkins—

"Christo – get away from me—"

Her voice sounded wet and heavy, grew ragged. I cancelled her comm-link: she was gone. Her blip flashed – med-alert activated but for long seconds still reporting life-signs. What was the Reaper doing to her? A bead of sweat broke on my upper lip, and I licked it back—

Moving again—

—Kaminski—

"Stay in formation, Kaminski!" I ordered.

"Say again?" Kaminski said. I saw his blip moving fast, saw the explosion of grenades as he went. "Unclear – I don't copy that—"

Of course Kaminski had heard. He was chasing Jenkins, unable to resist the bait. The Reaper knew exactly where to find him. *It's fucking enjoying this.* Kaminski fired off an EMP. Went down almost immediately afterwards, in the same corridor section as Jenkins.

Martinez vanished shortly after that.

In less than ten seconds, it was all over.

Eight deaths.

Hundreds of metres apart.

Fast, bloody, pointless . . .

. . . and yet, there, on my bio-scanner was a signal.

Not in formation – nearer to my coordinates than any of the team had been when they were finished off.

"Are all troopers extracted?" I questioned, over the comm. "Is anyone left?"

No response. What had I expected? The silence of the alien structure was almost crushing.

I wondered for a moment whether the Reaper had left one of them alive. Perhaps Kaminski or Jenkins: bleeding out in one of those dark corridors, yearning release from their simulant. But a quick analysis of my HUD revealed that was impossible. All bio-signs were completely extinct, and extraction had been confirmed.

Whatever else was in here wasn't from the *Colossus* expedition. It was something different.

I activated my suit-speakers. "What's out there?"

The real Shard? Another example of their twisted engineering?

A whisper answered me in the dark.

Words, but indecipherable. Inside the sim, my hearing and vision were advanced to a suprahuman degree: and the combat-suit only further enhanced my abilities. It was a female voice – a young girl? – but it was maddeningly unclear.

Simultaneously, a blazing-hot bio-sign flashed across my HUD. Near enough now so that I could sense a heartbeat: the rapid throb of a bio-system. It moved off, away from my position – became a firefly, luring me into the darkness. The reading wasn't moving fast but whatever it was it knew the terrain. The ghost didn't hesitate, didn't pause, and moved on from one junction to the next.

I gave chase immediately. If the Reaper was done with the rest of my team, then I would be next. Death was a certainty; it was how long I lasted that counted. If I learnt anything from this body, then that would be a victory.

There was a portal ahead – the same iris-style manufacture as the outer airlocks. As I crossed over into the room, the door whispered shut behind me. I found myself inside a large circular chamber – bigger than anything I'd seen inside the Artefact so far. The cuneiform on the walls began to softly illuminate, throwing out a pale light. Consoles rose soundlessly from the floor. Had to be some sort of self-assembling technology, something that the Alliance hadn't encountered before.

The bio-sign was somewhere inside the room with me – just beyond the reach of my suit-lamps – but had stopped moving.

"What are you?" I yelled.

My own voice taunted me; echoing into infinity, bouncing off the hard metal walls.

As it diminished to silence, another answered me.

"Turn off your feeds!"

I know that voice . . . I felt an ice-cold core forming in my chest: a black hole erupting inside my ribcage. I was paralysed. It was as though the speaker had commanded me to stop.

This isn't possible, I insisted to myself.

It's probably just another element of your fractured psyche, talking to you, the *Point's* holo-psych dictated to me. *But you're about to die in a few seconds anyway: you have nothing to lose.*

With that in mind, I cancelled everything via thought-command. No video, no audio, no scanner. I was truly isolated now: no connection at all with the *Colossus*.

"It follows your suit-feeds," the voice responded. "You're bleeding data like a stuck pig."

There was a figure in the shadows.

That weakness inside of me leaked into my limbs, spread through me at a terrifying rate. *Holy Mother Earth* . . . It held me like a vice; I was gripped with sick fascination. I lowered my gun – it would do me no good any more.

You see what your imagination is doing to you now? the psych taunted. *You're torturing yourself. That's how fucked-up you've become.*

I dropped my EMP to the floor and I tore my helmet free. I had to see this with my own eyes – to judge for myself. Nothing else would satisfy me, because I knew how utterly impossible this was. The reconstructed visuals of the tactical-helmet HUD could be faked, could lie. I hoped that my own eyes were more dependable.

A familiar face looked back at me.

Sweet Christo.

"Conrad?" Elena asked.

I couldn't speak. Couldn't do anything but stare at Elena, at the woman I had lost. Whatever incredible physical feats the simulant was capable of, right now it was useless to me. Every drop of strength had been drained from me, like I was infected by the most deadly Krell bio-toxin. I wanted to speak to her, to tell her how I had missed her, of how sorry I was that I had let her go – but I could do none of those things. Could do nothing but watch this impossible creature as she emerged from the shadows: so fragile, so precariously vulnerable.

I froze, my fingers wrapped so tightly around the grip of my rifle that I could sense the plastic deforming: the powered mechanisms in the gauntlets activating. What I was seeing was beyond impossible, beyond credibility.

And yet, here she was. Here was Elena.

But something was wrong.

Her expression – her reaction to seeing me – was almost as surprising as finding her here. She stared intently and her brow was knitted. It was a pained, hurt expression: directed at me. She narrowed her eyes and evaluated me. The look pulled me from my trance, brought me back to reality.

"Is that really you?" she asked, in a hard voice.

*   *   *

Elena had been gone for eight objective years.

Not a day of those eight years – even in hypersleep – had passed without me thinking of her. I'd dreamt of our reunion for such a long time. Sometimes, the dreams had been so intricate – so real – that on waking I'd hated myself for daring to imagine something so visceral that its absence was sheer agony.

I'd never considered that our reunion could be in circumstances like this. Not aboard an alien Artefact, in the deeps of the Maelstrom.

Perhaps worse, in flashback and dream Elena had been as I'd remembered her. She was a pure memory construct. The Elena Marceau in my tri-D photos, in the worn-out vid-clips: she was a fixed point of reference.

The Elena that looked back at me, with those enormous brown eyes, wasn't the woman I remembered at all. She was unkempt: exhausted, pallid-fleshed. Her long hair was clasped at her neck but lank strands escaped over her face. She wore a vacuum-suit; the yellow plastic grubby and tattered – torn at the elbows, shredded at the thigh. *That won't take exposure to vacuum*, I immediately concluded. In the low light of the chamber, I saw the UAS *Endeavour* crew badge on her shoulder – scuffed and faded so that it was barely visible.

Elena watched me examining her, eyes never leaving mine. There was a rigidity to her posture – like a feral animal about to take flight. She stepped back from me.

"Are you really here?" she said. Her voice quivered. She added, more abruptly: "Are you real, Conrad? I need to know!"

"It's me," I said: again taken by the strength of her response, by her unexpected reaction. "I'm real."

There was some irony there, I supposed. Here I was,

finally seeing the woman that I had pursued in dream and thought for eight long years – and it was she who doubted my existence. If this Elena was a construct of my damaged psyche, then she certainly wasn't reacting as I would have imagined.

"Are you alone?" she asked, sharply.

"I – I had a squad—"

She scowled at me, defiantly. Her body was so small compared to my enormous armoured frame, and she was shaking. Whether that was with anger, or some other emotion, it was hard to tell.

"Where are they now?"

"Gone. Dead."

"Are you sure?"

"Yes."

"Always keep your suit-feeds switched off when you come here," Elena snapped in admonishment. "That will give you more time before it finds you. It senses the data; it'll smell you – just like the Krell do."

"All right," I said, nodding. "I . . . I can't believe that you're still here."

I took a step towards Elena. I wanted so desperately to touch her – to feel her in my arms, even if those were only simulated. Despite her condition, she looked barely any older than when I'd last seen her. Maybe that was some trick of the Rift, caused by the localised distortion of time-space—

If she is here at all, the voice of reason muttered.

"Why would they send you?" she asked. "Is this a trick?"

"It's me," I repeated. "Have you been here all this time?"

She gave me a hard look. "How do I know that you haven't been compromised?"

"You'll have to trust me."

"I don't know if I can."

"How did you get here?"

Just as Elena seemed to doubt me, I needed some validation; some evidence that she was real. I took another step towards her and reached for her. Her eyes burnt with anger and she backed away again.

"They sent me back. To bring help. I have – or at least had – a shuttle in the moon-fields."

"I've got to get you out of here—"

She cut off my words. "I'm not going anywhere with you. Like I said: I need to know that you haven't been compromised." She pursed her lips. "The others were."

"What do you mean?"

I had so many questions – wanted to ask a million things.

"I need to know that I can trust you," Elena started. Her entire body was taut as a coiled spring. "I need to know that it's really you—"

For just a second Elena looked beyond me.

I felt the Reaper's presence in the room. I just knew that it was in there with us.

"Go!" I shouted. "Go!"

Elena moved fast. Stepped back – running before I had even turned.

The chamber came alive.

Something black and nightmarish exploded from above.

The Reaper was suddenly everywhere, and I had nowhere to run.

I grabbed another EMP from my suit-harness, and thrust the grenade into the dark mass. My gloved hands came into contact with the living metal and it flowed around me. Even in my sim, I cringed as I made contact with the material.

I plunged my fist into the Reaper. My shoulder-lamp wildly skittered over the shimmering entity – like a searchlight on an oil spill.

The grenade activator stud flashed a cool blue.

"Fuck yeah!" I roared.

Soundlessly, the EMP went off.

The Reaper froze.

I pulled my hand free. The blast radius was small, and Saul was right – the suit systems were barely touched by the EMP. But none of that mattered: instead, I searched for some sign of Elena – some indication that she had been real, and that she was safe. *Have to make sure that she makes it away from here!* Protective instinct drove me on. The rifle was in my hands and I jammed it into the Reaper's underside. I fired. Plasma pulses hit the entity, sent flickering electric discharge all over the dark metal – a miniature lightning storm.

The construct shrieked a devastating sonic wail. I staggered back, ready to fire again—

The Reaper rebooted.

A hundred spear-tips reached from the dark: weapons formed from the living metal of the alien construct.

It punched a multitude of barbs through my chest.

It was over.

In the blink of an eye, I made transition back into my real body. This time, I ignored the simulated pain that exploded across my body. Without pause, I fumbled with the interior tank controls. My hands were numb and unresponsive to my commands, but I tried to jam a finger onto the COMMENCE TRANSITION control.

I expected that buzz of transition – the plunging sensation as I inhabited the new sim, readied for launch in the drop-bay.

Instead: nothing.

"I have to go back!" I shouted. "I have to go back! Get me out there!"

I was vaguely aware of a medtech outside my tank. Hands open, palms up, defensive: repeating something again and again. Someone was trying to talk to me through my ear-piece.

"I saw her!" I shouted into my respirator. I wanted the whole damned ship to hear what I had to say – no one was going to stand in my way any more. "Elena is in there!"

The viewer above my tank displayed COMMAND OVERRIDE: TRANSITION CANCELLED.

"We need to go back," I said. "Elena is in there."

The Legion looked on sceptically and the room was silent.

"I'm going back."

Williams laughed under his breath. "Whatever, man."

"Shut the fuck up, Williams," Kaminski muttered.

Williams had dismissed the Warfighters for the day, and everyone else sat around the SOC. Professor Saul was hunched over the bank of monitor screens. He had set up the system to display all nine streams from the Legionnaires and the Warfighters. The combat-suits were set to broadcast from the moment we left the *Colossus*. They collected and broadcast more data than I was capable of assimilating in a simulant – streaming the encrypted material for later analysis.

Jenkins pulled a tight smile. "We've all been under a lot of stress. The number of transitions we've made, in such a short period of time: it's messing with our heads."

"Yeah," Martinez followed. "The Reaper isn't like anything we've ever seen before. Maybe it's, you know, affected you?"

"We've all got limits," Mason added.

Three transitions – coupled with three violent extractions – over a couple of days was exceptional. Our bodies might've

248

been intact but we were all showing the strain. The argument was logical and considered: but I wasn't thinking with that part of my brain any more.

"You're not hearing me," I said, as firmly as I could. "I saw her. She's real, and she's inside the Artefact."

"Maybe Professor Saul can assist," Dr West said, in her usual placatory tone. "Your combat-suit would have broadcast your feeds—"

"I turned my suit-feeds off."

"And why did you do that?" Williams asked.

"Because Elena told me to. She said that the Reaper follows our transmissions. It's using them to track us."

Williams laughed again. "Christo. This is unbelievable."

"What about before you switched the feeds off?" Dr West offered. "Maybe there is some evidence of the bio-sign you've described."

I remembered then that I had seen the bio-sign before I'd cancelled the feeds. It had probably only been a few seconds' worth of data but it was better than nothing.

"Yes, yes," Saul said. "Perhaps that is possible, ah, validation."

We all watched as Saul operated the SOC system. Nine video-feeds filled the screens. There was nothing exceptional about the earlier parts of the recordings. I watched myself fall from the *Colossus*, land on the Artefact. Saul sped through these parts, watched them at double speed.

Then all nine operators were inside the Artefact.

The Reaper arrived shortly afterwards. It appeared as a flurry of motion, without a distinct shape.

The Warfighters died first.

Then the simulated Mason died. She tried to toss a couple of EMPs but the Reaper was faster. Spike through the faceplate. Jesus. That had to hurt.

I watched the real Mason's reaction. She clutched a hand to her chest, gasping for breath in synchronicity with the simulated death on the vid-screen. She had taken it hard: one of her eyes was so bloodshot that it had almost turned black. That was the stigmata – the overspill of physical reaction from the simulant to the real operator.

Maybe she's reaching her limit as well, I thought. *Or maybe she already has.*

Jenkins was next.

Then Kaminski.

Martinez went last.

The Reaper was everywhere. I watched it at multiple angles, from the cameras of the dead troopers.

Just me left.

Saul spoke over the recordings. "At this point, Captain Williams and Sergeant Jenkins had been the two simulants nearest to your location." He pointed to a wireframe map of the explored portions of the Artefact; to flashing indicators. "You were making good progress towards the Hub. The sergeant died here, and the captain died there."

"What about our feeds?" Jenkins asked.

"The broadcast degraded as you made your way deeper into the Artefact. Captain Williams' feeds actually became unreadable in this corridor here."

Saul turned back to the screen, pointed out the location. The vid-streams were crippled with interference, had become infuriatingly difficult to decipher. The bio-scanner-feeds were no better.

"This is immediately before Major Harris cancelled his feeds," Saul continued. He shook his head in dismay. "The transmission quality isn't sufficient to reach any conclusion."

Jenkins sighed uncomfortably. "We don't know what the Artefact is capable of. The Shard technology might be causing hallucinations." She looked to Saul. "What about the Rift? Maybe this is a by-product of cosmic rays?"

Saul shrugged. "I can't rule it out."

Jenkins was taken with the idea. "Finding Elena is something that you want to happen. You really want to see her. Maybe the Rift or the Artefact is causing you to see things—"

I slammed a fist onto a nearby table. "Will someone listen to me? I'm Lazarus. I don't need scanner-feeds or transmission to prove anything. I know what I saw, and I saw her. Dr Elena Marceau is alive in there."

"It's impossible," Williams added. "Dr Marceau vanished years ago. So she's been hanging out on this Artefact for all that time? On her own? We've all seen the Reaper – seen what it does to simulant bodies. We can't survive in there – how the hell is she doing it?"

"I don't have all the answers. Not yet."

"And where is her ship? How did she get aboard the Artefact?"

"She said that she had a shuttle; in the moon-fields."

"Which Loeb hasn't found from ship-scans?" Williams added. "It just doesn't make sense, Major. I agree with Jenkins." He smiled in her direction; the exchange didn't go unnoticed by Kaminski. "You're seeing what you want to see."

I looked between Jenkins and Williams. There was a difference in their positions, even if Williams wanted to present a united front. Jenkins didn't believe what I'd seen; but she wanted to. Williams, on the other hand, was only interested in discrediting me: wanted this whole thing for himself.

"Still smarting because I didn't let you board the Artefact first?" I asked.

Williams frowned at me. "That has nothing to do with it. You're losing it, Major."

I stood, paced towards my simulator-tank. It was impassive and cold: patiently waiting for the next transition. My data-ports ached and I yearned to get back out there. I almost clambered back into the tank.

"Elena insisted on something," I whispered, looking at my reflection in the glass canopy. "She wanted to know whether I was real."

"What the fuck does that even mean?" Williams asked.

"I'm going to find out. I'm going back out there."

"Not tonight you aren't," came a voice from the entrance to the SOC. "Listen up!"

Loeb filled the doorway, chest puffed up with self-importance. Lincoln slinked around his feet, never taking his eyes off Saul. The professor seemed to wither, his enthusiasm dwindling, whenever the dog was around.

"The Damascus Rift is acting up," the Buzzard said. "A localised ion storm has developed out past the moon-fields. I want additional safety protocols in place. Until the storm passes, I'm suspending any further expeditions."

The sense of relief from the others was palpable. Mason's shoulders sagged, tension draining.

"And in case anyone has missed it, today is Alliance Day. Ship's universal clock confirms it." Loeb glared in my direction. "I've read today's debrief. A little downtime probably wouldn't go amiss."

He turned and left, his dog in tow.

CHAPTER TWENTY

ALLIANCE DAY

Alliance Day marked not only the founding of the Alliance, but through engineered coincidence also the end of the Martian Rebellion. When I was a kid, the annual celebration had been a big deal – a chance for disparate and often fractured communities to come together in a common cause. I could still remember the street celebrations. Fireworks, hot food, a late night: such simpler times. The few fond memories I had of the Metro seemed to revolve around Alliance Day.

This was a pitiful affair in comparison. It was held in the mess hall; the room cleaned out for the event. Tables were pushed to the edge of the room, lights dimmed, some music piped in through the ship's PA. Loeb had issued an open invite to the *Colossus*' officers and all off-duty personnel but few had attended. Those that had were in a sombre and withdrawn mood. Ordinarily it would've been an easy trip between the *Colossus* and the other ships in the battlegroup – a short shuttle ride – but the storm had locked down inter-fleet transport. I'd heard that similar gatherings were being held across the fleet, and couldn't help wondering whether those parties were any better than this.

The only positive aspect of the gathering was alcohol. The last supply run had ferried some crates of alcohol as well as the usual food rations. A few thousand cans of Alliance-issue beer, together with some stronger spirits: enough to take the edge off.

James and Scorpio Squadron had opened up the adjoining rec room. That was a small, cramped chamber, with a holo-pool table in one corner and a very amateur-looking bar in the other. A deckhand was playing the role of bartender; mixing ad hoc cocktails and distributing bottles of beer.

I couldn't stop thinking about Elena.

Did I really see her? I wanted to believe that she had been real. But even I could appreciate that there were so many unanswered questions, too many improbabilities. I had to make another transition. *This time*, I told myself, *I'll know for certain*. But I couldn't make transition without arousing suspicion. I had to pick my moment.

So I did what I do best: I got drunk.

I sat at a table in the rec room. Lieutenant James perched at the bar beside me.

"Credit for your thoughts?" he asked.

"I don't feel like talking."

"I heard about what happened."

I changed the train of the conversation. "You ever change that flight-suit?"

"Not if I can help it," he said, taking a deep swig from his beer.

"I thought that you said that alcohol didn't affect you?"

James smiled. "I said that I filter out the good stuff before it can act. But there are ways around that." He indicated to the line of empty bottles on the bar top. "Namely: speed.

If I drink a lot, and I do it fast, then it'll work for me. Just don't tell Dr West."

I laughed. The lieutenant popped off his barstool, pulled up a chair at my table.

"Like I said: I heard about what happened."

"I'll bet everyone has. I guess that it's the talk of the ship."

"I didn't mean it like that. You saw what you saw; nothing else to be said."

Above James, an ancient two-D viewer played a speedball match. Although it had probably finished a decade ago in real-time, the flyboys were oblivious to the party going on around them and were intently viewing the game.

"This place is getting to us all," James went on.

"You seeing things then?"

"No," James said, shaking his head. "Nothing like that."

"Then what?"

"I'm a soldier without a job," he said, letting the words roll out slowly.

"You're a pilot, James. Not a soldier."

"Same difference. It's just that, what with your new approach plans – using the drop-capsules – there isn't much room for the Aerospace Force any more."

"I guess," I said.

James looked dejected; now that we knew the Artefact's defence plan involved taking out space fighters, his squadron was without a proper role. The mission had moved on and James had become redundant.

"Be thankful for the downtime," I said.

"I'd rather be in the saddle, killing bad guys. The Legion gets all the best jobs."

I took in the Legion, dispersed around the room. Kaminski sat in another corner of the rec hall, alone. His eyes were red and he looked tired; today had taken its toll. He was quiet – very unlike Kaminski – looking over at Jenkins. She wore a cling-film green dress, exposing her chest in a decidedly more feminine fashion than usual. How she had acquired the dress was beyond my alcohol-blunted brain: I was sure that she hadn't brought it out here. As she danced, Jenkins occasionally looked over in Kaminski's direction, making fleeting eye contact, grinding against Mason, or swinging the younger girl around in a circle. They were all pretending to enjoy themselves, doing impressions. The Legion was haunted. Mason's face was a ruddy mess of lacerations; that one eye still filled with black blood, a warped reflection of Saul with his milky blind eye.

But James wanted to talk, and he kept going. "Nine years in the Force, Harris. I've seen it all: been to Ipcress Quadrant, fought the Krell in the Van Diem Straits. But this is different. It's not just dying on that approach to the Artefact. I've seen your vid-feeds of the Reaper. This thing – whatever it is – gets to me."

"Well," I said, "if you've seen our feeds, you'll know that this op is a bit more complicated than just killing a bad guy. Even our plasma rifles are bouncing off that son of a bitch."

"At least you're doing something," James said. "Even dying on the Artefact is better than sitting around here and waiting for new orders."

I finished my beer. James nodded at the bartender, passed me another. As I took it, I noticed that my hands were shaking – almost uncontrollably. *Fuck; I need to make transition so bad.* James saw it too but gave me a weak smile and pretended not to notice.

"I got a wife and kid," he said. "On Alpha Centauri."

"Good for you."

James ignored the sarcasm. "Not so much. I haven't seen my wife in what feels like for ever. I've been away for so long, I'm not sure how old my daughter'd be in real-time." For a moment, I was afraid that he was going to get the family photo out; impress on me that his child really was the cutest in the township. "Doesn't mean that I don't think about them every night. Anyone ever threatened them, I don't know what I'd be capable of doing."

"Is there a point to this conversation?" I asked.

James laughed. "Just do what you got to do, Major. To protect the ones you love."

We sat for a long while, drinking our beers, old men on a house porch at dusk. That was how I felt: old and used up. I was far from drinking my fill but I was out of touch with the rest of the room. I didn't recognise the music, didn't recognise the faces. Even Jenkins and Kaminski; they were more than just soldiers. They were people beyond the gun and the armour—

There was a sudden commotion at the end of the bar.

The atmosphere around me – such that it was – suddenly crashed. Although I was drunk, my senses immediately sharpened.

Kaminski bolted from his table, across the hall. Jenkins was standing over at the rec bar now, laughing. Williams was beside her, leaning close into her personal space. From where I sat, I couldn't tell whether the attention was invited or not: Jenkins' back was to me. The crowd parted, and I saw a flash of Williams' hand on the small of her back.

"Hey!" Kaminski yelled, jabbing a finger towards them. "Asshole!"

Williams immediately withdrew his hand; faked ignorance of the angry trooper shouting across the room.

"Just leave it, 'Ski," I called after him.

"What the fuck you doing?" Kaminski said, his voice dripping with Brooklynese. "I'm talking, you fucker!"

The party seemed to freeze, officers and crew standing aside to let Kaminski through. He stormed across the room.

"Hey, man," Williams said. "Way to go to spoil the mood. I'm just talking to the sergeant about old times, is all. Butt out and sit down."

"I can handle it, 'Ski!" Jenkins said. She glared indignantly at Williams too; making it clear that whatever his intentions, she wasn't interested.

Kaminski bobbed his head, pressed on: in Williams' face within seconds. Before I could follow him, Kaminski balled a fist and threw a punch.

"Whoa, Private!" Williams canted.

He ducked the blow with surprising speed. Kaminski connected with a bottle of beer on the bar, smashing it. Onlookers retreated in a wide arc of the two fighters.

Kaminski set his jaw. I'd seen that look on his face before; and knew that he wouldn't be cowed. He lashed out with another right hook. This time the blow caught Williams squarely in the mouth. He reeled back.

"Y . . . you fucking hit me!"

There was a bright smear of blood on his lip.

The Warfighters were suddenly behind Williams. They bristled bad energy; just drunk enough to take out their frustrations on anyone who got in their way. Looking at the big Martian's death-stare, considering his enormous bulk, I didn't want to have to take him on in my own skin.

"We were just talking about old times, man!" Williams repeated. He wiped blood from his mouth with the back of his hand.

"'Ski!" Jenkins roared. Her eyes flared and she immediately

looked a whole lot more like a soldier, regardless of what she was wearing. "I said I can handle this myself!"

I considered what to do. Martinez and Mason were on either side of me now.

"I'd like nothing more than to put that big red bastard down," Martinez said, pointing at the Warfighter. "New Girl is with me."

I didn't want this deteriorating into an all-out bar brawl: not in a pressure-cooker environment like the *Colossus*.

"Stand down," I said. "Kaminski, step away."

He reluctantly backed from the bar but kept his eyes on Williams. A blonde medtech – a woman I'd seen around the Medical Deck – moved to Williams' side, wiping at his split lip with a wet towel. It didn't look serious; had been more of a warning shot than a serious assault. Just as Kaminski cycd Williams, the medtech kept eyes on Jenkins: the look that told me, whatever the truth of the situation, she thought Jenkins was somehow to blame.

"We need to talk," I said to Kaminski. "Everyone else, I think it's time to call it a night. Williams, see to your people."

Williams nodded slowly, senses dulled by drink and the recent blow. He waved over to his team. The two female troopers came to his side, the big Martian following shortly after.

"I'll take you down to the infirmary," the medtech said, coddling Williams' jaw. "Get you fixed right up." Under her breath: "They're damn animals."

I watched them leave the mess hall, Williams making the most of his injury.

I turned to James. "Nice talking with you, Lieutenant."

He lifted his beer in my direction. "And you, Major."

Then I marched Kaminski outside, grabbing a bottle of vodka from the bar as we left.

* * *

We rode the elevator all the way up to the starship's top deck. Kaminski remained in petulant silence throughout: arms crossed, breathing through his nose. Suited me fine.

"Where are we going?" he eventually asked.

"Hydroponics. You need some space to cool down."

The Hydroponics deck was huge – several hundred square metres, crammed with gene-spliced plant strains. Arranged into oversized and automated feeding troughs, the plants provided a back-up oxygen-source and in an emergency could yield limited foodstuffs. On a ship this size, both of those aims were likely to be missed by a long way – we'd surely starve and suffocate should life support give out – but it was somewhere quiet. Overhead, banks of hanging halogen lamps flickered on as we entered. I squinted against the strong illumination; switched some of the lamps off. Satisfied with the artificial twilight, I picked my way through the jungle. Kaminski followed behind.

"What was that about?" I asked him.

I wandered around the edge of a planter, senses overloaded with a variety of exotic pollens. The smells were alien to me: nearly choking.

"Nothing."

"You want to spend your whole career as a PFC?"

"Not especially."

"Then hitting a senior officer, even if he is an asshole, isn't a very good idea. Williams is a captain, for fuck sake."

Kaminski fumbled around another planter, setting off the watering system. He jumped back – cursing as water pumped across the monstrous roots of the plant.

"Where I come from, there are no plants like this," Kaminski grumbled. "There are no plants. Period."

"You can quit the big-time Brooklyn front, Vinnie. I know where you come from, and you know where I started too."

An avid gardener had assembled a couple of deck loungers, like those found on the pleasure decks of interplanetary cruise liners, in one corner. From the piles of empty beer cans and ration packs that were piled beside them, I reckoned that the operation had been conducted without Admiral Loeb's approval, but whoever was responsible was long gone.

Reluctantly, Kaminski helped me move the loungers into a better position, beside one of the floor-to-wall view-ports.

"That's better," I said. "Now sit. We need to talk."

I sat on my lounger and cracked open the unlabelled vodka bottle. I took a mouthful of the harsh liquor. I liked vodka: drunk neat, it had an immediate and honest effect. I felt that numbness begin to creep through me, moving me one step closer to being properly drunk. I passed it to Kaminski. He flopped onto a lounger as well. Took the bottle and drank deep from it.

"That would strip paint," he said.

"It's alcoholic," I said. "It'll do."

Kaminski stared around the deck. "This place is nasty. Why'd you bring me up here?"

"To give you some space. You're the longest-serving Legionnaire, and you know that I cut you slack whenever I can, but that was out of order."

Kaminski stared at the floor for a beat. He looked a lot like a big kid.

"Are you listening to me?" I asked.

"Yeah," Kaminski said. "I hear you."

"I can't condone you hitting an officer."

"Even Williams?"

"*Especially* Williams."

"I know. I'll apologise to him."

"Good."

"Doesn't make it right . . ." he started. "He had his hands all over her . . ."

"I'll dress it up, make it look like you were at fault. I know it's not easy, but I warned you about keeping this professional. A couple of nights in the sack doesn't make Jenkins your weakness all of a sudden, does it?"

Kaminski smiled weakly. "Guess not."

"Because you can't think like that, Kaminski. Not in this job."

Kaminski gave a long sigh. He looked pained all of a sudden. "She's all I have," he said. I passed him the vodka but he waved it away. "Do you know the first thing that I did when we got back from Helios? I commed home. I haven't done that in years. An automated message every Christmas, the occasional birthday comm. That's the contact I got with home. That's how my old ma remembers me. Or how she used to remember me. She had Alzheimer's before we left."

"I guess the time away didn't help?" I offered.

"No," Kaminski said. "It didn't. I didn't begrudge it one bit but I blew a whole year's wages on an FTL link. We talked for a while. She didn't recognise me at all. I haven't got anyone left, except Jenkins."

"And the Legion."

"Yeah – and the Legion."

"Just watch it, is all. I know that Williams is bad news. He's a lazy bastard I'd rather be without, but Cole chose him. You can't let your private life interfere with work."

Kaminski nodded. "Understood."

"Now, get an early night and sleep it off."

I polished off the vodka, in several uninterrupted mouthfuls, and let the stuff hit me. I'd quickly reached the sweet spot of being just drunk enough: the boundary between being incapable of coherent thought, and being comfortably numb. I dropped the empty bottle into the pile of trash. We both stood, pushed our way through the artificial jungle.

But my night wasn't over; not by a long way.

I knew that the SOC would be empty by now. Anyone left awake would be at the party. This was the perfect time to move. After making sure that Kaminski had actually got back to the barracks, I fumbled my way into Medical. The entire ship was on night-cycle and the med-bay was deserted. That suited me just fine.

I desperately needed to know whether she was real; whether the woman I'd encountered on the Artefact really was Elena.

"She's all I have as well," I whispered to the dark. "And I need to go back."

I stripped out of my fatigues. I activated my simulator-tank and the intimate electric hum filled the air. Through the glass canopy, it glowed with an effervescent blue light – holding such promise, seemingly just beyond my reach. I'd seen this done so many times before that I was more than qualified to do it myself.

Just one more death, that might be all it takes, the voice taunted in my ear.

"I doubt it," I said, steadying myself against the tank exterior.

Slowly, swaying under the influence of a bellyful of vodka and a gut-load of disappointment, I realised that there was another light in the room: another blue glow, from the corner of my eye.

Williams' simulator-tank.

Not only was his tank operational but he was inside it. Caught in the cradle of data-cables and feeder tubes, his hardcopy bobbed tranquilly. I watched him for a long moment, processing what I was seeing – in my state, that took longer than it should have done. His eyes were tightly shut and the muscles of his face occasionally twitched.

Where Kaminski had hit him, there was no injury at all.

Was I imagining this as well? Maybe things were getting worse.

The monitor above his simulator was in sleep mode – had been running for a while, I reckoned. It flickered to life as I approached.

```
CAPTAIN LANCE WILLIAMS: TRANSITION
   CONFIRMED . . .
MISSION IN PROGRESS . . .
```

The timer was running.

"Well I'll be damned . . ."

Where has he gone? I asked myself. Surely not somewhere aboard the *Colossus*: someone would've seen him, called the incident in. The same went for the other warships in the fleet. I struggled to see any purpose in making transition, to board one of those vessels. There was nowhere else for him to go but the Artefact. Just the idea that he might have seen Elena: it somehow stirred the coals of my anger. She was mine, and whether she was real or not Williams had no Christo-damned right to see her.

"Get a fucking grip. We don't even know if he can see her."

Of course, the holo-psych suggested, *if she's real, then he will definitely be able to see her*.

I frantically searched the other tanks, ensuring that they were unoccupied. Maybe I was so drunk that I'd missed it, that the rest of his simulant team were engaged as well. But the other tanks were empty.

I thought for a moment about extracting Williams, about hitting the emergency override and bringing him – or at least his consciousness – back to the *Colossus*. I dismissed that idea: I needed to know why he was out there, and what he was doing.

Only one way to find out.

I lurched over the SOC control system. Slowly punched in the relevant command codes. Christo knows how I managed to obtain a firing solution for the drop-capsule, but I did. In double-vision I reviewed the destination of Williams' capsule. I was right; he had boarded the Artefact. There: near the frontal facing. If it was good enough for him, it was good enough for me. I selected the same coordinates.

Clambered into my own simulator and let muscle-memory do the rest: jacking in my data-ports, clasping the respirator to my mouth.

I hit the COMMENCE TRANSITION button.

I'd operated a simulant in most environments and in many conditions. When you've done this as many times as I have, it's very easy to think that there's nothing left to be learnt from the technology.

But I was definitely learning something from this transition.

I was pushing my mental and physical boundaries. As I slammed the operating controls, I realised that I had never actually done this drunk. Aboard the *Liberty Point*, the medtechs and psychs wouldn't have allowed it. I imagined their frowning faces outside the tank: peering in, disapproving. Beyond disapproving: I was quite sure that I would be seriously reprimanded. A major in the Alliance Army – with so many years under my belt – should know better than to operate heavy machinery while drunk.

The experience was disconcerting, to say the least.

One second I was raging drunk, having difficulty focusing on the world around me, nausea creeping through my gut.

The next I was absolutely awake, utterly sharp.

Simulant senses took over and I became hyper-aware. I was instantly sober; like I had jumped off a cliff, been hit by an air-car, shot with a gun. The drink and that cloying deprivation of senses that it brings with it just vanished.

My HUD came online, flashed with boot messages, and I stared out into the familiar dark. I was inside my combat-armour, in a drop-capsule, inside a firing tube aboard the *Colossus*.

CANCEL LAUNCH SEQUENCE? the AI asked me, reading the state of my biorhythms.

FUCK NO, I transmitted. CONFIRM LAUNCH.

CONFIRMED. T MINUS FIVE SECONDS UNTIL DROP.

I lay still in the capsule and let the ship do the rest.

I made the descent.

Drunk, I'd forgotten almost completely about Loeb's prohibition on further simulant trips until the Rift-storm had abated.

Sober, I recalled the fact immediately.

It was a very rough trip down. Once I'd breached the null-shield, near-space became a storm-tossed sea. Not in the physical sense: space looked just as calm and serene as it ever had. But while there was nothing to see, the instrumentation on my suit and capsule told a very different story. The region was being bombarded with squalling particle matter; engulfed by a tsunami of magnetic waves. The *Colossus* and her sister ships had advanced protective measures for such an occurrence – weather patterns like this were

266

unfortunate, but hardly unexpected in the wilderness space of the Maelstrom. Once the hatches were battened down, the storm was of limited threat to the starships.

To me, travelling through the void in the drop-capsule, sealed within my combat-suit, it was potentially lethal. My suit rebooted twice; shorted by electrical spikes. Alarms started to flood my head. I very quickly realised that I was losing control of this drop.

"Fuck!" I shouted as the drop-capsule jinked and wove, battering me inside the tight confines.

Something shorted out with a spray of sparks, so close to my head that it left scorch-marks on the outside of my face-plate. My combat-suit administered dizzying, poisonous levels of sedative and anti-sickness drugs. I began to think that maybe this wasn't such a good idea. Maybe the Buzzard had made the right choice in restricting expeditions while the Rift was active—

Williams must've done it. I can do it too.

Then the drop-capsule shed around me. I triggered my thruster pack. I was through the worst of the storm; inbound on my set coordinates. It wasn't a pleasant drop, by any stretch, but it was suddenly manageable. The urgent need to vomit subsided.

I landed near an airlock.

Safely down on the Artefact, I took in my surroundings. In miniature, the *Colossus* hovered above me – kilometres from my position. I thought of the party in the mess hall: now just a tiny dot of light on the hull of the warship. I had bigger things to worry about. I wasn't part of their world any more.

The rest of the fleet – those sixteen other anonymous starships – was positioned in a precise arc around the Artefact. The Damascus Rift was unusually bright tonight, and cast the ship hulls in a green nimbus. The display was perversely beautiful. A reminder of nature's unchecked ferocity.

"Jesus . . ." I said to myself, as I registered the rad-dose my suit was absorbing. It'd be enough to kill a real skin outright. "Imagine what this is doing to Elena . . ."

Clutching my plasma rifle, I waited as the airlock cycled open.

Even the terrifying can become routine with repetition, I thought. The sense of *déjà vu* was almost overwhelming and I struggled to stay focused.

I moved off.

CHAPTER TWENTY-ONE

KRELL

Once I was inside the Artefact, I switched off my suit-feeds and activated my bio-scanner. I decided that I would use that judiciously. If what Elena had told me was correct – if she was real – then I suspected that the Reaper could track me with passive returns on the scanner as well.

Almost immediately, I got a single result. I wondered whether that might be Elena, but quickly discarded the idea. It was moving slowly and within a previously mapped sector. Had to be Williams. *What is Williams doing out here, on his own?* Had he seen Elena? I doubted it, given his reaction during the debrief, but Elena's words haunted me: "How do I know that you haven't been compromised?"

I found Williams in an open corridor. I thought about dropping some drones – letting those creep up on him – but the data-bleed concerned me. Returns on my scanner gave me limited information on his status. His suit-feeds were, I noticed, all cancelled.

I crept along the corridor behind him, staying a junction away until I had caught up with him. He was fully suited, armed with a plasma rifle. Crouching, he clutched something in the pool of light cast by his combat-suit-lamps.

The corridor emitted a dull metallic glow – barely enough light to see by even with enhanced vision but damn better than the constant dark. I watched him intently. I couldn't see what he was doing. No IFF beacon, I realised.

"Hello, Harris," Williams suddenly declared, over the comm.

"How'd you know it was me?" I asked.

I stood to block the corridor. Tensed with my plasma rifle; for some reason half expecting to need it.

"Had to be you. No one else would think of coming in here alone. That, and you make too much noise. Maybe your hearing is letting you down. You sound like a Krell primary on a rampage."

Williams stayed on the ground, but turned on his enormous boots to face me. Behind his face-plate, he was grinning broadly; face underlit by his helmet.

"You saw me on the bio-scanner, I take it?" I said.

Williams sniggered. "You got me, man."

"What the fuck do you think you're doing in here?" I demanded. "I didn't give you clearance for an expedition."

"The Buzzard restricted all operations," Williams said, "which technically means that you shouldn't be here either."

"Repeat: what are you doing, Captain?"

Williams nodded at the floor beneath him. "See for yourself."

He was, I realised, standing among a sea of corpses.

Krell corpses.

"I found them during the last operation," Williams said. "Thought I'd come aboard and take some samples."

"Why didn't you tell anyone what you found?"

Williams looked surprised. "I didn't think to bother anyone. Seemed like more important things were happening, what with the whole Dr Marceau issue."

"And why didn't you tell me that you were coming back aboard the Artefact?"

"I tried to comm you. The watch officer was off-duty – probably at that damned party."

"So you just came aboard alone . . .?"

"I haven't been sleeping so well. Bad dreams. That, and the fat lip your private gave me wasn't exactly comfortable."

"Then see Dr West. Get some 'gesics. This is an unauthorised expedition."

We walked among the dead, crunching remains of ancient Krell specimens underfoot. For the most part they were desiccated to the point of ossification. Shrunken through exposure, heaped sometimes three bodies deep, erratically positioned all along the corridor. Their physiology and appearance was so familiar to me that I could classify them easily. Mostly primary-forms but several secondary-forms as well. The bizarre tableau went on for a few hundred metres, skirting the edge of the area Williams had explored on today's mission. At the last safe junction, a huge leader-form had slumped against the wall: raptorial arms deployed ready to strike some imagined enemy. Dead eyes long boiled, now just empty cavities staring back with indignant hate.

"Cause of death?" I asked.

"Probably that Shard asshole. These aren't evolved for ship-to-ship combat."

I agreed with him. The bodies were standard Krell primaries. A lot more resilient than a human soldier but no match for the Reaper.

"I'd be hard pressed to decide which side to bet on in a fight," Williams added. "But it's a match I'd like to see."

I frowned at the nearest corpse. There was no obvious cause of death, and considering the alien physiology, it was unlikely that we'd be able to reach a conclusion. The Krell corpses had died suddenly, in flight. Some had fallen on to their forelimbs, tails extended.

"They were running," I said. "Towards the Hub."

Williams nodded. "Maybe."

"It was a blind run," I said, considering the pattern of corpses. "The Krell don't usually think like that. They're a Collective. They don't have individual thought streams."

"Yeah, well . . ." Williams said.

It was like he had lost interest in the Krell. I found it strange that someone so experienced at fighting Krell didn't see that little detail. Sure, Williams was a bonehead, but he also had a couple of hundred transitions under his belt.

I pointed up ahead. An ornate Shard bulkhead sat at the terminus of the corridor: iris-lock fully contracted, surrounded by depowered alien runes. I made sure to get a good look.

"Must be something big behind that door then," Williams offered. "I'm sure that Saul would love it."

He slung his battle-rifle over his shoulder. It was disarmed, I noticed; the activation studs glowing red. He sighed loudly. Leant against the wall.

"Strange fish, isn't he?" he said.

I paced the corridor some more. This was a unique location aboard the Artefact and I didn't want to miss any detail that could be used against it. I was unsettled by the presentation of the Krell bodies.

"You mean Saul?" I asked.

"Yeah. Real strange fish. Has he shown you his little shrine in the chapel? Fucking Gaia Cultists – freak me out, man. All that religious nonsense about Mother Earth and the rights of inheritance."

"Don't worry about it, Captain. Just do your job."

"I'll try. He's started converting some of the crew. He's apparently holding some sort of mass up there. Mind if I smoke?"

Williams gave a guilty grin behind his face-plate. Lightning quick, he reached for his helmet and opened it with both hands. There was a brief hiss of escaping air and he dropped the helmet to the floor.

"You have to grow it strong," he said, "if you want it to have any effect on the simulant physiology."

He reached inside the collar of his suit and produced an oversized cigarette. Fingered the tip with his glove, and it ignited with an orange ember. He took a long drag.

"You think I won't bust you for breaking regs?" I said. Made sure to look as unimpressed as possible.

"You're not that kind of CO," Williams said, cocky as anything. "Sir."

"Must've taken some work to get smokes into your sim."

He nodded. "Not easy but it can be done. First, my stash in Hydroponics had to be strong enough to affect my sim. The herbs have been growing up there for a long time. Second, I got access to the firing tubes down in the drop-bay. Third, my combat-suit has had a little modification."

He tapped the status indicator on his chest. On most suits, the small panel was hardly visible: with the camo-field activated, it wasn't individually distinguishable from the rest of the chest-plate. But on Williams' armour, the indicators visibly pulsed red.

"You've disabled your medical suite?"

"Sure, man. And not just this suit: I've disabled *all* my medical suites. It's a hack I picked up."

I wasn't sure what I was more disconcerted by: the idea that he had done it alone, that he might've received help from someone on the *Colossus*, or that here was someone who knew simulants better than me. The whole thing made me uneasy.

"I want that shit shut down, Captain," I said.

Williams nodded, but also took another long drag on the enormous cigarette. "Barely works anyway. Doesn't seem like it was really worth the effort."

"It's a breach of protocol."

"Will you listen to the man? Lazarus, lecturing a lowly captain on breach of protocol."

"Everyone has their limits."

Williams held my gaze. The malicious joker façade was suddenly gone: replaced by an angry, hungry bastard of a man. "And has this place pushed you to yours? I wonder if it has. Because, you see, Major," he emphasised that last word, like I was of a different breed to him – a proper simulant trooper, "you're not going to break this place. No matter what you've done out there in deep-space, I'm better at this."

"Cut that shit out."

Williams' crooked smile was fixed, unbothered. "Sure, man. You're in charge. But I'm going to do this. The Warfighters will finish this puzzle."

"I beat the one on Helios. Damascus is no different. And you're right about one thing: I am the one in charge. You are not to come aboard the Artefact unless I personally approve the order. Understood?"

"Yes, sir."

"I'm watching you."

"We want the same thing, I think. Sir."

So far as I was concerned, the conversation was over. "Extract," I ordered.

With practised calmness, Williams flipped the buckle on

his sidearm holster and plucked his PPG-13 plasma pistol. "You serious?" he asked me.

"Deadly."

"What about the Reaper?"

"I'll risk it," I said.

"Your call."

Williams placed the pistol beneath the chin plate of his helmet. His eyes were fixed on mine and he stood rigid. Perhaps he expected me to back down. If he did, he was very wrong.

"Do it," I said.

He pulled the trigger.

The combat-suits were good but there was probably no personal body-armour in existence that could withstand a pulse from a forty-kilowatt plasma pistol at that range. There was an instant flash of white light, and the pulse fired up through the weak spot in the chin guard. The weapon gave a pitched hiss: nothing more, and the sound barely travelled down the corridor. The contents of Williams' head splattered the wall and ceiling. His body was stiff for a second, then crumpled in a heap.

"That's going to give you one hell of a headache."

Williams' cigarette butt lay discarded on the floor. It looked peculiarly out of place – a human relic aboard the monstrous alien vessel. *What would the Shard make of it?* I wondered.

I seemed to be doing a lot of things for reasons that I couldn't really explain. I lifted the cigarette butt and scanned it with my chemical-analyser. The device was a recent Sci-Div upgrade: something I rarely had the opportunity to use, but that I knew would one day come in handy. The probe – a small needle – extended from the tip of my right index finger. I pinched the cigarette.

The results of the chem-analysis were almost instant. Data scrolled down my HUD. Williams was right – it was a very strong narcotic combination – a chemically enhanced strain of marijuana laced with a methahydride. No surprises there. The stuff would have to be especially potent to have any impact on a simulant's nervous system. I stored the analysis results in my wrist-comp.

"And now to do what I came here to do," I whispered.

The signal appeared on my bio-scanner almost on cue. A lone blip, flickering in and out of existence.

"I'm here!" I shouted.

I flipped the catches on my helmet, let my atmosphere supply mingle with that of the Artefact. I needed to breathe the same air as Elena; to share the same experience.

The anticipation of seeing her was almost too much to bear. I resisted running to meet her: recalled her tense posture and angry response on my last visit. She had to come to me. So I waited at the end of the corridor, got another look at the runes circling the door. Their luminescence increased as I approached – encouraging me onwards, to an almost certain demise. The language was indecipherable: the tightly scripted symbols, an almost living ebb and flow to the writing.

I had seen it somewhere before.

At the foot of the Artefact, in the sleeting rain; bleeding out. The alien command console, rising up from the desert. Kellerman, lifting the Key into the air like a madman.

"It needs the Key . . ."

The structure around me was silent, and the Artefact itself offered no explanation.

I deactivated my null-shield as Elena appeared in the distance.

* * *

She had no weapon and looked the same as when I'd seen her earlier that day. There was no reaction from her when she saw the stacked Krell corpses, and she deftly picked her way through the bodies. Williams' body, on the other hand, evinced an instance response. Her eyes went wide.

"It's okay," I whispered. "He's dead."

"Is there anyone else with you?"

I shook my head. "Not now."

"Where are they?"

"I have a ship. A whole fleet."

"Did you tell them about me?" Elena insisted, glaring through her brows at me. "Is he one of them?"

"I don't know who you're talking about, Elena, but I'm here to rescue you."

There was still an impossible distance between us. Every fibre of my being wanted to close it. But that guarded expression on Elena's face told me that I'd have to wait.

"They would send you, I suppose," she muttered. "My weakness. Perhaps they don't know how we left things . . ."

"I can undo it all."

I could've given her the time since our parting in months, days, hours; expressed it in whatever measurements she wanted. Unconsciously, just because I couldn't stop myself any longer, I began towards her.

Elena glared at me. "Don't come any closer. Before you do anything, I need to believe it's really you."

I swallowed back emotion. My mouth felt impossibly dry.

"Azure," I said. "We lived together on Azure."

That answer didn't seem to satisfy Elena. Her expression remained fixed. "Anyone could know that," she responded. "I need real proof!"

Elena took a step back – half-subsumed by shadow now – and I knew that if I didn't think fast, she would be gone.

I threw my rifle to the floor. Held my hands open. My simulant body was still a weapon, and Elena knew Sim Ops well – knew what I was capable of even unarmed, but it was a gesture.

"I told you about my father. About how he died. About killing himself."

Elena froze. Pursed her lips.

I went on: "We were on a train together, going to my promotion ceremony. I insisted that you wear that black dress."

Her icy veneer seemed to crack, just a little, and her shoulders sagged. A tenderness began to dawn in her beautiful eyes.

"I . . . I made us take the train. There was a bomb."

Elena's face dropped. "You didn't make us. It was me."

"You were pregnant. We lost a baby. I came to the hospital."

"Stop it!" Elena hissed. She looked away from me, to the floor.

"I wasn't there for you, and you felt that you had to take this job to get away from me—"

"Stop it!" she said, louder now.

"You sent me a message. Told me not to forget you."

"Stop it!" she screamed.

She shook with rage or sadness or maybe both. Big, wet tears flooded her face; left dusty tracks down her cheeks. She held her ground as I went to her. I closed the distance in a couple of strides and flung my arms around her.

For a terrible, fraught second I imagined my hands passing through nothing – through the phantom-creation of my own anima.

But Elena was solid, physical matter.

She pounded against my chest – against the armour

plating – with her small fists, again and again. I held her until she stopped. Her body went limp and eventually she pulled me close. I lifted her off the ground, and Elena wrapped her legs around me. Her weight was nothing. We kissed – a long, animal connection: the release of eight long, lonely years apart.

"It's you," she said. Kept repeating: "It's you. It's really you."

Sobs of emotion swept over her. I buried her head into my chest, felt her hair against my face. Drew in her scent.

I had Elena: nothing else mattered.

"I need to get you out of here," I said.

I took Elena's hands. She wore no gloves, but her palms were soft and, unlike the rest of her, unblemished. She had stopped crying and her face had taken on a relaxed – almost acquiescent – quality.

"I wish that you could."

That was my primary mission; now my only objective. I worked through the logistics of the operation. "You'll need a new vacuum-suit," I said. "Those rips are too severe to use a sealant. Do you have a replacement?"

She had to have equipment; supplies aboard the Artefact. But Elena shook her head. "No. I have nothing left. I came here alone. Do the Artefact's defences still work?"

I remembered the Artefact's space-based defences: the kiss of the energy weapon as I'd approached in the Wildcat. Losing a simulant hadn't mattered but the idea of losing Elena again, after so many years and for real, filled me with dread.

"Yes, but perhaps we can jury-rig a drop-capsule." Maybe I could get Lieutenant James to assist – to send out a Wildcat? Reverse engineer a capsule? "A transport could move beyond the Artefact's perimeter, and pick you up."

"There's more to this than just me," Elena said. "The *Endeavour* sent me back. The expedition has suffered such losses. The crew is dying. They need help as well."

"Where is the ship?"

Something had changed. Elena's back arched, and she pulled away: searching the corridor. The air started to hum.

"It's found us . . ." Elena whispered.

A shriek sounded deep within the Artefact.

"Get somewhere safe," I ordered. I picked up my rifle. "I'll turn on my suit-feeds – draw it to me."

Elena nodded, stepping back from me now like I was a live bomb.

"Please come for me, Conrad. I want to go with you."

Her eyes pleaded with me: I couldn't imagine how she had done this for so long.

"What do I need to do?" I asked.

"Follow me."

"And how do I do that?"

"Turn the Artefact on."

Then Elena was gone. Her bio-sign was already dancing away, within seconds moving out of my scanner range and vanishing completely.

I thought-activated my feeds.

Simultaneously, the shadows around me began to buzz with activity. Like a hive of wasps, an ant hill stirred from long hibernation. I saw flashes of activity in my peripheral vision.

Then the dark took shape: sharp, angular. Two burning red eyes formed in the mechanical's skull cavity – or an approximation of that – and a mouth shaped to speak.

"Fuck you!" I roared.

I pumped the underslung grenade launcher.

Fired once, then again for good measure: using hi-ex grenades.

The Reaper's face translated an approximation of shock—

Then the grenades went off. Primed for a micro-second delay, the explosions were inside the mechanical. The noise was deafening and even the dampeners couldn't stop everything from getting through.

Something told me that I had seconds to live – most likely less – and so I took the advantage. I ran for the door, reactivating my null-shield as I went.

I sensed the Shard moving behind me.

"Come on!" I yelled. I had to make sure that Elena had got away.

My hands touched the runic impressions around the door.

To my surprise, the lock suddenly gave way. The metal leaves of the iris-pattern door opened, *schlicked* back into the wall.

Beyond the door, the corridor opened into a vast chamber. The ceiling far above was so covered in shadow, it was impossible to make out the real dimensions of the place. A thin, precarious-looking bridge crossed a chasm, leading to an elevated platform in the middle of the room. That structure was glittering with light – almost looked as though it was composed of light. It didn't look like it would take my weight, but I was willing to risk it. I ran, my boots against the alien construction.

Whatever is up there: that's the target.

Black crystalline edifices, bigger than a simulant, erupted from the floor. Those were knife-sharp, etched with the same sort of markings that I had seen on the Key.

This had to be the control chamber: the Hub.

I just kept moving. Kept running.

Looked down from the bridge: the ground was so far below that I couldn't make it out. The bridge itself was littered with Krell corpses—

Something slashed at my suit.

Again and again, a barbed whip.

The null-shield lit, but failed—

I registered multiple breaches across my back, both legs, shoulders. The pain was intense and immediate. I collapsed forwards, only just managed to stay on the bridge. Face-forward, I hit the ground hard.

EXTRACTION IMMINENT, my suit warned.

I managed to roll onto my back. Better to see what was about to kill me, I decided.

The dark spewed into the chamber.

Another tendril slammed into me: hit me somewhere in the chest. Something metallic and sharp pierced my suit. I felt wet, warm blood welling inside my armour, pumping from my debilitating wounds.

Right lung punctured. That'll do it.

The transition from drunk to sober had been unpleasant and jarring.

The extraction from sober to drunk was a hundred times worse.

I managed to stop myself from vomiting into my tank – knew that I wouldn't have the strength to clear up after myself – and lay in the simulator for a long while. Inebriated, I was finding it difficult to process what had just happened. The emotional upswell must've been tempered by my medi-suite, back on the Artefact, because now I was in my own skin – driven by natural human chemical reactions – my recollections were jumbled and hard to order.

I considered my next move. The SOC looked as I'd last left it: dark, deserted. I noted Williams' empty tank. I probably had a few hours before the morning shift started, and Sci-Div began to ready the simulators for the day's work.

It didn't take me long to reach a decision.

Fuck it. I have to go back.

I reached for the tank's internal control console. I punched the COMMENCE TRANSITION key, and closed my eyes – waiting for the absolute clarity of simulant senses—

Nothing happened.

I frowned, hit the key again.

Still nothing.

I tried again and again: but no response from the simulator.

I rested my head against the inside of the tank. The world outside was spinning, and my natural vision was doubling, but I could just about read the viewer-screen above my simulator. Words were flashing there.

"What the fuck . . .?"

COMMAND OVERRIDE.

I pressed the TRANSITION key again, but the error message – or whatever it was – flashed on the overhead monitor.

Something had to be wrong with the neural-link. Maybe Loeb had placed a system block on the simulator operations; or perhaps something had been damaged during the last transition. I was too damned drunk to work around the problem.

As the simulator-tank door opened, I realised that I'd forgotten to purge the amniotic – such a basic mistake – and the used fluid sloshed across the SOC floor. I stumbled out of my tank, unsteady on my feet, and slipped on it. Too late to make any secret of what I had done. Fighting back nausea, I got to my feet and dressed. I didn't bothered towelling myself dry – the fabric stuck to me uncomfortably.

I managed to get in front of the SOC control system and attempted to resolve the system message. Very quickly, it became apparent that this was beyond me. Punching keys in the correct order was too much, let alone accessing the system menus. I needed someone with technical knowledge, or at least someone sober. *Maybe Kaminski*, I thought. But he wasn't here, and if it was a hardware issue then I'd need proper Sci-Div support. That would mean explaining how and why I'd come to make transition badly hammered.

It'll have to wait, I decided.

Although it took me twice as long as normal, I got back to my quarters and successfully evaded any Naval crew.

I collapsed onto my bunk. Head spinning, eye sockets throbbing. Maybe it was the proximity to the Rift, or the cumulative effect of having died so many times in the last few days, but the drink had affected me far more than usual. Although I knew that I needed to confront Williams, I was too drunk to do anything about him now. I wanted the Legion behind me on this.

"Should've checked the percentage on that damned vodka . . ." I muttered to the dark.

"You shouldn't have started drinking," the dark answered back.

"I wish I'd never stopped."

It took me a moment to realise that I was talking to someone else in the room. I struggled to my elbows, sat up in bed. Scanned the cabin for an intruder—

"Computer?" I slurred. "Who else is in here?"

"Good morning, Major Harris," said the AI. "You are currently the only occupant of cabin sixteen, deck A-11. Do you require medical assistance?"

"No. Wake me immediately if anyone enters this cabin."

"As you wish, Major."

There was silence for a second, then the dark began whispering again.

"Are you going to lose everyone you love? Because in real life they don't come back, Connie."

I rubbed the data-ports in my forearms until I finally slept.

CHAPTER TWENTY-TWO

GOODBYE

Twenty-seven years ago

After my parents passed, Carrie and I drifted.

Both separately and together: the bond shared between siblings never broken, but strained by our increasing differences.

As I became a teenager, and Carrie was within reach of adulthood, our interests diverged. Carrie's was singular but regularly changed: the drug of choice on the street. That was something that I knew would set her down a dangerous and self-destructive path. The drug might've been different, but I'd seen it all in my father.

Carrie meant what she'd said to Nelson, about becoming a pacifist. Maybe she rebelled because of our family's military history, and the miserable home conditions only made things worse. I never really knew, because I never spoke to her any more. As we grew older we became more and more distant.

We moved around a lot in those days but the last place

that we stayed with was Aunt Ritha and Leeroy. After that move, Carrie rapidly deteriorated. She spent as much time as possible away from the cramped apartment. The typical teenage girl behaviour began – dyed her hair, lost weight – but much more as well. Was it Aunt Ritha that got her started on the scolometh? Should I hate her because of it? Probably.

It was the last week in June, the day after her eighteenth birthday, when Ritha threw her out. Carrie came home blazed on meths, angry and abusive and terrified. Ritha couldn't understand that, because the scolometh only ever made her tired and stupid. I slept through most of the exchange: it had become next to normal. Only, this time, the row had stirred Ritha from her couch – torn her from her self-inflicted torpor, away from her tri-D programmes.

I felt the prickle at the back of my neck that told me this argument was different. Half-heard words penetrated the walls. Even if I couldn't make out the specifics, I understood the emotions being conveyed. I swiped my civilian wrist-comp, saw the time flash on the display. It was still early morning.

Carrie burst into our room, face stained with kohl and tears: eyes wider than a Centauri moon. She stood over my bunk.

"I'm going," she declared. "I'm finished."

How many times had I heard that said before? It was a weekly mantra. She'd go shack up with one of the older boys in her tribe, spend a few nights there. Then, when the drugs and the money ran out, she'd be back – contrite, apologetic.

"All right," I said, rolling over, pulling the thin blanket over me.

Carrie wasn't the only one who had learnt feigned

indifference. I was a teenager too now and I'd started to deploy the same techniques. If anything, I'd got better at it than her.

"I'm not coming back, Con," she said.

She grabbed clothes from the floor, thrust them into a canvas bag. The tri-D photo cubes from under the bed; the only physical reminders that we had of our parents. Those were supposed to be shared but I was too proud to tell her to put them back. She was packing every possession important to her.

"You've said that so many times before. You'll be back."

"She damned well won't!" Ritha warbled, from the hall. "I'm having one of my fits, missy! My programmes is on! Your mother'd be—"

"She's dead, Ritha!" Carrie yelled. She continued scooping up items. "They're both dead, and do you know why they're dead? Because of the war."

I sighed. This was her favourite topic: the war.

"Okay," I said. "Whatever. I'm really not interested."

"You want to say goodbye to me?" Carrie leant over my bed again. "Because I'm going for good."

"That's exactly what you said last time."

"This isn't like that at all. I really mean it."

I recognised then that there was something different about her voice. *Maybe*, I suddenly panicked, *this is actually going to happen*. I sat up in bed, watched her cleaning out her possessions in the darkness.

"Meet me down at the terminal," she said, talking breathlessly, working fast. "Tomorrow. Ten."

"Maybe," I said.

Over the years, the Detroit Metro Off-World Terminal – the downtown spaceport – had grown in size and use. Once it had served as a launch pad for sub-orbitals – for those with money to burn, a quick way to get across the globe. Now it processed thousands of passengers a day, all looking to escape the confines of Old Earth: one of the UA's largest spaceports. While it was nowhere near as big as the Seattle Main Port, the Off-World Terminal was a source of something approaching pride for the locals.

I arrived much earlier than Carrie had suggested – or rather insisted – that we meet. I still wanted to believe – still believed – that this was another of Carrie's stunts; that she wasn't going to go through with it. But just in case, I'd turned up early – to make sure that I didn't miss her.

I waited outside the main passenger terminal. The port was busy and noisy. Greyhound buses lined up on the parking lot; windows concealed with heavy metal shutters, flanks pocked with burn marks and bullet holes. The nearest bus had the gun hatch open – a lazy contractor selling smokes from the roof. Two police spinners sat at the port's main entrance, harness-bulls observing the throng and throb of the crowd as it surged into the terminal.

There was a demonstration going on outside. Protestors with homemade, poor-quality holo-placards: chanting anti-war sentiments at anyone who would listen. Some carried loudhailers wired to speakers on their shoulders. Pacifists, one and all.

Carrie stood away from the crowd. Just as the cops eyed protestors, Carrie's eyes were always on the cops. She didn't look exceptional, didn't look different from the rest of the crowd: waif-like, hands plunged into the pockets of a plastic raincoat. Her face had an angular, hungry turn to it; eyes become deeper set over the last few years. Blonde hair braided and dirty. She didn't see me; didn't even appear to be looking for me. For a couple of minutes I watched her from the parking lot, took in this girl who was once my sister.

Although the clock over the main entrance still flashed ten minutes to ten, I started to fret that she might walk away – that she might decide that I wasn't coming. I wandered down to meet her.

"You came," she said. Face breaking in a restrained smile.

"I did," I said, coolly. "But I still don't think that you're really going."

Carrie grimaced. "Then you're wrong, little brother."

"I'll bet that you don't even have papers."

Carrie kept one hand on her bag at all times. Eyes still on the cops, she scooped inside and produced some crumpled plastic sheets. Immigration papers; an off-world visa.

"This time, I do," she said.

"How'd you get them? Are they real?"

"I've been doing some extra work," Carrie said. I didn't ask what that was, and she didn't offer to explain: better that I didn't know. "And of course they aren't real."

"Then how do you know that you'll get off-world?"

"Because I paid well for them, and I'm meeting people. I'm not travelling alone."

Panic overcame me. I thought about calling out to the cops, ratting on Carrie. The sudden and terrible feeling that I would be left alone with Ritha and Leeroy filled me—

"You can't go," I said. I didn't have the words to express it. "Please stay."

"I can't."

"Why?"

"I've got to be something more than this," Carrie said. "There are people dying on Ventris II. They need help."

More of Carrie's pacifist bullshit. The lapels of her plastic raincoat were lined with badges: beatnik symbols, peace slogans.

"I don't believe you. Ventris II is a Core World." I didn't know the specifics at that age, but I knew enough: Ventris II was light-years from Sol. "It'll take months of objective time to get there."

The trip would also likely cost thousands of UA dollars. It all sounded remarkably unlikely.

At least it did until I looked into Carrie's eyes. Cold determination, vicious certainty: those were the things dwelling in eighteen-year-old Carrie Harris' eyes.

"I'll come back," Carrie whispered. She reached out to touch my face; a gentle, caring brush of my cheek. "Eventually. Give it a few years; let me find who I am. You said it yourself: I always come back."

I swallowed. Implications were dawning on me. "Even if you do make it back, what about the debt? We'll be out of synch by years."

"I'll find a way. I have to do something, Con. Something more than die down here."

"How are you going to do that?" I asked. "By murdering the Directorate with love?"

"No. By being another pair of hands."

"That's rubbish, Carrie. And it isn't really why you're leaving, either."

I nodded at her forearms. Her coat was transparent, exposing her frail and pale arms through the plastic. Clear needle tracks lined the inner aspects: bruises that varied in colour between vibrant blues and violent reds. Those told their own story, and it had nothing to do with leaving Earth because of any peace movement.

"I'm off that now," Carrie said. "For good."

"Yeah? When'd that happen? Those look fresh to me."

Carrie shook her head. I wondered whether she would turn and leave – plough on through the mire of bodies and into the passenger terminal. She looked down at her overlarge black boots – military-grade: a poor attempt at irony.

"You ever think of that body we found in the drain?" she asked me.

"No."

"Well maybe you should."

"It was a body. Some kook. You remember what the cop told us."

"It wasn't a prank. That was a real soldier. No one thought anything of it. A Directorate trooper – a Chino soldier! In a uniform, of all things. You called the cops, but they didn't even care. No one cared. Because none of it matters any more."

"I don't understand what you're trying to say."

"You never do. That's your problem, Conrad. You don't think past the words. You take everything literally."

"Explain it to me then."

She let out a long sigh, from deep enough within that her slender body shook. "They knew what we'd found. They knew it wasn't some lunatic in fancy dress. It was a real Directorate soldier, and no one gave a damn. You called the police – did the whole 911 thing! What did they do? They covered it up."

I thought about that for a long moment.

"Because they already knew," Carrie said. "Because they were already here. Because they've been here all along."

Carrie shrugged at me, tilted her head to observe me. I tried to look like I understood her words, but the understanding was only skin deep. Perhaps it was my age; or perhaps I just didn't want to understand.

"Maybe wearing a uniform," she said, "carrying a gun, having a badge: all of those things are irrelevant now."

Carrie clucked her tongue, disappointed with me. She rifled in her bag some more. Eyes darting to the cops again, she pushed something towards me – kept it covered with both of her gloved hands.

"No way, Carrie," I said. Tried to back away into the crowd, kept my voice low. She knew that I never touched the stuff. "I don't want anything from your stash—"

"It isn't my stash, Con. It isn't leftovers."

It was an old wooden box. Looked in good condition; letters printed in gold leaf on the lid. Not much wider than Carrie's handspan but a lot longer.

"Take it," she insisted. "It was Jonathan's." She baulked, and I thought that she might even cry. "It was father's."

I took the box. When I wrapped my hands around it, I found that it was heavy.

"Maybe you can sell it, make some money from it. That's all those things are good for."

"Don't go. Please."

Carrie smiled. "I have to."

"You'll waste your life."

"So will you."

Someone called her name. Another young girl, a carbon copy of my sister: down to the kohl-stained eyelids and the plastic raincoat. A group of older youths were gathered at the foot of the terminal; mixed sex, but the same mould as Carrie. She gravitated towards them.

"Who was that?" a Carrie-copy asked, putting an arm around my sister's shoulder.

"No one," Carrie said.

"You sure? You look upset."

"It was nobody," she said, firmly this time.

I watched her go.

Soon her group was engulfed by the crowd and Carrie was gone.

I sat on a bench in the parking lot for several hours.

The Greyhounds came and went.

The police spinners changed shift.

Shuttles lifted off from the spaceport compound.

They were noisy and too far away for me to see much. I didn't know the terminology then, but those were heavy-lift VTOLs. Civilian pattern: nothing military-grade. Each would leave the atmosphere, join up with a waiting starship in low orbit, or dock with Orion Station. A few might go straight to New Chicago, the UA Luna colony.

Once they lifted off, the shuttles quickly accelerated. Within seconds they became nothing more than twinkles of light. Artificial stars on the horizon: burning far more brightly than the real thing, given the light pollution from Michigan State.

Part of me hoped that immigration control had clocked Carrie's documents. That her papers had been badly forged; that she had been detained as a meth-addict.

I waited, divided my time between watching the sky and the terminal entrance. But I knew, deep down, that one of those stars – leaving Earth for good, no matter what she said – was Carrie's.

I pulled up the hood on my jacket. Hid my face deep inside. Like it was some armour from the rest of the world – a barrier between me and them.

The wooden box sat on my lap. I had almost forgotten it, but as night fell – and I began to think that maybe I should get back before the district curfew began – I inspected it. The box was old, machined well before my time, or even my father's. I slowly flipped the metal clasp on the lid.

My father's old revolver sat inside.

CHAPTER TWENTY-THREE

SECTION EIGHT

By the following morning, the Rift-storm had subsided. By the start of morning shift, Admiral Loeb had lifted the restriction on expeditions to the Artefact.

Although my head raged and I ached, I wasn't going to let that stop me. *Today*, I decided, *is the day that I rescue Elena*. Elena was the priority; especially after what she had told me last night. I had to deal with Williams' insubordination but that would keep. He was probably nothing more than an upstart: eager to take the prize of reaching the Hub, to walk away from this operation with his share of the glory.

I called for an early-morning meeting in the SOC.

The Legionnaires were ashen-faced, exhausted; the Warfighters were no better. They carried a body odour of stale alcohol: the sort of residue that couldn't be washed out by shipboard shower units. Mason stared back at me across the tactical display, her face looking even greener than usual. Jenkins looked leaner than before. Kaminski stood beside her, a fraction too close to be less than lovers.

Martinez fiddled with a cross around his neck, was mumbling something under his breath.

Professor Saul and Dr West milled around the edge of the room, readying the simulator-tanks for the day's operation.

"Before we start," I said, "let's clear something up. We're in this together, people. Last night was unacceptable."

The Warfighters stood at one side of the SOC, the Legionnaires on the other. Neither looked particularly like making peace.

"There's a chain of command for a reason," I said, staring down both men. "Let's try to avoid that sort of behaviour. Kaminski – you have something to say?"

"Yeah," 'Ski said. "Apologies."

Williams sucked his teeth; Kaminski gave a slight nod. The pair were never going to be friends and a temporary truce would have to do—

Williams' lip, I noticed.

Last night it was completely uninjured; I remembered seeing that while he was inside the tank. Today, it was badly bruised; a single steri-strip over the split. It wasn't a serious injury by any stretch but it was much worse than last night. It didn't make sense.

How much of this is real?

Jenkins took the briefing that morning. We were going to drop to the same coordinates as the previous day; to approach the Artefact through previously explored corridors and chambers.

"I want all suit-feeds disabled," I interjected.

There was silence in the SOC for a long moment.

"You know that it works, Williams," I said.

I stared at Williams across the SOC, sought some recognition of what had happened aboard the Artefact. I'd expected him to want to speak with me privately; maybe explain himself. But he hadn't even tried: he was just the same ineffectual Warfighter, slightly more sullen as a result of his loss of face.

He frowned. "Why? Because your dead wife told you so?"

The big Martian sniggered. I shot him a cold glare and he suddenly stopped.

"She wasn't my wife," I said. "And it's because I survived for longer as a result of doing it."

"Are you sure that you're feeling up to this?" Martinez asked of me. "I mean, a lot has happened recently. Maybe, *jefe*, you should sit this one out . . ."

"Don't '*jefe*' me, Martinez," I growled. "I'm in charge out here. No one forget that."

Martinez nodded.

"All right," Jenkins cut in, taking the floor. "The major's plan might work. Perhaps I should drop to your coordinates. Try to use the same airlock as you."

I considered the idea. Elena might not show up if Jenkins was with me. But if Jenkins saw Elena – if she even picked her up on the bio-scanner – that would be some proper supporting evidence. Then the rest of the Legion would have to believe me, and I could mount a proper rescue operation. It had to be worth a shot.

"Let's try that."

Jenkins looked relieved by the decision, nodding profusely. "Everyone else has their orders. We move in one hour."

The Warfighters and the Legionnaires filed out of the SOC, ready to conduct final mission prep before the drop. I lingered back for a while, watching Saul and Dr West work.

"Anything that I can help with, Major?" Dr West asked me.

"No. I just wanted to apologise for leaving the SOC in such a state."

Dr West looked bemused. "What state? I don't understand."

I grimaced. "Look, I don't want this to be an issue with the Buzzard. I know I broke his restriction on off-ship expeditions. I made transition last night. Dropped to the Artefact."

Dr West's expression remained unchanged. She wasn't the type to mess with me; wasn't a joker like Williams or Kaminski. Saul stopped working, looked over in our direction.

"That's not possible," Dr West said.

I filled the hour before we were scheduled to make transition with a hundred checks. Had Dr West and Saul working feverishly, to do something – anything – to confirm what I had done in the SOC the previous night.

"The SOC was in perfect condition this morning," Dr West explained. "There was no mess at all."

"I opened my simulator-tank door early. Before the tank had finished purging. There was amniotic all over the floor!"

Dr West shook her head. "No. I was on the first shift this morning. I've been here since oh-four-hundred hours. That just didn't happen."

I paced the SOC, raging. Had I really imagined it all?

"Check the surveillance footage for the whole Medical deck."

Saul did as ordered. Called up grainy tri-D vid-feeds for the entire deck, even the SOC itself. Nothing. No one had come into, or left, the SOC during the entire period.

"I'm sorry, Major," Saul said, detecting my frustration and responding to it. "But there's no way into this centre without being caught by the cameras."

"Then check the transition logs. They'll show that

299

Williams and I have made four transitions, and everyone else has made three."

Saul rapidly keyed the relevant command. Data scrolled down the viewer-screen above us, showing the performance statistics for the Legionnaires and Warfighters.

Everyone showed as having made three transitions.

Even Williams' record demonstrated the same stats.

I stared at the screens. "Someone has corrupted the data. Just like Elena told me: we've been compromised."

Saul swallowed, looked sideways at Dr West. Neither of them believed me – about Elena or the unrecorded drop to the Artefact. The transition data was held on the *Colossus'* mainframe computer. It was highly encrypted and very difficult to tamper with.

Maybe it was all in your head, that taunting voice suggested. *And perhaps you've finally gone Section Eight; just like your grandfather.*

"The drop-bay launch data doesn't show a drop either," Saul said. He was talking fast, reading directly from the insides of his glasses. He repeated: "I'm sorry, Major."

I stood in front of my tank. Checked the holo-patch on the chest pocket of my fatigue; the device that recorded the number of transitions I'd made. The only statistic that mattered between operators. *It should show 228, if last night really happened . . .*

The number "227" flashed on the display.

By now, the drop held no surprises.

My capsule began to break up and I felt the by-now-familiar shift as my combat-suit thrusters fired, slowing my descent to the Artefact's hull.

Jenkins cut in on the private channel. "I'm coming in on your six."

I landed on the Artefact, mag-locks activating. An airlock sat ahead of me. Instead of going inside immediately I watched as Jenkins' capsule broke up. She made a smooth landing beside me. I couldn't remember having passed command over to her, but it seemed that she'd taken over for today's expedition. Her mouth moved soundlessly behind her face-plate – issuing orders, talking over the squad channel, conversations that I wasn't privy to.

She fell in step behind me, peered into the airlock and nodded in my direction.

"You want to take point?" she asked.

I crouched and scanned the inside of the lock with my suit-lamps. It looked the same as every other time we'd made the drop: dark, empty.

"Do you believe me, Jenkins?"

I heard her sigh over the comm. "Sure. Course I do."

"You don't sound very convincing."

"Let's just get inside, run some scanner sweeps. If your tactic of switching off the suit-feeds works, that should buy us some more time."

"It's not my tactic. It's Elena's."

"All right. If . . ." – Jenkins paused; as though saying her name would in some way endorse the truth of what I'd seen – ". . . Elena's tactic works."

"I don't need you to protect me."

"Whoever said I was protecting you?"

"I know what I saw."

I pushed off, activated my thruster pack to move into the outer lock. Jenkins glided alongside me.

The Shard Artefact opened for us.

"All suit-feeds terminated," Jenkins ordered.

I methodically cancelled my video- and audio-feeds, and

disconnected my communicator. The transponders that indicated the position of each of the simulants disappeared from my HUD. No one knew where anyone else was any more; and we were completely cut off from the outside world.

"Copy that," Williams said. "Command suits you, Jenkins."

"I'm not in charge, sir," Jenkins replied.

Inside, the sense of isolation was greater than ever before. I was glad of Jenkins' presence; glad that I wasn't completely alone in here. *How had Elena managed it?* I asked myself.

I popped my helmet. The only suit-system left activated was my bio-scanner, displayed directly onto my wrist-comp. I kept that under review – vigilant for the bio-sign. I noticed that Jenkins copied me; as though she was replicating an experiment, trying to achieve the same results as me.

"She might not appear if you're with me," I said.

"How will she know?"

"She just will."

Jenkins clipped her helmet to her belt. "How did she know to approach you, Harris? I'm not saying that I doubt you. Just that – well, it seems a little far-fetched, is all."

"What, like you and Kaminski?"

Jenkins fell into a sullen silence. I didn't feel like coaxing her into further conversation.

I tried to take the same route through the Artefact as I had the previous night. The structure around me had started that reverberant humming; that noise that went beyond a noise. It was a pervasive reminder that we were in Shard territory.

"Where are we going?" Jenkins asked.

I answered as I moved. "Just follow me and be my witness."

I desperately wanted to tell Jenkins about what I'd done, and about finding Williams aboard the Artefact. But I couldn't do that, because she would never believe me. So I was searching for proof. There had been Krell bodies in the tunnel: something that no one else had so far reported. Even better, we would find Williams' self-executed simulant in here.

"Elena wants me to activate the Artefact," I said.

"That so?" Jenkins replied.

"And I know how. It wants the Key."

"I don't think that's a very good idea—"

"She wants me to bring the Key into the Hub of the Artefact. Bring it to what is left of the Shard."

Jenkins stopped behind me. She gave a loud sigh. "Give it up. This is ridiculous. You want her back so desperately that you're willing to risk everything. I get that. It's a natural human reaction. But this quest to bring her back? It's getting old."

A plasma rifle sounded in the distance. I thought that I smelled the scent of smoke in the air. I turned back to look at Jenkins, caught her in the arc of my shoulder-lamps. I was several metres away from her now, and she was barely visible in the dark. It would be so easy for the Reaper to appear, to take her before I'd even noticed.

"I have to save her," I said. "With or without your help."

"Then maybe it'll be without. Maybe it'll be without the Legion. This operation is getting to everyone. Have you seen Mason's bio-statistics? Martinez hasn't slept since we got here—"

Ping! Ping! Ping!

I froze, filtered out whatever else Jenkins had to say. My

bio-scanner lit with a single return: at the periphery of my equipment's operating radius.

"I'm getting a signal!" I yelled.

By my reckoning, I was only a junction or so away from where Williams had discovered the Krell massacre – exactly where I'd last seen Elena. Her bio-sign danced, moving off my scanner completely. I started to give chase. Heard Jenkins moving off as well – still a way behind me. *Just round the next corner; the Krell bodies will prove everything—*

"I . . . I don't see anything!" Jenkins shouted.

"Your scanner is still out of range," I barked back at her.

"Stop, Harris! There's nothing—"

Her voice was cut off by an emergency tone over the comm. I kept running but I jammed my ear-bead back into place, angered by the interruption.

Got to keep moving!

A warning appeared on my wrist-comp: PRIORITY SIGNAL FROM COLOSSUS COMMAND.

It couldn't be more serious than finding Elena.

"Keep up, Jenkins!" I shouted.

Jenkins' footsteps suddenly fell silent. There was a muffled crunch – armour plating colliding with a wall or floor. I slowed, looking back the way that I had come.

"Get up!" I shouted.

Jenkins' body lay collapsed on the floor, eyes utterly vacant. She still clutched her rifle but her fingers were slack on the weapon grip.

EMERGENCY EXTRACT, my combat-suit said. ALL OPERATORS.

"Elena!" I bellowed.

My ears were filled with the whine of static feedback—

A familiar numbness spread through my limbs. My vision

abruptly faded, everything around me blackening. My heart began a thunderous, shifting beat: not the rhythm of this body.

I fell to the floor with my eyes pinned open. The last thing I saw was a wide and empty corridor, Shard glyphs glowing on the black walls.

CHAPTER TWENTY-FOUR

THE DARK PROTOCOL

The neural-link severed smoothly and my consciousness followed the golden thread across the void between the Artefact and the *Colossus*. Then I was back inside my simulator, among the data-cables and the feeder tubes. This time, I hadn't succumbed to some debilitating injury or condition: someone had called the extraction.

I opened my real eyes to find the SOC in disarray. Medtechs frantically dashed between simulators. Dragging operators free of the tanks, making sure that they were clothed and – I realised, with some alarm – armed. I pressed my hands against the inside of my tank canopy, sucked in warm air from the respirator.

A technician appeared outside my tank. He slammed open the door and helped me out. I scrambled into a waiting set of fatigues, the man hurrying me along.

"What the fuck is going on?" I asked.

"Admiral Loeb has declared an emergency. All hands are to remain on-ship. Take this."

The tech was clearly panicked. He held out a security-sealed shock-pistol in both hands – eager to get rid of the item, like it was incriminating evidence. I took it. Turned the gun over in my hands.

Lots was going on around me. A klaxon whined overhead, echoing through the halls. Outside Medical, I heard the tramp of boots on the metal-plated floor: orders being shouted. Could only be Marines and flyboys.

"Preparing to go dark in T-minus sixty seconds," the AI declared. "All systems will be entering—"

"We need a medical assist over here!" Jenkins called. She was half-covered by an aluminium blanket, crouched in front of me.

I hadn't noticed until then that Mason lay on the floor. She'd collapsed from her tank: naked, barely moving. She was foaming at the mouth. Blood trickled from her ears.

"Assist!" Jenkins yelled above the din. "I don't think she's breathing!"

A medtech answered her call, fumbling with a hypodermic. Mason's eyes were closed, her skin fish-belly white. The flesh around her data-ports was puckered.

What is my obsession going to cost Mason? I asked myself.

"Going dark in T-minus fifty seconds . . ."

"Admit her to the infirmary," Dr West declared. "Twenty ccs of methaline-alpha. Get the rest of them out of here!"

Mason was shot-up with a cocktail of drugs by one of the techs. Jenkins stood, glared at me: an ice pick through the commotion.

"Stay with her," I commanded Jenkins. "No matter what they say."

Martinez and Kaminski gathered around me, exchanging worried glances. They didn't look much better. The weight of so many transitions, in such a short period of time, weighed heavily on them.

"All personnel to take emergency measures!" Dr West shouted. "Vac-suits and breathers!"

"Is it Krell?" Kaminski asked. "Are you people expecting us to protect you with these things? We should be skinned up."

I couldn't help but agree with him. The weapons weren't fit for purpose. A Kiwati-Teslek shock-pistol wasn't an anti-Krell weapon: it was a law-enforcement sidearm.

"Let's get on with this," Williams shouted. He was already dressed in a vac-suit and had paused at the doorway to Medical, checking on the rest of his team. "We better get down to the CIC and check out what the problem is—"

The SOC lights suddenly dipped. A ripple of concern flowed through the twenty or so gathered personnel.

"Going dark," the AI declared.

Dressed in another of the bright yellow emergency vac-suits, and armed with a shock-pistol, I jogged ahead of Kaminski and Martinez. Williams' Warfighters were in close pursuit.

All active systems aboard the *Colossus* seemed to have gone into shutdown, save for gravity and life support. The elevator grid was off-line – we used the maintenance tubes to move between levels. I slid down the greased ladder rails, my booted feet hitting the ground.

A troop of Alliance aerospace pilots ran past us at full pelt. Helmets under their arms, respirators dangling at their necks, clad in metallic flight-suits: they were one step from war. *Maybe James will get his wish, and he'll get a piece of the action*, I thought. The squadron was gone before I could question them about the dark order.

"Scrambling fighter ships," Martinez declared, as we ran, "must mean we've got company. Got to be xenos, *jefe*."

That cold void had started to form in the pit of my gut:

that feeling that the calm was over, that the *Colossus* wasn't so safe after all.

I was sweating heavily by the time we reached the CIC. The route had been tortuous and awkward in the heavy vac-suits. We pushed through the Navy staff to the tactical display. Whatever was happening to the rest of the ship, power still flowed here. Ordinarily the multi-levelled chamber was expansive. Now, with every station occupied and so full of crew, it was like the chamber had shrunk. Intelligence officers wore sensory deprivation helms, charting near-space on holo-consoles. Sailors were physically jacked into consoles around the perimeter of the chamber. Above me, pointed towards the nose of the warship, weapons crews were mounted in specialised pods: hovering on suspensor arms.

Admiral Loeb presided over the circus. Flanked by junior officers on both sides, Loeb seemed to be utterly at ease with the situation – a veritable island of calm. He and his officers were the only personnel not wearing vac-suits. He glowered at the tac. The display didn't show the familiar close-up of the Artefact any longer – instead, a holo-projection of near-space. As I went towards Loeb, two Alliance Marines barred my path.

Loeb's eyes flickered from the display for just a fraction of a second. He waved a hand noncommittally in my direction. "Let them through."

The Marines lowered their guns.

"What's the sitrep?" I asked.

"If you're going to be here," Loeb said, "then the least that you can do is to behave with proper Naval decorum. Just stay out of the way."

"They're moving within an AU, sir," an officer reported. "Accelerating rapidly."

Oh, shit: they're here . . .

I realised exactly what the CIC was focused on.

An enormous Krell warship brushed the edge of the fleet's sensor range. On the feed – only a recreation of the data being captured by the scanners – the vessel looked almost too big to be real.

"Holy Christo . . ." Kaminski muttered.

"Category ten," someone declared. "No ID on primary threat—"

"This is Scorpio Squadron," a nearby communicator crackled. It was Lieutenant James: I could imagine him ready to gun the engine on his Hornet, finally able to get some kills in for his squadron. "Awaiting a go command, Admiral."

"We read, Scorpio One," a Navy officer replied. "Be on your mark for launch."

"Wait," Loeb said. "Just wait. Let's see their numbers first."

More bio-ships appeared on the tac-display. One at a time, popping into reality. Whether they had dropped out of Q-space, or had just now been detected by our sensors, I couldn't tell. It probably didn't matter: the undeniable fact was that a war-fleet was in near-space, and it was big.

"Weapons officers at the ready," someone else declared. "We have a target lock on primary threat."

"Wait!" Loeb said again.

The bio-engines trailed organic components; living tendrils pushing their way through the void. Even the green holographic projections looked threatening. Titan-sized, the ships were a shoal of predatory fish in the great sea of space: eyeless, their threat undimmed by the cold desolation.

I evaluated our position, watched the enemy fleet moving slowly – so slowly – through the moon-fields of Damascus Space. That sense of powerlessness rose within me again.

A long minute passed.

"Eleven Krell warships detected, sir."

"Are we dark across the fleet?" Loeb asked.

There was another heavy, aching pause.

"Confirmed, Admiral."

Loeb nodded. Wireframe holos of the Alliance fleet, all cordoned around the Artefact, sat at one end of the display. The Krell fleet was moving across the other.

"They might miss us," Kaminski said.

"If they were in Q-space, why'd they drop out here?" Martinez asked, rhetorically. "Space is big, and God doesn't do coincidences."

I said nothing; had no choice but to watch this play out and hope that we lived through it. Loeb's tactic was dangerous. By reining in his primary threats – the longer-ranged railguns and the Hornet fighter squadrons – we remained under the Krell's sensor-grid. But if they found us, then we would lose the element of surprise. And in space, a loss of initiative could be fatal. The consequence of playing his hand now, though, was that the dark order would be lifted. The *Colossus*, and thereby the Alliance fleet, would be immediately visible to the encroaching Krell . . .

"There are a further twenty-five possible warships in near-space, sir," another officer reported. "But the readings are unreliable. The moon-fields are causing a significant disturbance to the scanner . . ."

"Now reading forty-six hostiles," someone corrected.

"I'd strongly advise that we launch the fighter squadron," the ship's XO – the executive officer – said. "The Krell are about to enter the ideal kill zone."

"Scorpio One ready and more than willing," James replied over the comms. He was using an internal, closed circuit:

the only safe method of communicating, with the Krell so close. "My finger is on the launch button . . ."

"Who is in command of this damned ship?" Loeb said. His eyes never left the display, and he barely raised his voice.

No one responded to his challenge.

I'd never seen so many Krell warships in one place. The First Krell War, as some xeno-historians had labelled it, had involved many ship-to-ship engagements. I'd seen the vid-casts of those battles: many battleships on each side, duelling it out across the dark of space. But even those tri-D recordings – the stuff of legends – paled in comparison to the war-fleet I was witnessing. The ships were huge; and there were so many packed into the debris field. In the shadow of each of the motherships, smaller vessels flitted. There was no way that the Alliance fleet at Damascus would be a challenge to the Krell Collective. We would be nothing more than a hindrance.

"Keep those sensors on low-yield," Loeb ordered. "I don't want anything reading our presence."

"Aye, sir."

"Absolutely no external or inter-fleet comms until the threat has passed."

"Affirmative, sir."

The holo flashed with warning markers indicating the deployment of stealth systems. Every ship within the Damascus battlegroup was equipped with high-end covert gear; even running without comms, we could still send a beacon out into space that would gather every Krell between here and the homeworld. The thought sent a shiver down my spine.

The CIC sat in tense silence for another minute.

The Krell fleet was almost, but not quite, through the

moon-field. My pulse raced; that chemical tang in the back of my throat that could only be fear.

"Are they attracted by the Artefact?" I asked of Loeb, desperate for an answer.

Loeb looked at me through the thatch of his eyebrows. "The Artefact isn't broadcasting. I'd hazard a guess that they're moving towards the Quarantine Zone." He rubbed his index finger against his lip, staring down at the holo. "Perhaps they are concerned about using Q-space in the vicinity of those moons. Whatever the reason, they won't find us. We're running dark. The entire fleet has stealth systems engaged. They don't seem to be deviating from their flight path . . ."

The holo froze.

The Krell alpha-predator was still entangled in the shattered segments of a dozen moons, but she wasn't moving any more. Neither were the gathered smaller shark-ships around her.

The holo of the *Colossus* – suddenly incredibly small, barely capable of supporting over two thousand human crew – had started to glow crimson.

"*Colossus* is broadcasting!" a red-faced lieutenant shouted in disbelief, standing from her station. "I'm detecting an encrypted broadcast from inside this vessel!"

Loeb's calm façade shattered like one of Damascus' moons. "Get me the location of that broadcast, immediately!"

"Tracing location . . ." the lieutenant replied.

She started to work, but before she could get a result, as suddenly as it had cancelled, the stealth system was back online and the ship's icon turned a friendly green.

I let out a long breath.

"The Krell fleet is moving off again."

In reality, the stealth system had probably been suspended

for only a second or so: but that was enough. If the Krell had been looking for us, they would've found us. Something broadcasting from aboard the *Colossus* had rendered us immediately vulnerable.

One by one, the Krell ships blinked from existence. The mothership vanished last of all.

"The Krell are clear of the moon-field. The war-fleet is moving through Damascus Space."

"Confirmation that the Krell fleet has jumped to Q-space," a lieutenant indicated.

That wasn't worth much. Unlike human tech, the Krell ships left little in the way of evidence when they jumped. I stared down at the map, willing space to remain empty. Thankfully, it did.

"Permission to lift the dark order, sir?" an officer enquired.

Loeb was quiet for a long moment. As senior officer on the fleet, only he could impose or lift the order. It was a significant restriction on starship capabilities: under a dark order, the only functional tech was the null-shield. The *Colossus*, and the rest of the fleet, couldn't use their weapons or Q-drives. All power was routed to the extensive stealth systems. I didn't pretend to know how those worked – Sci-Div regularly updated stealth capabilities, to keep a step ahead of the Krell bio-tech.

Finally, Loeb muttered, "Lift the dark order."

The CIC overhead lights suddenly rose, and across the tac the various fleet assets disengaged their stealth systems. I heard captains from other ships reporting their safe status; a surge of relieved voices over the communications network. With the Krell having jumped to Q-space, there was no way that our inter-fleet communications could be traced by them any more.

"Is it over?" Kaminski asked. Like me, he was bathed in

sweat, and uncharacteristically for Kaminski he didn't seem to be smiling.

"I think so," I said.

The admiral was still looking over data from the display. He rubbed his chin, deep in thought.

"Those ships could have been part of a larger fleet," he said, slowly. "And who the fuck sent that transmission?" He turned to one of his comms officers. "Do we have a trace on it yet? I can't believe one of my crew would be stupid enough to send a transmission during a dark order."

"Whoever it was, they must've been in a damned hurry to get information off this ship," Martinez whispered. "Weren't comms supposed to be shut down while we are in the Maelstrom?"

"You remembered the safety briefing . . ." I said.

"I try, *jefe*," Martincz said with a shrug.

There was a brief pause while the comms officer worked.

"Status on the trace is a positive. It was an encrypted neutrino transmission, sent from somewhere in the lab deck. I have a fix on the terminal location."

Loeb read something from his command console. His face remained fixed, but I could see that the findings concerned him. He glared at me again.

"I'm retiring to my quarters. Major Harris, Captain Williams – your presence is requested."

Then he stormed out of the CIC, scattering officers and service personnel in his wake.

I'd hardly noticed the Warfighters throughout the incident. They stood at the bulkhead door to the CIC, all cockiness and certainty drained from their faces.

The Krell changed everything.

They always did.

The arrival, and subsequent disappearance, of the war-fleet could only mean one thing: that they were looking for something. Damascus Space was a dangerous pocket of the Maelstrom; as perilous to the Krell as to Alliance forces. It was surely not an area regularly patrolled by the Krell. So, the question remained: what were the Krell doing out here?

Loeb prowled the edge of his stateroom, tossing his cap onto his desk, then dragged out a chair. He noisily threw himself into it. I stood in front of his desk, a Navy lieutenant on one side of me, Williams on the other.

Loeb's answer to the Krell problem was blunt and uncomplicated.

"We're pulling out."

"Impossible," I said. "We have unfulfilled orders. We can't leave yet."

And more than that, Elena is waiting for me inside the Artefact. It suddenly occurred to me that I hadn't been able to touch her with my real body; that our only contact had been simulated. The idea that she might be stolen away from me, that Loeb might abandon the mission, made me feel sick to the stomach.

"Get me a scotch on the rocks," Loeb barked.

The lieutenant jumped to action, pouring liquor from a decanter and *clink-clinking* ice cubes into a glass. The sound alone gave me a thirst.

"Our mission was to secure the Artefact," I said. "And there is no way I'm leaving Damascus Space until we've achieved that objective."

"Things have changed," Loeb countered. "My orders were to provide Naval support to this operation. I've dutifully executed the same."

"Then I'll overrule you. I'm mission commander."

"I know exactly what you are. I've read the damned

debriefings. We're out of communication with the *Point*. Considering your impaired psychiatric condition, I could have you detained for further evaluation. I'm not going to do that, yet, but I am calling time on this operation."

"You can't do that!"

"I can do whatever I damned well please, Major. This is my ship, and I am fleet commander of the Damascus battle-group. Don't make me pull rank on you. I have a duty to inform Command of what we've just seen. The only way to relay that information is to jump back to the *Point* and deliver the news in person. Given the circumstances that is the only method that we have available."

"We both know that's a lie," I said. "It has nothing to do with method."

Loeb had made plain that he'd wanted off Operation Portent from the start. I remembered our conversation in this very room, only a few days ago. Loeb had been looking for justification to withdraw from Damascus Space and now he finally had it. The arrival of the Krell war-fleet was perfect.

Loeb saw the way that my mind was working. "Sending a tightbeam communication to the *Point* from inside the Maelstrom is too risky, what with that Krell war-fleet roving around the galactic neighbourhood. No; going back in person is the only way."

He gave a self-satisfied, smug smile. If someone inside Command did have the gall to investigate his decision, he'd already planned his defence.

"We're on the verge of cracking the Artefact. I just need a little more time!"

"Time is the one thing that we don't have," Loeb said. "The *Point* needs to be informed immediately— "

"Then send a single ship back. Repurpose one of the freighters! The *Northern Pledge* has a fast Q-drive."

Loeb's eyes were steely cold: he'd already made up his mind. "The War is on again," he said. "The only way to crush this problem is a full-scale show of force. Not cloak-and-dagger tactics, not reliance on new-fangled technologies, and certainly not through exploiting the remains of some aeons-old xenos' wreck."

He thrust his finger at the view-port, at the Artefact outside. I had to consciously avoid looking at it, because even the suggestion of the Artefact made my data-ports ache. Tired as I was, I wanted to be back out there all over again.

Williams fidgeted uncomfortably beside me.

"I agree with the admiral," he said. "I'm sorry, man, but I didn't sign up for this."

"What exactly did you sign up for?" I shouted.

Williams had demonstrated that he was no Legionnaire. His words to me, when we'd first met, echoed in my mind: "I'm only interested in the glory work." Sailing through the Maelstrom, in the midst of a Krell fleet of such magnitude: there wasn't much glory in that.

He pulled a face. "Just not this. That was a big fleet, man. Got to be a serious security risk. The *Point* should know about it."

Loeb took in the exchange: savouring the animosity between Williams and me. "There's more, and maybe worse," he said. "Much worse."

Worse than leaving Elena aboard the Artefact? Worse than abandoning her in deep-space for a second time?

"Saul is part of the problem," Loeb said. "Professor Saul sent that transmission."

His words shook me from my pit of frustration. He slid a print-out in front of me: I scanned it, but couldn't focus on the contents. Transmission logs – encrypted messages being sent from the *Colossus*.

USER NAME: SAUL, ASHAN (PROF).

I guessed what was coming. Fought to stay standing.

Compromised. That was Elena's word.

Loeb went on: "Saul has sent several communications through the lab deck. He's been using the FTL transmitter, employing an encryption algorithm used by them." Loeb's face looked almost smug as the words tripped off his tongue. "Saul is Directorate. He has been sending his research to an unknown receiver somewhere beyond the QZ."

"That fucking bastard . . ." Williams muttered in disbelief.

This was too much. How could it be happening again? The Asiatic Directorate seemed to have agents everywhere, always one step ahead of me. Always under my skin. In some terrible way, it made sense – was completely explicable. This was Dr Kellerman all over again. Sci-Div seemed to be the vulnerable underbelly of the Alliance military complex: an easy target, filled with little men and their personal schemes.

"And so, you see, even if I wanted to continue this operation, I have no choice. I'm ordering the arrest of Professor Saul. Don't make me add your name to the detention warrant, Major. We're taking Saul back; he can be Mili-Intel's problem."

"I want to speak with him," I said. "I need to know what he has been doing out here."

"Once he's in custody, by all means. Preparations for launch back to the *Point* will take some time. You have two days to undertake whatever further investigations you want. But I'm prohibiting any further expeditions to the Artefact." Loeb looked at me levelly, predicting my response. "Don't try anything silly. We can all walk away from this with some dignity."

The hint of a smile played at the edge of Loeb's lips, but I didn't see anything funny in what was happening.

"Dismissed. Both of you."

I stormed out of Loeb's quarters, in the blackest mood I'd experienced since our arrival in Damascus Space. Williams followed behind me.

"Maybe this is for the best," he said, with a tone bordering on joviality, like the news was a relief to him. "It'll be good to get back to *Liberty Point*. Maybe I'll buy you a drink—"

I turned on my heels and grasped at the collar of his fatigues. In a single motion, I lifted him off his feet and pushed him hard against the wall.

The pounding in my head was becoming overwhelming. It was all I could do to keep my rage in check; not to take it out on the worthless trooper. Williams scrambled and gasped. I enjoyed the look in his eyes – the realisation that even old and skinless, I was a force to be reckoned with.

"Shut the fuck up, Williams, or I'll finish what Kaminski started."

"Yeah, man . . . I . . . understand—" he stammered.

"That's just it: you don't understand. You don't understand at all."

"C . . . copy you, man," Williams managed. "I mean – sir."

"You done?" came a voice behind me.

I held Williams for a long second. Let the anger drain out of me. I eventually let him go. He slid down the wall, to his feet.

"Just about," I hissed.

Jenkins stood at the end of the corridor. She gave me a disapproving look.

"If you boys have finished . . ." she said.

Williams ducked out from underneath me. He smoothed his fatigues, ran a hand through his hair. "I'll see if I can help with that arrest," he said. "I'll let you know what the Marines say, sir."

"You do that, Captain," Jenkins said. "I'll take care of the major."

Williams disappeared off down the corridor, shaking his head.

"Was any of that really necessary?" Jenkins asked me.

"I've had enough of that asshole. Captain or not. Cole promised me the best; instead I get unmotivated fuckers like that."

"Yeah, well. Seems like I pick them."

"Loeb is pulling the plug. We have two days to wrap things up. No more expeditions to the Artefact."

"I know. He sent a directive a few minutes ago. Figured you might need someone to talk to."

She meant well, but there was nothing that my crew could do to help me. What could I really do? Mutiny was a fleeting, fantastical possibility. But even if I skinned up, even if I managed to persuade the rest of my team that this was the right thing to do, Loeb still controlled the *Colossus*.

"Is she all right?" I said.

"You mean Mason?"

"Of course I mean Mason."

"Nice of you to ask. Seems like your priorities have been elsewhere recently."

"Don't start with me, Jenkins."

"Mason hasn't been right for a long time. Haven't you noticed?"

"Don't get smart with me."

"I mean it," Jenkins said. "She's been struggling."

"So what's her condition?"

"She's in a coma; possible neurological feedback. The medtechs think she needs proper attention back at the *Point*."

"She'll live," I said. "She is no reason to leave."

"She *might* live. No promises, but she's stable for now."

"Aboard the Artefact," I asked, "did you see her? Did you see Elena?"

"I thought that this was about Mason, not Elena," Jenkins tutted. But she knew that response wouldn't be enough for me, and added: "I was behind you, and my bio-scanner couldn't reach so far into the structure—"

"Did you see her?" I asked again, my voice rising to a near shout.

She shook her head. "There was nothing there, Harris. My scanner was empty."

I followed Jenkins to the mess hall, where the remains of the Lazarus Legion waited.

Kaminski and Martinez occupied the recreation room, just off the main hall, and Jenkins had abandoned a half-eaten meal in one corner. When I entered the hall, the rest of the team stopped: eyes on me. A couple of Navy officers darted out of the door. Eager to avoid me.

"It's over," I said. "Loeb wants to recall the fleet."

"That was expected, after what we saw today," Martinez said.

He was talking sense; but I wasn't interested in sense. I was interested in results.

"We heard that Saul is in custody," Kaminski said. There was no surprise in his voice and the words were spoken with an undercurrent of disappointment, like he had always expected someone on the team to be a traitor.

"With Mason in the infirmary," Martinez said, "maybe, just maybe, this is for the best. She needs help."

I pulled a chair from under the table, slumped into it. Put my head in my hands. I wanted a drink now more than ever: needed something to numb the pain in my head, my heart and my data-ports. Beneath all that, my rage flowed like the tides of the Maelstrom. Jenkins' eyes flashed towards Kaminski; a barely perceptible gesture that spoke of joint concern. The idea that they might've been talking about me, might've shared worries, made me even angrier.

I shook my head. "Elena was concerned that I'd been compromised. Maybe the operation was compromised from the start . . ."

"Leave it, Harris!" Jenkins said. "We gave it our best shot. It's over."

"Elena wants out," I said. "I can help her. She wants me to activate the Artefact. I'll do it with or without your help. I'm not leaving this place."

The Legion said nothing. I sat back in the chair, looked into the eyes of each of them. I realised then that I didn't care any more whether they believed me or not.

I believed. That was all that mattered.

"I'm going to argue this out with Loeb," I insisted. "He can go fuck himself if he thinks I'm leaving in two days. Tomorrow morning, assemble in the SOC as usual."

None of the group immediately responded.

"Understood?" I said. "And make sure that Williams keeps that traitorous bastard in custody. I want him interrogated; I want every detail of his operation exposed."

"Affirmative," Jenkins said, with more than a little reluctance.

I thought about going to the SOC and making transition again, but figured that it was too soon. I'd be seen, and in the current climate Loeb was looking for any opportunity to undermine me. As difficult as it was, I had to wait again.

But Jenkins' words had wounded me. And so, a guilt that I couldn't repress drove me down to Medical. I was angry with myself for putting Mason in danger; for allowing her to end up like this. Dejah Mason was a trooper under my command and she was my responsibility.

The infirmary occupied one corner of the Medical Deck, and was even more clinically sterile than the rest of the med-bay. Decontamination docks sat open and a medtech was at a workstation just inside the ward. I got her attention.

"I need to see Private Mason."

She was a small blonde woman of Martian stock. The name-tag on her chest read TREENA BAILEY, MEDTECH GRADE A3: I vaguely recognised her as the girl I'd seen with Williams at the Alliance Day party.

Bailey looked up and gave a brief smile. "Of course. She's in bay three."

"How's she been?"

"You have security clearance to access her medical data directly."

"I don't want data. I want to know how she is."

The tech's brittle smile flashed again. "Sorry. We're all kind of on edge, what with the news about the Professor. I still can't believe it."

I shrugged. When the girl realised that I wasn't interested in trading scuttlebutt, she went on, "Dr West is her treating clinician. The working theory is that she suffered some form of neurological feedback during extraction."

That was a rare but not unknown complication for a sim operator. I'd probably increased the chances of such an occurrence by putting my people under too much pressure.

With so many extractions, in such a short period of time, it wasn't surprising that one of the team would break. Maybe Mason just wasn't up to it. Maybe she wasn't really Sim Ops material after all.

Maybe none of them are up to it, that voice whispered.

"She's currently in a medically induced coma. Dr West is running some blood tests and further scans. She'll be on shift in the next hour if you want to speak with her. Or I can comm her direct, if you'd prefer."

"No. I just want to see Private Mason."

"Go on through."

I've never liked hospitals. The smell of medical equipment; the lighting. It's the same wherever you are, whatever word you use to dress up the location.

Sub-chambers lined the edges of the main ward, rigid plastic curtains partitioning them from the rest of the room. A robot auto-doc – all white plastic shielding and gleaming apparatus-tipped arms, like a mechanical octopus – sat at the end of the ward. The doc's clamshell-design canopy was open, the moulded treatment couch unoccupied.

I pulled open the plastic curtain to Mason's cube. She lay in the bunk, in a hospital gown, covered to the chest by a clean white sheet. She looked haggard; eyes faintly shut. A plethora of medical devices were wired to her body: feeder tubes, data-cables, reader pads.

"Good evening, Dejah," I whispered.

She didn't respond. Only lay there, still, chest faintly rising and falling. In rhythm, a machine beside her emitted a sibilant wheezing. A plastic rosary lay on her pillow, next to her head. That had to be from Martinez.

I lifted a data-slate from a holder beside her bed. I linked my wrist-comp to the terminal and downloaded the material – her medical history and case notes – just in case I might need it.

"I shouldn't have brought you out here," I said.

Mason just looked on. Impassive, calm: next to death.

I touched the young trooper's hand. It was cold, rigid. Mason reminded me of my sister: her youth, her determination. Seeing her like this – immobile in the hospital bed – made the comparison even stronger. I shook my head, forced back the memories.

"This is my mission," I said to Mason. "It's always been my mission, and I'll complete it alone. Sleep well."

I slipped the data-slate back into the holder. Pulled Mason's bedsheet up to her neck. She didn't rouse.

I slid out of the cube, closed the plastic curtain behind me.

By the time I left the Medical Deck, the *Colossus'* night-cycle had commenced. The late watch staff had taken over, and the ship was generally quiet.

There was nothing else for me to do but sleep. It had been a long and tortuous day.

As ever, my dreams were troubled. I kept waking up on the Buzzard's Run. The openness terrified me – all of those stars, reaching out to infinity. I thought that I could hear Elena's voice, calling to me across time-space. I felt so cold, hands pressed against the glass corridor walls.

Except that when I woke up, I was back in the tiny officer quarters aboard the *Colossus*, and it wasn't cold at all. Quite the contrary: I was drenched in sweat, in the grasp of a feverish headache.

I heard – or at least, thought that I heard – voices from outside my room. Speaking in whispered, accusatory tones.

"He's crazy. Proper Section Eight."

"We're going to have to relieve him of command. Nobody back at the Point*'ll question that decision."*

The voices sounded like Kaminski and Jenkins. There was laughter as well; hushed, malicious laughter.

"Right on, sister. But I'll do it if we have to; I'm captain."

That had to be Williams.

Had they – Kaminski and Jenkins – been in on this with Williams from the start? Jenkins had been laughing with Williams at the Alliance Day party. Had the entire confrontation between Williams and Kaminski been staged, a way for Williams to get aboard the Artefact alone?

Williams spoke again. *"We've got to think of ourselves now. There's no way that Dr Marceau is aboard the Artefact."*

I tried to move but found that I couldn't. A great weight was on my chest, pushing the atmosphere from my lungs.

"Sleep now," said another familiar voice.

It's best this way, whispered the voice in my head.

I realised that they were one and the same voice: a voice I'd heard so many times in dream and reality that I should've recognised it immediately.

Elena sat in the corner of the room, dressed in her yellow vac-suit. She smiled.

I went towards her. Tried to pull my body from the bed.

"Lie back, my love," she said. "I can wait. I've waited this long. The dead have patience, if nothing else."

"I tried . . ." I said. My voice dried up in my throat.

"Maybe just not hard enough. What's it going to take? To actually make you stand up to all this. To make you realise that only you can change it?"

A figure sat in the opposite corner of the room. Half in shadow, I could only make out the lower portion of the spectre's face. Most certainly a man, chin speckled with irregular and patchy stubble. His breathing was laboured, sibilant.

But no matter how hard I tried, I couldn't move my body – couldn't twist that extra distance to make out the rest of the face.

The stranger sat with his hands – about as worn and tired as his face – on his lap.

Sweet Christo . . .

There was something in those hands. The glint of metal: a familiar object that I hadn't seen in such a long time. Something I thought that I had lost for good.

My father's revolver.

Whoever the stranger was, his face twisted in a ragged smile: an expression that was filled with cruel malice, and chilled me to the core.

Elena laughed. "Only death seems to motivate you, Conrad."

CHAPTER TWENTY-FIVE

RUINS OF THE OLD WORLD

Twenty-three years ago

I was nineteen years old when Carrie came back.

Demarco and I were on the thirty-eighth floor of what had once been the Penobscot Building. The Penobscot was the tallest remaining tower in the Detroit financial district: in the ruins of the old world. I'd chosen our location carefully – above those levels already plundered by the street scavs, out of range of the security drones and probes. They could fly but they were only anti-grav: even those machines had their limits.

"Good spot," Demarco said. He nodded at the window. "I can see across most of the Metro from here."

I snorted. Drank from my flask – a nice metal model, something I'd acquired on my last hunt. The water was warm and bitter.

"Nothing I want to see out there," I said.

I'd seen the results of the bomb too many times. I had a portable Geiger counter on a lanyard around my neck;

the plastic casing scratched and scuffed. It purred a regular background noise: a reminder that every hour, minute and second I spent in the blast zone was time shaved off my life.

Fuck it. It was decent work and if *I* didn't do it then someone else would.

Demarco stalked between a pair of blackened office desks, keeping low. Save for the jagged glass fragments lining the frame, the window behind him was completely blown out; casting the black office interior in dull morning light.

"Just sit down and eat," I said. Pulled the goggles from my face, let them hang around my neck. "We've been going at this for hours."

Just elevated from boyhood; Demarco looked much younger than his actual age, but he talked much older – had the lingo of a kid who'd seen things beyond his years. His hair was cut short, patchy in places. Like most of the Metro, he was a child of the bomb: carried glaring white welts on his neck and shoulders. Those were the product of long-term radiation exposure, of a lifetime spent searching the bombed-out tenements and the decayed inner city.

I sprawled on the floor, facing the window, and opened my shoulder bag. It bulged with recovered relics. Simple low-value items like handheld electronics, packets of cigarettes, even a couple of food tins. I carefully scattered the items across the floor.

"You're missing out," Demarco said.

He was almost as good a scavenger as me; save for that dangerous streak of curiosity. He grinned in the dark, peeking over the office desk at the rectangle of grey light outside.

"Keep away from the window," I ordered. "That's how they find you, more often than not."

"It's quite a sight . . ."

Demarco was referring to the remains of old downtown, the rotten heart of the Metro. Of course, I'd seen the views from the towers as well. Maybe, to someone, they were impressive; the jagged black skyline, the fused glass and steel monstrosities that had once been buildings. But it just reminded me of what the Alliance and Directorate had done to each other. There was evidence of that all around me. The thirty-eighth-floor office of the Penobscot had been working as usual the day that the bomb dropped on Detroit Metro. Some of the employees still sat at their desks; now eternally tethered to the melted plastic workstations and swivel chairs. A body sat a couple metres from me. It was impossible to tell whether the blackened husk of a corpse had once been a man or a woman. More bones and dust than flesh: all moisture sucked from the body by thirteen long years in the dark. The thing grinned that dead smile – a stylus still held in desiccated fingers, ready to operate a computer that was equally spent.

I jumped up, grabbed at the skeleton's hand. It was a good-quality stylus; something to add to the day's meagre trawl.

Demarco eventually came to sit in my sheltered spot away from the window. He was covered in a thin sheen of sweat and dust; eyes peering out of a matt facemask of ash. I watched him empty his own bag to the floor: very careful to separate his treasures from mine. He shook his head. Fished in the pockets of his coveralls – we both wore those, marked up with the insignia of some long-deceased Earth-bound corporation – and poured some smaller items onto the ground as well.

"Bad show, Con," he said. "Not much for a morning's work."

"Better than Rachi's gang," I said. I pulled open a chocolate

331

bar with my teeth, bit at the contents. It tasted soft and stale. "They spent the whole day out on Eleventh Avenue; came back with nothing."

Neither of us had anything of especial worth. I knew enough about nuclear war to understand that the electronic devices I'd foraged would probably be fried; I figured maybe I could break those down, sell on some of the components. The other items might get me a few credits, and the tinned foods looked edible, but none of it would get me past the next meal.

I took another swig from my flask.

"It's getting harder," Demarco said. "You got to admit it."

"Maybe," I said, swilling the warm liquid around my mouth. It was laced with anti-rad drugs. Not the high-end stuff that the clinics sometimes handed out, but the street version. Not as effective; much easier to acquire. "If you're so worried about the rads, then drink up. I haven't seen you take a taste all day."

Demarco gave me a sideways smile. Broke out an inhaler from his coveralls: a dirty plastic amphet sucker. He took a mouthful from the device.

"I ain't worried about rads," he whispered. "I'll be long gone before Geiger takes his dues."

Making a living was getting harder: much harder. The lower levels of the office buildings and towers of the business district had long ago been searched and plundered. That drove those looking for pre-war treasures deeper into the blast zone, increasing the risk to radiation exposure. I didn't know the exact location of the blast zone but my best guess was that we were a couple of klicks from ground zero.

It had been thirteen years since the single nuclear warhead had dropped on Detroit. Successive governors installed to oversee the Michigan State – puppet politicians talking the Pentagon's war-rhetoric – had promised to repopulate the downtown. It all cost money: the UA didn't have enough of that to go around, and Detroit downtown fell to the bottom of a long list of priorities.

"What you thinking about, boss?" Demarco asked me.

"Nothing much. Just the war."

"It wasn't a war, man," he said. He gave a muted laugh. "Congress called it a 'tactical nuclear exchange'."

"Sounds like a war, shits like a war. Probably is a war."

Demarco grinned again. "You heard about the real war? The xeno war?"

"Course. I hear just like everybody else."

"They're saying that there are bug-eyed fishmen coming from beyond the stars. Invading human space. Taking prisoners and all that shit."

"You really believe it?"

"I want to believe. I want to believe that we aren't alone – that there's something bigger than this." He paused, scratched at the tumours on his neck. "More than that: I want to believe something is going to come down here, and mop up all this crap – to force us to start again."

"But fishmen? Sounds like bull."

Demarco shrugged. "I got an uncle in the UA Army. He's a sergeant or something. Came back from the Rim; started telling stories about aliens. Real nasty bastards."

There were plenty of stories going round about the new threat to Alliance security – to human security – but nothing confirmed. Back then, I wasn't sure what to believe: the politicos and the military were quick to debunk the rumours as Directorate propaganda. It seemed inherently unlikely; but the rumour mill was gaining momentum. Time-delay on civilian space comms meant that news we received on

Earth – hundreds of light-years from the edges of explored space – was years old.

"Wasn't your old man in the military?" Demarco asked.

I sighed. "No. He wasn't. And he sure as fuck didn't fight fishmen."

Jonathan Harris. My father. I never spoke about him; never thought about him. Out here – in the blasted inner-city wasteland – no one cared where you really came from. I made my own bio; lied when I needed to. I watched Demarco as he rearranged his day's take. We'd inevitably part ways soon, and my real history wouldn't matter. That, or as Demarco had predicted, Old Death would come calling for him. Children of the bomb as gifted as him didn't last long. I'd move on to another gang – change my story again.

"You ever think about joining up?" Demarco said. "Getting off this rock?"

"No. Can't say that I have."

"Maybe we should."

"What, and fight your uncle's fishmen?"

"It'd beat scraping a life down here in the piss and the shit."

"Not for me. Not when there's still plenty for the taking down here."

I waved my hands at the desiccated building around us.

"Maybe you're right," Demarco said. "Come on. We should be getting on. Still another six floors above us—"

Up until that moment, the building had been maddeningly quiet. We only had the dead for company; the other scav crews knew that we were working the Penobscot, wouldn't dare to encroach onto our territory.

The silence was broken by a barely audible whirring.

Demarco went to one knee, scrambling with his bag: eyes on the big empty window.

"Maybe it was the building?" he babbled. "Maybe the structure is coming down?"

While that was possible, the noise had nothing to do with the building coming down and we both knew it.

The noise was unmistakably an anti-gravity engine.

A drone.

It appeared at the window, hovering outside: as though it was afraid to enter the structure. As big as a man, the drone was armoured and spherical. Faceless, it was equipped with a handful of multi-vision sights that blinked and flashed. Its frontal facing was interrupted by several cylindrical devices: the muzzles of unidentified projectile weapons.

"Oh, fuck, Con!" Demarco said. His face was splashed with sweat, neck corded with distress. "We're done!"

I already had my shit together, had started backing up to the door we'd used to get in.

"Stay low and follow me."

"We're fucked! They have infrared, motion sensors—!"

"You don't even know what any of those things are."

"They'll kill us, Con!"

I agreed with that.

Although the blast zone was dead, unoccupied, it was still owned. Big business wouldn't relinquish its hold on the existing structures and the contents: still regularly used security patrols. This far inside the blast zone, the drones were the law. They didn't ask questions, didn't care about our reasons for being here. They terminated trespassers with extreme prejudice.

Demarco and I scrambled into the corridor outside. Vaulted a displaced filing cabinet.

The drone lost its compunction about entering the tower. I heard it crash through the window frame, the whine of its engines growing ever nearer. A searchlight popped on behind us; sent jagged splinters of hard light over the darkened interior of the corridor.

Getting out of the building had become our only objective.

Smaller than me, faster than me, Demarco dashed on ahead. He made for the stairwell. The floor was at an angle, slowing us.

The searchlight spun behind me. There was more crashing as the drone went through a wall. Brickwork and dust poured along the corridor.

"Go, go!" I shouted.

The building creaked, expressing disquiet at the drone's invasion. How had it gotten so high? I was no technician but all scavengers had a basic understanding of how the drones worked. It was common knowledge that their anti-grav engines only operated close to the ground—

Not this one, I answered, as the drone gained on us.

We both leapt through an empty window, into another blasted office space. Demarco skidded on a pool of water – something dripping from above him – and rolled into the remains of a Penobscot employee. He gasped, jumped back in revulsion: an unconscious, human reaction to something we'd both witnessed a hundred times before. I grabbed his collar, dragged him between a line of desks.

Everything fell silent for a moment. I braced behind the desk, breathing in short, controlled gasps. I kept one hand on Demarco's chest – could feel his beating heart through the bones of his ribcage – because the look in his eyes told me that he was going to run at any moment.

"Stay with it, Demarco!" I whispered.

"Maybe it's gone?" he murmured.

Just because that was what we wanted didn't make it so,

but it was quiet enough for that to be true. I listened. Could only hear the regular creak and whine of the tower. I relaxed my hand. Demarco righted himself and peeked over a stack of gutted computers.

The drone suddenly rammed the office doorway with such force that part of the ceiling came down. It used the bulk of its great spherical body to batter its way through the wall, clipping the frame without concern. The chase was on again.

"Just move!" I ordered.

The drone emerged from the dust cloud created by the collapsed ceiling at full speed: metal shell barely touched. It collided with a desk, hard enough to ram it aside.

"This way!" Demarco yelled.

"No," I shouted back, above the noise of the advancing drone. I pointed in the opposite direction. "It's through there."

Demarco shrugged, moved off on the route he'd indicated.

Coughing, mouth full of carbon fibre and plaster dust, I paused for just a moment: paralysed by indecision. The insides of the towers looked similar at times; could be misleading.

With the drone metres behind me, I decided to follow Demarco.

The drone was relentless. It moved at full pelt, searchlight inadvertently illuminating my path.

We emerged into another corridor – somewhere dark, without any natural light. It stank of rot and wet. Pools of rainwater collected on the warped floors. Demarco pounded ahead, wheezing so hard that it almost hurt to listen to him.

"This way!" he bellowed. "Th . . . through here—!"

He hit the double safety doors at full speed, slammed them open with his shoulder—

There was light beyond the doors.

Light from outside.

Demarco stopped. He pulled back from the ragged edge of the collapsed floor.

Instead of a stairwell, the building terminated in a wide void. It looked like an entire section had fallen in on itself, creating a thirty-metre drop to the next – equally unsafe – floor.

Demarco wobbled at the edge of the drop. He turned to me, arms out to steady himself. His expression recognised that we'd gone the wrong way.

The drone crashed behind us.

Demarco's eyes snapped to the other side of the collapsed floor. It was a good six metres – a difficult jump in ideal circumstances, an impossible one in these. I immediately realised what he was going to do.

"Demarco! No – you'll never make it!"

He underarmed his satchel and hurled it across the gap. The bag crashed into a wall on the other side.

The drone's engines were just outside the doors now: it would be on us in seconds.

"Better to die trying than not try at all!" Demarco yelled.

Demarco took two steps back.

I went to grab him, my own bag slipping off my shoulder – into the hole in the floor.

Demarco jumped.

He shouted – a loud, guttural roar – as he went, his arms winding, legs outstretched.

The drone paused at the door. It wasn't programmed for surprise; had no way of expressing that emotion on its fixed metal features, and yet I felt a wave of bewilderment emanating from the machine.

Demarco reached for the far floor, fingers clutching at the air as he went.

He missed the other side of the hole by metres. His wiry frame sailed down through the hole.

I looked away. He made a loose, wet thumping sound as he hit the floor.

Dead.

The drone swivelled on the spot. Caught me in its searchlight. I gingerly raised my hands, palms up. It was over. There was no point in running any more.

It wasn't until then that I realised there was an insignia printed on the drone's hull.

ALLIANCE ARMY.

"Harris, Conrad?" the machine asked in abrupt monotone.

I nodded.

"Harris, Conrad?" it asked again. "Provide verbal response."

"Yes!" I shouted. "I'm Conrad Harris!"

"Identification accepted. Accompany this drone to the ground floor."

"Fuck you!"

The drone retreated, back the way that it had come.

"Accompany this drone to the ground floor," it repeated. "Alliance Army personnel require your attendance."

I took the stairs down all thirty-eight floors of the Penobscot. It had taken Demarco and me hours to get to our position – we'd arrived pre-dawn, to make the most of the darkness – and the journey back down was demanding. Condensed into less than an hour, and without the safety webbing we'd used on the way up, it was a miserable and punishing experience.

The drone was always at my shoulder; watchful and

coaxing. It wouldn't answer my questions. Always waited until I was a few metres ahead, then crashed through the wreckage of whatever room we had just left: probably a latent safety control to ensure that it didn't bring the whole building down on me. Maintained that searchlight behind me to keep the way ahead illuminated.

"Just kill me and get it over with," I said, more than once.

The drone always responded in the same way: "Accompany this drone to the ground floor. Alliance Army personnel require your attendance."

Most of the ground floor – or at least what was left of it – was taken up with a reception room. The marbled flooring was cracked and aged; remaining windows cast a misted sepia, due either to the initial nuclear blast or to the decade of neglect since. Water drip-dripped from above; wires and maintenance cables trailed from the soggy holes in the ceiling tiles.

The drone chimed, moved close to me. Coaxing me onwards into the destroyed lobby.

"For fuck sake! I'm going, all right!"

"Accompany this drone —"

"You've told me that already!"

I stumbled through a pair of glass doors; frames twisted and torn, wedged open by a pile of brickwork.

What was I expecting down in the lobby? I hadn't even considered what I was about to find – why the Alliance Army might want anything from me. It surely couldn't be something positive. As I marched through the reception area, towards the Penobscot's main doors, I began to think about ways to get out of this. I had a knife holstered inside my boot. The drone would be a tough target. It was big; armed with several kinetic or energy weapons, capability unknown. The armour plating would likely deflect a direct knife-blow.

It must have a control mechanism somewhere, an override panel—

"Conrad Harris?" came a stern voice across the lobby.

There were four men outside the building, gathered at the entrance. All military men: wearing khaki fatigues and dull green body-armour. Behind them, a few metres across the street, was a small wheeled vehicle: a jeep or a buggy.

"Mr Harris?" the lead man called again, impatiently. His voice bounced around inside the lobby, competing with the sound of dripping water. "Can you identify yourself?"

I approached the exit. No one had told me to, but I put my hands up anyway. At least three of the four soldiers were armed – two with rifles trained on the deserted street, the third aimed in my direction – and it seemed like the right thing to do.

"Yeah. I'm Conrad Harris."

The lead soldier was a middle-aged man, spoke with a Detroit twist. He had a respirator over his lower mouth. Pulled it free and smiled.

"You're a hard man to find, Mr Harris."

None of them wanted to stay here any longer than was absolutely necessary: that was obvious from their body-language, their entire presentation. I couldn't say that I blamed them.

"What do you want?" I said. "Am I under arrest?"

"No," the lead soldier said. He had no weapon that I could see; just nodded in the direction of the buggy. "Not at all. It's more complicated than that. Can you come with us?"

"What do you want?"

My mind absently returned to thoughts of escape: of the best route out of this street, of the available resources to win a fight against three armed men.

"It's about your sister," the soldier muttered. "You do have a sister – Carrie Harris? Daughter of Jane and Jonathan Harris? Immigrated to Ventris II?"

I swallowed. My throat had suddenly and inexplicably closed; chest tightening with forgotten emotions. I thought of Carrie leaving on the forged papers: of whether any admission I made would get her into trouble, whether it was better just to lie—

I answered before I'd considered the implications. "Yeah. That's me. Has – has something happened to her?"

The soldier didn't introduce himself but I recognised his shoulder stripes as those of a sergeant simply because that had been my father's rank.

"She died on Ventris II," he said, as we drove through the remains of downtown Detroit. "We've been looking for you for two months."

We were all buckled into the ATV – six big wheels clambering over the debris-strewn highways. The buggy was open-topped; although it only had five passengers, there was room for a full squad. The drone had been docked at the rear and diligently covered our wake: ready to fire at anything that fancied its chances. One of the soldiers occupied a gun-mount in the passenger cage, panning back and forth over the empty buildings. Whispering into his comm all the way.

Those little details occupied me. Because what the sergeant was saying was too much to focus on.

"The aid workers are dropping like flies," he continued. He shook his head. "Always getting caught in the cross-fire. We're a new task force; supposed to track down next of kin, to formally identify the bodies."

"Sure," I said, watching blackened shadows on the walls that had once been people.

The ATV eventually rolled out of the blast zone. Past the enormous battered signpost – words only just visible beneath a gloss of graffiti and dirt.

ENTRY TO THIS AREA IS PROHIBITED UNDER MICHIGAN STATE LAW AND DETROIT CITY BY-LAW – EMERGENCY SERVICES DO NOT COVER THIS AREA.

Two desiccated corpses hung from lamp posts beside the sign. Not victims of the bomb; these corpses were far too fresh.

It took another hour to reach the government sector. Would've been much faster in an air-car, but the ATV had to do. I phased out the sights and sounds of the living city.

Carrie is dead.

It sunk in by degrees.

The squad took me to a medical facility, then through to the DETROIT MORTUARY. The room was small and dark and the cold hit me as I entered. One wall of the chamber was taken up by fridge units, shelves closed. The sergeant and another of his team paused by the door.

A medtech appeared. Dressed in a dirty white smock, he jabbed at a data-slate: looked up at me over scratched glasses.

"This him?" he said. "Conrad Harris?"

"Yeah, this is him," the sergeant answered for me.

"Can I see her?" I asked.

The mortician scoffed. "That's what you're here for, son."

He slid open a freezer.

Carrie lay inside.

Not the Carrie I had known. She had died four years ago; at the Detroit Metro Off-World Terminal.

343

This Carrie looked older, but not as old as I'd expected. Time-dilation had played its part and she had probably spent a good deal of the years since our parting in hypersleep. The young woman who lay flat out on the slab was a different version of Carrie. A blanket covered her lower half, torso naked: her skin a pale blue. Her eyes were closed, giving the impression that she was sleeping rather than deceased. She looked peaceful.

I touched her shoulder. The flesh was cold.

"You came back, Carrie," I whispered. "You always said that you would."

I hadn't noticed them at first, but now I saw that there were ugly bruises on her temples – half-covered by her unruly blonde hair – and a deep blue laceration on her chest. Black stitches tapered together a wound there.

"How did she die?" I asked.

The sergeant read from a holo-dossier. "Executed. Directorate Special Forces. They sometimes take hostages from the aid workers. They don't usually want anything in return – not really – but it's a terror tactic."

"She was an aid worker?"

"Yeah. Looks like she used false papers to get on-world, then started using her own name. Went in with a whole clan."

"Did she suffer?"

"Not likely. Her contingent got ambushed. Whole crawler of aid workers was taken. She was executed the following week."

Her arms were positioned at her sides, over the blanket. I touched her right hand. Felt the calluses on her palms; saw the grit and blood under her fingernails. I could see that she'd worked hard at what she'd been doing. She had believed in it.

"When did she die?" I asked.

"Objective: a few months back. We've had the body on ice since then."

I stared down at her thin arms, at the frail blue skin.

Bare arms. No tracks. No habit.

"You did it, Carrie. You said you'd kick it, and you did."

The emotions that I felt were almost disabling. I struggled to process the mixture. Guilt, because I'd let her go, and thereby I'd been complicit in her death. I could – and damned well should – have done something to stop her. But more than that I felt pride, because Carrie had done it. Carrie had become something greater, escaped the Metro. Just as she had promised.

"You okay?" the soldier asked.

"I'm stone cold," I whispered back. "Have . . . have you found the soldiers that did this to her?"

"Do we ever?" the sergeant replied, with a knowing snigger. Maybe realised – given the circumstances – that it wasn't such a clever comment. Corrected himself: "The Directorate aren't like that. They're ghosts."

"Can you positively identify this corpse as your sister, known as Carrie Harris?" the mortician asked. His voice was cold and even.

I nodded. "It's her."

He pulled my hand free from the body, gently slid the freezer tray back into the wall.

"Thank you, son. If you'd like to follow the sergeant, he will show you out."

Carrie's placid, peaceful face disappeared: hived away with the dead.

I felt numb.

That was the only way to describe it: the absolute absence of any sensation. I wanted to feel rage, wanted to feel purpose, but I couldn't muster either of those reactions. Both would be futile, because I had no outlet for them.

Who was I? A street scav: one among a million, riffing off the remains of the old world. Who would I be in twenty years? No more or no less than I was right now.

I wanted to make a difference.

I paced the medical centre lobby. It was a quiet, empty space: much bigger than I was used to. The sergeant sat with me, watching me. He hadn't spoken since we'd left the mortuary. A security droid was in one corner, tracking me with empty eyes, but I guessed that I'd been biometrically tagged – given some leeway because of what I'd just seen.

It felt like I'd been running all my life. Felt as though the drone, the cops, whoever – had always been chasing me. They'd chased Carrie too, but she had stood up to them. She had made a difference. Everything that she had said she'd do: she'd made good on those promises.

I wiped at my eyes with the backs of my hands.

"Why'd they send someone?" I asked the sergeant. "To find me, I mean?"

He smiled. It was a crooked, world-weary expression. "It's a tick in a box somewhere: a positive statistic for the war-effort."

"I don't believe you."

He went to say something; to conjure some explanation that would support what he'd said, but instead he just nodded. "You're a clever kid."

"Then tell me the truth."

"I recognised the name – Harris – on the death-docket. I knew your old man. We served together years back, during the Rebellion. He looked out for me a couple of times. When the name came up," he shrugged nonchalantly, "I took a chance."

"It's a long way to come for one body."

"Not if you knew Jon like I did. He was a good man." He stated the fact flatly, as though that was the only justification he needed. "If you could be half the man he was, you'd do okay."

"I'm not sure that I can be," I said. "Not here."

"You got any more family? The municipal records aren't so clear any more. Lots of deletions. Things get lost all the time."

"There's nothing left here for me any more."

I think that, in the medical centre lobby, I'd gradually become resigned. Finally realised that I was done with running: that sometimes the inevitable had to be faced.

"There's not much left for anyone," the sergeant replied.

And just like that, without thought or reflection, I said the words.

"I want to join up."

The sergeant didn't ask me to explain, didn't seem to want an explanation. "All right, kid."

"I want to make them pay," I said, my voice rising to a near shout. "I want to take this to the Directorate. There's no point in running from it any more."

The UA Army had set up a recruiting office downtown. When that was flooded with applicants, they set up another two. Eventually there were recruitment offices on every street corner, or at least it felt that way. Even then, there were always queues that reached around the block: eager faces looking to sign up for a tour.

I found an office off Wood Street; an armour-plated booth big enough to accommodate a single trooper, behind a plas-glass screen.

I queued in the heat with the other applicants. Most looked

like they were more interested in a hot meal and a decent bed, but that was fair enough. A digital display on the outside of the booth read NO FITNESS CHECK – NO ENTRANCE REQUIREMENT – NO ONE TURNED AWAY.

When it came to my turn, the Army man looked me up and down. He was a big, stocky man in a digital camo uniform with a vaguely amused smile on his broad face.

"You want to sign up, boy?"

"I wouldn't have queued for an hour if I didn't."

"Got a comedian here, do we?"

"Just saying it how it is."

He passed me some hardcopy papers, in a tray beneath the glass barrier. "You read? You write?"

"I can do both. Got an education centre diploma."

"A regular Einstein. You know who that is, kid?"

"I know of the name."

"Well, that's a great start. You know what branch you want to join?"

"Somewhere off-world. Away from here."

"A man after my own heart," he said, marking an electronic application. "Follow in the footsteps of our brave forefathers, out into the distant stars."

"Somewhere away from here is all I want."

"You running from the law?"

"Not any more."

"Good enough for me. Sign here."

CHAPTER TWENTY-SIX

EXECUTION

I was awake.

I scanned the room. Found that it was empty and quiet.

"What time is it?" I called to the AI.

"Oh-four-hundred hours, Major. Do you require sedation in order to sleep?"

"No. I've slept enough."

"There is a communication on the *Colossus'* server for you. I was directed to wait until you were awake for the day."

"I'm up. Give it to me."

"Captain Williams wishes to see you in the ship's brig."

Had to be about Professor Saul, which made it urgent.

"I'm on my way," I said to the AI.

I needed to see the traitor with my own eyes; to stare down the Directorate bastard. I stumbled out of my bunk.

I stormed through the corridors of the *Colossus* and towards the brig, full of righteous hatred. The dream – of Carrie's death, so many years ago – felt visceral; fresh as a new bullet-wound. My head ached – an incredible pressure building in my temples. Anyone or anything that stood in my way had to be dealt with.

Saul had tried to do just that.

Two voices vied for dominance: a devil and an angel.

Which was which?

He's a Kellerman in the making. Except that you can stop him; you can nip this treason in the bud.

You don't know what he is yet. This – execution, reaching judgment without evidence – isn't the Alliance way. If you're wrong . . .

"Shut the fuck up!" I yelled, thumping a hand to my cranium. I didn't want to hear the voices any more; didn't want the cajoling whispers. There were hard choices to be made here and only I could answer for them. "I wasn't wrong on Helios, and I won't be wrong now."

"All right, sir," Kaminski said. He had fallen behind and out of step with my pace. "No one's questioning what happened on Helios."

I'd forgotten that Kaminski was even there. Both he and Jenkins flanked me, dressed in body-armour. Not full combat-suits – those were reserved for the simulants – but borrowed Marine gear. The black flak-vests looked out of place against their khaki fatigues.

"Whatever you decide to do," Jenkins said, "we're here to back you up."

She gave me a nod. It was probably meant as a supportive gesture but I interpreted it as patronising.

"I get it, Sergeant. Now fall in line and do as I order."

I still didn't trust either of them; couldn't decide whether the overheard conversation last night had been real or imagined. Of late, I seemed to be having a lot of trouble separating those two strands.

The checkpoint entrance to the brig sat ahead. Four Alliance Marines in flak-suits paced the corridor; shock-rifles slung across chests, goggles strapped onto tactical helmets. One was eagerly cracking his knuckles.

"The prisoner is this way," he said. "Captain Williams is already inside."

He manually cranked the locking wheel on the hatch and showed us through.

The interrogation room was small, with a low ceiling. Stud-lights above were at full illumination and dowsed the room in pure white light. It was boiling hot; caused either by the presence of so many personnel gathered in one tight space, or by the heightened state of emotion.

Strange: how so much fear in one place focused like a light until it became a laser.

There was such fear here, but an equal measure of hate.

I breathed it in, felt the emotions hit my bloodstream like a drug.

"Saul . . ." I whispered.

He had seen better days. He was shirtless; thick black chest hair sweat-matted, shoulders marked with heavy red welts. My would-be nemesis sat in the middle of the room, on a chair positioned very specifically beneath a metal table. His forearms were both held in front of him, fingers splayed.

When I entered, he looked up at me with terrified eyes, and his lips moved without speaking. He shook uncontrollably. I'd seen the behaviour before: in civilians pushed over the edge, in a state where sanity became like a fine mist. He was either shitting himself or a damned good actor.

That was the fear part of the room dealt with.

Now the hate.

Williams paced behind Saul. Finally: he had the anger in

his eyes, looked like a real soldier. He loured at the door as the four of us entered. The muscles along his neckline trembled, spoke of barely restrained emotion. He had a small semi-automatic pistol in his hand, and both of his hands were swollen, with minor scuffs across the knuckles. That explained Saul's condition.

Lincoln the dog appeared between the legs of the table, feeding on the hate and negativity in the room. He let out a bark in Saul's direction and Williams scattered him with a loose kick.

"This is the traitor," the Marine added, quite unnecessarily. He took up a spot by the bulkhead. "Admiral Loeb says that he has to be guarded at all times."

A seat had been set up directly in front of Saul: empty. Williams nodded to me, indicated to sit. "I didn't want to start without you, Lazarus."

I took up the position. Saul started whimpering.

For a long moment, I just watched him. Watched the flicker and flit of his eyes; noted his inability to make eye contact. The easy tells that I was staring at a liar. Was he an Alliance liar or a Directorate liar? That was the question. That was what I was going to find out.

"When did they get to you?" I asked.

Saul gave an exaggerated frown. He glanced over my shoulder, at Kaminski. Then at Jenkins; perhaps hoping that a female face would improve his chances of getting out of this alive.

"I . . . I don't understand," he started.

"Don't fuck with us!" Williams shouted. He pressed his mouth against Saul's ear, made the man cringe. "This is Lazarus you're dealing with here."

"Everyone has a price," I said. "Everyone has a breaking point. What was yours?"

"I'm not what you think I am!"

"Then what are you, Saul?"

"Please! I haven't done anything wrong!"

"Shut the fuck up!" Williams roared at him. His voice was like a weapon: piercing but impossible to aim in the contained area. "Don't lie to us, Saul!"

"I've dealt with your kind before," I said. "Don't forget what happened on Helios."

"I'm not like Dr Kellerman!"

"Then why have you been sending unauthorised transmissions from the *Colossus*?"

"Yeah, using a Directorate encryption package!" Williams added.

"I . . . I was following orders . . ."

"That's what they all say," Williams sighed, shaking his head. Sweat was dripping from his brow, in big ugly droplets.

"Please; there is nothing to tell! Don't do this! I deserve proper procedure. I'm an Alliance citizen, of the Arab Freeworlds—"

"You're a fucking terrorist," Williams spat.

The room degenerated into yelling. The dog began to bark again. Saul was shouting the same old answers, the answers that any traitor would give. Williams was in his face, repeating the accusation again and again.

The noise in the chamber was becoming unbearable.

None of this is real, I decided. *None of this matters*.

Williams slapped his sidearm on the table in front of me. The noise was loud enough to cut through the rest; to temporarily silence the cacophony.

"You're the CO," he said. Not at all like the useless, combat-fresh operator I'd come to know over the last few days. "You make the call. But I say ghost him. No telling what he has planned."

Elena tried to warn me, I thought. *I brought a traitor to Damascus.* I imagined him planting viral traps in the *Colossus'* AI, malware backdoors to the rest of the fleet's defences. Williams was right: there really was no telling what damage Saul had already done.

The room froze.

Kaminski and the Marine over one shoulder; Jenkins at the other. The devil and the angel.

Saul's lower lip was quivering.

"Ghost him," Williams said. He turned to the Marine. "Security eyes are off, right? He tried to escape, got capped."

The Marine nodded. "I didn't see a thing."

"Maybe," Kaminski said, "the captain has a point."

Saul shut his eyes.

I picked up the gun. It was a Berringer M-5, a standard Army sidearm. The weapon felt good in my hands. For a device designed to kill, it was perhaps perverse that it immediately made me feel more alive. The arming stud was depressed, ready to fire.

I aimed it at Saul.

"Tell me what I need to know," I whispered. "Who were you broadcasting to? What were you broadcasting?"

"By the Earth Herself," Saul snivelled, "I am not a terrorist."

I jammed the pistol into Saul's forehead. He went cross-eyed, glaring up at the muzzle.

Pulling the trigger on the pistol would be a mercy.

It would be for Elena, and what we had lost.

For Carrie.

For my mother.

The Directorate has taken them all.

"I know what it is," Saul suddenly blurted. "I know what the Artefact does."

"I'm listening," I said.

"It . . . It's a gate."

"Yes?"

"Or rather, it can open a gate. A Shard Gate."

"Go on."

"This Artefact connects to the others – will allow travel through the Shard Network, through time-space. Beyond Q-space. The Key will give access to the entire grid."

He's lying, I decided. *But let him speak. Let him trip himself up, so there is no room for doubt.*

"Does it still work?" I said.

"P . . . possibly."

"How do you know this?"

"I've had access to Command's complete Shard database, to the findings of all research."

"Go on."

"Th . . . they are an artificial life-form."

"Something made them?"

"No. They advanced beyond the flesh. The ruins on Tysis World prove that they are thinking machines."

Tysis World was a name I recognised; a planet on the border between the QZ and the Maelstrom. There had been fighting there, during the First Krell War – with many lives lost on both sides.

"And Tysis World was one of the planets on which the Alliance discovered evidence of the Shard?"

Saul nodded. "Yes. During the War, certain structures were uncovered. Nothing as grand as an Artefact, but very old and very detailed relics. We've been able to interpret several of the markings found there. I think that the Reaper is just an emissary, programmed to seek communication."

"Why would they want to communicate with us?"

Saul shook his head. "Not us. The Reaper wants to

communicate with the others – to rejoin the rest of the Shard Network. They never left us, Harris. They're still out there."

"More," I snarled.

Saul talked quickly. "The Krell and the Shard fought in Damascus Space. This was the site of their largest engagement. The Shard won; reduced the Krell to scavengers."

"That isn't what Kellerman told me."

"Kellerman was wrong about a lot of things."

"When did this happen? Why haven't we seen any evidence?"

"It was thousands – millions – of years ago. So long ago that we can barely measure it. The Shard left the Krell imprisoned in the Maelstrom. But they underestimated them; misunderstood the true nature of organic life. They thought that they had killed them all, but their methods were imprecise. They let them rise again."

He swallowed, shook so hard that I thought that he was going to pass out. "The Shard moved on to the next galaxy – left behind the Artefacts. The site on Tysis allowed us to decode parts of the outer hull cuneiform. It shows that the Damascus Artefact was once a node, a part of a much greater Network."

"You can travel through it?"

"Yes," Saul said, "to elsewhere in the Shard Network."

Williams interrupted Saul with a sarcastic laugh. "This sounds an awful lot like bullshit."

"Why were you broadcasting in contravention of Loeb's orders?" I said. "What were you broadcasting?"

Saul's voice dropped. "I am an agent of the Alliance Science Division. My orders were to report directly to a classified location."

"Without telling me?" I said, my voice rising in volume.

"Specifically," he said, nodding. The bones of his forehead pressed against the muzzle of the pistol; when he moved, I saw that the gun had left an imprint on his head.

I was mission commander, and I knew that there was no way Sci-Div or Command would've approved such an order. There were huge risks in sending out communications this far inside the Maelstrom; risks that Saul had completely ignored. He'd put us all in peril. I was losing my patience with him. His revelations were becoming more outlandish; more unlikely.

"Why?" I yelled.

"C . . . Cole didn't know who he could trust. My orders were to avoid comms with *Liberty Point*."

"Then where did you send the data, Saul?"

"I don't know. Just star coordinates."

"And why were you using a Directorate encryption package?"

"I wasn't," Saul said. His voice had become a nasal whine. "I really wasn't. Loeb has that part wrong."

Williams let out an exasperated sigh. "Just waste this asshole. Cole selected us, man. He trusts us, not him."

I focused on Saul. "Why would Cole tell you to do any of these things?" I asked. "None of it makes sense."

"It was in case I, or the mission, became compromised."

That word again. Elena's word. Dropped so innocuously into the conversation, it immediately set me on a different path. *This whole episode is a damned diversion*, I thought. *A diversion from Elena, and from what really matters.*

"Tell me about Elena," I said. "I want to know everything."

Saul nodded. "She was here, but that was years ago."

"Did they do it?" I asked, eyes widening. I could barely contain my rage; could barely stop myself from pulling the pistol trigger. "Did Elena operate the Artefact? Did she use the Shard Gate?"

"I don't know!"

"Where did she go, Saul?" I shouted. The pain in my head was almost all-consuming: and the only way to end it was for me to end Saul. "Where did Elena go?"

My vision wavered and my hand had started to shake.

"I've told you everything," Saul said. "I have nothing else to say. I want a lawyer."

"Ghost him!" Williams yelled. "This is all lies!"

Maybe this is the only way.

Saul shut his eyes again – eyelids twitching with stress – and began to mumble something under his breath. It sounded a lot like a prayer.

"That's enough," Jenkins said. Her hand was on my shoulder with a firm but gentle grip. "No one's getting ghosted. He deserves a proper trial. Put the gun down."

I was on a knife edge; could go either way.

A nice clean headshot would do it . . .

Fuck it.

I dropped the gun to the table.

It clattered on the metal surface. Quick as a Krell primary-form, Jenkins whisked the pistol up and stepped back. She glared at Williams; dared him to challenge her.

"Don't forget what happened here," I said to Saul. "Remember how this could have gone."

Saul let out a pained sigh. "Thank you, Major."

"Don't thank me," I said. "Not yet. Not until Alliance Command has decided what to do with you." I turned to the room in general. "Make sure that he's watered and fed. I want him kept alive until we can hand him over to the proper authorities."

I scanned the gathered personnel. I couldn't trust Williams to do the job: I suspected that he would kill Saul the first chance he got, and the Marine standing behind me was likely to turn a blind eye to the murder.

"Kaminski," I ordered. "Keep guard on Saul until we make the Q-jump."

"Solid copy," Kaminski said.

"No one else is to be allowed access to the brig."

The Marine sergeant gave a glum but accepting salute. He looked about as disappointed as Williams that he hadn't seen Directorate blood spilled.

"Get him back to his cell," I directed. "Everyone else out."

CHAPTER TWENTY-SEVEN

THE RUN

I left the brig reeling from Saul's disclosure.

He was the one under investigation, but it felt as though the interrogation had yielded as many questions as answers. I could think only of Elena. Where had she gone? How had she got onto the Artefact?

The *Colossus'* crew wasted no time in preparing for launch back to Alliance space. Everything about the ship set me on edge. Everywhere I went, there were cargo-loaders hauling materiel to safe locations; crew members laughing and joking, looking forward to returning to the *Point*.

I had to get away from it all, had to find my own space. I had to get my focus back.

If the Run can't calm my mind, I thought, *then nothing can*.

I took off my wrist-comp and placed it on the floor beside the elevator door. The end of the corridor looked an impossibly long way away; not helped by the infinite blackness that stretched off around me. I took a deep breath, psyching myself up, and got ready to move off—

Something flickered at the edge of my vision. Moving fast; black against the starlight. I wasn't far from the Hornet landing bays but from the dimensions and trajectory it wasn't a fighter. Something more familiar moved beyond the glass corridor, floating above me, barely metres from my position.

A barb ran through me.

That's impossible. I'm losing it. I'm actually losing it.

It was a Directorate Interceptor. Those waspish engine units, enormous gun pods and the iconic black armour: the ship was a symbol of Directorate supremacy on the worlds upon which it was deployed.

The Interceptor delicately hovered in position on VTOL engines. There was no way that this was an Alliance ship that I'd mistaken for Directorate. This was the real thing. The hydra and sword emblem of Directorate Spec Ops – brazenly printed on the nose-cone – confirmed that.

"Oh fuck . . ." I whispered.

My instant and overriding reaction was that I had to get out of there – had to take cover. I turned for the elevator, thumbed the control.

"Identity not recognised," the AI chirped.

"Come on!" I shouted, swiping my thumb again. "Red-clearance – Major Conrad Harris!"

"User not recognised."

A hundred thoughts ran through my mind and I fought to order them. What was the ship doing here? Why hadn't it tripped proximity alarms across the *Colossus*? Where were the Christo-damned space jockeys when I needed them? The H-28 laser cannon tracked my movements. Mounted on the Interceptor's nose, the cannon was standard Asiatic

Directorate equipment: deployed to eradicate heavy infantry and light armour.

I was neither of those. If that thing fired on me directly, I was vapour. In a split second, my eyes flickered to the armour-glass corridor ceiling. Would it hold against a multi-kilowatt laser discharge?

I was about to find out.

The Interceptor fired.

Bright laser pulses slashed the glass, and I had no doubt that I was the target of the attack.

I turned and started the Buzzard's Run.

I ran like I'd never run before.

The glass audibly cracked, the corridor giving in all around me. I knew that I would be losing atmosphere in seconds.

Run!

As soon as the glass broke, there was a flash at the end of the corridor. It was the safety lock-box, containing vac and security gear. There would be a breather.

I was engulfed by noise: the pitched whine of the laser firing, the shriek of escaping atmosphere, even the pressing hum of the Interceptor's engines.

A shadow fell across me, across the remainder of the Run.

Keep going! Keep going!

Lactic burn spread through my legs, my arms. I went from rapid breathing to stilted panting; oxygen suddenly finite, every mouthful precious —

The elevator door felt so far away.

The temperature was dropping rapidly – vacuum leaching away the ship's heat —

Then gravity collapsed.

I didn't know how – possibly a malfunction in the grav-generator, maybe some localised damage caused by the Interceptor's gunfire – but it was a gift. Every footfall became a bounce, my body unable to comprehend the immediate shift, and I kept running. The forward momentum carried me on and I sailed towards the elevator door. In a step, Vulture's Row loomed over me. Automatically, I outstretched my arms, breaking my fall as I collapsed against the wall.

The Interceptor continued firing, churning up the corridor floor behind me.

I grappled the wall for the emergency box. My body was numb with the ache of exposure to vacuum and I broke open the cabinet seal. The respirator kit floated free. I grabbed the mask with both hands.

The Interceptor swept around, better positioning herself to take me out.

The kit was made for use in an emergency. As soon as I placed it on my face the seals attached. A pair of plastic goggles fixed over my streaming eyes; a small oxygen bottle dangling at my neck. Alongside the respirator kit was a button labelled EMERGENCY. A shipboard shotgun. I palmed the button with one hand, pulled out the shotgun with the other. I floated off the deck, but anchored myself with both actions.

The elevator door remained resolutely closed.

I've been set up, I told myself. *Loeb has to be behind this.*

The Interceptor was directly over the Run, so low that I could almost touch her. She grazed a metal spar from the ruins of the corridor against her armoured undercarriage, and I felt a brief wave of heat generated by the VTOL engine.

Last stand. This has to be how it ends.

It was no small irony that the last time I had seen a ship like this, she had turned out to be my salvation. This time the opposite was true: she was death incarnate.

One man with a shotgun against an armoured gunship.

Even Martinez wouldn't like those odds.

The ship paused. Waited.

The black angular lines of the vessel looked so similar to those of the Artefact, to those of Shard technology. That had been what the Directorate wanted all along, and at Damascus they had it all. An Artefact, the Key, and a repository of operational Shard tech.

"Better to die trying than not try at all!" I shouted.

I lifted the shotgun and fired at the Interceptor's belly.

The Remington 900 is a shotgun approved for use in pressurised environments. Specifically, the Alliance Navy approves its use aboard starships. The standard munition is a solid-shot ball-bearing anti-personnel round: the sort of ammo that causes non-lethal injuries to unruly crewmen. With low armour-penetration, a stray shot is unlikely to cause a hull breach.

The Asiatic Directorate Interceptor is a multi-purpose aerospace craft. A generalist rather than a specialist, the Interceptor is equipped with heavy hull armour.

All of this ran through in my mind, in the space of a heartbeat. Braced against the elevator door, equipped with only the shotgun, I'm not sure what I expected to achieve.

The double-barrels fired simultaneously. In an environ with gravity, the kick would have been jarring. Here, in zero-G, the recoil was crippling. The feedback slammed me into the elevator door, sent intense kinetic force up both arms.

Eyes still streaming, I watched the rounds impact the underside of the Interceptor.

The ship didn't even falter.

She had weaved and pivoted throughout our encounter,

but now she was completely still – save for that nose-cannon, which twitched like the muzzle of a hungry dog. I imagined the pilot savouring my image on the HUD as the cross-hairs closed in.

I racked the slide and fired again. A read-out on the stock of the gun flashed with remaining ammo: another eight shots. Even if I'd had a hundred rounds left, I was quite sure that they would do me no good.

The recoil caught me again, sent me spinning back into the elevator door. This time I readied myself for the impact – expected to feel the hard metal against my back and elbows as I made contact—

Except that I didn't.

Gravity sucked me in.

The door behind me was open and I collapsed into the elevator. Someone caught me, hands grappling around my shoulders.

Williams. It was Williams.

"What the fuck's happening out here?" he yelled, over the rush of escaping atmosphere.

He wasn't wearing a respirator and must've overridden the security protocols as the AI would've stopped the elevator from calling at this level without his clearance. He was unarmed, and looked about as shocked as I'd felt when I first saw the Interceptor. Poised at the elevator door, he repeatedly keyed the EMERGENCY CLOSE switch.

The Interceptor wheeled about like an angry insect – drawing ever closer to the elevator. The nose-gun erratically darted left and right—

The doors finally shut.

I fell to the floor, fingers wrapped around the shotgun out of deep-seated instinct rather than conscious thought.

"Wh . . . what's going on?" Williams stammered. "What was that thing?"

I tore off the respirator, flung it away. Gasped mouthfuls of processed ship air. "It was a Directorate Interceptor."

"What's it doing out here? How did the Directorate—?"

"How the fuck should I know?" I shouted back. "My best guess is Loeb."

Panic detonated across Williams' face. "Are you serious?"

"Do I look serious?"

"Fuck, man! Just fuck!"

"How else could the Directorate get that close to the fleet? Maybe he's working with Saul."

Williams swallowed hard, his Adam's apple bobbing against his fatigue collar. He was shit-scared.

"This real enough for you?" I asked.

"Just about."

"Am I so old and used up now?"

"No, but you are bleeding."

I used my free hand to wipe liquid from one ear and then the other. Everything sounded like I was underwater; subdued, muffled. I had to concentrate on what Williams was saying to understand him.

"If you're going to stay standing, you need treatment," Williams said. "This shaft leads down to Medical."

"I'm fine." I wasn't at all, but there were more important things happening on this ship than my loss of hearing. "Forget about me. Where's the Legion?"

"I . . . I don't know."

There's still time to undo all of this – to put things right. I racked the shotgun, ignored the deep ache spreading throughout my body.

"I need to get my team out. If Loeb has turned traitor, then he might've brought the whole ship down with him."

366

Williams nodded uncertainly. "Unless we try to hand ourselves over – ask for mercy or something . . ."

"You're an Alliance soldier, goddamn it!" I yelled, right into his face. I was a hair's breadth from hitting him.

Williams squirmed beneath my gaze, but composed himself. "I was in the mess hall," he started, "when the proximity sensor went off. Someone must've overridden it, because it only sounded once. I just had a hunch you'd be up here – trying to beat that record. I think Kaminski is still covering the brig. I haven't seen the others."

Fuck. With Mason in the infirmary, that was a lot of distance to cover. I needed proper firepower, needed something more robust than my real skin.

"And the Warfighters?"

Williams rubbed his face. "I don't know. The crew quarters, maybe."

The barracks were even further away from our location. I made a decision. "We need to get to the SOC."

"You want to get your sim?" he asked, raising his eyebrows in a way that would be almost funny if it wasn't obvious he was in deep shock. "What if the Directorate have control of the tanks? That sounds like a bad idea."

"The Directorate don't have sims," I said. That was the age-old mantra of the Alliance military. "Or at least I hope that they don't, because if they do we're all in the shit."

The elevator pinged down another level. I thought that I heard shouting outside, but my ears were still ringing with nightmare tinnitus and I couldn't be sure.

"All right, all right, whatever you think is best."

"Stay with it. We need to get my crew, get into the sims, and organise our defence." The elevator came to a stop. "You still have clearance?"

Williams put his thumb to the DNA reader. "I think so."

"I've been deauthorised." The machines had been erratic before, but I was certain that I'd now been removed from the database: that someone had deliberately locked me out. "You're going to have to get us through ship security."

I watched as the doors peeled open. I pointed the shotgun at the corridor beyond: my finger poised over the trigger in case of incoming hostiles. As it turned out, the area was still and empty; disconcertingly quiet. Bright lights overhead, the atmosphere a reasonable temperature. As though I'd imagined that whole encounter up on the Run.

"I need a gun too," Williams muttered, following me out of the elevator.

"That isn't a priority right now," I said. Armed with a projectile weapon like a shotgun in his own skin, I wasn't sure whether he'd be a hindrance or a help. "Where's the nearest communications station?"

"Two corridors away. I can use the reader to access—"

I held up a hand, called for silence. Williams abruptly complied.

A body lay on the floor ahead of us. A bright red splash indicated blood up the wall.

I fell into a combat-crouch. Moved up as stealthily as I could and held my breath until I was on top of the body. I nudged it with the muzzle of my shotgun.

"Oh sweet Jesus Christo . . .!" Williams started. "This cannot be happening, man. This cannot be happening!"

She had been a soldier. Not a turncoat – not Alliance – but a proper Directorate commando. Her helmet was gone, exposing a pale but grizzled face that was almost androgynous: hair shorn to a single strip across her scalp. Features distinctly South Asian – Korean or Chino. Clad in sleek black body-armour; segmented, like a human version of the Interceptor gunship. There was a hole punched cleanly through the commando's gut, with pureed organs and bodily tissue inside.

"Directorate Special Ops," I whispered. A sword emblem, against a stylised image of Mars, was displayed on her armoured chest. "They call themselves the Sword Battalion."

Highly trained and well equipped, the Swords were the Directorate's response to the Simulant Operations Programme.

"Where'd they get the name?" Williams asked.

I pointed to the sword scabbarded at the commando's waist. It looked so archaic as to be almost absurd: flat-bladed, nearly as long as my arm. Not the sort of weapon that had been employed in the last few hundred years by any civilised military. But I knew better than to be taken in by the simple appearance of the blade. It was a powered mono-sword; capable of slicing through reinforced ablative plate with ease.

"The Swords of the South Chino Cluster," I said. "I once read that the battalion took the name from a historic reference – back before the Directorate had even been formed." My brain was too addled to dredge that up. "She didn't get here on her own. This isn't a solo operation."

"How many more can we expect?"

"Enough to take the ship. You fought the Asiatic Directorate before?"

"No," Williams said, recoiling from the body like he really didn't believe she was dead. "Any tips?"

I flipped the body back onto its back. The trooper had a backpack wired to her suit; it blocked heat signals and gave limited life support. Her eyes were still wide open: yellowed and bloodshot, like she hadn't slept in months. Bar-codes and battle honours were tattooed over both cheeks, down the neck.

"Probably hopped up on methaline and battle drugs. Probably been awake for a long time before she died; dropping

369

adrenaline tabs." I pointed out a row of dulled metal staples in the back of the woman's head. Those reached up the nape of her neck, into her skull and the strip of dyed-blonde hair. The surgery looked crude but I knew it to be effective. "Those are nerve staples. Makes them fearless and resistant to pain."

The small metal studs were chemical-inducers: rough neuro-surgery. At specific programmed points, they would cause a near battle frenzy. The Directorate states had a long history of drug abuse in their militaries and corporate structures. The staples were another dirty example of the drug-race.

"Best advice I can give you is don't let them take you alive."

The overhead lighting abruptly went off. We both froze, and I cocked my head to listen for the tell-tale sounds of battle. Instead, that non-audible hum generated by shipboard systems wound down: the gentle vibration of the air that you hardly ever feel, unless to note its absence.

I knew what was happening before the declaration came.

"Preparing to go dark in T-minus sixty seconds," the AI declared.

Luminous arrows appeared on the floor. A guide-path to the nearest evacuation pod or safe muster zone.

"Shit, shit, shit . . ." Williams whispered. "This is so not fair . . ."

"We've got more company inbound," I said. "Let's move." I edged towards the nearest corridor junction. "Which way is Medical?"

Williams pointed down the corridor. "Next sector. We should be able to find a comms station there as well. Needs be, we can defend the place: it has a lockdown facility."

"Good enough for me."

Minutes later, we arrived at Medical. Amber lights were inset around the big bulkhead door, which was thankfully open. Whatever was happening elsewhere on the ship, at least Medical was still functional.

We entered the main corridor dividing up the SOC and the infirmary.

"The SOC is this way," Williams said, pointing in the opposite direction to that in which I was moving.

"I need to check on someone first," I said. Shotgun up, I stayed low to the ground – made for a smaller target. "And the infirmary is this way."

Williams mimicked my movements. He looked like a gangly teenager copying combat moves he'd seen on a tri-D action flick rather than a trained soldier.

"Why are we going this way?"

"Because I said so."

Mason. She was the reason. I had to see to her first. Get her into an evac-pod, if I could, or at the very least I'd make sure she was comfortable – whatever that meant in the circumstances.

A figure moved at the end of the corridor, from behind a desk. Wearing a *Colossus*-issue yellow vac-suit which almost glowed in the low light.

"Hello?" someone called.

"Stand down," Williams rumbled, grasping my shoulder. "It's just a tech."

A medtech emerged from the infirmary area, from behind the reception desk. It was Bailey; the girl I'd seen when I'd last checked on Mason. She raised two gloved hands in the air and stepped out into the open.

"Don't shoot," she called, far too loudly for my liking. "I was about to evac Medical . . ."

"Shut up!" I hissed. I beckoned that she stayed low behind the desk. "The ship is under attack."

The woman's face slackened. "Oh. Sorry."

I turned to Williams, looked back into the empty corridor we had just come from.

"Don't ever tell me to stand down," I said to him. "Not when there are Directorate aboard my ship."

Williams gave a nod. "Yes, sir. Sorry."

Back to Bailey, I said, "Where are the rest of the staff? Where's Private Mason?"

"Almost everyone else has already left," the medtech said. "The private is in there."

She pointed to the plate-glass doors leading into the infirmary. Those were closed and the area beyond was mainly unlit. The familiar location had suddenly taken on a frightening aspect; everything immediately new, rendered horrifying by the basic absence of light.

"Williams, get us inside."

"Yes, sir."

Williams moved up, thumbed the DNA scanner beside the door. In a ragged formation, with me covering the corridor with the shotgun, the three of us deployed into the main infirmary. The amber warning bulbs in the central ward area illuminated in response to our presence, leaving most of the side-chambers in darkness. Two of those were still partitioned off with plastic concertina-style curtains. At the end of the ward, the auto-doc sat at the ready to receive its next patient – or was that victim? – with a variety of surgical implements gleaming in the low light, all poised over the reclining treatment couch.

I nosed the shotgun into the room. Panned left and then right. The immediate area was empty.

"Seal the doors," I ordered Williams.

"Solid copy, sir."

The doors slid shut behind us.

"I'll lock down Medical as well," he declared. "That bulkhead on the way in is six inches of hardened steel. Nothing is coming through that door without a demo-charge or a plasma rifle."

"Fine."

The tech scurried ahead, to a drug cabinet on the wall beside the auto-doc. She noisily and anxiously started to sort through medicines – no easy task considering that she was wearing vac-gloves.

"You look like you need something for your ears," Bailey said. "What caused the injury?"

"An unplanned decompression incident."

"You want me to take the gun?" Williams asked.

"No. I'll keep it."

"Then you mind if I smoke? I always need a smoke when I get nervous."

"Whatever. Just stay frosty."

He pulled out an oversized cigarette. Flipped the ignition, and the tip lit. The smell of chemical compound immediately filled the infirmary ward.

"We need access to the comms station as well," I said to Bailey. "Williams, get it working."

Williams dragged hard on the cigarette. "I'll try."

"The comms station is in the SOC," Bailey said. "We can go there afterwards."

She gave a feeble smile. Tapped a syringe, shook a bottle of tablets. "The injection will deal with air in the blood, and these smart-meds will keep you running until we can get you some proper attention."

"I just need to keep going, is all. Make sure that my team is all right."

I took the smart-meds from her and swallowed down a handful of them. Big, dry tablets; they were medical nano-tech, designed to repair internal damage at the cellular level.

How they worked wasn't really relevant to me; far more important was that they just worked. They did that almost immediately.

"Forget about the injection," I said, dismissing the large hypodermic that Bailey had produced.

"Are you sure? I'd advise that you take it."

"Forget it." I looked back at the exit door to the infirmary. "That the only way out of here?"

"Yes," Bailey said. "The SOC is on the other side of Medical, straight down the main corridor."

"All right. Now I need to see Mason."

Bailey nodded. "Of course. She's over here."

She pointed to a cube off the infirmary. Not the same cube Mason had been assigned last time I'd visited, I noticed. The curtain was pulled across, and I couldn't see inside, but a light shone through the thin plastic material. Bailey went to the handle, fumbled with it inside her gloves, and turned to give me a half-smile.

There was a metal trolley beside the cube and for just a second I caught Williams' reflection in the mirrored tray on top of it.

I had the shotgun over my right shoulder, cocked. My finger tightened on the trigger.

Suddenly, for no reason that I could really explain, everything in the room just felt *wrong*.

A dark realisation hit me. That awkward smile wasn't scared: it was fake.

Bailey pulled back the curtain, all the way, and dodged sideways.

A body lay on the bed. Wearing a smock, but so heavily bloodstained that it was almost impossible to tell that the fabric had originally been white. Arms dangling freely from the side of the bed, eyes open, mouth smeared with even more crimson fluid.

"What have they done to you, Mason . . .?" I said.

Not Mason: Dr West. Her wild grey hair escaped into a frizzy mass, now slicked with her own blood.

"Now!" Bailey screamed. Her eyes flitted in Williams' direction.

Williams and Bailey tried to take advantage of my surprise, to capitalise on my shock at seeing the body.

But I was already reacting. Before I'd properly registered the thing behind the curtain, I spun sideways. Gun up: aimed at Bailey.

Whoever or whatever she was, she was not a professional soldier. Instead of moving out of my kill zone – the shotgun only had a limited range – she froze, put her hands up to her face.

Williams slammed his bodyweight into the right of my ribcage – hard enough to disrupt my aim. I fired the gun once, just missing Bailey. Shotgun pellets sprayed the wall of the cube and peppered the ceiling.

"You useless old fuck!" Williams yelled.

We crashed against the far wall. Williams was much stronger than he looked. I dragged the shotgun around to face him with one hand, grabbed for the slide with the other. Damned thing needed to be reloaded before I could shoot again.

He punched me in the face: a full-on blow. I felt a cheekbone snap, hot blood gushing from somewhere.

"Get him on there!" Bailey shouted, with a determination that marked her as a long-term accomplice. "The auto-doc!"

I scrambled against Williams. Brought the gun up again. He slammed into me once more. My fingers fumbled with the slide and I lost my grip on the shotgun.

I was shaking, so weak.

Bailey glared back at me. Smirking.

The smart-meds, I realised, weren't smart-meds at all.

Williams' elbow rose up. Connected with my face. I stumbled back, now feeling even more sluggish.

Bailey and Williams appeared in triplicate—

Jesus Christo.

Couldn't speak.

I collapsed against the side of the auto-doc, then into the waiting pod.

I felt the contoured plastic treatment table moulding around my shoulders, restraining me. There was no need for that: my body didn't seem to want to respond to my orders any more. The auto-doc's canopy whined as it descended over me – sealing me inside. It was an automatic reaction to snake my arms back, to avoid being caught as the pod sealed. The machine itself powered up with a nauseating purr.

An array of the auto-doc's medical tools was mounted inside the canopy. Wicked bladed forearms hovered overhead; laser-tipped probes cycling through treatment functions. Like a twisted metal spider, suspended in a web.

"Just kill him!" Bailey commanded.

Williams shook his head. "It isn't that easy. He's been a pain since he got here, and I want my pound of flesh."

"There's no time for that!"

"Like I said, it'll be the Warfighters that crack the Artefact. The Lazarus Legion is history."

Everything was blurring, sickeningly so. The room lights above me flashed. Williams loomed closer, a blot over the sun – a grinning idiot.

The auto-doc began to stream audio warnings so quickly that I couldn't keep up. Williams punched some keys on the control unit beside me. I pounded against the reinforced transparent plastic but it was useless. I was trapped inside.

"Shit out of luck this time, Lazarus," Williams said.

He roared with laughter. The auto-doc is a revolution in medical treatment, capable of treating the most hideously injured military personnel. If not healing, then at least getting them back on their feet. Williams didn't give a shit about those aspects of the machine. He wanted to inflict maximum damage. Bailey stood beside him, arms crossed over her chest, and they both looked down into my pod.

Inhumanly fast – machine fast – one of the super-sharp blades came down on my left arm. It was a clean, medical cut, but the location was random: piercing the mid-wrist, through muscle, through the ulna and radius bones. It missed the data-port in my forearm by mere centimetres.

The pain would've been unbearable, I'm quite sure, but at least Bailey's poisoned drugs had taken the edge off. Even so, I screamed – a slurred, drunken sound. This was real pain in my real body. I thought of Carrie. Thought of the tired old veterans with their metal hands. I remembered in that instant how I had feared ending up like them. Now it was happening.

The blade scythed right through my limb: powering down as it completed the amputation. Arterial spray coated the inside of the canopy and, seen through it, the two faces above me. I shouted some more through gritted teeth, tried to move inside the cramped confines of the pod. The procedure took seconds to complete. The auto-doc probably didn't like doing this sort of work: the continuous warning chime was evidence of that.

"By the way: that run up there?" Williams said. "It doesn't count. You used zero-G to finish it. So looks like you come second again."

He took another long drag on his cigarette. He had stopped smiling, was now just looking down at the pod—

Then, for the second time that day, something completely unexpected happened.

CHAPTER TWENTY-EIGHT

I'M LAZARUS

Bailey's head exploded.

At first, I thought that the blood was mine. But in my drug-induced, pain-wracked fervour, I realised that the blood now spraying the auto-doc canopy was from outside the pod.

In my debilitated state, I registered the sound of the gunshot a second later.

Bailey's blonde hair was a wash of brain and bone and blood. She slumped against the canopy.

Williams appeared as surprised as I was. He had no weapon – had been so sure of himself that he hadn't bothered to pick up my Remington – and turned on the spot, face contorted in angry disbelief.

Another gunshot.

It hit him in the upper chest, reducing his fatigues to a black pulp. He managed to remain standing – mouth open to yell something that he never had the chance to voice. The barrel of the Remington was suddenly jammed into his face: point-blank range.

Dealing with unruly crewmen. Exactly what it's for.

The shotgun barked again.

Williams' head exploded with a single well-placed shot.

I lay still in the pod, trying to evaluate what had just happened. The auto-doc's savage blades powered down. Like an insect drawing its legs up before flight, the medical tools adopted a relaxed position.

A friendly face appeared over me.

Tired, sallow; but friendly.

Private Dejah Mason.

"Jesus fuck, sir," she shouted, loud enough that I could hear her from inside the pod. "What's happening?"

I was weak – haemorrhaging from the open stump of my left arm – and didn't have the strength to explain. "Activate the cauterisation protocol," I said. "Now. Before I bleed out."

Mason nodded, and the machine began that stomach-turning buzzing – started its work again.

Uneducated Army grunts aren't typically trained in the use of the auto-doc. It's a precision device: carrying a significant price-tag. That said, trauma-models like that in the infirmary were often programmed with automated routines. Some commands are a matter of pressing the right keys and issuing the correct commands. That was exactly what Mason did.

It took about five minutes to seal the wound with a medical laser, then less than a minute to pump me with real smart-meds to deal with the pain. I felt like I was floating: either the result of the blood loss or because I was in severe shock. The machine ended the treatment programme by sealing the stump with a thick layer of transparent plasti-skin.

"Treatment is now complete," the auto-doc said. "Have a nice day."

Mason stood over the control console. Dressed in a tank top and shorts, barefoot; the salvaged Remington shotgun was still in her hand.

"Good work," I croaked. "Never let your gun out of your sight."

"You okay, sir?"

"I'll live. And you?"

"I've felt better," she said. She rolled her head around against her shoulders. "But I guess I don't really have grounds to complain."

She stared down at the stump of my left arm. It had been severed completely at the wrist. Under the water-proofed false skin, nanos were working away inside my body to coagulate my blood, making sure that I wouldn't bleed out. I was drenched in more than enough of that.

My severed hand lay on the treatment couch – fingers curled in a death-claw, already turning a sickening white.

"That's going to hurt when the drugs wear off," was all Mason could say.

"I'll worry about that when it happens." Perhaps it was a result of the smart-meds, but my dead hand was bizarrely hypnotic. It took some serious willpower to pull my eyes from it. "There's work to be done."

"I was in the cube, when I heard shouting," Mason said. "How long have I been asleep for? And since when was Captain Williams trying to kill you?"

"Since the whole world went to shit." I swivelled my legs out of the auto-doc and off the treatment couch, winced as I sat in my own blood. "It's a long story, but all you need to know right now is that the Directorate are here. On the *Colossus*."

"Where and how?"

"Unknown to both. We need to scramble the Legion, get

them operational. Listen Mason, I'm so sorry. I should never have pushed you like that."

Mason gave a nod. "Forget it."

"I'm going to make sure that this is done right. Make sure everyone gets out of this in one piece."

She gave a guilty smile at that. "Except for you."

"This is nothing that can't be fixed. A week in a regeneration tank and I'll be good as new."

That wasn't quite true; I was grossly oversimplifying things. Regrowing a hand in a regen tank wasn't easy and I'd heard that it was also an extremely painful experience. But I didn't want to think about that, and especially didn't want Mason thinking about it.

"I'm Lazarus. I always come back."

"For the Legion," Mason said.

"Let's get the comms station over in the SOC working. You take the shotgun."

"Affirmative."

I stepped over the corpses of Bailey and Williams. There was a lot of blood; pooled around the bodies, leaking out onto the white floor tiles. Among the remains of Williams' head, still on his lips but badly crumpled during the fall, was his cigarette.

"At least Williams is down," I said. "That's one less traitor to worry about . . ."

I paused, looked at his corpse. Maybe it was the blood loss. Maybe it was some deep intuition. Either way, something about his bone structure – about the underlying muscle tissue – bothered me.

I saw him with a split lip. I know that I did.

I reached down and scooped up the cigarette. It had absorbed a lot of blood: gone completely red.

"Mason, activate the chemical-analyser on the auto-doc."

She did as ordered, without hesitation, although she couldn't possibly have understood why I needed the analysis done. Only I'd been on the Artefact that night, and only I had seen Williams' bizarre behaviour with the cigarette.

It was just a hunch, nothing more. But as I considered the idea, it became less and less fanciful: more plausible.

The auto-doc sucked the remains of the bloodstained cigarette into its analyser. It took a few seconds to work. Then a read-out appeared on the monitor.

We both stood, looking at the results.

I wasn't sure what to say; wasn't sure what could be said.

"Does that mean what I think it does?" Mason eventually asked.

"I think so."

The chemical breakdown of the cigarette was concerning enough. The same analysis as that night on the Artefact. Extreme narcotic content, not just grown in Hydroponics but combined with other chems: no doubt provided by Bailey, in the perfect position to lift supplies from the infirmary and medical, right under Dr West's nose.

More worrying was the sub-analysis of the blood content. Three words glowed on the screen:

```
SIMULANT BLOOD DETECTED
SUBJECT: CAPTAIN LANCE WILLIAMS
```

"Williams," I said, "or at least *that* Williams, was a simulant."

"I guess that explains why it took two shots to put him down," Mason whispered. "But how is that possible?"

"When we first arrived here, Dr West bragged that the next-generation simulants were for more than direct combat. She even said that you could live in one indefinitely. That the sims were becoming second skins."

"Holy shit . . ."

"Williams isn't dead – not really dead, anyway." The cut on his lip: gone the next morning. It suddenly made sense. I nudged the body on the floor with my foot. "This body is a next-gen simulant."

It was the perfect cover. A traitor right under our noses, using next-gen simulants to minimise the risk to himself.

"I met him on the Run," I whispered. "He didn't come to save me. He came to make sure that I was dead . . ."

"Then where is the real Williams? Where's his real skin?"

"Who knows?" I said, thinking it through. "He could be hidden somewhere else on the *Colossus*. Hell, there are more than enough hiding places on this ship. Or maybe he's on one of the other Alliance warships; there are sixteen others in this fleet."

"We'll never find him," Mason said. "What about the other Warfighters? You think they're in on it too?"

"You ask a lot of questions," I said. I mustered the best smile that I could in the circumstances. "And I'm all out of answers. We need to get to the SOC, and we can investigate from there. One more thing before we go."

I reached down, and dragged Williams' body to the auto-doc. Given I only had one hand, that wasn't as easy as it should've been: Mason helped me get him into place. Then I activated the vibro-scalpel and sliced off his hand. *You took my hand, now I'll take yours.* Not that he noticed or cared. This version of him just looked back at me with half a face, eyes vacant and confused.

"I think that we might need this."

Mason cautiously covered every aspect of the deck as we moved, but we found the SOC as deserted as the rest of Medical.

"At least we've got power," she said. "But someone has already been here."

The simulators usually sat in two rows, facing each other like pieces on a holo-chess board. The Legion tanks were impassive, in sleep mode: a welcoming blue. All of the Warfighters' tanks were missing. The outlines of their simulators were imprinted on the floor, connecting cables strewn nearby.

"You think our tanks are safe?" Mason asked.

I quickly inspected them. They appeared intact, no obvious damage. I activated each in turn. Checked the diagnostics panels on the outer canopy.

"They look to be operational. They haven't been obviously sabotaged." I shook my head. "Williams was too damned sloppy for that."

"What would you have done?" Mason asked, as she powered up the communications station. Although the room was still cast in darkness, it seemed that most of the terminals were capable of running on emergency power.

"I'd have taken these tanks out the first opportunity I got."

"What about the sims?" Mason said. "Maybe they've been sabotaged."

"Only one way to find that out."

My missing hand throbbed, but my data-ports ached even more. I'd never felt the urge to climb into the tanks so strongly. Just by clambering in, by making transition to the waiting sim in the belly of the *Colossus*, I could end the pain in my arm, in my head, everywhere in my body. The idea of living in a sim – combat or next-gen – seemed more than appealing.

"Communications off-line," the AI chirped over the SOC speakers. "This starship is in a dark cycle. Authorisation required. User not recognised."

Mason swiped her thumb over the DNA reader attached to the comms station. Cursed as she received the same response.

"Williams must've locked me out."

"Let me," I said, nudging my way to the terminal.

I used Williams' dead hand. Swiped his cold thumb over the reader. It left a print in blood. "I knew it'd come in handy," I said.

Mason gave me an unimpressed stare.

"What?" I asked. "I'm facing certain death on a Directorate-infested starship, and I can't make a joke?"

"I thought you said that we were going to make it."

"I don't remember saying that at all."

"Maybe it was the meds talking."

"User recognised," the AI interrupted. "Communications active."

The general channel suddenly erupted with sound. Gunfire, screams. Shouts in Chino – I'd heard the language enough times to understand when it was being spoken, even if I didn't understand the words – and Standard.

"Can you identify the brig?"

Mason shook her head. "The individual stations are still locked out."

"Then can you open to broadcast on all decks?"

"That I can do, but it's a one-way link." Mason manipulated the controls. "Go ahead."

I leant over the station, into the microphone. "This is Major Conrad Harris."

Mason watched me very keenly. The irrational, misplaced optimism that surged behind her eyes was almost crushing.

"Many of you will know me as Lazarus," I said. I let that sink in for whoever was listening. "The *Colossus* is my ship, and I know her well. So long as I breathe, I'm not going to give her up. I want every goddamned Directorate fuck on this ship to understand one thing: I'm coming for you. For every life you take today, I will take ten. No one is going to be left alive."

I imagined my words streaming out of the speakers across the ship. Through the corridors, through the crew decks. If there was anyone loyal left alive on this ship, I just hoped that they would give them a glimmer of hope. Some sliver of assurance, to encourage them to keep fighting.

"For the Alliance," I whispered, then closed the line.

Mason and I stood there for a little while: listening to the sounds of battle developing around us. Those were unmistakable now. Not nearby, but drifting through the air-ducts and maintenance shafts. I wasn't sure how long we'd have before they reached Medical. Williams' words haunted me: "That bulkhead on the way in is six inches of hardened steel. Nothing is coming through that door without a demo-charge or a plasma rifle." The Warfighters had both of those things.

"What do we do?" Mason asked. She was still clutching the shotgun.

"I'm skinning up."

"Then I am too." She nodded. Stepped for her simulator.

"No," I said. "I can't allow you to do that. I want you to guard the SOC. Break out whatever weapons they have in Medical, but stay here."

"You can't go alone."

"I'll use my tank, make transition, and head for the brig. Kaminski will be there. If I'm still alive, I'll move on the CIC."

"Why the CIC?"

I stripped out of my fatigues. They were crusted with dry blood. "Because I need to see how high this goes. If

387

Loeb's Directorate – and I've reason to suspect he is – then I'll take him down first."

"Aim for the head, and sever the command chain?"

"Something like that. And Mason – one more thing," I said, pausing as I climbed into my tank.

"Yes, sir?"

"You did good, New Girl. You did real good."

"Thanks, sir. I appreciate it."

I nodded. The amniotic fluid of the tank was warming. The canopy snapped into place and the respirator attached to my face. I sealed myself in my tank. Began to jack-in with the cables.

"If they make it through that door," I said, into the communicator, "then you know what to do."

"I won't let them take either of us alive."

She smiled; harsh and practical. Martian, through and through.

I bobbed in the simulator. Blood streamed from my tortured arm, clouding the perfect blue amniotic. The liquid was acidic against the open flesh and stung painfully – probably breaking down the cauterised layer, maybe even the plastic coating that the auto-doc had treated it with.

With my only hand, I keyed COMMENCE TRANSITION and closed my eyes.

I was resurrected.

I was whole again.

I flexed both hands and felt the powered gauntlets of the combat-suit responding. The aching in my head that I'd felt since the incident on the Run was completely gone. The dizziness caused by blood loss was replaced by hyper-vigilance.

TRANSITION CONFIRMED, my HUD indicated.

"This is more like it," I said, my voice filling my helmet.

The combat-suit was booting up. The firing tube started to thrum. Machinery prepared to propel my drop-capsule out into space. Every remaining copy of me was inside the launch bay, every sim prepared to fire on the Artefact. But, for now at least, my fight was elsewhere.

My combat-suit read my thought-stream.

ABORT LAUNCH? the HUD asked.

"Abort," I confirmed.

It was dark inside the capsule and I couldn't see what was happening outside, but I knew the firing mechanism had begun the abort sequence. There was an abrupt jolt as the capsule was removed from the launch queue.

CAPSULE REJECTED – REMOVING TO LAUNCH BAY, my HUD explained.

I was being shunted past the queue of waiting sims, each individually sealed in drop-capsules. I felt the safety webbing relax. The capsule slid back up the firing tube, back into the launch bay.

"Open capsule."

The coffin door slid open and I clambered free.

It felt like I was rising from the grave.

"You there, Mason?" I asked, over the comm-link. "Talk to me."

"Yes, sir."

"Transition confirmed. I'm in the launch bay."

"I don't have visual down there, but I've called up deck plans for the *Colossus*. Let me know what I can do to help."

"I need you to be my eyes and ears. I'm broadcasting my vid-feed; patch in so you can see what I'm doing."

"Affirmative. I have your signal."

Like the rest of the ship, the launch bay was in darkness. That was no hindrance to me: my tactical-helmet activated night-vision. There were numerous other firing tube hatches set into the floor, each housing dozens of pre-armed and pre-armoured simulants: the Legion and the Warfighters.

I cycled my M95 plasma rifle and slaved it to the auto-targeting software. The HUD illuminated with indicators. I fixed a heavy strobe light to the rail mount, tested it against the wall. The bright lamp flicked rapidly: was often used to blind opponents, employed during ship-boarding operations. I had in mind just that use.

I did a cursory check of my equipment and weapons.

Assorted grenades on my chest harness.

Power cells clipped to my belt.

PPG-13 plasma pistol holstered on my right thigh.

A flame-thrower unit, with a full tank of juice, strapped to my back.

Sim-issue mono-blade sheathed on my left boot.

Null-shield generator attached to my right forearm.

Wrist-comp attached to my left forearm.

A full complement of twelve surveillance drones mounted in my backpack.

Thruster pack primed and ready to fire.

Oxygen tanks charged and good for twelve hours EVA.

There were crates of weapons in the corner of the bay, still sealed and awaiting distribution. I sorted through those; clipped some more grenades to my suit. Smokes, hi-ex, incendiary: anything that might be useful. I took two demo-charges, smaller low-yield versions of those Jenkins usually carried. I attached a simulant-sized shotgun to my back-plate; a monstrous Westington Mk 6 – a weapon that made the Remington 900 look like a toothpick. I took a portable plasma welder and clipped that to my belt.

"Do you have enough weapons now?" Mason asked.

"That last choice wasn't a weapon. I have everything I need but I'm not done yet."

I took one final look around the launch bay.

Each of the tubes set in the floor was labelled with the name of an operator. I crouched over four of the tubes, inspected the hatches. I primed four hi-ex grenades, twisting the manual activation caps, and tossed them down the tubes. Then I ran towards the bay exit doors. The grenades had a five-second fuse, and as I made it to the doors I felt the floor beneath me absorb the force of the explosion.

All four of the Warfighters' firing tubes were disabled.

"Will that help?" Mason asked.

"I don't know. I expect that they have simulants among the fleet elsewhere. Even if it doesn't, it sure felt good."

"I copy that."

I glanced back at the mess; savoured the sight. Smoke trailed from each of the armoured hatches, now buckled and shredded. The firing tubes for my squad were safe and useable but if Williams or the other traitors tried to make a drop direct from the *Colossus*, they would be shit out of luck. That felt like a small victory.

"Plot me a course to the brig," I said to Mason. "Kaminski will be my first objective. Having two operators in the tanks will significantly improve our odds."

"I can always make transition. I'm feeling up to it."

"Negative, Mason. Stay put; defend the SOC and Medical."

There was a lot more to it than that. I didn't want Mason in the tank because I feared that she wouldn't come back: that dying in her sim would mean real death. I had more than enough blood on my hands. True: another simulant would make a huge difference, but I'd already gambled with her life once, letting her come here and allowing a green recruit on the Legion.

There was a long pause, as though Mason was considering refusing the order, before she finally answered, "Affirmative."

"Can you get the bay doors open?"

"I can do that. Williams' DNA lets me into lots of the systems. He must've programmed viral loops into the *Colossus'* AI."

The enormous doors suddenly ground into motion, parting before me. I covered the corridor beyond with my plasma rifle. Let my bio-scanner probe the shadows.

Nothing.

The scanner could probably probe this deck; the ship's heavy metal construction made the device less reliable in predicting signals above and below my location. Whatever was happening on the ship, it hadn't yet reached the cargo decks. That didn't mean much, because the launch bay was in the very bowel of the starship, but it gave me some breathing room if nothing else.

"Hangar bays are seeing the most activity right now," Mason said. "I have some partial spy-eye footage."

"What are they doing?"

"Docking and unloading Interceptors. Looks like they have a lot of manpower."

"How many ships?"

"I don't think that you want to know. I'm broadcasting the route to the brig right now. I'd definitely recommend you stay away from the hangar decks."

The hangars were several decks directly above me. I scanned over the downloaded maps, considered the best course.

I crept out of the launch bay, closed the doors behind me. Once that was done, I activated one of my drones.

SENTRY MODE, I instructed.

The drone bobbed in the air. Hovered obediently above the bulkhead door.

"Stay with me as I go," I said to Mason.

"I don't have anything better to do."

"And you never know," I said, grinning in the dark, "you might even learn something."

"Be careful, Major. You don't know what you'll find out there."

"Don't worry about me. I'm stone cold."

A corridor or so from the drop-bay, I found the first Alliance casualty.

A crewman in Alliance Navy fatigues. Hanging upside down, by the ankles, from a rafter in the ceiling. Although the body was still warm, vitals were completely extinguished. The man's head had been punctured with two shots from a kinetic slug-thrower; a heavy-calibre pistol, I reckoned. The Directorate were old-fashioned like that – they preferred kinetics to energy weapons.

"Is that what they do to captives?" Mason whispered over the comm.

Thick blood pooled beneath the corpse. The man's hands ended in stumps; likely hacked off with a sword or bladed implement. Probably one of their mono-swords, but through unarmoured skin that would be total overkill. I followed the line of the body to the ad hoc binding above me: noted that the poor bastard was missing his feet as well.

"Looks that way. I don't have time to cut him down, but log the location on your terminal."

"Affirmative."

I edged around the corpse. It gently swayed.

"Do you remember Far Eye?" Mason said. She spoke slowly; almost reluctantly.

"Of course."

"In the corridor outside Saul's lab, you told me that the Krell always seemed to do just fine. You said that the Krell are one of nature's bad jokes."

I recalled the conversation well enough. "I remember."

"You maybe think that we're the other one?"

"I've known the answer to that for a long time."

With nothing more I could do for the crewman, I prowled onwards.

Soon there were more dead.

Several had been displayed like the Navy man. Almost all looked as though they had been caught by surprise – execution-style shootings, sometimes at workstations or en masse in corridors.

"Let's hope the Legion are buckled down somewhere," Mason said.

"Just as long as they aren't like that. No way for a soldier to die. I'll save them all, then I'll save Elena."

"What was that, sir? I didn't copy."

"Nothing, Mason. Just talking to myself."

"You're coming up on the brig."

"Ah, shit," I whispered.

The bulkhead doors were all open and there was no one alive at the checkpoint. An Alliance Marine had been executed where he sat. I sent a drone ahead of me into the brig. It was dark and still inside, and I used the remote camera to ensure that the area was secure.

Jesus. Secure is the wrong word.

Inside the perimeter, another Marine had been shot in the stomach. Many of his organs were sluiced across the floor.

I switched on my suit-speakers. "Kaminski? You in here?"

No response. The drone reported no heat signatures, no movement. I stalked further into the brig, plasma rifle up. I was just looking for an excuse to shoot someone or something.

"Kaminski!" I called again. "Saul!"

Saul's cell was ahead. It was dark and empty; the metal-barred door open. I flicked on my rifle-lamp: threw a beam of white light into the chamber. Better to see this with my own eyes – to face the horror of it.

A body had been hung from the ceiling. Same as the others: hands and feet gone.

"Fuck it!" I roared. "I'm too late."

"There was nothing you could do," Mason implored. "You went right to him—"

This body had been inexpertly hung. It had been tied with a length of cable, enough slack that the body twisted about-face. One of my drones flew ahead and scanned the corpse.

I frowned. Moved up on the cell, my lamp jittering over the body. It was surely dead – my HUD confirmed the lack of any heartbeat – but it was also wrong.

"It . . . it's not him!" Mason stammered.

The body in the rafters was a Directorate Sword. Armour stripped back, face wearing an expression of surprise. Neither rifle nor sidearm were with the corpse; even the commando's sword was missing from the holster on his leg.

"The blood," Mason whispered. "Look down."

There was plenty of it – liberally sprayed on the ground, up the walls. From the spatter-pattern, I guessed that the Sword had been killed in this chamber. Maybe coming to investigate Saul, maybe coming to free him. Could it be Kaminski in waiting?

"Yeah, I see the blood," I said.

"Not that – I mean the marking."

Daubed in blood, the crude drawing was instantly identifiable. A pyramid, with an eye at the pinnacle.

The Lazarus Legion.

Beneath that was an arrow, pointing back into the outer brig. The whole thing had been drawn beneath the corpse; like the insane iconography of some cult practising human sacrifice.

"He's alive," Mason said. "Kaminski, I mean. He wanted you to know."

I followed the arrow, lighting up the floor with my rifle-lamp. Another appeared. Then another. All pointing to the back wall of the crew station. I traced the objective, searching for indications that someone was left alive back there.

"The wily little shit . . ."

The wall ahead of me was marked with the same symbol, on a piece of sheet-metal. That immediately looked out of place and I quickly identified that it was from the ceiling. I panned my light up, but found no movement. Instead, I wrenched the sheet of metal from the wall.

Behind the sheet was a warning in bold letters: EMERGENCY EVACUATION POD. A terminal screen – previously concealed by the metal cover – flashed with an update: POD FIRED – PLEASE PROCEED TO DECK A-19 FOR FURTHER EMERGENCY FACILITIES.

I smiled to myself. It wasn't much of a plan, but it had obviously worked.

"So, that's where he's gone," Mason said. "He's alive."

Some hope was better than none. Kaminski was probably, as of now, floating in near-space – with or without Saul – inside an evac-pod. It would be cramped but they'd survive for a few days; they had food and air. The pod would broadcast a distress signal, would await pick-up.

"I'm moving on," I declared to Mason. "I need to get to the CIC – track down the rest of the Legion and order a pick-up for Kaminski."

"There are likely hostiles all around your location. You might want to be ready for a fight. I'll send the fastest route to your suit."

I checked over the maps again. On foot, it was a long journey to the CIC. The elevators were all down; I'd have to use the ladders and other access shafts. Even in a sim, that wouldn't be an easy journey . . .

My audio pick-ups detected a sound nearby.

A child's voice. Whispering from the crawlspace above.

"Carrie?" I asked. "Is that you?"

It was the voice I'd heard on the Artefact, when I'd first seen Elena.

Something moved in the ceiling, where the metal covering had been removed. There were airshafts and maintenance ducts up there; kilometres of empty tunnels used by the air-recyclers. Just like the storm drains. I heard someone moving above me, an encouraging whisper.

"Come on, Con," came my sister's voice. "You scared?"

"No, Carrie. Not any more."

Mason was babbling over the comm, asking me who or what I was talking to, but I filtered her out.

My bio-scanner glowed with hot targets: too many to individualise. The sounds of gunfire and screaming had become defined. In the distance, my enhanced hearing detected the *boom-boom-boom* of heavy footsteps: someone or something starting a slow plod across the deck. I couldn't tell what that was, but I didn't like the sound of it one bit.

"I'm not taking the direct route," I said. "These fuckers aren't going to know what's hit them."

"If you say so," Mason answered.

I gave chase.

Once I was in the tunnels, Mason's maps didn't help me any more. I was off the grid: only guided by Carrie's voice. Sometimes, I saw her ahead of me. But she was always too fast to catch; always coaxing me onwards.

The tunnels were damned tight. They were barely wide enough to accommodate my sim in full armour and not made for supporting that sort of weight. But if I crawled on my belly with my rifle beneath me, they were just big enough; and although occasionally the structures creaked as I moved, they held firm.

I made fast and effective progress through the *Colossus*. No one suspected that Alliance personnel would use these tunnels. They stank of chemical residue, were sometimes scalding hot with steam-flows. I just switched to my internal oxygen supply and got on with it.

"They're ahead!" Carrie called. "Don't let them see me."

"I won't let them get you this time."

I saw spikes of yellow light breaking the gloom: a grate set into the floor of the shaft. I shuffled into position. The grate was barely a metre wide but gave a perfect vantage point into the corridor below. The heartbeat sensor on my HUD identified four live targets.

"What are you waiting for, pussy?" Carrie said, with my mother's laugh. She lingered further down the tunnel, still half in shadow.

The Directorate commandos were in formation, moving slowly: rifles up, covering the corridor. The graphics on my tactical-helmet painted them in perfect clarity. They were so close. Bloodlust arose within me like a hunger.

I disengaged a surveillance drone from my backpack.

REMAIN HERE, I thought-commanded.

ORDER ACKNOWLEDGED, the drone responded.

The Directorate commandos were directly beneath me now. I fought the compulsion to reveal my position.

I took a hi-ex grenade from my harness; checked the diameter. It was small enough to fit through the grate. Then I shuffled off further down the shaft, leaving the drone behind. I moved fast: conscious that I didn't want the commandos going too far.

Once I was a few metres away from the grille, I issued more commands.

COMMENCE AUDIO ALARM, I told the drone. MAXIMUM VOLUME.

ORDER ACKNOWLEDGED, flashed on my HUD.

The drone suddenly began a loud beeping.

The Directorate Swords paused, all rifles aimed at the noisy drone.

I flipped a grenade. It bounced along the tunnel, between the spars of the grate and to the ground below.

A brief, irrelevant volley of gunfire stitched the thin metal surfaces around me. Then the grenade went off and the Directorate fell silent. I was well out of the threat radius. The explosive rattled the structure around me, releasing dust and fine particulate into the air, but the explosion was too far away to cause a collapse.

The four heartbeats on my HUD were extinguished: dead.

It went on from there. I remained quiet and used surprise whenever possible. It was easy to tag the Directorate: they were in far greater numbers than the Alliance resistance, and they were always on the offensive.

When I found the Swords, I killed them.

I used my combat-suit to mimic voices, called recorded phrases in Chino over my loudspeakers. When the commandos came to investigate, I dropped grenades from the concealed shafts, flipped overcharged power cells. Always moved on before they could find me; used smoke and flash-bang grenades as cover. Carrie's aim was always true.

"I'd never have thought this was your style," Mason said to me.

Her voice was a comfort in the organised chaos, but also an intrusion into the world I was suddenly sharing with Carrie.

"What do you mean?" I grunted, negotiating a bend in the corridor.

"Doing things discreetly."

I gave a cold laugh. "Then there's a lot you don't know about me. I was Alliance Special Forces before I was inducted into Sim Ops."

"I know. I read about it. But I thought that you'd left all that behind."

"You never leave it behind. Fear is a weapon; you've just got to know when to use it. How many have I killed so far?"

"I'm not sure," Mason said. "Thirty-seven?"

The sounds of battle were becoming more intense; the shaft walls and floor sometimes reverberating as a heavier weapon was discharged. People were shouting, yelling not in confusion but in a more ordered fashion. Someone was giving orders down there.

"How far to the CIC?" I asked.

"Your exact location isn't that clear on my map, but maybe two hundred metres."

"All right."

"I've managed to reprogram some more of the spy-cams from the main approach corridor. It looks clear, if you're quick."

"Which way do I go?"

"I'm not sure."

"I wasn't talking to you, Mason," I said.

Ahead of me, Carrie was crouching in the tunnel: her eyes reflecting the low light like two small jewels. She grinned.

"This way, Con."

By the time I reached the end of the tunnel, Carrie was gone.

I braced myself against the shaft wall. There was a hatch beneath me, near to a corridor junction. I raised both feet then slammed hard against it. The metal gave way with a gentle thump. I dropped from the shaft into the corridor below.

Gunfire, boots bouncing off the deck plating: both were nearby, but the activity wasn't immediate. The distant mechanical thumping; probably a couple of decks away. *What is that noise?* There was no time to investigate. I dropped a smoke grenade and dashed for the CIC.

The bulkhead door was shut but it had taken a heavy toll. Burn marks, laser-fire and frag dimpled the outer door. That told me something. Loeb might be loyal after all. It also meant that the Directorate wanted the *Colossus* in one piece: if they had really wanted to burn the operation, they would have demo-charged the whole CIC. I reasoned that the officer cadre, or what was left of it, was probably locked down inside.

Behind me, two automated sentry guns dangled from the

ceiling: no operating lights, no hint of movement. In ordinary circumstances, those would be tracking targets like crazy – defending the CIC. I registered Alliance Marines piled outside. The last line of defence, spent.

A lone security camera peered down from above the door. I looked up, let the lens focus on me.

"Callsign: Chicago."

CHAPTER TWENTY-NINE

YOU HAVE THE CHOICE OF SURRENDER

The doors to the CIC slowly opened, revealing the chamber beyond.

"R . . . response: cl . . . claret," someone stammered in my direction.

My HUD flagged twelve Alliance Marines. They aimed carbines at me, laser dots from their weapon sights skating over my camo-skin.

"The area is secure," I canted over my suit-speakers. "Get this door shut, and those guns out of my face."

The officer in charge of the security team gave a slow nod, lowered his weapon. The others gradually did the same. The door hummed shut behind me.

I stepped over the threshold into the CIC and took in what was left of the *Colossus'* crew. There were twenty or so officers, all hooked into their consoles. Loeb, over at the tactical display, with Flight Lieutenant James.

I blew the catches on my helmet. Made eye contact with as many personnel as I could.

"Anyone in here wants to declare Directorate affiliation, then do it now. It'll be easier that way. I promise: if there are traitors here, I will find them. There's nowhere to hide any more."

No one dared move. No one came forward. I kept my finger on the firing stud of my rifle; watched for any reaction. The CIC was frozen.

I nodded. "Good. Then let's save this fleet and as many Alliance souls as we can."

Lieutenant James was in his simulant, dressed in his G-suit. He gave me a crooked smile. Loeb pointed an angry stare in my direction, but gave a slow nod. His dress uniform was in disarray, bald head sweated. I had never seen him look so dishevelled.

"We heard your performance over the PA," Loeb said. "And rest assured that we want the same thing. But it could be too late."

"It's never too late. Who gave the dark order?"

"The Directorate have a fleet. When the initial proximity alarm went off, we mistook it for a Krell war-fleet. I issued the dark order."

"Show me."

Loeb swiped a hand at the tactical display. A holo of near-space appeared on the desk. The only familiar aspect was the Artefact – the ever-present focal point. The rest was completely new: the fleet was in total disorder, the cordon replaced by a ragged line of Alliance ships. Warning markers flashed over several of the holos, indicating severe structural damage. Smaller, unidentified starships flittered around the *Colossus*. Worst of all, the AI seemed to be having difficulty separating friend from foe – even as I watched, some vessels flashed red as hostiles, then flickered to green.

"We can't even rely on our own systems any more,"

Loeb said. "This will give you an idea of the scale of the problem."

He called up some real-time vid-feeds from external cameras across the Alliance battlegroup.

"Jesus . . ." I whispered.

The Asiatic Directorate built their ships well. The Directorate had been in space for as long as the Alliance. The People's Republic of China, as it was once known, had been one of the first Old Earth nations to enter the Space Race. They had been constructing ships, specifically warships, for a long time: honing the science, perfecting the art.

I took in every detail. The nearest Directorate starship was within a klick of the *Colossus*, moored alongside her. A name was printed on the flank – the tac-display gave a translation as *Shanghai Remembered*. She was much smaller than the *Colossus*, and in a stand-up fight would probably be outgunned and under-armoured. But this was no stand-up fight. From the jagged black-plated flanks, to the sharp-nosed bridge module – she exuded the menacing aura of an assassin. Small lights blinked along her belly as she disgorged another flight of Interceptors. Weapons pods mounted on her spine were trained on the *Colossus*. I couldn't identify what firepower she was packing, but I guessed railguns of some description. *Shanghai* was the pinnacle of ship-building art; a primary example of the Second Space Race and the dark rewards it had yielded.

"She's a destroyer-class starship," Loeb muttered. "A fast-response ship. Manoeuvrable and light as they come given her pattern. There are sixteen of them out there."

Directorate battleships mingled with the Alliance fleet – several destroyer-class vessels, but also a handful of other Directorate ships. They shared that common heritage: angry-looking, almost insectile in design, low-albedo.

"They're using advanced systems jamming software," Loeb said.

"Can we counter it?" I said.

"We're trying, but our entire system has been compromised; even the back-up redundancies. There are a number of sleeper viral and malware programs infesting the AI – probably inserted into our command suite by Directorate agents. The rest of the fleet is in just as bad a condition."

"Can you cancel the dark order?" I asked.

"I've been locked out of command access."

"I'd say that they planned it that way," said James. "Catching us when our guard was down."

"I know who's responsible," I said.

"I assume Saul," Loeb said. "But how could he have orchestrated this from the brig?"

I shook my head. "We were wrong when we identified Professor Saul as the traitor."

I mentally crumpled at the thought of almost executing the Professor; stayed only by Jenkins' hand.

"Then who is responsible?" Loeb said. "They must've had someone on the inside to pull this off—"

"Williams is the defector," I said. "Mason killed him. Well, kind of."

"That sly bastard . . ." Loeb gave an exasperated sigh, looked down at the floor. "What do you mean 'kind of'?"

"He tried to kill me in the infirmary, but Mason shot him. We ran some tests on his blood: he was using a next-gen simulant." I let that sink in, then added: "Mason can send the results to the CIC, if you want proof. She's manning Medical."

"But the Warfighters only have access to combat sims," James said. "How could he . . .?"

"I don't know. And right now, all that matters is that he

isn't to be trusted. I reckon that he has been using next-gen sims to get around the ship. The Warfighters' tanks are gone from the SOC. They could be anywhere."

"I'll issue a detain-on-sight order," Loeb said.

"I'd make that shoot on sight," I corrected. "For him, and the rest of the Warfighters."

Lincoln padded around the edge of the tactical display, snarling in my direction. An officer held him back, pulling at his collar. I shot the dog a glare and made a sudden movement with my head. Lincoln immediately leapt back, cowering from me.

"Looks like your method of sim detection just got a whole lot more complex," I said. "Lincoln won't do any more. Why aren't the Alliance space force taking on the Directorate ships?"

James shook his head. "Because most of my flight crew are pinned down in the mess hall. They can't get to the docking bay, so they can't fly. And there's another problem . . ."

"Tell me everything," I said.

Even more colour seemed to drain from Loeb's face. "Twenty-three minutes ago a Krell Collective made real-space in the Damascus moon-fields."

This was getting worse by the minute. The tac-display expanded to show the entire Damascus Rift region; that shattered graveyard where the Krell had previously appeared. The shoal of xeno-ships was hunting through the assorted debris again. The sensor-reads were poor – sporadically descending into gibberish – but the message was clear enough.

The Krell were back.

"The same Collective as yesterday?"

"That's what the bio-signatures suggest," Loeb said, sullenly. "It seems like more than just a coincidence. The

Directorate attack came within minutes of our detection of the Krell incursion."

"God doesn't do coincidences . . ." I whispered.

"They haven't detected us yet but it's only a matter of time. I don't know what stealth systems the Directorate ships have, but it looks like they are running hot."

It made a perverse sense. The Directorate had been organising this raid for a long time: it had probably taken months of planning. Their starships were faster than ours but even with a top-end Q-drive the journey from Directorate space to the Damascus Rift would've taken months of real-time. I rapidly made the calculations in my head and decided that the enemy fleet had likely embarked shortly after we'd left *Liberty Point*. I wanted to probe the implications of that – had the Directorate known about the mission? – but I reined my thought-stream back.

"The Directorate ships were probably waiting in Damascus Space," I said. "Perhaps they were invisible to our sensors, but not those of the Krell war-fleet. Maybe the Krell were drawn here as a result."

I considered the situation. Our guard was down: the Directorate were aboard the *Colossus*, and we couldn't fight back.

"We need to take the *Colossus* back," I said. "What about the Lazarus Legion? Where are they?"

Loeb punched more keys on the terminal. The holo shifted to show the mess hall, a direct vid-feed from security cameras. The place had seen better days. There were upturned tables across the hall; makeshift barricades which Alliance military personnel were using as cover. There, behind one of the tables, were two familiar figures: Jenkins and Martinez. Both in their real skins, dressed in shipboard fatigues. Looked like they had a shotgun between them, maybe a flare gun:

no proper hardware. Other figures moved behind them, laying down a veil of covering fire.

I could see that Jenkins had been hit. She was bleeding from somewhere; a black stain over her stomach.

"I have to save them," I said. "I have to get them out of there."

"It's gone too far for that," Loeb said. "I have a duty to the Navy, to the Alliance. I can't risk classified intelligence getting into enemy hands."

"Then what are you proposing?"

Loeb sighed. "I have to blow the *Colossus*' energy core and destroy our data-stacks. I should have given the order already, but we're locked out of some of the subroutines. Lieutenant Udin thinks he can countermand those."

Self-destruction. The ultimate sanction: a weapon to deny the enemy not just the starship, but also the intelligence engines that it carried.

That was an option of last resort. I wasn't going to allow that, not on my watch.

"There has to be an alternative," I said.

"I can't see one."

There was still anger in him; still the coals of hate, but he was tired – almost a spent force. *Aren't we all?*

"We need to create a distraction," I said. The pieces were falling into place: slowly but surely. "A really fucking big distraction."

"That would take the heat off the Alliance fleet," James said. "Surely you can't be suggesting . . .?"

"The Krell," I said. "We call the Krell here."

Admiral Loeb let out a pained laugh.

He faltered, and went chokingly quiet, when he realised that no one else in the CIC had joined him.

"Are you out of your mind?" he said. "We've got more than enough to deal with from the Directorate. And you want to bring another threat to our doorstep?"

I met Loeb's gaze. A tension arose around me, between us, and the CIC settled into another anxious silence.

"The Krell are already here. It's only a matter of time before they find us. I want to give the Directorate a distraction they can't ignore. And I can't think of a bigger threat than a Krell war-fleet."

It was a simple matter of logistics: a callous numbers' game.

Loeb pointed to the Krell fleet, still nosing through the moonlets. "If we alert them to our presence, they'll destroy us all! They won't care whether we're Alliance or Directorate! It'll be a death-sentence!"

James interjected: "I don't want to do this either, but right now the Krell are the biggest Christo-damned guns we have at our disposal."

Loeb searched the faces of his nearest officers – for allies among his staff.

He found none.

"How exactly do you propose to execute this plan?" he asked.

"I want to take the Key into the Artefact. I'll take it to the Hub. I'll activate the Artefact and it will start broadcasting. It'll draw the Krell here."

I left out that I also intended to save Elena; that my plan gave me another excuse to get aboard the Artefact and rescue her too. It was a selfish goal, but I couldn't leave here without getting her out of that accursed place.

"That isn't a plan," Loeb went on. "You don't know how long it will take the Artefact to start broadcasting – how long the Krell will take to respond! There are too many variables, and in the meantime the fleet are caught in the middle."

"There's more," I said. "Saul told me what the Artefact really is."

"And no one thought to share that intel with me?" Loeb said.

I left that question unanswered. Every passing second was wasted time, while my team were pinned down in the mess hall. While Elena was still aboard the Artefact.

"Saul told me that the Artefact is a gateway – a portal. I don't know how it works, or even if it will work. But if he's right, then we can use it to jump Damascus Space. Is the lab still secure?"

Loeb called up some security schematics, a handful of poor-quality vid-captures. He zoomed in on the spy-eye in the laboratory. The area was swarming with Directorate commandos. Terminals had been set alight, machines overturned. There, in the centre of the lab, still encased in the glass prison, sat the Key. It sparked, flickered: as though it was responding to the horrors elsewhere on the ship. Even the Directorate knew that it was too precious to be handled except by specialised staff. Those would come later, once the *Colossus* had been pacified.

"If you do this," Loeb said, begrudgingly, "then what do you want us to do?"

"I want you to fight back. Get comms up and running – work on cancelling the dark order. I'm going to the mess hall to get my squad and the flight crews. Two more simulants will turn the tide of the war on this ship, and the Legion can escort the flyboys to the launch deck. We'll get the Hornets spaceborne."

"Even if your sergeant is injured?" Loeb asked, brusquely.

"She'll do her duty," I said. "If she's alive, she'll want to make transition."

Loeb didn't know that my real body had been injured

too. Just going on: that was what real soldiers, and especially sim operators, did best.

"Priority is to make a pick-up," I said. "When the Directorate attacked, Kaminski and Saul evacuated the ship in an escape pod. I want fighters searching for him. Make sure he's aboard. That'll give us two points to defend: the SOC and the CIC. The SOC is a priority. It's the weak underbelly of any simulant operation. Meanwhile, I'll get down to the lab deck and retrieve the Key."

"That's a lot of distance to cover," Loeb said. "I want to believe that you can do this, but I can only give you an hour. If you aren't done by then, I'll have no option but to blow the core and initiate self-destruct."

I nodded. "And if I activate the Artefact – if Saul's theory about it acting as a Shard Gate is right – then be damned ready to use it."

"Understood," said Loeb.

I slipped my helmet back on, watched my HUD dance with graphics. All this talk was getting to me. There was fighting to be done.

"Good hunting," James said.

I nodded. "Get ready to move on the hangar bay."

Loeb saluted me, as I turned back towards the CIC doors. Marines and crew parted, eyes on me: their last and only hope.

"I can do this," I said. "An hour will be plenty."

I double-timed it through the ship.

The whispering was back – Carrie's footfalls leading me on. She always seemed to know the way; the best routes, working them out before Mason. The disorder across the *Colossus* allowed me to move on my objective quickly. I avoided combat; didn't want to get bogged down in a protracted firefight.

"What else can I do, sir?" Mason asked. "I want to help."

"You're helping plenty, Mason."

"I want to get back into my sim. The Legion needs me. Maybe I could follow you over to the mess hall—"

"No. You're doing more than enough."

"But . . ."

"I want you to sit tight. That's an order."

"Solid copy."

"I have to do this, then I can get the Key," I said, running a checklist of objectives in my head. "Have you got visual on the mess hall yet?"

Mason paused, and I thought that I heard her swallow hard over the link. "There are lots of Directorate. They're moving from the lab deck to the mess hall. They've got the place under siege. Looks like they are setting up barricades—"

That enormous thumping sound continued all around me.

"What is that noise?" I asked. It had been plaguing me for some time; always just out of detection range, but drawing closer wherever I went. "Sounds like machinery . . ."

"I'm not sure," she said. "I've just lost the hangar deck cams. They were unloading something big, but I didn't see what it was. I . . . I'd say that they know you're coming. There's an air-shaft above you. Maybe you could use that – drop down behind them—"

"The thing about stealth," I said, interrupting Mason, "is knowing when not to use it."

"Copy that. Good luck. I'm going off-line for a while – I'll try to work on a security patch, see if I can get some more cams working."

"You do that."

I didn't want any distractions from the task. I was done with stealth. This called for a direct assault. I wanted them to know that I was coming; wanted them to fear me.

I activated my external suit-speakers.

"You have the choice of surrender. I can guarantee that you will not be afforded any rights under the New Geneva Convention. I will treat you as you've treated my people; without compassion or mercy. I will make it fast, although not painless."

I unclipped a smoke grenade from my harness. Primed it, then tossed it around the corner.

The action was met with a volley of kinetic gunfire. Hard rounds churned up the corridor wall but I was back around the corner before any could hit me.

With a thought, I activated my drones. *Scout ahead. Be my eyes.* They silently detached from my suit. Although they broadcast grainy, low-res imagery, the drones used the same multi-vision modes as my suit. Suddenly, I could see the Directorate.

What am I dealing with here? They had the mess hall entrance under siege. There was smoke and debris everywhere, makeshift barricades established every few metres. Twenty, maybe thirty, Directorate Swords. Their suits were good; they emitted very little heat, and barely showed up on infrared.

It won't be enough. They are all dead.

"Come out, Alliance!" someone shouted in poor Standard.

I suspended my looped message for a second.

"Fuck you," I yelled back. My suit translated into machine-Chino.

Then I activated the loop again.

Someone whistled further down the corridor.

"This guy is crazy," my suit AI translated.

"Something like that."

I crouched, rolled another grenade along the corridor floor.

"Respirators!" a Sword shouted.

I viewed the scene through my drones. They hovered in the smoke, behind the enemy barricades; innocuous enough, barely a threat, the enemy ignored them. I saw the Sword commandos pulling respirators over their faces, closing their visored helmets, and aiming Klashov 1500 assault rifles in my direction.

The grenade bounced along the ground. Hit the first barricade.

I'd like to think that the soldier behind it realised his mistake, in the split second he had to react.

The grenade exploded.

Not a smoke: a hi-ex.

The barricade had once been an officer's desk. Pulled from one of the sub-chambers, welded to the floor and wall. It was a poor shield from the explosive blast and the grenade tore through the thin metal surface easily. The soldier was thrown backwards, losing his grip on his rifle.

The soldier next to him started firing, almost randomly, into the smoke.

I popped around the corner of the junction, my M95 up. I thought-activated the strobe mounted on top of the gun: in the low-light conditions, the scene was rendered in frightening stop-start motion. Only a small advantage, but it was something. The battle-rifle produced its own light as I fired. The M95 was a Krell killer at this range; against Directorate troopers, even Swords, there was no contest.

There are professionals, and there are simulant operators. Then there is the Lazarus Legion.

I whetted my lips, was so eager for the kill.

The second man went down in a volley of plasma pulses. His black armour lit white – a hole through the chest-plate, then another in his helmet. I reached the barricade behind which he had sought shelter in a single stride. My boot up, I slammed it aside, clearing the area.

More shooters popped up out of cover. Hard AP rounds slashed the area; tracer fire directing the other soldiers to my location. They were using depleted uranium shells, my AI told me: likely to puncture my combat-suit on impact.

"You have the choice of surrender . . ."

That was if I got hit, of course. My null-shield illuminated, taking the brunt of the enemy fire. Still firing with one hand, I dropped another smoke grenade with the other. Smoke and debris filled the corridor, just how I liked it. I controlled the battlefield: it was my decision as to how this played out.

". . . I can guarantee that you will not be afforded any rights under the New Geneva Convention . . ."

A Directorate commando was pinned behind the next barricade. On his back, helmet discarded, he'd abandoned his rifle and was aiming up at me with a semi-automatic pistol. His face contorted into a mask of hate and he fired at me again and again. Pumped with chemical courage: there were nerve staples across his forehead, plugged into his temples.

For a split second, I thought I recognised the man. The storm drain. The pitiful soldier Carrie and I had found.

I wasn't going to show weakness this time.

I fired until the man was ended. The recognition was instantly gone: he was just another corpse. Dead like all the others.

I moved on. Even though the occasional round breached my null-shield, the bullets only grazed my combat-suit. So long as I stayed operational, none of that mattered. I wasn't concerned about damage limitation. Speed was the key – I needed to get into the mess hall.

My armour camo-skin gently shifted, mimicking the movement of smoke across the surface: in contradiction of the malevolent soul within. I lifted my booted foot, stamped down on another commando's chest. There was a reassuring crunch as the soldier stopped moving.

"*. . . I will treat you as you've treated my people; without compassion or mercy . . .*"

Fear and awe were my two best friends.

I fired wherever I saw movement.

They killed my mother. They killed Carrie. They killed my child.

The Directorate hadn't considered me or the crew they had cold-heartedly slaughtered. None of them had considered Elena, what we had lost all those years ago, back on Azure. I blocked the thought: cut off that neural pathway. Easier to forget – to become an instrument of war.

Another Sword leapt from a side chamber, firing his Klashov on full auto. I felt the jarring impacts this time. A round penetrated the armour of my left shoulder. The bullet slashed through tissue, lodged in the bone, shattered. The pain was momentary and intense: uranium had a painful effect, even on a sim. My medi-suite responded with a dose of adrenaline and a painkiller shot.

I didn't even pause.

Pain is good, I told myself.

I discarded my plasma rifle. I could see the soldier's face behind his goggles. Despite the drugs and the fatigue, there was terror in his wide pupils. Not even the staples could touch that. He froze as I reached for him. I clamped my enormous gloved hand around his neck. The insignia on his uniform marked him as an officer of some stripe, maybe the equivalent of a sergeant. I effortlessly lifted him off the ground and snapped his neck. I couldn't even hear the response – such was the roar of gunfire, now all around me – but the body went limp.

"*. . . I will make it fast, although not painless . . .*"

I tossed the soldier aside. In the same motion, reached for my pistol. The trusty PPG-13 activated, powered-up and good for another twenty shots.

The loop started again: "*You have the choice of surrender . . .*"

INCOMING, my AI notified me. TAKE EVASIVE ACTION.

I twisted on the spot, held my left hand out. My three-sixty-degree cameras showed a grenade had been thrown at me by someone behind my position.

Three more attackers, in fact. Trying to flank me.

I fluidly caught the grenade. Just as fluidly threw it back. The three attackers scrambled the way that they had come, yelling to each other to take cover.

"*. . . I can guarantee that you will not be afforded any rights under the New Geneva Convention . . .*"

I turned to the mess hall bulkhead. Less than a hundred metres to go.

I fired my plasma pistol with one hand – aimed to keep the Swords down. By now, there were smoking holes in the walls and floors. The barricades behind which the soldiers sheltered were so much molten slag, destroyed beyond recognition. I unclipped another grenade – incendiary this time – and threw that further down the corridor. More screaming – bodies aflame, unsure of whether to run towards me or away. I caught two of them, snapped more necks.

"*. . . I will treat you as you've treated my people; without compassion or mercy . . .*"

My plasma pistol eventually ran out of power. I stormed the next barricade, slammed it aside with my shoulder. The soldiers behind it scattered, leaving rifles and grenades on the floor.

"*. . . I will make it fast, although not painless . . .*"

I was suddenly outside the mess hall.

Another couple of stray rounds pinged against my null-shield. Shooters from behind me, attracted to the sounds of battle.

I reached over my shoulder and grabbed the next weapon available to me. That was the flame-thrower: a huge incinerator unit surely not approved for use aboard an occupied starship. I primed the flame-thrower's firing mechanism and the pilot light immediately lit. Then I took up a position behind the last barricade, although in my combat-suit I was so big that it barely provided me with any cover at all.

There were shouts down the corridor. Boot-falls against the deck. Another ten or so soldiers. Although many of my drones had been disabled during the battle, I still had enough circling the zone to inform me of their location.

Fifty metres and closing.

Not close enough.

I waited. A heartbeat, a second.

They started shooting and my null-shield lit. Of course, they knew exactly where I was. But that was hardly the point.

Where they were: that was what this was all about.

Twenty metres.

Close enough.

I lurched up and over the barricade; extended the flame-thrower, aimed high, and fired. A jet of super-heated combustible fuel poured over the area between me and the Directorate troopers, creating a wall of flame. I panned left and right. A sheet of white fire consumed the deck and covered the corridor. Kept my finger jammed on the trigger – I didn't care about ammo consumption.

The Swords were screaming.

The nearest to me suddenly ignited – ragged outline flagged by my HUD – and a grenade on his belt popped. The remains of the body collapsed among the burning wreckage of the corridor. As an afterthought, I tossed another couple of incendiary grenades further down the corridor. There was more screaming, the energetic *pop-pop-pop* of ammunition cooking off in the heat.

My HUD tagged twenty-two dead bodies. More than I'd expected, not as many as I'd hoped.

The *Colossus'* emergency response routines finally responded: dispensing green halon gas over the funeral pyres, putting out the fires.

As the mist cleared, I saw that it was done. Nothing stirred in the corridor.

The mess hall doors were open ahead.

I kept my flame-thrower poised – ready to fire again – as I entered and found that it was deathly quiet inside. *Am I too late?* I questioned.

Any encouragement I'd felt from the firefight in the corridor immediately left me. The hall was the site of an unmitigated massacre. Alliance and Directorate bodies littered the floor. Gunfire stitched the walls. Like the corridor outside, impromptu defences had been erected from tables, chairs, whatever furniture was on hand.

"Anyone alive in here?" I called.

A bedraggled figure emerged from behind a barricade. *Martinez.*

An immense wave of relief flowed over me. Battered, bruised – but mostly alive. Other dirtied faces peered from hiding places as well, aimed weapons in my direction. I recognised a handful of Scorpio Squadron's aerospace pilots. They were holed-up in the rec room, behind the servery.

"Stand down, people. He's a friendly," Martinez called. He carried an oversized Navy flare gun. "Fucking A, *jefe*."

I opened my helmet, flung it aside. I was immediately assaulted by the scent of roasting flesh and burning plastic; the cloy of halon spray.

"Where's Jenkins?" I asked.

"Down here," Martinez motioned. He gave his diagnosis bluntly: "She's hit. It's bad."

I followed Martinez behind an upturned table at the far end of the hall, backed against one of the floor-to-wall observation windows. Those had been sealed to space: heavy shutters deployed so that the mess hall was now a closed environment.

Jenkins lay on the floor, clutching at a wound in her stomach with a torn-off strip of uniform. Thick blood had soaked through her fatigues. Turned everything a black-red.

"Thought you'd never make it," she said.

"Stay still," I said, crouching beside her.

Jenkins' skin had gone a waxy white; she was sweating unnaturally. Hair plastered to her forehead. She still held a shotgun over her chest – protectively, like it was all that was keeping her alive.

"Pistol shot," Martinez said. "I'm not sure where the bullet lodged."

"Somewhere painful, is where!" Jenkins said, baring her teeth. It was a bad impression of a smile. "But I'm okay. I can still fight."

"Like fuck you can," I said. "You given her anything?"

Martinez shook his head.

"Except for offering me last rites," Jenkins said. "But I think I'll give that a miss."

I flipped open the medi-suite panel on my combat-suit. The kit was intravenous, hardwired to my nervous system, but if Williams could unwire it then I was sure I could too. I disconnected the analgesic supply.

"That would be nice," Jenkins said. "As much of it as I can stand."

I hooked up a redundant hypodermic and stabbed Jenkins in the leg, through the fabric of her fatigues. She hissed with the pain, but sat back. I imagined it wasn't much compared to the agony in her gut.

"What the fuck's happening to this ship?" she managed.

"We're being invaded by Directorate commandos. Williams and the Warfighters are defectors. He has access to next-gen sims."

"He what?"

"Get back into cover. I'll explain."

With my improved sim-senses, I could already hear the pound of boots and the distant chatter of gunfire. The Directorate were moving to our location, sending whatever resources they had to the mess hall.

"Positions!" Martinez shouted.

The survivors scrambled as one.

I started again. "Williams is Directorate. Mason killed him in Medical, but he was using a next-gen simulant. He must have a supply somewhere aboard the *Colossus*, or the fleet."

"Christo . . . When did they get to him . . .?"

I shook my head. "No time for that now."

There was a sudden, muffled explosion. The faraway *wer-chunk, wer-chunk, wer-chunk* of machinery activating; a giant's footfalls echoing around the empty corridors of the *Colossus. That sound again . . .*

Jenkins ignored the noise, quickly asked: "Have . . . have you found Kaminski?"

"He's okay. He's evacuated the ship, in a pod from the brig. I think that he has Saul."

"And Mason?" Martinez said.

That distant mechanical sound was undeniably moving in our direction now. Something big was coming our way. The flyboys bristled behind their barricades, all eyes on the mess hall entrance.

"She's in the SOC, covering the simulators," I said. "That's where you need to go."

I didn't add that she'd gone off-line, that she might be dead. The fact that my real body hadn't given up yet had to be some evidence that Mason was still alive. I glanced down at my wrist-comp and saw that the connection to Medical was still down. Whatever Mason was doing, she was still off the grid.

"I have a plan," I said, speaking faster now. With the metallic booming coming nearer and nearer, I got the distinct feeling that time was running out; that this hiatus was about to be shattered. "I'm going into the Artefact. I'm going to call the Krell here, give the Directorate fleet a run for their money—"

Wer-chunk, wer-chunk, wer-chunk . . .

"And I'm going to open the Shard Gate."

Jenkins nodded. She'd been in the interrogation room when Saul had revealed the existence of the gateway.

Near, nearer: *wer-chunk, wer-chunk—*

"As soon as the Shard Gate opens, we use it to leave Damascus Space."

I left out that we didn't know whether the Gate worked, that Saul's research had probably been hypothetical, and that even if we did use the Gate we had no idea where it might lead . . .

"If that fails," I said, checking my wrist-comp, "in less than forty-nine minutes none of this will matter anyway. Loeb will blow the *Colossus'* energy core and the data-stacks."

"How are we going to get to the SOC?" Martinez asked.

"Get a pilot over here," I ordered.

Martinez waved to the nearest flyboy. He dashed between barricades.

"Is there a crawlspace beneath us?" I asked.

He nodded. "I . . . I think so. I used to serve on the maintenance team."

"Is it pressurised?"

"No, but we have respirators." He nodded at a pile of bright yellow masks. "There are enough to go around."

"Good. Get into the crawlspaces, leave this deck. Put on the respirators."

I unhooked the hand welder from my belt, and tossed it at Martinez. He deftly caught it.

"Look after these two," I said. The flyboys were in their sims; their real bodies safe in the tanks. "I mean that: your crew might be disposable, but mine aren't."

The man nodded. "I copy that."

"What are you going to do?" Martinez said.

"No time to explain," I said. "Go now. Just make sure that Loeb doesn't leave without Kaminski."

"Good luck, Conrad," Jenkins said. The words were quietly resigned.

Emotion stirred within me; that boundless well of anger. "Solid copy."

Martinez started signing to the pilots, and, as one, the survivors moved off to an access plate mounted on the floor. He had it up within seconds.

Each titanic footstep made the deck vibrate.

424

I sat behind the metal table and watched as my bio-scanner began to fill with signals. Alliance and Directorate life-signs, but the Alliance were distinguishable – they were moving away from the mess hall now, slowly but surely. There were far more Directorate signals: those were swarming across the exterior corridors, all converging on my location.

There was shouting from the corridor. Harsh, angry.

I unclipped my remaining gear from my backpack. A demo-charge sat on the ground beside me, and I began to synch it to my suit systems. I slapped it against the nearest window shutter: the magnetic locks activated, holding the charge firm.

They would be here soon—

CHAPTER THIRTY

WAR NO END

The barricade exploded with enemy fire.

Hot frag showered the mess hall. I rolled sideways: not quite fast enough. My shield caught most of the debris, but enough hit my torso to cause a suit breach. I felt white-hot pain blossom in my pectoral region; slivers of frag poking from the ruptures in my armour.

I was immediately glad that Martinez and Jenkins weren't here.

Fighting against the pain, and without an active medi-suite, I scrambled into alternative cover – a crate metres from my original position. I loosed off a handful of shots with the military shotgun: watched as figures began to loom through the smoke. The gun had a terrifying blast radius and several bodies exploded.

Wer-chunk, wer-chunk, wer-chunk, came the sound again. It was now so near that it was almost on top of me, dominating the chamber, coming right down the main corridor.

It has to be a heavy mech, I decided.

I peered out from behind the barricade. My breath caught

in my chest, and I felt a ripple of anxiety through my simulated skin. The Directorate troopers hadn't been proper, real quarry. Here was the challenge. This was an undeniable threat – something capable of taking not just me out, but a squad of simulants.

My mind raced with combat scenarios. A direct assault against the mech would be suicide; worse than suicide. To call the machine a tank on legs was an understatement. Walkers based on the same chassis had almost replaced the tank, and had become commonplace among the ranks of the Asiatic Directorate. It was much bigger than a man – bigger than a simulant in a combat-suit, even. Equipped with a heavy flame-thrower under one arm, with an assault cannon under the other; a half-spent rack of anti-personnel missiles mounted on the monster's back. Pistons and attenuators were half-concealed by thick ablative plating, all cast in the same matt black as the Interceptors and foot troops.

I'd seen the Xi-989 before, but never this close. It was a bunker-breaker, used for shock value as much as combat potential. The single pilot was cramped inside the semi-mirrored cockpit; cranium a mess of wires and cables that directly connected him to the machine. When his head pivoted, the mech responded: moving left and right, sniffing out prey—

More thumping.

Another mech plodded along behind the first. The pair slowly advanced into the mess hall.

I popped a few cartridges into advancing Swords. The flash of the discharging weapon gave my position away and soon the crate was being pounded with fire.

"Surrender!" the lead mech squawked with an electronic voice, from a soundbox on its shoulder.

The mech advanced on me. Behind, Directorate Swords swarmed around the feet of their bigger brothers.

"Mason, you there?" I asked over the comm.

I cringed as more gunfire poured over my location. I hugged the floor. Rounds ricocheted off the armour-glass windows behind me, chewed up the ground around me. My continued existence in the mess hall was becoming increasingly finite.

My comms bead crackled. "I'm back, sir. I copy you."

It was difficult to judge, above the roar of weapons discharge, but the tone of her voice sounded different.

"Get ready. I'm about to make extraction."

The lead mech advanced, the pilot's face just visible inside the cockpit. An angry look crossed the man's brow. Maybe he was frustrated because I wasn't cowed by their show of fire superiority.

I smiled to myself. The Directorate were all over the mess hall now, both mechs inside the chamber. A swathe of flame poured from the second mech's incinerator, torching the floors and barricades – making sure that no one would leave this room alive.

Which was exactly what I'd planned.

"I am Lazarus," I shouted. "I always come back."

My eyes flashed to the demo-charge, attached to the observation window.

The lead mech twisted its torso in that direction—

Someone shouted a command—

My wrist-comp display flashed.

CHARGE ACTIVATED.

The blast-shutters and the armour-glass compound were tough – strong enough to withstand glancing gunfire impacts, maybe even a plasma pulse – but the explosive was a shaped nuclear charge.

There was a brief explosion.

All of the wall-to-floor windows were gone.

The metal shutters, then the armour-glass beyond.

On the other side, there was only vacuum.

The hall decompressed immediately.

The Directorate scrambled towards the door.

None of them were quick enough.

The *Colossus* emergency subroutines kicked in again, and this time not so sluggishly. The bulkhead door slammed shut, sealing the mess hall from the rest of the ship. We were all trapped inside the doomed chamber, and the ship was working fast to make sure that the breach was sealed.

On this occasion, I was grateful for that.

The Directorate wanted the *Colossus* intact. That was their weakness: they couldn't blow the hall, because they wanted the ship in one piece. I was desperate. I didn't care any more. So long as my people avoided capture, that was good enough for me.

Debris was sucked out into space. Mostly, that was made up of cartwheeling Sword commandos: slamming into one another, colliding with solid objects. Corpses sailed past me, limbs flailing at awkward and foreign angles. There was gunfire, but it was disorganised and irrelevant. Directorate bodies floated all around me, their weapons and armour a cloud of detritus that erupted from the mess hall window.

The real prize came next.

Both heavy mechs slid along the deck. They were too big for mag-locks: instead, they were clawing at the floor for purchase. One flew past me, close enough that I could see inside the cockpit. The pilot was panicking; jabbing at controls on the illuminated panel in front of him, yelling into his communicator.

I gave him the finger as he went, grinning with malice.

I knew that it would only be a temporary set-back to the

invaders. The mechs were probably space-proofed; would rely on their internal atmosphere supplies until they were back aboard the ship. But equally, it would do the Directorate no good for their heavy machinery to be floating outside.

Of course, the vacuum got me just the same as everyone else, and there was no time to revel in my victory. I'd already discarded my helmet and my life support was redundant. Within seconds, the grip of vacuum took me and wouldn't let go. *Not even Lazarus can escape this one.* Once, I would have dreaded that icy grasp: the agonising stab of cold invading my lungs, every cell of my being.

Now, like an old friend, I welcomed it.

I was part of the great cosmos now.

I extracted.

I opened my eyes.

The pain was only bearable because I knew that it wasn't real. This time I didn't make a sound – just let it flow through me.

Another sort of suffering spread through my body. My head ached so badly. My severed hand trailed blood and the amniotic had become a murky, impure purple. That deep-seated wooziness that comes with blood loss nagged at my consciousness, threatening to pull me under. I suspected that only the smart-meds were keeping me awake, let alone alive. *Just ride it over. Just let it go.* I was experiencing the worst of both worlds: pain from my real and simulated bodies transposed.

"Extraction confirmed," I groaned.

A figure appeared outside my tank and looked in.

Am I hallucinating again?

It was Mason, but not Mason: much bigger, meaner.

"What have you done?" I said.

"I couldn't let you do this alone. The Legion needs me."

She was skinned up, in her simulant.

Armoured, armed, enormous.

Over her shoulder, in double-vision, I made out her real body. Curled inside her tank.

Her simulant smiled, and she said, "War is a crucible, Major. You either rise from it, or you die trying. Whatever happens, I'm not going to go down without a fight. There's something waiting for you in your capsule."

I nodded, not understanding her words. Everything seemed so distant and I had to fight the urge to sleep.

"Hurry," Mason said. "Loeb's countdown won't wait."

"How long h . . . have I got?"

"Forty-three minutes."

My finger paused over the console, inside the tank: over the control labelled COMMENCE TRANSITION.

I made transition and the pain vanished almost instantly.

I was back in the dark of a drop-capsule, bound in place as I'd been so many times before. I flexed my limbs, began to acquaint myself with the new body –

I felt something different in the capsule with me. With such little room to move, every additional item on the sim was immediately recognisable. I felt my thigh. A holster was there; and in the low light I could see the glitter of glyphs on the shaft. Shard glyphs.

The Key.

Mason had delivered the Key to me.

There was something else strapped to my waist.

A sword, the hilt slick with black liquid. Blood.

The launch countdown timer began on my HUD.

"You read me, Mason?"

"Affirmative, Major."

"That was some good work. I'm impressed."

"You needed the Key. Should give you some additional time to reach the objective. And the sword was – ah, forcibly liberated, shall we say."

"All right. I'll be out of communication as soon as I leave the ship."

I paused. Listened to the distant crackle of the comm-line.

"See you on the other side, Mason."

"Affirmative, Major."

For what it was worth, I didn't think that I would be seeing Mason again in this life.

If I was a gambling man, I'd have bet that I wouldn't be seeing any of the Legion again.

The firing tube activated and the drop-capsule was ejected from the underside of the *Colossus*.

I braced – half expecting to be shot down as I left the ship. The Directorate might be watching for vehicles leaving the *Colossus*, hoping to pick off anyone fleeing the warship. But as the seconds after ejection passed, I dismissed that: the drop-capsule's anti-tracking systems were engaged, meaning that the only way to trace my progress properly would be by eyeballing me as I dropped.

I activated the remote cameras of the drop-capsule, to take a look at surrounding space.

The Directorate were everywhere.

Z-5 Wraith gunships – the Directorate equivalent of the Dragonfly – circled the Artefact. The Shard tech fought back, firing energy beams into the invaders when they got too close, but the Directorate had the weight of numbers. Like Krell, they simply did not care about casualties. The Wraiths were disgorging squads of foot troops, and some of those were getting through the defences. Commandos in hard-suits – vac-proofed heavy armour – were all over the hull of the Artefact. Even worse, the Artefact's rules had not changed and the airlocks were opening: allowing the Directorate onboard.

The entire scene was cast against the backdrop of the Damascus Rift. It seemed to glow especially bright: an insanity-inducing, effervescent green. My cameras scanned the mass of moonlets tumbling around the Damascus Rift. Something out there flashed red-and-yellow. That had to be the tell-tale pattern of an evac beacon. An idea occurred to me. I activated my receiver and began to search through the Alliance distress frequencies. My suit found the relevant band quickly, began to decipher the decoded transmission.

"Kaminski?" I asked. "That you?"

"Major?" He sounded relieved.

"Affirmative." I had to keep it brief; at any given second I might move out of comms range. "Any injuries?"

"Negative. I . . . I don't know what the fuck just happened. I was guarding Saul, when all hell broke loose. Jesus. It was bad."

"I copy that. Hold tight. You're going to be okay. We're retaking the *Colossus*. Once James has control of the flight deck, your pick-up will be the priority."

"Where are you going?"

"I'm making a drop to the Artefact." There was no time to explain the plan, so instead I just said, "I'm calling in some back-up."

Kaminski said nothing, and the line crackled and popped with interference from the Rift.

"You still there?" I asked, after a long pause. I was worried that I'd lost the signal.

"Yeah, Major. I'm still here. Don't leave that pick-up too long, if you can help it. The pod's atmospherics will hold out for a few days but we're being bathed in radiation from the Rift. We'll run out of anti-rad drugs before we lose oxygen."

"I copy. Hopefully we won't need that long."

"Major!" came another voice: Saul. "I need to speak with you urgently!"

There was some movement at Kaminski's end of the line.

My drop-capsule made another course correction, and the transmission suddenly became even more static-heavy.

"I'm not sure it matters any more," Saul said, dourly. Sounded like he had no preconceptions of survival either. "But you need to know what happened—"

The line abruptly went dead: descended into a wail of white noise.

"Saul?" I yelled. "Kaminski!"

I cycled the bands again, furiously tried to reach them, but every band was claimed by feedback. What did Saul know? Fuck. What had happened out here?

I gradually shed the remainder of my drop-capsule. The safety webbing loosened, slid free. My retro-thrusters fired. I landed on the outer hull of the Artefact and my mag-locks activated.

The Directorate boarding party was still scattered, disorganised. Two soldiers advanced on my location – firing Armtrade X-90 laser rifles – but I dispatched them with a volley from my M95. Even in hard-suits, they dissolved to plasma. In the distance, flagged on my HUD as major threats, a heavy mech had just made landfall. I wondered whether any of those had already breached the Artefact: whether I'd have any Directorate opposition once I was aboard.

Only one way to find out, I thought. *I'm coming to get you, Elena.*

A ubiquitous iris-airlock sat in the hull beside me. It slid

434

open. With a gentle nudge from my thruster pack, I launched myself inside.

The familiar tug of gravity, the glowing blue corridors.

I crossed the threshold.

I crouched, my rifle held in my left hand – a hand which my real body no longer possessed – and slid the Key free with my right. My HUD sparkled with error messages as it sought to recreate an analysis of the Key's energy output. The device began that cyclic flashing, the glyphs along the blade alight. The Artefact on Helios had yearned for activation. This cold, dark station was no different. I was going to give the machine exactly what it wanted.

"Elena!" I shouted. "I'm here! I have the Key!"

The Artefact creaked and groaned around me. A noise like the distant beating of drums, or the churning of ancient machinery, fell in rhythm with my heartbeat. In the distance, I could hear the rattle of gunfire. I was sure that the Reaper was doing its thing: there would be plenty of Directorate targets.

"We aren't so different," I shouted to the Artefact. "We both want the same thing."

My bio-scanner began a regular chiming.

There. A single bio-read; a flashing blip moving towards me.

The air tasted of ozone, of burning, but there was no sign of fire. The cuneiform on the walls gently strobed and pulsed. My skin crawled for no good reason. It felt as though something was awakening from a long slumber. Every footfall, it lingered just beyond my field of vision. Liquid shadow pooled wherever darkness fell, but then abolished under the light of my combat-suit lamps.

My sensor-suite was going crazy. There were spikes of electrical activity all around me. The biological read was always tantalisingly out of reach; a corridor away no matter how far I got into the Artefact. I shouted Elena's name, but my voice was claimed by the moaning of the Shard machinery all around—

The Reaper suddenly took shape in front of me.

It hovered, almost in vacillation: torn between two paths – I could sense the agony coming from the thing in waves – and undecided what it should do with me.

I breathed hard, fought the urge to shoot. The Key was still in my hand and I held it out to the machine. I knew that fighting was useless – knew how this scenario had played out so many times before – but I couldn't let it just kill me. Too many people depended on me.

The black mass squirmed under my gaze; took on a humanoid form. A skull-like face appeared, mouth open in a machine scream. My audio-dampeners reacted a second too late and the noise pricked my consciousness. The tactical-helmet began to stream a series of errors; fuzzing with lines of static.

Fuck. Not static. Something else.

Words rapidly scrolled across the interior of my face-plate. The machine-shriek wasn't just a sound. It was a data-burst.

The Reaper was speaking to me.

Query: organic?
Exterminate organic! Not Shard!
Non-organic?
Shard, no shard
Execute command: <one>
//Not one!//
<<Shard many>>
//Shard one!//

436

Execute: unity
<End now>
<<No Shard: end>>

There was so much more to the noise than just those words. It spoke of incredible loss, incredible pain. Emotions that I knew too – but on a level that I couldn't understand. Didn't want to understand, because this was the suffering of ages. It was beyond the ken of human measurements.

Unity: it wanted to be one again.

"What are you?" I asked.

Sharp appendages formed from the Reaper's body – a million black chrome needles, poised to launch at me. But instead of attacking, it spoke again.

//Execute command: guardian//
<< No time log >>
Long time: too long–
//Command: no end//

Eternity washed over me: thousands of years out here, alone and undying. The construct was angry; so very angry. It wasn't just a guardian for this place. The Reaper *was* the Artefact. The structure and thing in front of me were one and the same, and they yearned to be part of the Shard Network. The Reaper's words were mere expressions it was using so that I could understand; representative tools, nothing more.

It screamed again: another burst of machine-code.

<<War no end>>
<<Initiate protect Network>>
//War no end//
Command execute: protect
Unity–

Something exploded from elsewhere in the Artefact. The floor rumbled, the structure amplifying the distant violence. I guessed that it was the Directorate; maybe a shuttle crashing on the hull, or perhaps the heavier machinery being used to breach and secure the Artefact.

"Finish them," I said, tossing my head back down the corridor: towards the airlock.

The Reaper hesitated. Its facial expression – if you could call that monstrous mimicry, cast in living black metal, a face – flickered with confusion. I didn't know how this would play out, and kept my rifle at the ready. The construct's proclivity for sudden and lethal violence naturally made me wary—

As abruptly as it had appeared, the Reaper recoiled back into the walls: instantly gone.

"Conrad?" came a familiar voice. "You came back."

Elena. She emerged from the shadows ahead, her face panic-stricken.

"What's happening?" she asked.

"The Directorate are here. Our ship has been invaded and this place isn't secure. We have to act fast. Were they on your ship? Were the Directorate on the *Endeavour*?"

Elena nodded. "They were with us all the way."

We embraced. "I told you that I would come back. We have to get you off the Artefact."

I broke free from her, looked down into her wide eyes. She looked so tired, so vulnerable. This close, I could see every pore of her unblemished skin; see the perfect structure of her face in every detail.

"I have the Key," I said. "We have to get you out of here, but I have so many questions . . ."

"You know what you need to do," said Elena.

"The rest can wait," I said.

Before us, glowing so bright that the light scorched my eyes, was the portal to the Hub.

*　*　*

The doorway yawned open.

"The *Endeavour* is beyond the Rift," Elena began, talking as we ran. "You have to follow me – save all of us. You cannot let the Directorate know where we are."

"Stay behind me," I said. "We can talk soon—"

Her tiny hand was inside mine, and I had to be so careful not to hurt her.

Elena shook her head. "This is important, Conrad," she insisted. "More important than me. The Directorate have eyes and ears everywhere. I'm sorry that I couldn't tell you before." She shivered. "There are so many things that I want to say."

"There will be time."

I wrestled with the urge to know, to question her further, but danger lurked everywhere. With Elena behind me, that guise of invulnerability that I enjoyed inside a sim was gone. If she died, all of this was for nothing. If I died, she would either be trapped in here for ever, or worse, she would be captured by the Directorate. Loeb's countdown could be up at any time: my HUD was still scrambled and I had no way of knowing how long I had left. Every second counted.

"I'll never let them get to you," I said to Elena.

"I have things to tell you. I need to explain it all."

We prowled across the bridge, towards the raised platform in the middle of the cavern. I avoided looking over the edge, into the deep chasm over which the bridge was constructed. Just once, curiosity got the better of me. *Shit*. I couldn't make out the purpose of the chasm, but it was deep. I repressed a crash of vertigo; kept my eyes on the ground in front of me. My rifle lowered to illuminate a distressed, pitiful xeno body: an ancient cadaver crawling towards the cavern's centre.

We finally reached the other side of the bridge and set

down on the platform. This was completely unchartered territory: the very heart of the Artefact. Mist circled around my feet, like dry ice; dripping off the edge and disappearing into the chasm below. There were alien structures, cast of black rock and crystal, all around us. An atonal humming – maybe generated by the machines – caught the air.

"It's this way," Elena said.

There was a raised dais sat in the centre of the platform, and something was self-assembling on top of it. Formed of living metal, shivering with an artificial heartbeat, the thing was an alien control console – like no tech that I had ever seen before. Snippets of radio transmissions reverberated from the console and the semi-mirrored surface flayed with images. Reflected transmissions, caught in Damascus Space: bouncing off the moon-fields for ever. Those memories, like the Reaper, would never be allowed to die.

I could feel the heat emanating from the Key. It yearned for unity in the same way as the Reaper.

"I'm sorry," I said to Elena. "For what I did. For everything. I'll make it right."

Elena nodded. "We can both make it right—"

The distinctive pitched tone of a plasma rifle firing suddenly filled my ears.

Elena reeled backwards.

Three shots, all to the chest.

She didn't even have time to scream.

I did. "*No!*"

She staggered towards the edge of the platform.

I reacted, dropped the Key and my rifle – because, if I lost Elena, those things wouldn't matter anyway. I went prone, belly-down, and lurched towards the edge of the chasm. As she fell, I grabbed for her with my right hand. Caught her just in time, as she was about to drop. I closed my gauntlet around her left hand so hard that I feared I'd break her. She dangled at the edge of the platform, her whole body swaying over the edge.

"It's okay," I said. "I've got you. It's okay!"

I knew that it really wasn't. All three shots had hit her in the torso; punched right through the vac-suit, exposing burnt skin and bone. There was no way that she would survive the plasma wounds, and if I let her fall into the chasm then the drop would surely kill her.

"Hold on to me!" I yelled. "Don't give up! Never give up!"

I clutched her hand – palm to palm – and tried to grab her with my other hand as well. Her fingers were already growing limp, beginning to lose traction against my glove. There was blood everywhere. It bathed my hand and hers, made it difficult to get proper purchase. I couldn't get the leverage to drag her body back up.

Another plasma volley erupted around me.

Elena lurched – like she was suddenly able to see through the fog of pain, grasp some transient clarity – and scrabbled against the wall. Her glassy eyes fixed on mine.

"I'll get you out of here!" I roared.

"Do it, Conrad," she said. She swallowed, her hand slipping through mine. "Then find me . . ."

"Don't let go!" I shouted. "Don't leave me!"

Her face went slack.

She was already gone.

The strength in her hand seemed to evaporate.

Elena let go, and fell from the platform edge.

Grasping for thin air, I watched as her body faded into blackness.

CHAPTER THIRTY-ONE

THROUGH THE RIFT

I wanted to shout.

Wanted to rage against this cosmic injustice, to tear the universe apart.

But the words wouldn't come to me. Desperation clouded my thought-process; made it impossible to think rationally. This couldn't be happening. Not after everything that we had been through.

I just saw Elena die.

The hurt was so enormous that I couldn't deal with it. The humane, human, parts of my neural matrix began to shut down. I felt the pathways withering: felt positive emotion being stolen from me.

Elena is dead.

Elena's suffering – waiting here, for some purpose that I still didn't fully understand – had been for nothing. Eight years of hope and dream and finally its realisation all gone. To be so close, and to have my objective ripped away from me: that was the story of my life.

Gone.

Elena was everything.

Without her, I was nothing.

I was hollow.

I looked down at my gloves. Just seconds ago Elena was in my grasp, and now the only evidence that she'd ever been here was the blood soaking my combat-suit. It covered my palms, ran into the creases of my fingertips.

I'm gone.

Was it worth going on any more?

My answer came from an unexpected angle.

"Hey, Harris! You kill my woman, I kill yours. Sounds like a fair trade."

My combat-suit wasn't expecting the surge of feeling – of pure, unadulterated hatred – that detonated inside me. The medi-suite tried to compensate; began to flood my system with dangerous levels of combat-drugs in an effort to keep me optimal.

I didn't need that any more. My psyche began to reboot, rebuild. I became a machine calibrated only for violence. Something new pulsed through my veins – filled me like a Krell venom, consumed me.

Hate.

I stood. Didn't even bother with my plasma rifle, because I wanted to see Williams' face when I killed him. This had to be up close and personal. I looked down, saw the weapon sheathed at my belt: the Directorate mono-sword that Mason had liberated. Standing, invulnerable, as plasma fire rained all around me, I drew the sword. The blade lit immediately and I swung it to test the weight. It was a heavy, solid weapon, with a killing edge. I was no swordsman but sheer and brutal determination would make up for lack of experience.

All four of the Warfighters were in the mist, their outlines illuminated by the muzzle-glow of firing rifles. They advanced through the Shard structures, trying to encircle me.

"Give it up, Harris!" Williams shouted. "This is a waste of time. The Legion has already surrendered. They're back aboard the *Colossus*, safe and sound."

You don't reason with a rabid animal, Williams. I was a cornered street dog; an animal with no purpose any more. Attack was the only option.

I shouted a war cry, long and violent, then ran at the nearest Warfighter. It didn't matter which: I was going to kill them all. Exactly who had fired the killing shot was irrelevant. They were all guilty.

A Warfighter was trying to outflank me: moving through the mist to my left. Without any conscious thought, I grabbed a fragmentation grenade from my suit-webbing. Primed it, tossed it sideways. The grenade exploded, sending red-hot frag across the area. I felt something hit me in the ribs – maybe a plasma pulse, maybe debris from the blast – but the injury wasn't enough to put me down and I ignored it.

One of the female Warfighters was suddenly in front of me. She went to fire her rifle.

"He's here!" she shrieked. She had discarded her helmet, and I could see every trembling feature of her face. "I have him!"

We worked in different time-scales: two different realities.

She moved with glacial slowness.

I moved with blistering speed.

I held the sword in a two-handed grip, and with the force generated by my run I thrust it towards her abdomen. This close, I was under her null-shield. She twisted – far too slowly.

I stabbed the blade all the way through her combat-suit.

Soundlessly, the trooper crumpled onto the weapon. Her blood sizzled along the blade edge: boiled against the powered filament. Her eyes met mine for an instant. There was some small consolation in the fact that the last face she saw before death had been mine.

On instinct alone, I knew that there was another of the Warfighters behind me. I jerked the blade free. Whirled about-face; sweeping the sword in an arc. It left an afterimage as it moved.

I finished the second trooper with a flurry of thrusts, cuts, slashes. I was driven by absolute rage. There was no technique to my assault at all. The important part was that she was dead.

"I'm coming for you, Williams!" I yelled.

I slammed a smoke grenade to the floor and darted back into the cover of the Shard structures.

I found the big Martian next. He bumbled through the mist, reeking of over-confidence. He shot his rifle from the hip as he moved, splitting the air with plasma pulses, compensating for lack of accuracy with the quantity of fire.

I lurched out of cover. Caught his head with the hilt of the sword. Like the others, he had no helmet and the blow was hard enough to break his nose. He screamed – blood fountaining from his face.

I reacted fast, brought the sword up to finish him. The blade was keenly sharp and made a pleasing whistle as it cut the air. It hit home: the sweet spot between armour plates on his collar bone. The blade crackled as it slit the armour. I grunted as I forced it into his flesh.

The Martian slumped to the floor, sword still embedded into him.

No time to pull it out.

Williams stood at the foot of the dais, before the Shard control console, with his rifle trained on me. He was smiling, but the expression looked practised: looked more frightened than frightening. He had good reason to be scared.

"You fucking killed her!" I roared. Spittle flecked the inside of my face-plate.

"Give it up!" Williams yelled back.

Plasma fire throbbed all around me. With every other footfall I was encased in a white sphere of energy as my null-shield illuminated. One shot whined past my head so close that it made my face-plate polarise.

Move or die. I ran at Williams: head down, body lowered.

I fired my backpack thruster as I closed – a juggernaut now, moving faster and faster. The backpack was made for use in zero-G, for manoeuvring in space. Inside an atmosphere, it roared as it discharged – and I exponentially accelerated, became a killing force.

I covered the distance between us in a heartbeat.

Williams braced.

Our bodies collided, an immovable object meeting an unstoppable force.

We spun across the chamber.

Williams slammed into one of the Shard structures, hard enough to shatter the crystal and send black splinters across the area. Both null-shields activated and failed: that line of defence rendered irrelevant.

I pinned his arms, threw him back. Another aeons-old Shard structure was smashed apart under the force of his weight. Another piece of irreplaceable Shard tech was demolished.

I knew that it wouldn't be enough to put him down, because I knew that it wouldn't be enough to put *me* down.

He tried to break away from me. In response, I grappled with his webbing and pounded a fist into his face. It was a solid, murderous blow: with powered gauntlets, hard enough to smash a Krell skull, probably decapitate a hard-copy man.

It did little to slow Williams. His face-plate shattered, sent fragments of plastic bouncing around inside his helmet, but it did nothing to stop him.

I punched again and again: roaring as each blow connected. Not just with his helmet, now. I felt bone crunch, felt tissue snapping—

Williams dived out beneath the last blow. Too slow to react to his evasive manoeuvre, I pounded a fist into the floor. I cracked both the metal surface, and my knuckles. Pain shot up my forearm, momentarily stunning me.

Williams took the advantage. He pivoted about-face, kicked out with a powered boot. The blow landed in my abdomen. The armoured plates protecting my stomach cracked. I felt something explode inside me – something break in the bone structure of my ribs – but I rolled backwards with the force of the blow.

Pain was fleeting and immaterial. I couldn't let it hold me back.

I lurched to my feet, lunged for Williams.

"Who are you?" I shouted, into his face.

He let out a long, maniacal laugh. He got purchase on my armour for a second, hoisted me by the shoulders. Before I could break free, he threw me across the chamber. I crashed against the dais. My medi-suite warned of another broken rib, of concerning levels of adrenaline—

"I could be anyone!" Williams replied, circling me. "I might be the neighbour you've known for thirty years. Maybe your commanding officer." His eyes twinkled with hateful glee. "I could even be the man sitting next to you on the monorail."

"Fuck you, Williams."

He was still standing, but only just. His helmet was destroyed and the bloody mess of his face peered out, his teeth white flashes among the gore. He tried to laugh again but the noise was wet and unpleasant.

"Don't you know, man?" he went on. "I'm a ghost. A fucking ghost, come back to haunt you." He pulled a face, leered at me. "I'm like the wind, passing wherever I choose. How's the hand?"

"It'll pass."

"I bet it will. Take more than that to put down Lazarus, eh?"

Williams kept his eyes on me, that grisly smile painted on his face, but I suddenly noticed the flash of something in his palm. A mono-blade: a smaller version of the Directorate troopers' sword. Williams quickly drew the blade back, lurched away from me.

I immediately realised what he was trying to do. This wasn't about taking me out any more: it was about tactical retreat. He wants to get out of this skin – to extract.

I reached for my sidearm – the holstered PPG-13 plasma pistol, still strapped to my thigh. I flipped the stud, grabbed the pistol grip—

—Williams brought the knife up: still smiling, the blade reflecting light as it charged—

—I had my plasma pistol in my hand—

—aimed it at him—

—the knife was at his own throat – ready to plunge it into his own neck, to achieve the fastest possible extraction—

—my finger closed on the firing stud—

I fired. A bright plasma pulse seared across the chamber, hit Williams in the hand in which he held that weapon.

"Fuck!" he screamed, looking at his right hand.

He dropped the mono-blade.

I dove forwards. Kicked it away from him.

The plasma pulse had bored a hole right through the glove, right through his hand. He collapsed to his knees. Grasped at the destroyed hand: looking in utter incredulity at the ruined appendage.

I took the initiative.

I fired twice into his legs, at the knee-caps.

Williams howled. Blood, bone, armour plating: it was all fused under the intense fire of the plasma pistol. He fell onto his back and writhed in agony.

"That's got to hurt – especially without a medi-suite," I shouted at him. "But you're not taking the easy way out."

"Fuck you!" he screamed. "Your nation is a relic! Your uniform means nothing! You think that you've won here?" He dissolved into an agonised choke, before continuing, "You're wrong, Harris! The Directorate is everywhere! It's us who are legion!"

"Shut the fuck up, Williams."

Debris was now falling from above us. Chunks of machinery lay strewn across the ground. I stood over what remained of Captain Williams. *How long until Loeb blows the ship?* I asked myself. This deep into the Artefact, I had no communication with the *Colossus*. I could have minutes left, could have seconds. I had to act now.

I turned to the dais. The control console rippled, straining to maintain stability.

"Let's do this," I declared, and started to climb the steps to the console.

Williams continued screaming behind me. "Is this what

you want? If that machine goes off, every fish head in this sector is going to be all over the fleet. None of us will get out of here alive!"

Up close, the console looked like black mercury – composed of the same poisoned quicksilver as the Reaper. There was nothing that I recognised as a control but I felt the Key in my gloved hands. I couldn't remember having picked it up. It was hot and heavy, as though it had gained mass since I'd entered the chamber.

Elena's blood was all over my fingertips – dark, indelible. On the index finger of my right hand the chem-analyser probe was extended: a tiny needle device, used to sample blood and other substances. The machine I'd used on Williams' cigarette butt, that night I found him alone on the Artefact.

"You're insane!" Williams yelled. "You want to open the Gate? Who knows what will come through?"

The Reaper was suddenly above me. It was bristling, angered by the inactivity. It wanted unity, but there was no understanding there. This thing was alien – was incomprehensibly machine. We were not allies. We were not friends—

ALERT, my HUD informed me.

Fragments of my face-plate still clung to the remains of my tactical-helmet. I'd ignored the error messages flashing there – had been focused on bringing Williams down – but now something caught my eye.

"You'll never save her!" Williams screamed at me. He had dragged his destroyed legs up the dais, pulling himself nearer to my position. "We will find her!"

Find her. Save her.

A persistent message flashed on my HUD: an urgent update from my chem-analyser. The hand that had touched Elena's ruined body, that had sampled her blood.

Something hot – blood or tears – welled in my eyes,

began to stream down my face so that the message was blurred and indistinct.

```
SIMULANT BLOOD DETECTED
SUBJECT: DR ELENA MARCEAU
```

She wanted to tell me that she was simulant-operational. *"I have things to tell you. I need to explain it all."* Then Elena's last words: *"Find me."*

That was how she'd existed out here: because she had never really been here. Her real body was somewhere beyond the Rift. Safe, I hoped, from the Krell and the Directorate.

"She's still alive . . ." I whispered. "And I can find her."

Hope – that most toxic and dangerous of emotions – poured into me, reinvigorated me. I was alive again: driven, awake, directed.

I turned the Key over in my hands. I knew this would be the last time I'd see it.

The Artefact rumbled again. More dust and debris began to fall from above. The Reaper shrieked, bubbling all around me. Williams screamed and screamed and screamed.

A portal opened in the console. The liquid metal flashed with glyphs, pulsed with unrealised power.

"There's still hope. That has to be something."

I inserted the Key.

I activated the Artefact.

It began to transmit a signal, broadcasting at a speed that no Alliance or Directorate technology could ever achieve. Like wildfire, it spread through Damascus Space.

I knew all of this as I stood at the console. The air around me was saturated with data – information flowing like an atmosphere. More than just a language: this was Shard lifeblood.

Beneath the churn and whine of the signal, I felt emotions. Loss and longing. Although they were not spoken, words formed: a message that repeated over and over until I understood the meaning.

Find me, it said.

I stood at the console for what felt like an eternity, although it might've only been the blink of an eye. Under the onslaught of such perversely advanced technology, my equipment was useless. My combat-suit was off-line. Unpowered, it was a dead weight on my shoulders.

The signal was building in volume and intensity.

Conversely, my sanity was evaporating.

I collapsed to my knees. Felt blood streaming from my mouth, my ears.

The Reaper was everywhere but it was glitching – bubbling with irregular shapes, struggling to control its own body. It had become an iridescent, mirrored silver.

"What the hell have you done?" Williams screeched over the noise.

Then the Reaper dissolved. It splashed to the floor like water, all semblance of form gone.

Its job is done, I told myself. *And now mine is too.*

I struggled with my plasma pistol. In the unpowered suit, every movement was a war. I prayed that the pistol would operate – that I could escape the Artefact. The chamber was shaking so violently, and the signal was so strong in my mind, that I couldn't focus on anything.

"Take me with you!" Williams wailed. "Don't leave me here! Let me out of this body!"

"Fuck you, Williams."

I put the pistol to my chin and fired.

* * *

"Come back."

I gasped for breath. Choked on a mixture of blood and amniotic.

"Stay with me."

I'm trying! I couldn't seem to make my mouth work.

The blue – focus on the blue—

I was sick some more.

I was back on the *Colossus*. Clambering out of my tank, supported by strong hands. I glared down at the ragged stump of my missing hand.

Martinez stood in front of me. He was saying something – babbling so fast in Spanish that I couldn't understand him. That didn't matter though, because I could read the urgency in his eyes.

"Slow down!" I said. "Slow down!"

Alliance Marines, in various states of battledress and injury, stood at the door to the SOC: carbines covering the corridor outside. I guessed that part of the plan had worked and that Alliance troops had managed to retake some of the *Colossus*.

I stumbled out of Martinez's hands, caught myself just before I collapsed. My vision was blurred; my world shaking violently.

"His vitals are all over the place," Mason yelled, standing beside Martinez.

Both were operating simulants. Their helmets were removed, and their faces bore minor injuries.

"I don't feel so good," I slurred. "The shaking—"

"It's not you, Major," Martinez said. He was shouting to make himself heard. "It's the ship."

The entire vessel shook – the deck beneath my feet, the walls around me. Medical equipment rolled across the floor, clattered against walls. I could still hear the piercing wail of the Artefact's signal ringing in my ears, but there was new noise around me. Mechanical groans echoed through the SOC.

"Whatever happened out there," Martinez said, still propping me up, "cancelled the dark order. We're operational again. The Shard Gate is open."

Mason helped me into some fatigues. With my missing hand and the pain in my head I was in no position to turn her down.

"Are the Krell here?" I asked. "Did the plan work?"

"Too well," Mason said. She grimaced. "They're everywhere."

"We've got to get to the CIC now, *jefe*," Martinez said. "Clear a path! Lazarus coming through."

A lot seemed to have happened. The corridors were cleared of hostiles but warning klaxons still sounded and the atmosphere tasted of smoke. There were bodies – Alliance and Directorate – strewn on the floor, and as we moved past one junction I heard the *crack-crack-crack* of an assault rifle firing.

The CIC was in utter chaos. There were officers everywhere, crew everywhere. No rhyme or reason as to who was in command – deckhands were plugged into control consoles, a couple of Marines occupied the weapons pods. Being alive seemed to have become a good qualification for taking command.

"All power to the aft null-shields," Loeb shouted across the CIC. He sat at his command station, surrounded by holo-feeds. "Now!"

"Damage sustained to the port-side generator. Shields running at twenty per cent, sir."

"Better than nothing. Get me power to the drive propulsion unit."

"What's happening?" I asked.

Martinez ushered me to the tac-display. Loeb looked down at my missing hand, went to say something, but was interrupted by another officer.

"We have fifty per cent thrust, sir."

"Bearing ninety-degrees!" the admiral yelled. "Keep the comm-line to navigation clear!"

The blast-shutters to the CIC were open.

The Krell had come back in force.

They had brought carnage with them. Debris scattered near-space. Brilliant explosions flashed across the view-port, impossibly close. Had to be a human ship cooking off, lost to the vacuum. A Directorate Interceptor passed, laser raking the underside of a Krell bio-ship. Plasma fire and kinetics seemed to fill space.

"Someone get me comms with any operating Alliance ships!" Loeb roared. "They need to know we're leaving!"

The Artefact was a black heart to the battlefield. It throbbed with new life. A beam of green light streamed from the Artefact itself, beyond the battle – out into Damascus Space.

I felt bile rising in the back of my throat; felt that sense of wrongness that only operational Shard technology could evoke. I clutched the display a little tighter to stay upright.

The beam pierced the Damascus Rift. Illuminated it; activated it. The entire Rift had turned an iridescent black – filled with stars, like some terrible mirror. That was where Elena had gone.

"Your Shard Gate is working," Loeb said to me. "We can't perform a Q-jump under our own power, so it's our ticket out of here." Back to his crew: "Issue the extraction order to Scorpio Squadron. We are leaving!"

"Where's Jenkins?" I suddenly realised that I hadn't seen her since I'd made extraction. Then another realisation hit me: "Please tell me that we've got Kaminski aboard . . ."

"It's not good news," Martinez said.

Jenkins was physically and emotionally in a bad way.

She was skinned and she had forced her armoured bulk into a comms officer's chair. She sat with her head in her hands; plastered with blood, a nasty wound on her temple still streaming black fluid. I knew that her real body must be in an even worse state – hoped that she had received some medical attention.

Mason and Martinez hung back as I approached, like they were frightened of Jenkins' reaction.

I soon understood why.

Kaminski's still out there; and he isn't coming back.

A static-riddled holo was projected from the desk in front of her. Kaminski inside the evac-pod: his appearance quivering and shaking with every disturbance in near-space.

Jenkins looked up at me sharply. She said nothing, but I could read the anger and hurt in her face. She pushed off from the desk.

"Harris?" Kaminski asked.

I leant over the console, into the camera mounted there. "It's me."

"Saul and I are going to be fine," Kaminski said.

"He isn't!" Jenkins shouted. "Loeb's leaving him!"

"Hey, Jenkins!" Kaminski insisted. "Someone can come back and get us. It's not a problem."

He has no damned right to sound so calm! I clenched a fist, with my only hand, and clutched Jenkins to my chest. Her whole body shook and bucked: on the verge of fighting me off. Saul and Kaminski looked back from the evac-pod, consigned to their fate. I locked eyes with Kaminski.

"I still have a man out there!" I shouted to Loeb. "We can't leave without him—"

"We've already tried to get him twice!" Loeb said. "Both ships were shot down, and every passing second the evac-pod is moving further into the moon-fields!"

Around us, the crew were preparing for launch. Orders were being exchanged.

"We have to go. There isn't time to send out another sweep. Inform any operational vessel to follow us into the Rift. I'm sorry."

"No! You don't even know if it will work—"

"It's not right!" Jenkins shouted. "We can't leave him!"

"Powering up propulsion drive."

There was a deep rumbling from the *Colossus*. Her drives were cold booting, getting ready to move off.

"All hands take safety precautions!"

The view out of the blast-shutters spiralled as we manoeuvred. There was another explosion – something hit the ship as we changed position. I half-expected to feel the prickle of lost atmosphere, the cold of vacuum, as we suffered some catastrophic damage.

The ship navigated towards the Rift. Jenkins broke away from me and slammed both of her fists into a bulkhead. She was sobbing uncontrollably.

"Closing in T minus ten seconds," an officer shouted above the din. "Nine . . ."

"No!" I yelled. "We have to stay!"

"Eight . . ."

A stray Krell bio-weapon glanced the *Colossus'* flank.

"Buckle in if you want to live," Loeb ordered.

"Seven . . ."

Mason and Martinez dragged me to a seat.

"Six . . ."

I struggled against them, yelled in defiance, as they strapped me in.

Gravity began to ebb and flow. Stray debris was being sucked into the gap in time-space. Ships spiralled end over end towards the Rift. I didn't know how we were managing to maintain our position.

"Five . . ."

Mason and Martinez were strapped in too now.

"Four . . ."

The Rift dominated the view-ports. I tasted blood at the back of my throat, felt my whole body constricting as we made the final approach.

"Three . . ."

Jenkins was still crying.

This, I decided, *is probably how it ends*. Lost in the Maelstrom, reduced to constituent atoms by an alien gravity well – blown across time by a technology that none of us understood.

"Two . . ."

The *Colossus* emitted an enormous groan. The clash of metal on metal, the grinding of the superstructure collapsing in on itself—

"One . . ."

There was only the Shard Gate.

My body was torn apart.

No, not torn apart. Disassembled was more apt a description.

But just as quickly, I was reassembled.

And I was in a hundred places at once.

Space and time became instantly malleable. I was somewhere beyond the touch of the natural laws of physics – a lacuna between planes of existence, the space between space.

The Shard Network eddied around me. It was a galaxy-spanning web of ancient Artefacts, connecting myriad planets and stars. Both transmitters – waypoints in the night, like the machine on Helios – and also gates, like that in Damascus Space. There were so many of them.

The Artefacts were truly legion.

I wanted to reach out and touch the worlds of the Network. To explore the terrible black holes of the Outer Dark; to reach the collapsed wormholes of the Xerxes Spiral; to fly the gas giants of Tia Star. These were worlds that no human explorer had ever visited. Such terrible beauty lurked in the tapestry of stars – an empire crafted by the Shard that had grown too vast for a single species to tend, and had long ago fallen into disrepair. And yet, as I saw those worlds, I knew that they were far from dead. I sensed Shards of the great mechanical mind – just slivers of the higher consciousness – and quickly recoiled from them.

There was no time to dwell on any of the visions that the Network showed me. As each galactic wonder appeared, it was gone just as quickly. The *Colossus* was moving too fast, blurring the lines between dimensions—

I detected something else in there with us. Something malevolent and terrifying; awakening so slowly that the passage of time was barely measurable. A Shard machine-mind incapable of comprehending lesser entities. It carried such hatred for the organic, the biological.

The war had never ended for the Shard. They had been gone for a long time but that meant nothing to them. Their lesser machines might feel atrophy – wither from the gnaw of insanity, the passing of lonely millennia – but the Machine did not care.

I heard Elena's voice.

She was crying, laughing, whispering to me.

"Surely you would cross light-years of time and space to be with me?"

"I'd cross the universe to be with you. Truthfully."

I saw the UAS *Endeavour*, the starship Elena had used to travel into the Maelstrom, lurking within the Network. The ship was suspended in space, among the familiar constellations of the Maelstrom. That was how she was able to broadcast to the Artefact. She had used the Damascus Rift, somehow managed to maintain the neural-link with her simulant. I saw the data-thread of her consciousness, weaving through the Shard Network.

Is this it? I asked myself. *Have I really found her?*

Then the *Colossus* was moving again, onward through the Network, to whatever destination the Shard builders had programmed. I tried to lurch from my seat, to yell to Loeb that we had to stop – we had to save her! – but the Network had a life of its own.

Our final destination, our translation back into real-space, was not of our choosing.

Crewmen were everywhere. Some hadn't been lucky enough to get buckled in before we made for the Gate: others had been thrown free of safety harnesses and webbing. Either the ship's gravity well had given up, or the Shard Gate was causing disabling distortion.

The *Colossus* was dying. Her hull roared and her frame groaned in response to enormous tidal forces. Her instrument banks were going berserk. Every system bleated warnings, protested against the Gate's violations of time-space. Striations of light flowed past at maddening speeds. Stars became white lines; galaxies multi-coloured waves. Space folded in on itself. Klaxons rang out all around – breach warnings, proximity alarms. A nearby console was aflame, and someone was fumbling with a fire extinguisher.

"Stay down!" I shouted. "You'll be torn apart!"

I tried to lift my body from my seat but I was pinned. Every muscle and joint was frozen. In my own skin, I could only take so much. My senses were being overloaded. I closed my eyes, wanted the noise and colour and damned sensation to *just fucking stop!*

When the blackness descended, I was grateful.

CHAPTER THIRTY-TWO

WRECK

I lay there for a long time, in the quiet and the dark.

Recently those had become such rare commodities.

I wondered whether I might be dead. Not simulated dead; really dead. But I was cold. If Martinez's sermons were anything to go by, my final destination would be a good deal warmer.

I exhaled, inhaled, felt the frozen atmosphere fill my lungs. I recognised the familiar tang at the back of my throat; the cloy of formaldehyde and cryogen. Images began to come into focus above me. An overhead light. A glass canopy. A safety label.

I was in a hypersleep suite. While that wasn't where I'd expected to wake up, it was better than being dead.

The capsule lid hissed open, lifted slowly. I pulled my aching body upright.

"Watch your arm."

Martinez stood next to my capsule. He was clean, dressed, in his own skin: a world away from when I'd last seen him. *Maybe even further*, I thought – remembering the Shard

Gate, the sudden jump through the Network. Martinez rubbed his small goatee, put a hand through his hair. He had obviously been awake for a while.

I clambered out of my capsule and realised I was still aboard the *Colossus*. The walls were plastered with battle-group insignia and deck numbering – but the capsules around me had been used recently. The crew had just been thawed.

"Where are we?" I asked.

"That would be a good question. Maybe approaching the *Liberty Point*."

He tossed me some fatigues. I went to catch them with my lost hand, and almost missed.

"I . . . I saw Elena's ship . . ." I started. "The *Endeavour* . . ."

Martinez gave an involuntary shiver and crossed himself. "We saw a lot of things when we went through the Shard Gate. Some that I would rather forget. You were in a pretty bad shape. The medtechs thought it would be best if you went straight into the freezer."

"Where are Jenkins, Mason and . . ."

Martinez pulled a face. "Come with me, *jefe*."

We walked the endless corridors of the *Colossus*, at my decrepit pace.

Everything still ached, churned and burnt. I couldn't stop looking down at my missing hand. That was bandaged now and, Martinez had explained, I'd received the best medical treatment that the *Colossus* had available. Still, the techs hadn't managed to save the real thing.

"We went through the Gate," Martinez said. "Loeb thinks that we were gone for a second of ship's time." He shook his head. He obviously didn't believe that explanation. "The AI says that we jumped the entire Maelstrom; made at least three stops before we finally became stable again."

"And that was when I blacked out?"

Martinez nodded. "Yeah, Major."

"Where did we end up?"

"Anyone's guess. The telemetry module and the universal clock got fried when the Gate finally dumped us. I'd bet the science pukes would love to know, though."

"The *Endeavour* is somewhere in the Network," I said. "But not here."

"Exactly, *jefe*."

"Then where are we? You said that we were approaching the *Point*."

"I said that we were maybe approaching the *Point*," Martinez said. "After we left the Network, we were in dead space. It was quiet: there was nothing on the other side of the Gate, no Krell or Directorate. We had no idea where we were, *jefe*. Loeb ordered a Q-jump back to Alliance space, back to *Liberty Point*. Everyone, including you, went into hypersleep."

I let the news soak in. I'd been out for the decision to jump to Alliance space, but I remembered parts of the rest. My temples still ached with the touch of the Artefact's signal. Subjectively, not counting the months I'd spent in hypersleep, my battle with Williams had only been a few minutes ago.

"So we beat the Directorate?" I asked.

Martinez stopped. We were outside the mess hall.

"I guess that we did, at least on the *Colossus*."

"Did any of the other ships make it?"

"No," Martinez answered, firmly. "They didn't."

I considered that. There had been sixteen other ships in the battlegroup. Likely thousands of crewmen: all dead. Either lost to the void, destroyed by the Krell, or captured by the Directorate. I wasn't sure which fate was worse.

Martinez nodded towards the mess hall. "Jenkins is in there. Go easy on her."

Martinez left me at the door.

There had been efforts to clean up the mess hall. New shutters were bolted over the observation windows – a makeshift repair job to keep the chamber pressurised. The fix gave the place a peculiarly claustrophobic feel.

Jenkins sat alone in the corner. Recently defrosted, she cut a haggard figure. An unsmoked cigarette – half-consumed by ash – was poised in one hand, and she stared at the shutters: like she was trying to see through them and into space outside.

"I'm surprised that you want to spend any time in here, after what happened," I said.

Jenkins turned to look at me. She moved sluggishly, putting pressure on her left side. I remembered that the gunshot wound had been to her right.

"Morning, Major."

"Morning, Keira," I said. I was unsure of what to say, how to put it. "I didn't think that any of us were going to make it out of Damascus Space."

Jenkins gave a slow nod. "Some of us didn't."

"I . . . I'm sorry. About Kaminski. But it's not over. We're Legion. We'll find him."

"The universe is a big place. And like Martinez says, God doesn't do coincidences. 'Ski is gone. No point in kidding myself." She gave a dry laugh. "I have terrible taste in men."

"You mean Williams?"

"Yeah. He was an asshole, but to think that he was Directorate? It's just beyond me . . ."

"He had access to next-gen and combat sims, but it goes

much deeper than just Williams. There were Directorate infiltrators among us from the start."

"Of Operation Portent?"

"No. From the start of the Simulant Operations Programme."

"Then when did they get to him?" she asked, frowning as though she'd been thinking about the question for a while.

"Who knows? Maybe they've had the technology for years. Maybe Williams was recently turned."

"Military Intelligence is going to have a field day with this."

"Are you wondering whether he was a turncoat when he was with you in Basic?"

Jenkins gave a blasé shrug, but I could tell that it was feigned. When she moved, it was obvious that the stomach injury hadn't been resolved: there were creases of pain on her face.

"Maybe there's no telling any more," I said. "Sim Ops is changing. A long time ago, someone told me this would happen. That we would change the whole system."

"Elena?"

"Yes."

"And what about her?" Jenkins said. "Did you find the answers you were looking for?"

The unasked question: was Elena real? Whatever had happened on the Artefact, back in Damascus Space: it proved that Elena was still alive. I'd only seen a simulant, only a glimpse of the real Elena, but that was enough.

"She was operational," I said. "I don't know how she did it, but she was using a next-gen sim as well." I sighed; wished that I'd learnt more from her.

"Didn't Dr West say that the next-gen project was a recent

development? The *Endeavour* left for the Maelstrom years ago . . ."

"Dr West is dead," I said, "so I can hardly ask her. But when we get back to the *Point*, I want some answers. Someone knows about that project, and about what happened to the *Endeavour*."

Jenkins nodded. After what we had been through – what we had uncovered – nothing seemed beyond possibility any more.

"I was searching through Kaminski's stuff," she said. "What he had left on the *Colossus*. I found this."

Jenkins opened her hand. She held something out to me. "Kaminski wanted Mason to have it. Maybe you should go see her."

I found Mason in the infirmary.

She looked a decade older than when I had last seen her. I wondered whether the *Point*'s facial recognition would even recognise the war-scarred veteran that she had become. A medtech fretted over her, offering her an injection to the forearm. She waved the man away with an angry scowl.

As I entered, she looked up, and her expression softened a little.

"I'm fine, Major," she said. She glared at the retreating medic. "Really. They just want to keep me here for obser-vations, until we get back to the *Point*."

I nodded. "I understand."

She didn't look fine. She had that glaze to her eyes; a look that I knew too well. The look of a proper operator.

"None of this will hold me back," Mason said. "I'm eager to get into the tanks again, as soon as I'm certified."

"If you're sure that's what you want."

"Never been more certain."

We walked to the end of the infirmary. Mason did her best to hide the obvious: that even the short distance was hurting.

"I have something for you," I said. "From Kaminski."

I held out my hand.

A fabric badge, like that sown onto all of our duty fatigues: a stylised pyramid with an eye atop it, the name LAZARUS LEGION printed beneath.

"Jenkins figured that you deserve to wear the badge. If you still want it, that is."

"I'd like that." She took the badge from me, held it tightly. "I'd like that a lot."

Admiral Loeb had asked to see me in his room, and I thought how different the circumstances of my last visit had been. The stately corridor outside his chamber had been almost destroyed in the attack, his chamber doors replaced. His room had no doubt been one of the first targets for the Directorate attackers.

An officer let me in; not the same lieutenant as the one I'd previously been dealing with. Loeb sat on his own by the view-port, a glass of liquor in his hand, dog at his heel. Both looked impossibly tired.

"Please, sit," he insisted. "Lieutenant Toms, pour the major a drink."

"What happened to your old assistant?" I asked, inspecting the new officer.

"A little problem of loyalty. He was one of the Directorate sleeper agents and I executed him myself." He sighed; a long, drawn-out expression. "And as you know, they killed Dr West. She'll be missed."

Loeb looked away, ran a hand through the fur on Lincoln's neck.

"You don't need to talk about it if you don't want to," I said.

"Whatever I want, I'm going to have to talk about it a lot. I guess you already know what that's like. Questions are going to be asked as to why an admiral – with over forty years of fleet experience – didn't realise that the Directorate had compromised his ship."

"It happens."

"Not to me, it doesn't. Not to me. Command will want to know how Captain Williams – if that was his real name – managed to infiltrate an Army Sim Ops mission, right under my nose."

It had been a large and well-planned operation, albeit one that had ultimately failed. *But had it?* I wondered. *Where is Williams? Where are the simulator-tanks that he and the Warfighters used?* The thought sent a chill through me. The new lieutenant returned with my drink, and I eyed her warily. The Directorate could be anywhere, now.

Loeb said: "Not a single enemy agent was taken alive. Even sleepers; they'd rather die than be taken prisoner."

I sipped the drink. It was an aged Scotch: a pleasant reminder of what I could expect back on the *Point*.

"I'm a fossil, Harris. A goddamn dinosaur. I'm being left behind. I don't understand this war any more. We went out there to investigate an alien Artefact with seventeen combat-ready ships. I thought there was nothing in this galaxy that could stand in our way."

"It's an easy mistake to make."

"You're too forgiving." He swallowed down the remainder of his drink; rolled the ice around in the bottom of his glass. "Listen: I'm sorry about your man. I'm sorry about what happened to Private Kaminski. And Saul too. I – we – couldn't stay there."

If Loeb had stayed in Damascus Space, we'd sure as shit all be dead. But even so, it was a decision that I wouldn't have been able to make. We hadn't just left Kaminski behind, but also a good deal of the Alliance fleet. Loeb's logic was faultless, but it still made no sense to me.

"We're at war, Loeb," I said. "It's going to happen to us all, sooner or later."

"I suppose so."

"All we can ask for is a good death."

Loeb motioned to his new lieutenant to pour me another drink. I accepted it, and we both sat in silence for a long while – watching the distant stars, worlds and systems tumbling past.

"When we jumped through the Shard Gate," I said, my voice barely a whisper, "I felt something in there with us. Something else, in Shard Space."

"We barely have any data on the jump," Loeb said. "The sensor-suite was FUBAR. Whatever tech the Shard had, it isn't like anything I've ever seen before."

"Whatever tech the Shard *have*," I corrected. "And that's my point: it felt like something alive, functional."

Loeb was quiet for a moment. "I felt it too. Sci-Div will shit themselves when they see the data."

I hoped that I'd done the right thing; that activating the Artefact – the Shard Gate – hadn't doomed us all. Not just a few thousand personnel – terrible as that was – but the entire human race.

"Martinez told me that we're approaching *Liberty Point*," I said.

"It's a bit more complicated than that. The journey through the Shard Gate caused a malfunction in the *Colossus'* telemetry module." He waved at the stars. "Astrocartography isn't a manual art any more."

"So where are we?"

"We should be approaching the *Point*, any day now."

"But we don't know?"

"Exactly. And as for when we are: the Q-jump might've cost us six months, or it might've cost us twenty years."

I started to probe the darker consequences of the time-lapse for Kaminski or Elena, but before I could really do that there was a chime over the ship's PA.

I noticed that Loeb started involuntarily, and his face then crumpled like he was angry with his own reaction.

"Admiral Loeb to the bridge," announced the PA.

All of us gathered in the CIC: Jenkins, Martinez, Mason, Loeb. Even Lieutenant James – in a healthy next-gen sim, dressed in the flight-suit that he never seemed to leave.

The blast-shutters were open again.

"What are we looking at?" Loeb questioned.

The CIC was only half-staffed. There was an air of anxiety among the personnel: from the clipped exchanges occurring around me, I also detected confusion. I automatically scanned near-space.

"Nothing, sir," an officer replied.

"Then why the priority summons?" Loeb barked.

"Because we've managed to get the telemetry module online, sir."

"Good. Then where are we?"

An officer down in the well of the CIC tilted her head, frowned at the readings in front of her. I looked over her shoulder and tried to interpret the data-feed myself.

"We should be on top of *Liberty Point*, sir."

"Do we have comms?" I asked.

"Yes, sir," the comms officer said.

"Then open the general channel!" Loeb ordered.

"... is an emergency broadcast ... Alliance FOB Liberty Point *has fallen* ... *All surviving personnel are to await pick-up* ... *Retrieval crews are inbound* ... *This transponder is set to repeat this message* ..."

"This is it," I whispered. "This is all that's left."

We all stood in silence, watching the black, as the wreck of home drifted past the view-screen.

Look out for

THE LAZARUS WAR: REDEMPTION

by

Jamie Sawyer

Taniya Coetzer is the chief engineer of the transport ship *Edison* on a routine cargo run to the military outpost *Liberty Point*. But she's also an ex-convict with a secret, and she's hoping to make peace with her estranged mother when they reach the *Point*.

Their family reunion will be disrupted, however, when a catastrophe strikes the space station. The crew of the *Edison* suddenly find themselves fighting for their lives – and amongst the chaos, Taniya will discover that she's not the only member of the crew with a secret . . .

See the world of the Lazarus War in a whole new light, in this thrilling spin-off novella from the new science fiction star Jamie Sawyer.

ACKNOWLEDGEMENTS

Writing any book is a collaborative effort, and I am grateful for the support and assistance that my family has shown throughout the process.

Once again, my wife Louise has been my frontline proof-reader and the ideal sounding board for the long list of ideas that seem to pour out like a stream of consciousness. As ever, thank you for encouraging and inspiring me.

My children have also put up with long hours of writing and weekends when I've had to be at war rather than in the park.

As with my first book, my agent Robert Dinsdale helped me to shape and direct this novel. His feedback and comments are always on the mark. And what do you know? The second book was a little less work than the first . . . But not by much!

My editor Anna Jackson and the whole Orbit team have also been hugely encouraging and assisted greatly in getting this book out there.

extras

orbit

www.orbitbooks.net

about the author

Jamie Sawyer was born in 1979 in Newbury, Berkshire. He studied Law at the University of East Anglia, Norwich, acquiring a Master's degree in human rights and surveillance law. Jamie is a full-time barrister, practising in criminal law. When he isn't working in law or writing, Jamie enjoys spending time with his family in Essex. He is an enthusiastic reader of all types of SF, especially classic authors such as Heinlein and Haldeman.

Find out more about Jamie Sawyer and other Orbit authors by registering for the free monthly newsletter at www.orbitbooks.net.

if you enjoyed
LEGION
look out for

ANCESTRAL MACHINES

by

Michael Cobley

Chapter One

Through Brannan Pyke's slow-waking mind, thoughts stole like foggy ghosts . . .

Death came . . .

He felt cold, lying on something soft, something weight-less.

Death came whispering . . .

Cold, yes, but not soft, not lying on anything.

Death came whispering orders . . .

Just hanging in zero-gee, he realised drowsily, hanging in the dark, with something glowing faintly red off to one side. Those words about death whispering seemed familiar somehow . . . then he remembered. It was poetry, something that Dervla had been singing yesterday . . .

Then Pyke awoke with a curse on his lips as it all came back in a black, bitter rush, the rendezvous with Khorr, the handover, the sleepgas ambush . . . and now here he was in some shadowed corner of the *Scarabus* where he spun lazily amid a cloud of angular objects that caught faint red glimmers from . . . from a solitary emergency lamp over the hatch.

"Lights," he said, voice hoarse in a dry throat. Nothing happened.

"Scar – can you hear or respond?"

Silence reigned in the gloom, which meant that the comms and/or the AI was offline.

Pyke coughed, swallowed, and realised he was in Auxiliary Hold 3, the place where they stored stuff that wasn't point-less and wasn't crucial but might be later. A variety of containers, plastic, card and fabric, drifted all around, some agape and surrounded by their contents, components, silver-wrapped edibles, unidentifiable disc things webbed together in tangled nets, trade goods maybe.

Well, he thought. *Still most definitely alive. But why would that pusbag Khorr do that? Why leave behind witnesses that could identify him . . .*

His imagination provided a variety of answers in shades of sadism and horror, and it was impossible not to think about the rest of the crew, Dervla especially. He had to get out of here, find out what had happened, whatever it was.

Several unsecured storage straps hung from the ceiling, drifting like strands of plaslon kelp. He stretched out and caught one with his fingertips, drew it into his hand, then hauled himself up to the ceiling and used the sling loops to get to the nearest bulkhead.

Loose boxes and tubes and bags hung in his way, reminding him of the number of times he'd asked Ancil to sort through this guddle and clear out the really useless tat.

Racks lined the bulkhead. Pulling himself across them he steered towards the hatch, anchored himself with the metal handle and prodded the panel of touch controls. As expected, they were dead so he reached down and twisted the manual release. The doorseal popped and he felt a brief but definite puff of air as pressures equalised. Wedging his arm between the hatch handle and the doorframe he slowly forced the unlocked hatch open. With a sigh of relief he floated out into the ship's starboard passageway, glanced either way and saw the same emergency lights shedding meagre red halos amid the murk. There were no sounds, just a muffled quiet. He hooked one arm around a wall stanchion and paused to think back.

The trade rendezvous had been set for the environs of a snowbound world called Nadisha II, in an unexploited system right on the border between Earthsphere and the Indroma Solidarity. The *Scarabus* had been in orbit for over an hour when Khorr's vessel finally arrived. The meeting had taken place in the *Scarabus*'s main hold, and was Pyke's first face-to-face with the client. Over subspace comms Khorr had claimed to be the descendant of higrav workers but in the flesh he was clearly much more, humanoid in appearance though possibly lab-coded for what headhunters referred to as non-civilian applications. Garbed in worn, leathery body armour, Khorr was easily seven feet tall, bald, and had a fighter's brawny physique, as did his two slightly less imposing henchmen. With the body armour and the heavy boots they resembled extras from the set of an exceptionally ultragothique glowactioner.

Pyke had taken the usual precautions: apart from Punzho and Hammadi, the rest of the crew were on hand to provide the deterrence of an armed welcoming committee. Khorr and his men had climbed out of their squat shuttle and strode leisurely over to where Pyke stood next to a waist-high crate on which sat the merchandise, resting within its shaped padding, a state-of-the-art milgrade subspace scanner-caster. When the three stopped a few feet short and crossed their arms, Pyke had heard one of Dervla's trademark derisive snorts from behind. Ignoring it, he had given a bright smile.

"Well, now, here we are, meeting at last. Very nice."

Khorr, face like granite, grunted. His dark eyes had flicked right and left at the rest of the crew for a moment before fixing on Pyke again.

"This is the device?"

Pyke gave the scanner's case an affectionate pat.

"You see before you Sagramore Industries' latest and finest scanner, factory-fresh and field-ready, conveyed to your waiting hands by my professional services. Which don't come cheap."

Khorr nodded, reached inside his heavy jacket and produced a small flat case just the right size for holding a number of credit splines. He held them out and waited until Pyke's fingers were prying at the release button before saying, "Here is your payment!"

Now, floating weightless in the half-lit passage, Pyke remembered how his danger-sense had quivered right at that moment but his hands had had a life of their own and were already opening the small case. A faint mist had puffed out and even though he had turned his face away from it he still caught a whiff of something sweet. He had felt cold prickles scamper across his face as he turned to shout a warning, but saw Ancil and Win crumpling to the deck a second before grey nothing shut down his mind.

And yet I'm still alive, he thought. *And that skagpile Khorr really doesn't seem like the type to leave behind loose ends.*

Grabbing handholds on the bulkhead, he launched himself along the passage towards Auxiliary Hold 4. He slowed and floated over to the hatch window, gazed in and swore at the sight.

Hammadi's corpse hung there, adrift amid blue and green spares boxes. Dead. The jutting tongue and noticeably bulging eyes spoke of suffocation by depressurisation, gradual not explosive, otherwise there would have been webs of burst blood vessels and more grotesque damage. Hammadi was – had been – chief engineer, a genius in his own way who had made the *Scarabus*'s drives sing like a chorus of harmonised furies.

But all Pyke could think about was Dervla. *Dear God, please no!*

Pyke pushed away from the hatch, turning towards a side opening, the midsection lateral corridor which led to the port-side passageway and the other auxiliary holds. He launched himself along it, driven to get it over with.

The quiet was eerie, unnerving. No mingled background murmur of onboard systems, no whisper of a/c, no low hum of micropumps, no faint sounds of crew activities, no music, no chattering news feeds. Just a numbed silence. But the air . . . He sniffed, breathed in deep, and realised that it was not as stale as it should be. Some backup ventilation had to be running somewhere, but how and why? More unanswered questions.

It was just as gloomy over in the port-side passage. From the T junction he glided across to Auxiliary Hold 2, grabbed the door stanchion and peered in through the hatch window. There was movement, and the surprised, bandito-moustached face of Ancil

Martel glanced up from where he floated, crouched next to the manual override panel.

"Hey, chief," came his muffled voice. "It's jammed on this side.

Can you . . . ?"

Pyke nodded, pried aside the outer panel and after several sharp tugs the hatch seal gave with a familiar pop. A moment later the hatch was slid aside enough for Ancil to squeeze through.

"Those ratbags chumped us, chief."

"I know."

"But why are we still alive . . . ?"

Pyke ground his teeth and shook his head. "Hammadi's in Hold 4, dead from air-evac. I think that's what that gouger Khorr had in mind, for us all to be in our quarters and dead from some massive failure of the environmentals. But something must have interrupted the scum . . . or he just made a bollocks of it and didn't know." He glanced along at the next hatch. "What about Hold 1? D'ye know if there's anyone in there?"

Ancil shrugged. "Only came around a short while ago. Banged on the wall a few times but I didn't hear anything."

"Better find out, then, hadn't we?"

So saying he pushed off along to Hold 1's hatch, grabbed its handle and swung in close to the window and . . .

"Feck and dammit!" he snarled.

Inside, near the rear bulkhead, the bulky, brown-overalled form of Krefom, the Henkayan heavy weapons specialist, drifted a few feet off the deck, still as a statue, sightless eyes gazing out of that craggy impassive face. In Pyke's mind he imagined Khorr and his men moving through the ship, dragging the unconscious crew along, imprisoning them one by one.

"That son of a bitch is going to pay!"

With the last rage-filled word he slammed one palm and upper arm against the flat bulkhead, making a sudden loud bang which reverberated along the passage. Then he gasped as he saw the Henkayan's still form jerk convulsively, eyes staring wildly around him for a moment or two. Then he spotted the disbelieving Pyke and Ancil at the window, gave a big grin and pointed.

"He was sleeping?" Pyke said. "Sleeping . . . with his eyes open?"

A frowning Ancil shrugged. "Maybe Henkayans can do that, chief. I've never seen him asleep."

Then Krefom was at the hatch, knocking on the window with a big knuckly fist.

"Can't open this side, Captain-sir," came his deep rough voice.

"Broke the emergency handle. Sorry."

"We can crack it from here, Kref," Pyke said.

Moments later the lock-seal was released and Krefom pushed the hatch aside with a single push of one mighty forearm. As the big Henkayan shouldered out of the hold he gave a gravelly chuckle and slapped palms with Ancil. Pyke intervened before they started swapping stories.

"Kref, I need to know what you have stashed in that cabinet up by the crew quarters."

"Some good stuff – shockbatons, trankers, concussion and smoke nades, some light body armour . . ." The Henkayan frowned for a moment. "And a tangler. You think them skaghats is still on board, Captain-sir?"

"Dunno, Kref," he said. "But I'll not be taking any chances. Let's go."

Together they floated back along the lateral corridor to the midpoint where a panel was yanked out to reveal an interdeck access shaft. Pyke went first, hand over hand up the cold alloy ladder. Near the top, where a hatch led to an alcove near the crew quarters, he heard voices and slowed. He made a silencing gesture to Ancil and Kref below him while listening intently. One voice was female and after a moment he smiled, recognising the unflappably sardonic tones of Win Foskel, their tactics and close combat expert. Pyke proceeded to snap open the hatch catches without trying to mute the noise, then gripped a ladder rung and pushed the hatch upwards.

"Stop right there!" came Win Foskel's voice. "Surrender your weapons – toss them out, no smart moves or I'll drop something down that shaft that'll fry you from the inside!"

"And what would that be?" Pyke said. "One of those gritburgers from the galley?"

Ancil laughed further down as Pyke pushed himself up and into the corridor. A rueful Win tilted her tranker away and nodded, then grinned as Ancil was next to emerge. Her glittering dreads wavered as she drifted over to him. Out in the corridor proper, Pyke found Mojag, a skinny Human, Punzho the Egetsi, and Dervla who seemed oddly calm when her eyes settled upon him. He was about to ask how she was but there was something in her features, in fact something in the demeanour of them all.

Then he realised what was wrong – three Humans, one Egetsi, but no portly, middle-aged reptiloid Kiskashin.

"Where's Oleg?" he said abruptly, even as he guessed.

Dervla floated over to him, grey eyes staring intensely from her pale face, her back-tied red hair looking almost black in the redness of the emergency light. She leaned in close and kissed him.

"That's for being alive," she said. Then with disconcerting suddenness she slapped him. "And that's for Mojag, because he's far too polite!"

"So you thought you'd take it upon yourself to act in his stead, is that it?"

Her gaze was full of smouldering anger but Pyke could see the hurt behind it. Oleg had been Mojag's copartner but in the four years since they joined the crew Dervla had built up bonds of friendship with the Kiskashin.

"You led us here, Bran," she said.

"Where is he?" Pyke said.

"And it was your idea, your deal."

"Where?"

Before she could answer, Mojag spoke from where he floated further along the darkened passage.

"Our cabin," he said in a quiet voice. "They must have sealed him in there then set the environmentals to evacuate. I don't know if he knew what was going on but when the temperature and pressure fell the hibernation reflex must have taken over." Mojag breathed deeply for a moment and rubbed his face. "He looks peaceful – he was probably in hibernation fugue when the air ran out."

"But they could only do that if they got into the enviro controls first," said Ancil, who then paused, and snapped his fingers. "The auxiliaries in the main hold."

Pyke nodded, anger leashed. "You're right."

"Wouldn't be any of them still aboard, would there?" said Ancil.

"No – once the deed was done, the filthy gougers would have left us for dead and scarpered, although we better be sure." By now the crew were gathered round, listening. "So what we're going to do is this – empty that armoury cabinet, make sure everyone's got something harmful and a torch, and maybe some armour, then we split up. Two groups, one sweeping the ship from bows to stern while the other heads for Engineering to see about getting the power and the environmentals back up and running. Okay? Let's get to it."

The crew seemed subdued, faces masked with sombreness and . . . something else. Sorrow over the loss of Hammadi and Oleg, certainly, but Pyke could sense some kind of reserve.

Perhaps Dervla wasn't the only one laying blame at his door.

The armoury cabinet had only been partially looted. Unearthed from a carrycase was a solitary pulse-stunner which Kref passed to Pyke, who looked it over, checked the charge, then pulled out the extendable stock, locking it in place. It was an ugly, stubby weapon done up in a horrible mud-brown colour scheme but for shipboard skirmishing it was highly effective.

Pyke chose Kref and Win to go with him to Engineering, while the others accompanied Dervla forward to start at the bridge. The *Scarabus* was a small ship, yet the journey back along grav-less, low-lit passages to the aft section was tense, almost nerve-jangling.

Pyke's group checked from the main hold back to the storerooms, the little machine-shop, the lower and upper generators and the aft maintenance niches, ending up at last in the narrow, split-level chamber that served as Engineering Control. It had taken twenty-odd minutes, and Dervla's group arrived just moments after them.

"Nothing," she said, balancing a black-handled shock-baton on her shoulder. "Not a sign, not a sound, not a soul."

"Just as well," said Pyke. "Then first order of business is getting the gravity back on. Ancil, you think you can manage that?"

Ancil screwed one eye half shut thoughtfully. "Eh, if Mojag lends me a hand."

Mojag gave a wordless nod and climbed up to join Ancil at the long console where he sat, prodding boards awake.

"Time we got as close to the deck as possible," he told the others. "Don't want anyone copping a sprained ankle or worse."

Lying flat out with his head propped up on one hand, Pyke thought about Mojag. He was a skinny guy in his middle years, dark brown eyes and short brown hair lightened by encroaching greyness. He and the Kiskashin, Oleg, had only joined the crew a year ago but the story went that back in his twenties, before he met Oleg, he had suffered head injuries so serious that nearly half his brain was replaced with a pseudo-organic cortical prosthesis.

While the injury and subsequent operation erased great swathes of memory, the prosthesis permitted the replacement of fact and images as supplied by members of his family. Whenever the subject arose Mojag insisted that before the injury he had been something of a planet-skipping, bed-hopping playboy, a claim most of the crew found amusing since the Mojag they knew was calm and meditative and self-possessed to the point of unreadability. Even now.

Once everyone was on the deck, Ancil gave a five-second countdown before bringing the grav-system back online. The return of body weight elicited a collective *oof!* a moment before the sound of crashes and clatters reverberated along the corridor outside and undoubtedly throughout the ship.

"The sound of our worldly goods rediscovering which way is down," said Dervla as she got up on shaky legs.

With a dry laugh Pyke forced himself upright. "Right, then, Ancil – can you activate some sort of comms?"

Sitting slumped in one of the bucket seats by the monitors, Ancil frowned. "Without oversight from Scar? I might be able to rig an open channel using the corridor voker network. You might have to shout, though."

Scar was the name Pyke had conferred upon the ship's AI.

"Aye, do it," Pyke said. "We'll get Scar back online, and then maybe we can find out what's keeping the air breathable."

"Bet it's another legacy system," said Dervla. "Y'know, the stuff that Voth dealer promised that he'd wiped from the substrate nodes. Six years since you bought this heap and we're still getting weird events like this."

"Well, aye, but this time it's kept us alive," he said. "Perhaps yourself and Win could go up to the main hold and restart the enviros from up there?"

"What about Oleg and Hammadi?"

"We'll deal with them once the *Scarabus* is up and running, and we have the sensors and weapons primed and ready, not before."

Dervla regarded him. "Should we go to the bridge afterwards, relight the boards?"

"No, I'm heading there myself in a moment or two." He offered a thin smile. "Get Scar woken up and bright-eyed."

"You and that AI are too close for my liking," she said, arching one eyebrow. With that she headed out of the hatch, followed by Win who smiled and rolled her eyes before leaving.

Watching them go, Pyke thought, *Well, if I didn't know any better . . .*

He turned to the others. Mojag and Ancil were still working at their elevated workstations, prodding and flicking screen glyphs and webby data arrays. Krefom the Henkayan was doing stretching exercises to firm up his relaxed muscles, while the Egetsi,

Punzho Bex, was still slumped on the floor by the wall. At two and a half metres he was average height for an Egetsi, a lo-grav biped species whose homeworld lay in the confederal alliance of Fensahr.

Pyke squatted down beside him. "How are you doing, Punzho?"

"I have been without gravityness for some time, Captain," the Egetsi said in his soft, double-larynxed voice. "I am with embarrassment at my body's incapacity. I should be aiding the recovery of our vessel."

"Don't you worry yourself about that – you'll be right as rain in a short while. I just need to ask you something about when that Khorr and his goons came aboard; did ye sense anything from them at all, any kind of threat?"

The Egetsi's narrow features were a picture of anguish. Pyke had hired him a year and a half ago on account of his voluminous knowledge of rare and valuable trade goods (especially arts and antiquities). He also possessed some low-level psi abilities that had proved useful now and then.

"Captain, I am with sorrow. I detected nothing from them, nothing at all. They were very calm—"

"Might have been shielded," chipped in Ancil from above.

"Or mind-trained," Pyke said, frowning. *Which would make for a very interesting skillset for a bunch of supposed smugglers.*

He patted Punzho on the shoulder and stood.

"Look, if they were able to shield their minds then there was nothing you could have done. Doesn't matter how they did it. So don't be getting bent out of shape over it, all right?"

Punzho raised one long-fingered hand, reached inside his pale green overtunic and took out a small dark blue pouch. He loosened its ties, opened it and tipped out a number of small, intricately detailed figurines. Sorting through them he picked out one and returned the rest to the pouch.

"You are right, Captain," he said. "I must winnow out the true guilt from the false, and in the enduring time regain my strengths. Gst will help me see the path."

Punzho was a follower of the Weave, a religion derived from the lives of nine holy seekers who lived at a time when the Egetsi had reached a tribal level of development. Believers memorised the Three Catechisms, the Three Inspirations, and the Three Obligations, and carried on their persons a pouch containing effigies representing the Nine Novices. The little figurines served as a focus for meditation on a wide range of topics, either on their own or in specific arrangements. Out of curiosity, Pyke had once asked Punzho if he ever employed the effigies as stand-ins for the crew but the Egetsi insisted that according to orthodoxy such a use amounted to allegory and was therefore inadvisable. Pyke wasn't sure how much of an answer that was.

"Good," he said. "And now I'm off to the bridge to get things humming there . . . Oh, and Kref, would you check the aft storage booths for breakages and damage? The sensors on some of the stackerbots are crocked so we may have to straighten the booths out by hand."

"I can do that, Captain," Kref said. "There'll be some good lifting in that."

Pyke grinned and left, following the starboard corridor to where a companionway led up to an offdeck up on a level with the high gantries that ran along either bulkhead of the main hold.

A viewport gave a view down into the hold where he could see Win Foskel inspecting the innards of a tall, hinged maintenance panel. Of Dervla there was no sign. Turning, he glanced at the smaller, thicker viewport in the bulkhead which was part of the hull; there was only a dozen of them scattered around the *Scarabus*, and all were double-sealed by the shipwide shutdown.

Getting them open again was high on his list, serving his need to see the stars. The Great Star-Forest, as his Granny Rennals used to call it, saying that there were many trails through the forest and not all of them were safe.

Well, you were right enough there, Gran. If I ever get back to Cruachan I'll have a few stories to tell you.

A couple of weak red emergency lamps scarcely pushed back the gloom on the bridge, otherwise broken by a scattering of glowing amber pinpoints. But Pyke moved with the ease of familiarity from station to station, switching on the six retrofitted overhead holomonitors. Silver radiance lit up the vacant operator couches and patches of the deck, while brighter luminance bloomed from console lamps and readouts as he started to bring the secondary systems online.

Moving over to the command console, he sat in his battered, leathery chair with the tilt-gimballed drink holder and watched the system indicators go green on his main holoscreen and felt a measure of satisfaction. The *Scarabus* was a Type-38 Ombilan transport, well known for its ruggedness, but the modifications he'd put in down the years had changed it from a reliable workhorse into a tough, fast multipurpose vessel capable of giving as good as she got. Now she practically amounted to an extension of himself and this shipwide reactivation was like a part of himself reawakening.

The AI Scar had not yet reached full-run status. From a standing start it was always the slowest to reach functionality, but since most of the secondary systems were now online Pyke decided to unseal the viewports, starting with the ones on the bridge. Three yard-long, foot-wide curves of lattice-toughened uglass capable of withstanding direct hits from pulse and beam cannon. Now the outer seals retracted into their hull apertures, revealing the world they were orbiting, a large planet banded in shades of dark blue and grey and adorned with a thin and perfect, almost delicate-looking orbital ring.

That's not Nadisha II, he thought. *I should be looking at a pale blue world in the grip of an ice age, not this . . . whatever it is.*

"Captain, where are we?" Win Foskel was standing in the entry hatch, staring in shock at the viewport. "That's not the ice planet—"

"I know that, Win," Pyke said calmly. "Now, if you sit yourself down at the nav-station we'll work on finding out what the situation is, okay?"

"Okay," she said shakily, going over to one of the couches. "But that's a gas giant, and we were orbiting a class P habitable before—"

She was interrupted by a brief, tinny fanfare.

"At last," Pyke muttered in relief. "Win, I have a feeling that we're still in the same system but I'm sure the expert can figure it out. Scar, y'back in the saddle yet?"

"Hello, Bran. Cognitives are at 98 per cent . . . now at 100 per cent."

Pyke smiled. The AI's voice was composed and purposefully synthetic, yet with a feminine undertone.

"Excellent, Scar. Priority request – verify astrogational location."

"Still trying to initialise main sensors, Bran. Crash powerdown has damaged several low-level data conduits . . . sensors initialised . . . scanning now."

Pyke glanced over at Win and said, "Wait for it . . ."

"Astropositional anomaly!" said the AI in a more urgent tone.

"Rebuilding stellar context array – gathering system comparators – matching with last known coordinates – Bran, I can confirm that the *Scarabus* is still in the Nadisha star system.

However, we are now 594 megaklicks from our original position, in orbit around Nadisha IV, a mid-range gas giant—"

"What's our orbital status?"

"Ecliptical intermediate, high stability."

"And just how long were we out?" Pyke said, thoughts racing.

"Seventeen hours and twenty-four minutes have elapsed since the crash powerdown event."

He uttered a low whistle. "That's quite a span of time – whatever they were up to they'll be long gone by now, I reckon."

Seated in her couch, Win Foskel looked over her shoulder at him. "Chief, I don't get it – if they wanted us dead why not just blow the drives instead of hauling us halfway across the system . . ."

"Look at it from their twisted, psychopathic side," he said. "Those scum wouldn't have known what precautions we might have taken, or who knew we were coming here . . . eh, Scar, was the ship ident still active through all that?"

"Yes, Bran, it was."

Pyke nodded. "Yes, they might have looked like low-brow brutes but they had some smarts among them. So anyone who came looking for us would lock onto our ident, follow it here only to discover that we were all victims of a tragic enviro-system malf. Which would keep attention away from the planet we were originally orbiting."

He sat back in his high-backed couch, enjoying the creak of the blue tove-leather as he thought for a moment, wondering why the ship had been moved and what might be happening back at their original location. Then he said:

"Scar, what's our general status? Are we fit to fly?"

"Hull integrity is optimal, as are shields and secondary propulsion units."

He gave a little nod and leaned forward to prod up a commlink on the holoscreen.

"Ancil?" In the holoscreen Ancil Martel looked round. "Ancil, I'm thinking we should set a course back to that wintry world we were orbiting before, see if we can find out what happened to our cargo and that gang of scum-sucking jackers. How are the drives behaving?"

"Sweet as a bell, chief. Field matrices should be ready in about ten minutes. Will we by any chance be making a microjump?"

"That's my thinking," Pyke said, pausing when he realised that the seat next to Martel was empty. "Where's Mojag?"

"Well, once the generators were up and running, everything was on track. Mojag knows his stuff, must have picked up a lot from, y'know, Oleg. So he says he has to take care of his quarters and I told him that's okay 'cos I'm on top of everything." Ancil frowned. "He seemed quieter than usual, but not himself."

"What do you mean?"

"When I glanced over a few times I saw him shake his head slightly or make that agreeing sound he makes, but nobody was speaking to him, and once I definitely heard him mutter to himself."

He shrugged. "Never saw him do that before."

Pyke nodded. "Mojag has a different load to carry than you or I. Got that chunk of hardmem in his head which makes dealing with grief complicated."

"Mojag is a very mellow fellow," said Ancil. "He's usually a calming influence."

"And I am sure that in time he'll find a way to cope with his loss," Pyke said. "In the meantime, how are those fields coming along?"

"A few minutes yet, chief, then we can shake the dust and be on our way."

"Good man." Then, sensing something he spun his chair round to see Dervla watching him from the port-side bridge hatch.

"You're really taking us back to the ice-world?" she said. "Could be risky, going by what we've just been through."

"I don't take kindly to being trussed and chumped by a bunch of overmuscled leatherboys," he said.

"Ah, so this is about your ego. Mmm, glad we're clear on that."

Smiling, Pyke poked one of the comm buttons. "Scar, set a microjump course back to Nadisha II, if you please."

"Yes, Bran. I shall be ready to commence a shipwide thirty-second countdown in two minutes."

"Thanks." He met Dervla's gaze. "And no, my flower, this is not about my ego. I take on jobs for business reasons, not thrills, and I think I'm quite entitled to remedy the situation."

"And get us into . . ." She shrugged. "Okay, so what's the plan?"

"Well, as we are in possession of neither the comm-scanner nor the payment we were due from that pus-stain Khorr, the idea is to return to the scene of the crime and see what clues we can find, ion trails, any stay-behind pieces, that kind of thing."

In the background Scar's voice announced the imminent hyperspace microjump and started counting down.

"So we're going after the scumbucket," Dervla said. "While not having any idea of what force he might have at his disposal. Y'know, there is such a thing as cutting your losses."

"And there's such a thing as self-respect!" he came back. "In any case, we actually need the money to keep the *Scarabus* operational . . ."

At that moment the ship's hyperdrive kicked in, bending the subquantal structures of space-time in very specific ways. Pyke felt the familiar squeeze-vertigo effect as it swirled through him, but he only paused for a moment or two.

". . . and . . . AND – it might be nice to buy some of that stuff they call 'food'. I'm led to believe that it actually has a taste, unlike that cyclo rubbish we've been . . ."

He stopped when Dervla, wide-eyed and uneasy, pointed over at the bridge viewports.

"Is that really . . . ?"

Even as Pyke swivelled his chair to look, the ship AI spoke.

"Planetary anomaly detected – stat conflicts across all main parameters – full macroscan in progress."

Nadisha II was a pale blue world, its continents buried beneath snow and blizzards that weren't due to start receding for another half a millennium. But what Brannan Pyke was seeing through the viewports was something completely different, a darkened world, swathed in angry cyclonic weather patterns. As he stared he felt a strange urge to laugh.

"Scar, what the devil are we looking at?"

"Scan results are incomplete but preliminary assessment is confirmed – although this planet occupies exactly the same orbital location as Nadisha II, and possesses the same angular velocity, it is another planet altogether."

Pyke nodded judiciously.

"Well, you don't see that every day."